THE
DARK SIDE
OF
REVERENCE

AN EPIC TALE OF RIVALRY AND REVENGE

BOOK ONE
ASCENDANCE TRILOGY

F. M. HEPTON

BABILI BOOKS

Cover Design by Francesca Hepton

1st edition 2025

Published Babili Books, a division of Babili Services Ltd, United Kingdom

ISBN: 978-1-0686081-5-5

To my sons Oliver and Eddie,
thank you for fanning the flames of fantasy and magic.

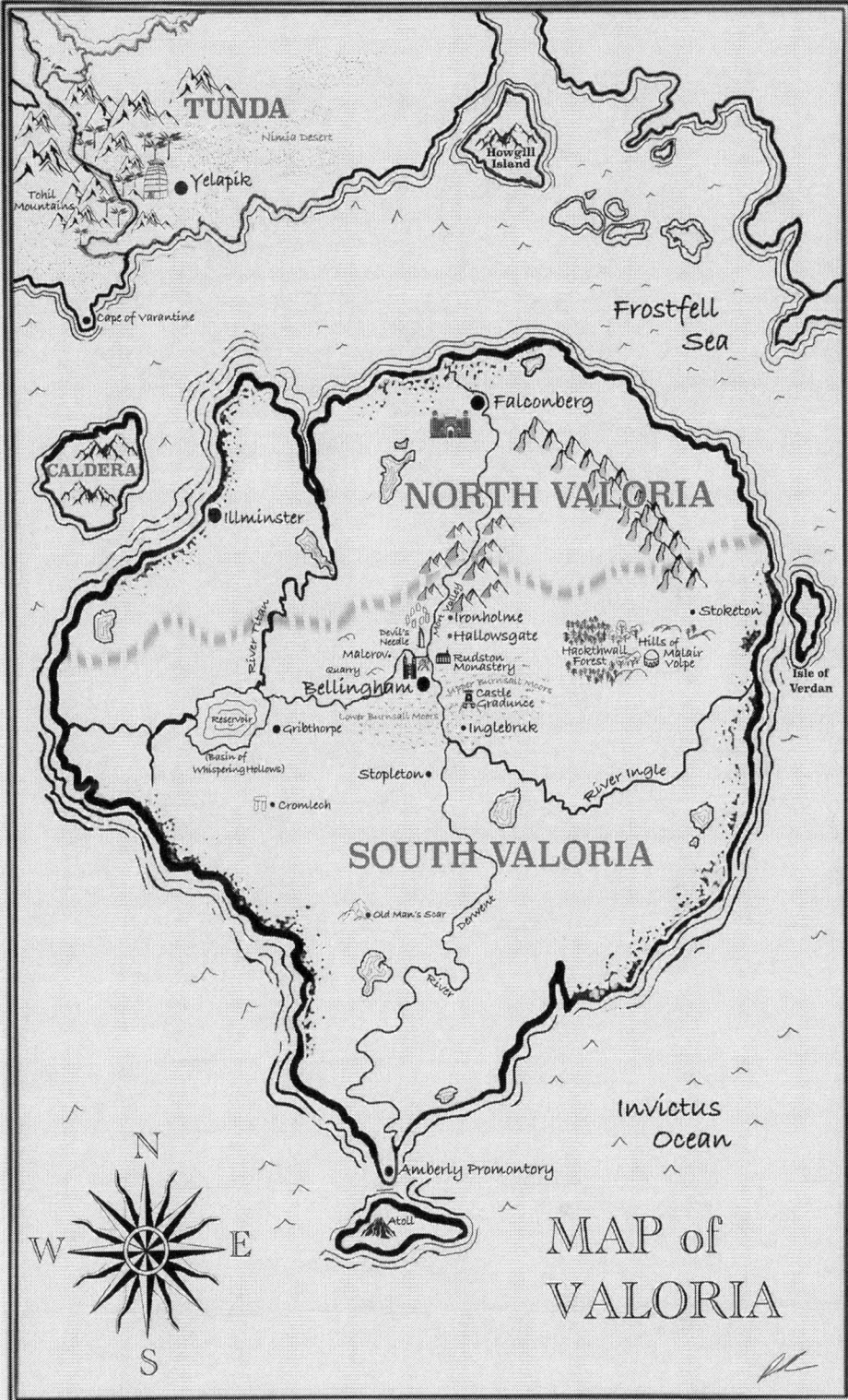

CONTENTS

ACKNOWLEDGEMENTS

Thank you to all my friends and family for joining and inspiring me along this journey.

I feel very lucky to have had the encouragement and support from my brother and sister-in-law (Stephan and Melissa), as well as their natural propensity for all things sword and sorcery—ready-made readers!

A big thank you to all my biggest supporters—Charlie Hepton, my parents, Suzy Wilson, Alison Thompson, Anne Watson, Rebecca Colby, Jess Pears, Alice Hepton and all the Haskertons—who believed in me, encouraged me, and helped make this story good enough to compete with the heavy word-power out there. And also for all the support and inspiration and thoughtful comments from my Facebook friends, you helped me turn some big corners and stay motivated.

Finally, a special thank you to my sons Oliver Graham for always being the hero of both light and dark, and Eddie Graham for widening the portal to the inner recesses of my imagination, so that others may now enter the virtuous and villainous world of Valoria.

PROLOGUE

Seeds of Revenge

S PARKLING COURTIERS GATHERED IN the Palace of Bellingham to witness the signing of the Valorian-Octule Peace Treaty. They convened in the immense throne room, a mosaic of light filtered through the long stained glass windows, creating patches of colour across the mostly empty stone floor. At the far end, sat King Valkarse, giving off an aura of kingly power and self-importance. His air of authority, carefully curated to mask his underlying apprehension. Atropa, his adviser, stood at his side. Her commandeering sapphire eyes and pale face framed by long, raven-black hair exuded a calm authority.

The king was about to finalise a treaty with the ancient race of Octules to secure them as allies. But it was more of a gesture of peace wrapped in an act of desperation. For decades, Valkarse had been reluctant to come to their aid after they had lost their homeland to a seismic natural disaster. Against his adviser's counsel, he had not wanted to surrender or part with a single inch of Valorain land. Now that the Octules had found a new domain to call their own, he feared them. They were larger-than-life beings, master engineers and full of wisdom. Even though they were known as a peaceful race, he believed you can never be too sure—Valkarse's own untrustworthiness ruling his decision. Yet, for all his pomp and circumstance, his offering, though impressive, was too late, too see-through.

"And take my adviser as a token of good faith." King Valkarse's words, delivered with ease, flew like poisoned darts into the ears of Atropa. Inside she screamed, concealing the wave of outrage and betrayal that burned through her. She had devoted her life to Valoria, to guiding Valkarse with great thought and care. She was not a pawn to be handed over as a bargaining tool.

Atropa spoke, her voice an icy blade she wanted to plunge into the king's tongue. "King Valkarse, always so generous, I'm sure the Octules have no need for me. We have great arts of beauty and an abundance of wildlife, surely, they'd prefer such tokens of homage."

Oblivious to the cauldron of rage boiling within his adviser, King Valkarse believed himself shrewd: offering the Octules a powerful asset to seal the peace, while planting a trusted Valorian within their midst to spy. To him, Atropa's protest was insubordination.

"I am your king—"

The panther-like Octule leader, Eldra, intervened. "Of course we accept this generous offer," he purred, deftly cutting short any potential conflict. With the flick of his long white cloak, he curved his towering body into a gracious bow, extending his slender hand to Atropa, who had no choice but to take it. Though stooped, his impassive eyes remained fixed on Valkarse and his regal frame was, as before, impressive.

"Few kings," he continued, "would be willing to part with such a treasure." His words, though smooth, carried a barbed message Valkarse clearly failed to understand.

Led away by Eldra, Atropa's respect for him remained intact. For Valkarse though, her soul seethed with a silent vow of revenge.

Chapter 1

CRUMBLING AWAY

CANE, AN IMPERIAL GUARD with a heightened sense of duty, and currently a keen sense of discomfort, stopped his horse at the edge of the castle grounds. The muggy air, heavy with clouds, promised rain but gave none. He was not one to bow to omens—nature's fickle predicators—but there was something about this place that sat wrong with him. The taste of it was sour, like iron on the tongue, and the smell, damp, old, like rot.

No one came to greet him. No lights in the windows, no movement in the shadows. Just silence. The walls were old, the stone blackened with age, and the cobwebs, thick as a man's fist, clung to every corner. Though he wore his valour like a second skin, it offered him no help in shaking the feeling that this place was dead. Not dangerous dead—just forgotten, left to crumble. Not fearful dead, but a reminder it had seen better days, and that anyone left inside didn't care about what it had become.

His boots made too much noise as he climbed the central stairway, the sound of them out of place in the stillness. Only when he stopped did he hear a voice coming from the dark corridor extending before him. Prying wasn't his style, and yet here he was, following the voice to a chamber, like the rest, dark, dank, and somehow marked with sorrow. Yet within, a woman, draped in green robes, her angelic face framed by silver braids, was cooing to an infant in her arms. It was incongruous, a soft scene in such a hard setting.

"You, you are *the one*. This time, I can feel it deep within me, you are *the one*," she whispered, her words heavy with an unspoken significance.

This did not sound good. 'The one' usually led to sacrifices, unstoppable public revolt or bloody wars. It felt off. An instinctual, hasty step back, slid Cane into the shadows. No sooner had he vanished than the woman swept from the chamber with the infant pressed tight against her bodice. Her green robes swirled like a leaf caught in a breeze as though the very air obeyed her whim. Cane's grand idea of following her for more clues immediately hit a snag when he found himself outmatched by her speed.

Although a clever man of many talents, he faltered. No one had warned him the mission would require the eyes of a hawk and legs of a stag! By the time he caught his breath, he was utterly lost in a maze of corridors, winding like the entrails of some giant beast, all furnished with that special decor one could only describe as 'neglected medieval dungeon meets castle burgled in haste' customised by a unique smell. It was overpowering, a fetid mix of decay and wet stone that stuck to the back of his throat. A stench that spoke of lives once lived and now long forgotten—a testament to the castle's slow, inexorable decline. His hand, gloved and trembling despite himself, pressed against the slick, cold wall, to steady him. But nausea crept up, relentless, as if the castle itself sought to purge him from its bowels.

He fought it. His duty called, and he pressed on, driven by the urgency of King Aurelius's orders. Somewhere in this dreadful castle, was a Baron. Not a Baron with gold or glory anymore, but a man stuck in the kind of ruins that screamed 'financial despair'. Rumours about disappearing servants, bones in moats, and ghoulish beasts played in his mind, and Cane cursed his luck. None of the other guards had volunteered for this mission, and now, he was starting to see why. Was it worth it? For king and country? For the slim chance of becoming Captain of the Guard or going on a real mission?

His musings were interrupted by the sound of voices—muffled, but clear enough to guide him to another room downstairs. Peering through a gap in the door, he saw the green-robed lady, now standing in what nobility would call a 'trophy room' but Cane thought 'the room with all the dead animals on the walls' was a more accurate description.

Instantly surmising it was not the opportune moment to introduce himself, he watched from the shadows as the woman approached a large, hulking figure hunched by the fire. He was warming his huge hands like he had all the problems of the world bearing down on his grumpy shoulders.

"Look, Baron, I brought your daughter." The woman's voice was a mixture of hope and desperation. The silent man continued to stare into the fire.

"Will you not look at her?" she implored.

When he finally spoke, his voice was rough, worn down by years of hardship and bitterness.

"Not again," he growled, sounding every bit like the overgrown bear he resembled. "I want none of this. None of you. None of... whatever *that* is." He waved his hand vaguely in her direction.

Kneeling before him, she held the child out as if offering a sacrifice. "Will you not at least turn to see her? Do you not want to hold this daughter of yours?"

When he finally turned, it was as if the villain in this tragic parody assumed his role in full. "That's no daughter of mine!" he boomed, making the walls tremble.

Towering over her, in one swift motion, he seized a poker from the fire and thrusted its glowing tip toward the infant's throat. Cane braced to intervene but before he could act, the child—so peaceful moments ago—unleashed a shocking fury. With a strength that belied her tiny frame, she lashed out, shattering the poker like a toothpick with her small, bony hands.

A scream tore from the woman and she fled past him, the baby clinging to her dress like a malevolent mongrel on heat digging its sharp claws in deep.

She ran, like a madcap chase scene from an absurd play, but no one was laughing. Cane, his instincts now on high alert, followed the sound of her frantic footsteps as she disappeared into the depths of the castle. He was fast, faster than most, but she moved with a speed born of terror, darting down the spiral staircase and into the darkness below with the spawn of something sinister digging its claws in ever deeper.

In the cellars, he lost her. Silent and still, he fancied he saw movement in the darkness—glimpses of eyes, or perhaps teeth—but when he looked closer, there was nothing there. Just the wild imaginings of a mind primed for danger.

A sudden clank of metal caught his attention—a heavy bolt being slid shut. Then, silence once more. He felt a gust of wind in front of him as though a noiseless cloud had rushed past. Groping the walls for a torch he found none. The darkness was complete, oppressive, but he had the distinct feeling that he was not alone. The rancid smell was unbearable. Whatever had been there was not revealing itself, and he was left standing in the pitch-black, his heart pounding in his chest. He could suffer the stench no more.

With a burst of speed, he dashed back up the stairs, two at a time, eager to escape the suffocating darkness. *No wonder there are wild rumours*, he thought to himself—and finally found his way back to ground level. Here, a new scene awaited him: servants. The contrast was jarring. Actual, real, bustling, food-preparing servants. And—was that the smell of a roast? Was that fresh bread? Had he crossed into a different household by accident?

With his best 'I'm an Imperial Guard' face on, he approached a woman who seemed in charge. Distrusting eyes above rosy cheeks, framed by auburn hair looked up and down his tall frame.

Steeling himself, striving to project an air of professionalism fitting for his station, he asked, "Excuse me, my lady, could you tell me where I may find Baron Gradunce?" hoping to have masked the whiplash of impossible chaos he had just experienced.

Clearly surprised to see a stranger in the castle, she treated him with wary caution. "Why yes, sir, but could you first tell me your business with the Baron?"

"I am an Imperial Guard to our sovereign King Aurelius." His sky-blue tunic embroidered with a flaming sun crest in golden thread would have already told her as much. "I am here regarding official matters."

"If you will kindly follow me," she said. With deadened feet he followed her back to the scene of the crime, a numbness replacing the confident thoughts and decisive actions that usually filled his mind.

⸺◈⸺

There, sitting like the lord of his crumbling, smelly domain, was the Baron, but he wasn't the scary bear Cane had seen moments before.

"Ah, Arabella," he said with warmth. She gave the slightest of nods in return. "And Cane of Cromlech!" smiled the Baron, who had switched from menacing to genial with the ease of a caterpillar transforming into a butterfly.

Well, this is interesting. The other lady must have been the nanny.

This version of the Baron spoke softly to the pretty woman named Arabella before turning his attention to Cane.

"Come, come," he extended his massive hand in the first gesture of welcome during Cane's visit.

Now that it came to it, Cane wasn't exactly thrilled to be standing in front of the dominating figure of Baron Gradunce, who looked like he could crush a man with a single hearty laugh. And there was a lot of laughing—at least from the Baron's end.

"I was wondering when you'd come," the Baron said, his voice as sonorous as a storm's rumblings. "I knew your father. Good man the Earl of Cromlech. Impressive man, very intelligent. Yet here you stand, with your golden skin, chestnut hair, and those striking hazel eyes—nothing like him at all." The Baron scrutinised Cane as if trying to spot a family resemblance that simply wasn't there. "You're more like a living incarnation of the god of beauty, than anything resembling him. I hope you got his brains, at least." More rumbling laughter. "Quite the scholar, your old man. Ah, those good old days are gone, but you've made quite a name for yourself at the Sovereign Games, haven't you? Is that why King Aurelius sent you on this tedious assignment? No one left in the circle he can trust?" More one-sided laughing. "No need to answer—I'll just assume the others were busy. What kept you so long anyway?"

Cane remained unmoved. He didn't appreciate the Baron reducing him to the 'son of so-and-so' or 'that guy from the Games'. Even though he outranked the Baron in Valoria's social hierarchy, Cane didn't stoop to play that card. This was official business, and the

Baron needed to understand that. No matter how convivial the Baron was, Cane wasn't in the mood to be treated like a greenhorn or someone's offspring. He kept his approach on an even keel.

"As you well know, King Aurelius is a noble man, Baron Gradunce. And yes, he chose me because he can trust me and since he thought he could trust you... Anyway, the real question here isn't the timing of my arrival, but rather the timeliness with which you will respond to the king's request to come to court, so that he may assist you in your time of need." Cane delivered the line with the seriousness he hoped would make the Baron realise this wasn't just a casual chat with a novice.

The Baron smiled—though whether it was out of respect for Cane's seriousness or just amusement at the whole situation, Cane couldn't quite tell. "The entanglement in which I find myself cannot be disentangled with financial aid, logic, or sympathy," Baron Gradunce said, looking off into the distance as if he'd just remembered something particularly unpleasant, like the time the castle roof caved in or dry rot had set in the bedrooms.

Cane caught the vacant stare. Definitely not happy thoughts. Baron Gradunce came back to the moment with a sudden grin. "But I hate to discuss business on an empty stomach, and as you can see," he patted his sizeable belly with a pride that suggested he'd never missed a meal in his life, "it's rarely empty. Though, at this rate, I'll soon be feeding off the servants!"

Cane noticed Arabella stiffen ever so slightly at the Baron's last words, her face doing its best impression of a calm lake. But the ripples were there.

"But none of that now," the Baron continued, all jollity and cheer. "Come, my dear, let us escort our most distinguished guest to the fine dining hall in this decrepit hovel we call home."

Arabella took the Baron's arm with the practiced grace of someone who'd done this a thousand times. Cane followed them. "We're having our final banquet," she said, her voice spiked with a touch of caustic humour. "It's our intention to enter our era of complete poverty in style."

If nothing else, this couple had a flair for the dramatic. It was as if Cane had wandered into a theatre production where every actor was stuck playing a role they did not want or wore disguises designed to confuse the spectators. *This whole scene is a perverse play of deception and pretence, I'm sure, with me cast as the sole audience member trying to make sense of it all—better that than the fool who gets duped or stabbed in the back in the final scene*, he thought.

Baron Gradunce pushed open two huge doors leading into an opulent dining room for their 'final banquet'—a farewell to riches in style, because why not?

Taking a seat near the head of the table, opposite the Baron, Cane watched him promptly tear into a very long leg of what he hoped was roast lamb. Arabella sat to his left, her plate untouched as she absently pushed around peas and potatoes. Cane looked at the meat on his plate. Lamb? At this time of year? He had faced many challenges in his career, but resisting the urge to bolt from the dining room and lose the contents of his stomach was quickly climbing to the top of his list. Abandoning his assignment wasn't an option, though. He would politely accept the meal, pretend he'd already eaten, and just hope his growling stomach didn't betray him.

The Baron, in contrast, thrived in the spotlight, holding court over the feast with boisterous gusto.

"Tell me, Cane," he said, between mouthfuls, "what news of the capital? What of that new Duke, eh? Duke Nieman. I hear things are getting rather interesting in Bellingham."

Unsure how much to reveal, Cane hesitated. "There's always something going on in the capital. Perhaps if you attended court, you'd be abreast of the changes. My role here is not that of reporter but to represent the king's wishes: King Aurelius is concerned about the state of Castle Gradunce and the rumours that have been circulating. He wants to ensure that everything is in order—"

Baron Gradunce chuckled, a muted rumbling. "Rumours, eh? And what do they say about old Gradunce?"

Cane chose his words carefully. "There have been reports of unrest in your estate, Baron Gradunce. Missing servants, unexplained occurrences, creatures described as ghoulish 'castle crawlers'... that sort of thing. Disturbing. The king is concerned, as any ruler would be."

The Baron's expression darkened. "Missing servants? Unexplained occurrences? I'd say it's more likely they've found better opportunities elsewhere. This castle may be old, but it's still my home, and I run it as I see fit. As for the king's concerns, tell him he needn't worry. I have everything under control."

Unconvinced, Cane nodded. There was something about the Baron's tone that suggested otherwise. The dinner continued in awkward silence, Cane's mind racing with unanswered questions. What was really going on at Castle Gradunce? And what role did the mysterious woman and her strange child play in it all?

As the meal came to an end, the Baron wiped his mouth with a greasy silk napkin and leaned back in his chair, clearly satisfied. "Well, Cane of Cromlech, it's been a pleasure dining with you. But now, if you'll excuse me, I have other matters to attend to."

Cane found himself being politely but definitively ushered out into the hall.

"We'll speak in the morning," said the Baron. "You may stay here tonight. My home is open to you."

Cane barely stifled a shudder at the thought. The place had all the charm of a haunted mausoleum, and he had no desire to discover which ghouls, real or not, might come knocking at his door. Feeling the prickling sensation of unseen eyes on him, he glanced toward the central staircase. Was someone lurking up there in the shadows? Probably. No, he would not be spending the night here. An inn nearby, in Inglebruk, sounded like paradise compared to the unsettling atmosphere of Castle Gradunce. He thanked his host for his generosity and left with the promise of returning in the morning.

Out in the courtyard, Cane took a moment to jot down some notes for his report. He was nothing if not diligent, and there was no way he was going to let this bizarre situation reflect poorly on his record. As he looked up at the starless sky, with the moon half-swallowed by ominous clouds, he couldn't help but think that this was exactly the kind of place where 'disturbing occurrences' were standard fare.

When he turned to mount his horse, he heard something—voices escaping from an open window above the courtyard. Normally, Cane wouldn't dream of eavesdropping. But these were far from normal circumstances, and frankly, it was the only way he'd learned anything useful since he'd arrived. So, once again, he found himself playing the snoop. Peering through the grimy panes, he hoped to snatch a clue about what the Baron was really up to.

What he saw was what he expected: the Baron and Arabella, snuggled up together in a cosy (well, as cosy as one could get in that castle) embrace on a pile of furs in the 'dead animals as trophies' room, the faint glow of embers providing just enough light to catch the loving look in their eyes. They were talking in hushed tones about their future together, apparently planning to travel to North Valoria after their last indulgent meal.

Just when he was about to turn and leave, the scene of domestic bliss took a turn to the unexpected. The woman in green stormed into the room, her entrance as subtle as a thunderclap. There was the Baron, running his hands through Arabella's long hair, when his nanny burst in on them. But it wasn't the Baron who complained.

"You are too cruel, sir!" the nanny sobbed, her voice thick with betrayal. "I have always shown you nothing but faithfulness and loyalty. How could you? How could you? I am your wife!"

Cane raised an eyebrow. *Oh! Not the nanny then.* This tragic play was turning into an overly dramatic farce. The Baron, the larger-than-life adulterous husband, was not impressed.

"You are nothing to me, you heinous scourge!" he snarled, practically spitting out the words. "You are a disgrace to womanhood and life itself. Get away from me, Agatha—you belong in a cage!"

Agatha, a sparrow to the bear, was now seething and looked as though she was about to spontaneously combust. For a moment, Cane was certain he saw something strange—a shadow that seemed to move of its own accord across her face. But before he could puzzle it out, the Baron stepped in front of Arabella, shielding her from his wife's wrath. The Baroness responded with a hiss that would have done any snake proud.

"Have her then," she spat, her eyes boring into the Baron's. "And may you always be together in infernal torment!"

If lightning had struck at that very moment, Cane would not have been surprised but instead, the Baroness simply turned and left, her head held high—now her turn to play the villainess, exiting stage left.

Still processing what he'd just witnessed, Cane decided it was high time to get out of there. Yes, this was all very intriguing, but it was also very much not his business. He was here on official duty, and that duty did not include getting involved in a marital meltdown. He'd stick to the rules, return early in the morning, and catch the Baron before he and Arabella made their grand elope.

As he rode off into the dark, moorland night, Cane couldn't help but think that whatever awaited him at the inn was bound to be more peaceful than anything that might unfold within the walls of Castle Gradunce.

Chapter 2

A TASTE OF THINGS TO COME

I T WAS NOT ALL cosiness and peace at the inn either. After a night of dreams so vivid he could barely separate them from reality, Cane returned to Baron Gradunce's home. Not that anyone would call that pile of gloom and cracked stone 'homey'. Today, though, something was even more off. More black clouds piled over the place like a bad mood, crows flapping around like drunk dinner guests. He half-expected them to start dive-bombing him, asking, "Are you here for breakfast... our breakfast?"

Inside, the castle was as lively as a crypt. No one greeted him, again. Cane thought nothing of it. He walked right into the back room or one could say, he walked right into the belly of the beast where the Baron had spent yesterday roasting his problems by the fire. Only, there was no fire this time. And there was no Baron. He could hear an unnatural groaning. At first, he thought someone was in pain, then he caught himself with the embarrassing thought, maybe it was a pleasure-induced groan. With the curtains drawn shut he groped into the darkness, tripping over—what was that? A bear's head on a rug? The groans grew louder, turning into screeches. He felt his way behind the large seating arrangement draped in furs and skins of wild bears where the two elopers had been canoodling. Tentatively moving in the dark, he pulled back the long, heavy curtains slightly. A shard of light pierced the darkness, revealing the noise maker. Instead of a canoodling couple, Cane found... well, something you'd find in a book titled '*Terrors Best Left Unseen*'.

There on the floor, squirming like something that crawled out of the wrong end of creation, was an ungodly large blob with *too many* limbs. Eight, to be exact. And two heads. One of which belonged to Baron Gradunce himself, making futile attempts to burrow into the floor like a trainee mole on its first day out. The other head? Arabella's.

"Baron Gradunce!" Cane's voice echoed like someone shouting in a graveyard. The Baron's eyes snapped up, and the sound that followed wasn't a groan, more like the netherworld itself screaming, "Run, boy, run!" The walls shook, the iron candelabra crashed to the floor, and Cane almost did an off-balance hop onto Arabella's head. That was it. He had to get help.

He bolted like someone who'd realised they were in the wrong life, trying to shout for help but only managing to choke on his own fear. Panic flooded his body like hot molten. In his over five million minutes of training, not one had prepared him for this.

Running through the desolate halls, he heard a gentle melody—so surreal it might as well have been playing in a dream—calling him. He followed it, like the hapless fool he knew he wasn't supposed to be, into a small, sunlit parlour. The room couldn't have been more different from the madness he'd just left. Sunlight streamed in, the music wrapped around him like a warm hug, and there, playing a harp with a serenity that made him question his sanity, was the Baroness.

She was stunning. Her fingers plucked the harp strings as though she were skilfully plaiting the silken hair of a goddess. She turned, startled to see him, but everything about her presence—her delicate features, silvery hair, bright green eyes—made him feel like everything was as it should be. All thoughts and sights of the gelatinous blob erased.

"Pray, who are you?" she demanded. Her voice was as sweet as the music but hard enough to bring him back to reality with a slap. He tried to explain, rambling on about the Baron's... condition, if that's what you could call it. She was walking away from him as he spoke, through the doorway.

"Your words are madness." She dismissed him, not believing a word, and led him down the hall.

"I shall call my husband." She made this threat as sternly as she could to evidently try and cover the tremble in her voice that was all too apparent to Cane.

Up close he saw she was much taller than he had realised. With her authoritative words and impressive height, he no longer saw her as a frail sparrow but a woman in charge. He followed her down the corridor towards the large kitchen that was bustling with life the day before. He implored her to listen to him, to make haste, to get help, to—

She ignored him.

"I said I'll call my husband and—" Upon reaching the kitchen, she stopped dead in her tracks and swung open the door. And that's when everything got infinitely worse.

Inside, ash-coloured figures—disastrous creations of a mad sculptor—feasted on the servants, stuffing arms and clumps of bloody flesh into their own chewed-up mouths. Some had overly long limbs, some had too few—most of them were just wrong in every sense of the word.

Instinctively, Cane acted before the Baroness could scream.

"Castle crawlers! Get out of here!" he yelled, pushing her out and slamming the door shut, though judging by her petrified face, he wasn't sure she'd heard him.

Warped bodies wrapped in glabrous skin advanced. *What are they?* Cane did not have time to think, just react. Sword drawn, he threw himself into battle. One imp-sized crawler jumped on his head digging its claws in. Reacting on reflex, he pried it off and shoved it into a pot of boiling soup... *Oh no, was that the baby?* There was no time to check before spinning to face the next wave of horrors.

Another one came at him, this one looked like he'd visited a blind barber for a close shave. Cane barely had time to block its scared face and gnashing teeth when a second squamous body pounced at him, its skin pale and gelatinous. Firmly caught in its stranglehold, Cane wriggled half circle to backstab it in the stomach, turning his blade in a brutal arc to gut the crawler and ensure its death. Straw-coloured blood splattered across the hanging pots and pans as its body hit the floor with a wet thud.

In its heyday, the kitchen would no doubt have been a hub of culinary commotion, where knives flew and roasts were carved with zeal, but nothing in comparison with the current frenzy of skewering and slicing. Now it was a whirlwind of human carnage. Cane fought like a man possessed, slashing, hacking, spinning with deadly precision. For each one he felled, another two seemed to take its place. With a clean swipe, Cane decapitated the first. The second, he kicked square in the chest to send it flying backward and land empaled on the roasting spit's rod.

There were too many. They kept coming, abnormal forms, sharp teeth in snapping jaws. Up close, their bad breath was enough to make him lose his step. Thrashing without stop, he felt the fatigue setting in. This was a fight he could not win by sheer force. He had to think fast.

His eyes darted around the kitchen, searching for something, anything. Then he spotted it—a large water silo perched above the rafters. A far-fetched plan formed in his mind.

In a move worthy of a bard's most legendary hero, Cane scrambled up the beams. A crawler lunged at his back, claws raking through his cloak, but he yanked away just enough to stomp on its head and send it sprawling. Using the momentum, he propelled himself up the beams, climbing higher as the crawlers screeched below. They would be on him in seconds, their malformed limbs clambering over each other in a frenzy to reach him. With his last ounce of strength, he cut through the cord holding the silo, sending a flood of water crashing down.

Water exploded into a downpour crashing over the kitchen, sweeping the crawlers off their feet. Cane watched from above as the cannibalistic assailants were engulfed by the deluge, their pasty forms thrashing and shrieking as the water overwhelmed them. Unearthly and agonising cries pierced the air, before they were silenced beneath the rising flood.

Cane held on to the beam as the water surged below, feeling the cold spray on his face. Mummy-like bodies writhed in the water, flailing in a desperate, futile attempt to stay afloat. One by one, they sank beneath the surface, their misshapen forms becoming part of the kitchen's flotsam.

Breathing heavily, and grateful for their lack of swimming skills, Cane leaped out of the roof's window and landed hard on the ground outside. Through the side window, he saw the water churn before finally calming to reveal the lifeless bodies floating in the deluge. He could not tell if the ordeal was truly over, but for now, the kitchen was silent.

After making sure there were no other castle crawlers around him, Cane's thoughts turned to the Baroness. Where had she gone? He scanned the courtyard and finally spotted her kneeling by the drawbridge, a tragic figure of grace and sorrow that clashed absurdly against the hellish backdrop. She looked as misplaced here as a lily in a wasteland. Her sobs to the indifferent, cloudy skies above grew louder, more desperate the closer Cane got.

"This wasn't how it was supposed to end!" she wailed. Cane, unaccustomed to dealing with wailing women, or women in general, placed a firm hand on her shoulder and spoke to her as a Guard on a mission.

"Baroness, it's time to go. Let's get you to a place of safety."

In the chaos, it seemed the Baroness had forgotten all about Cane. She startled at his touch, then gripped his hand like a drowning woman grabbing for a lifeline, her fingers tightening with a newfound strength.

Their eyes met, and a sudden memory flashed through Cane's mind—the child she'd been cradling the night before. "Where's your child?"

The Baroness blinked in confusion. "What child? I have no child!" Her voice wavered, teetering on hysteria. "I have no child. No husband. No home." Her breathing quickened, and panic twisted her features. "Where is my husband?"

"We can't save the Baron; he's lost, I fear. He and Arabella..." But before he could finish, the Baroness's knees buckled. Cane caught her, holding her upright as her weight sagged against him. "Are you sure there's no one else in the castle we need to rescue?" The child's fiendish body gripping onto her robes flared in his mind again. *Where was that child?* Had he lost it somewhere? Misplaced it? Dunked it into the boiling pot, mistaking it for a crawler?

The Baroness shook her head, her eyes hollow with grief, though her lips parted as if to speak. Before she could utter a word, her gaze seemed to sharpen, locking onto his. Her voice softened, soothing like a mother's lullaby. "There was no child, sir. Just monsters. You're mistaken. Like me, your mind has been razed by the horrors of that place."

Her words curled into his thoughts and smothered his doubts. No child. Of course. His memory must have betrayed him, frayed by the chaos of the night. There had only been crawlers and… the Baron!

"We need to get help," Cane said brusquely. "This situation is beyond me. There might be more of them, and I can't fight them alone. I must get you to safety."

The Baroness looked like she'd struggle to walk, let alone ride. Cane hoisted her onto his horse with ease. As they made their way out of the courtyard, his mind churned with questions. Had the castle been enchanted? Was the child he saw a figment of his imagination? What about the visions in the cellar—had they been real? Were they the crawlers he'd slain in the kitchen? His usually logical mind was teetering on the edge of uncertainty, a place he seldom frequented. Only one thing was certain: he had to get the Baroness to safety and bring back reinforcements.

After they crossed the drawbridge into the heather-clad moors, the Baroness's small, tremulous voice broke the silence. "Won't they come after us once they've finished… feeding?"

"No, I took care of that."

"But how?"

"Trust me. Whatever those things were, they won't be following us. They're as dead as my understanding of normality."

The Baroness slumped forward, her silver braids untying and falling across her face. Cane couldn't help but pity her. "I don't know what happened back there, but we need to find somewhere before night. Do you have family or friends nearby?" She shook her head. "Winter's closing in, and we've only got a few hours of daylight left."

They rode in silence for an hour, the vision of atrocities seen haunting Cane's mind. Even though it was the nearest option, taking her to the inn was not a good idea—too many prying eyes, too many questions. And he already had so many unanswered questions of his own. Bellingham was too far and his military barracks were no place for a lady.

"What really happened back there? Are the stories about Castle Gradunce true?" He knew it was a harsh thing to ask after all she'd been through, but he needed answers.

Her voice was small, barely audible. "I knew of the rumours, but those… things… I'd never seen anything like them. If I had, I would never have spent another night in that cursed place." Her words dissolved into sobs. Cane decided not to push her any further.

When the last light of day began to fade, they came upon an old monastery, its dark basalt walls hidden away behind a cluster of leafless trees strangled by rampant ivy. The place had clearly been abandoned for years, the stone walls weathered and worn, but to Cane, it was a beacon of hope.

"This will do for the night," he said, dismounting and guiding his horse through the rusty iron gates. As they entered, Cane read the weathered inscription carved into the stone: 'Rudston Monastery'.

It wasn't ideal, but it was a place to rest from the madness they'd just escaped. Three figures hidden under black cowls emerged between the gates, their hoods deep and shadowy. Unusual feathers adorned their habits, gleaming golden-brown in the setting sun. Cane's training urged him to continue to the Palace of Bellingham and seek help from the Imperial Court; his instincts told him to stay. They had nowhere else to go, and these monks seemed willing to take them in.

Inside, the corridors were silent, save for Cane's reverberating footsteps on the stone floor. His guard was up. Every step fell heavier with suspicion. He glanced at the monks who led them—tall, silent, their faces hidden. Who were these men? The monastery should have been empty.

The room they led them to was nothing like what he had expected. Lavish chairs, thick rugs, a grand fireplace—it was like stepping into a palatial room, not a forsaken monastery. The high ceiling was ablaze with the candles burning on a giant candelabrum suspended on heavy iron chains from the exposed dark beams. This scene was extraordinary enough for being found in such a place of worship where austerity should have prevailed, but it was further crowned by the most elaborate and majestic instrument imaginable: the organ.

On a larger scale, it could have been mistaken for a minster. If ever there was a reason to believe in the incredible power of a god, this spectacularly crafted organ was enough to sway even the most ardent of atheists.

When Cane saw the pale, smooth face of the monk at the organ, he was struck by how young he appeared. The young man flexed his svelte fingers and played a soothing tune. The melody stirred up an enchanting and soothing atmosphere.

Other monks seated the Baroness gently on a chaise longue, their movements precise, almost ritualistic. The room soon filled with the smoke of incense. They served them chamomile tea and scattered a mixture of herbs and petals around the Baroness, their hoods still drawn low. Cane stood nearby, his hand resting near his blade, just in case. His eyes lingered on the organ, then back on the monks who moved around them.

A few other monks entered. They gathered, humming low in their throats, their voices blending with the deepening notes of the organ. Cane could feel a hypnotic energy in the air as the young monk's singing grew louder.

Withering maiden at peace be
Withering maiden be set free

Countless dark nights
Countless bad sights
With this song we banish
With these petals they vanish.
Feel the sun of tomorrow
Feel no more deep sorrow
Withering maiden be set free
Withering maiden at peace be.

The song drifted on, its rhythm pulling at Cane's mind, lulling him into a deep sense of weariness. He tried to resist, tried to fight the sleep creeping over him, but it was no use. The sound was too soothing, too irresistible. His body grew heavy, and before he knew it, his eyes drooped shut. He fell into the bliss of a dreamless sleep, unconcerned if he would awaken again to a world that no longer made sense.

Chapter 3

SANITARIUM

W HEN CANE AWOKE, HE was still seated in the same chair. His neck had made a pact with discomfort, and his muscles had gone on strike. He could hear the Baroness breathing softly under a blanket dusted with petals, like some woodland nymph who had wandered too far from home.

Stretching his protesting limbs, Cane ventured into the stone corridors of the monastery. True to his other monastic experiences, the architect of this complex had clearly also been averse to light and comfort. After what felt like a bad rerun of his miserable labyrinthine misadventure at Castle Gradunce, Cane found himself following a much more promising scent—breakfast! If all else failed, at least here he wouldn't starve while searching through a cold maze.

He followed the tantalising wafts to a kitchen-come-dining room where five monks sat around a large oak table, looking entirely too cheerful for people who had presumably taken a vow of something involving 'lifelong suffering'. If they had burst into song, it would not have been surprising. The thought amused Cane, though the reality was simpler: they were merely enjoying breakfast. Apparently, being holy didn't mean you had to miss out on life's little pleasures, like crispy bacon and buttery toast.

"Ah, come in, my friend!" called out a particularly large monk with a black beard so magnificent it could well have been the nesting ground of several bird colonies, and no one would be the wiser. Cane recognised him as the man who had escorted them the previous night. "I trust you slept well?" he asked, as though implying Cane had spent the night in a feathered bed at a guest house, rather than a hard chair in a random monastery among strangers.

These monks didn't exactly match his expectations of pious puritans. They looked more like gentry who had accidentally been sent habits instead of doublets in the latest fashion delivery. His look had clearly betrayed his thoughts.

"Ah, don't be so confused, lad," Gerant chuckled. "We're not your average monks, I admit. But don't worry, we won't bite, or even baptise you!" This sparked giggles. "But you're not the average traveller either! I mean, who'd have expected Cane of Cromlech, Imperial Guard to the Sovereign Realm, son of the Earl of Cromlech, to be trotting around the moors with Baron Gradunce's wife?" The table erupted in laughter.

"How do you know who I am?" Cane asked.

"Well, besides that rather conspicuous tunic of yours," Gerant said with a grin, "everyone knows the Sovereign Games champion! You're quite the celebrity, my boy. Allow me to formally introduce myself. I am Gerant, Viscount of Stoketon, and these two young rascals you met last night are brothers Tristan and Percy."

The two younger 'monks' bowed in unison. Tristan, wiry and excitable, looked as though he had been powered by lightning rather than sleep, while Percy, his more serious brother, had the air of someone who enjoyed alphabetising things in his spare time. Their brown curls made them a matching pair, though Tristan's were wild and wind-swept, while Percy's were tamed with a significant amount of wax.

"We're not monks either," said the keen looking Tristan. "We are actual brothers... to each other." He wagged a finger between himself and Percy who was busy pushing an oversized mouthful of egg sandwich into his mouth. "Just in case you were wondering."

"Yes, thank you for clarifying, Tristan. And these fine gentlemen are Rowan and Blake," Gerant continued, gesturing at two more monks. Rowan, Cane recalled, was the organ player; with his pale complexion and soulful eyes, he looked more like a poet who had strayed from a library of forbidden lore. Rowan's smooth looks differed starkly with Blake's ruggedly handsome features, who sported an outlandishly large and lustrous black moustache.

"I know, it's hard to take in at first," Blake said, catching Cane's look of bewilderment as he stared at the moustache that would have been more at home at the end of a broom pole. "You've never seen such a devilishly handsome man, have you?"

"I think he is probably wondering how much self-restraint it takes not to give you a solid thump," Tristan teased. "You're like a walking target with that black squirrel hibernating under your nose and that smug grin—just begging for a slap!"

"Alright, alright, that's quite enough," interrupted Gerant, bringing a halt to the growing roasting of Blake. Cane, though momentarily entertained by their banter, felt a little lost.

He sat down, pulling up a chair next to the pallid, young Rowan, who seemed more preoccupied with writing in his small notebook than eating. Tristan happily shoved a plate of food in Cane's direction.

Tucking in, he let his eyes sweep over these strangers: Gerant, the cheerful leader with a penchant for theatrics, seemed to carry the mantel of authority, the two brothers, Tristan and Percy, two opposites if ever there were. Then there was Rowan, with his pale, poetic demeanor, who might have been composing an ode that very instant, and in stark contrast stood Blake, a burly slab of confidence with a moustache so absurdly magnificent it deserved its own title and coat of arms.

As much as Cane tried to relax into the setting, his thoughts kept drifting back to the Baroness, sleeping alone in the organ room. Would she panic if she woke up to find herself alone? How could he repay these men for their help? He'd imposed on them long enough.

"No need to fret," said a tall, stoic-looking man also wearing a habit, who had just entered the kitchen with a stride that suggested he was more used to leading marches than morning prayers. "Felix is with your lady friend, keeping an eye on things. And you'll repay us for our hospitality by lending us your skills." This new addition to the group gave Cane a fatherly look. "And no more thoughts of imposing. We're glad to help."

Cane stared at him. "How... how do you know what I'm thinking?"

The tall man grinned. "Oh, please, young man. You're not that mysterious. And I'm not that magical. You were wearing that 'I'm worried about my companion' look on your face like an ill-fitting toupée. Plus, you're a well-brought-up young chap and would of course not want to be seen as a charity case. I'm Bain, by the way, not 'bane', ha ha. Spelled with an 'i', not an 'e', though the others would probably disagree."

Bain extended a firm handshake to Cane. The twinkle in his eye belied the stern contours of his face.

The men all chuckled again, and Cane was beginning to get the impression that this was a regular occurrence. They were clearly used to each other's quirks.

Cane, however, had pressing business to attend to. "Well, as kind as your hospitality is, I must take the Baroness to her father, Duke Nieman."

Gerant gave Bain an uneasy look. "Ah, yes. About that. I don't think the Duke will be rolling out the red carpet for her. Or you, for that matter."

Cane, halfway through a particularly delicious mouthful of bread, almost choked. "What? Why?"

"Let's just say the Duke is no longer as fond of his daughter as he once was. She was supposed to provide him with a nice, neat little heir to push his political ambitions. Instead, there's been no heir, the Baron has turned into an impoverished recluse, and the Duke has washed his hands of them. Not only was no heir forthcoming, but since his marriage, the Baron has been a man transformed. He no longer tends to his lands; his income has dwindled, and he no longer appears in his usual social circles. His influence at court is all but gone along with it his usefulness to the Duke."

Though Cane felt an affinity for these men and they were well informed, he remained dubious about what role they played. Still, he decided to trust them. "But... I saw a child at the castle. An infant. Yes... but there was something not quite right with it... her." Cane battled through the flashes of what he saw. It would sound absurd. "The Baroness insisted it wasn't hers, but I could have sworn I saw her holding it!"

Gerant leaned back, now fully intrigued. "Oh, this does put a different spin on things. And where is this mystery baby now?"

"That's just it," Cane said, putting down his fork. "I'm not sure. At first, I thought maybe it was the lovechild of the Baron and Arabella, but that wouldn't explain why the Baroness was holding her, and well, I didn't exactly have time to fully explore—"

"Ah, so the Baron had a sweetheart," Gerant hummed thoughtfully. "The plot thickens."

Cane hesitated, suddenly unsure. His mind, a tangle of mismatched memories, mocked him. The Baroness's words echoed in his thoughts, dismissing the child's existence so convincingly that he questioned his own certainty. Could the shock have clouded his judgment? He rubbed the back of his neck. "There was something unnatural about the castle. Things happened so quickly. I'm not even fully sure there was a child, let alone if it was the Baron's."

Gerant looked at him sympathetically. "Things are more complicated than they seem, eh? In any case, rushing off to the Duke isn't the wisest plan." He paused before asking, "Weren't you commissioned by King Aurelius to seek a meeting with the Baron so that he may help him in his time of need?"

"How do you know all this detail?" asked Cane. "Regardless, I must take the Baroness to the Palace of Bellingham if she has nowhere else to go."

"An unwise decision," warned Bain.

"And why not?"

"Well, for starters, you'd be spotted a mile away in that uniform. The Duke's scouts would be on you before you had time to draw breath, let alone your sword. They could indict you for any crime they choose: kidnapping the Baroness for a handsome ransom, for example. And," he added, his expression darkening his stern face, "the Duke isn't half as generous as his reputation suggests. Don't be impetuous and tempt the jaws of fate. You might think you're walking into a gathering of house cats, but it's more like stepping into a lion's den."

Cane, suddenly feeling like a pawn in a game he hadn't signed up for, let out a frustrated sigh. "I'm not sure I understand. Why would Duke Nieman have scouts?" He was on the verge of questioning their claims, but the sickly strangeness of the castle crept back into his thoughts. His world had taken a sharp turn into the unknown. It might be wise to heed these men who seemed to mean well. "And if this is all true, what exactly do you suggest I do?"

Gerant's eyes sparkled with a knowing light as if waiting for that very question. "First, I suggest you listen carefully. There's more at play here than meets the eye. Welcome to the real world, my boy, where fairy tales have two heads."

That's not the only thing that has two heads, thought Cane ruefully, shifting uncomfortably on the creaky wooden chair. The image of the Baron and Arabella melded together in a grotesque mass of sagging flesh plagued him. Trying to focus on Gerant's words, he ignored the part of him desperate to whisk the Baroness away to King Aurelius and wash his hands of the whole affair. They had yet to broach the mind-bending matter of those mutant cannibals and the Baron's new 'look'. His assignment had taken on a demented dimension. It felt as though he was stumbling from one surreal scene to the next, where nothing and no one were what they seemed. Even these apparently trustworthy men wore masks to conceal their true stations in life. And what role did he play in all this? For the time being, he continued in the role of the hapless audience member—first drawn into the Baron's charade, now trapped in a creaky seat, watching a performance he had not bought a ticket for.

Accept it, life has taken a sharp turn off the normalcy map. There's no going back. He decided his best option was to listen to Gerant, however bizarre the tale.

———— ◆◇◆ ————

"This is not a fairy tale like those of old," Gerant began, his voice taking on a storyteller's cadence. "Yet it does start with the words 'Once upon a time, there was a kingdom'. The kingdom of South Valoria, to be precise, where the sovereign family has reigned peacefully for many a decade. The people were content, with no need for change. But, as in all such tales, an evil force arrived—a foreign presence in this tranquil land. And that, my dear boy, is where our Duke makes his entrance. He came with a small but impressive entourage, and where he came from, no one knows. What they do know is that he's a master schemer, and he's been chipping away at Aurelius's reign and allies, right under his old nose."

Cane's mind raced to keep up with Gerant's tale. He recalled the slight changes at court he had dismissed as insignificant over the past few years. The lands were at peace. Why would anyone want to unseat Aurelius? Was this some elaborate jest? But the seriousness in the Viscount's tone kept him silent.

"You must have noticed, being one of the Imperial Guards, that the influential dukes and earls who once stood by our sovereign leader are now bankrupt or missing," Gerant continued. "Those the Duke couldn't corrupt, he imprisoned. His goal? To seize control of our lands." Gerant paused. His expression sombre. "Your father, the Earl of Cromlech, was one of his victims. He wouldn't yield to the Duke's demands, wouldn't be swayed by empty promises. For his loyalty to the Sovereign Realm, he and your mother were imprisoned."

"No! They died!" Cane cried, jumping up. His chair clattered to the floor. "Why do you tell me such lies?"

"You know only what the Duke wants you to know. Remember, this tale has two heads: the one you see and the one you don't. The truth is in the hidden head. This man is sick to the very core. An evil hand guides his will. Your parents were taken, forced into servitude along with others who resisted. Duke Nieman uses his victims as labourers, making them dig in the mud to help create a reservoir at Gribthorpe in the west. Death would be a mercy to them."

Staring at Gerant, stunned beyond words, Cane wondered what this man was trying to achieve. Why invent such hurtful lies about his parents? As if sensing his scepticism, Gerant went into the pantry and returned with a chest full of papers.

"Here are the letters the Duke sent to each of us, summoning us to Malcrov Court or, in other cases, on a fictitious expedition to North Valoria."

Cane pulled out one of the scrolls from the pile that bore the symbol of the Duke's seal. Gerant continued, "Numerous key figures have stopped attending the king's court sessions these past two years. You've noticed this, I'm sure."

Sinking back into his chair, Cane listened in a daze. These men did not know that he would be there that day. It seemed impossible for them to prepare all these documents on such short notice or concoct such a story merely for his benefit. In fact, the more he thought about it, the more their observations and explanations pointed to the opposite being true. He cast his mind back to two years ago when he had just been promoted to the position of Imperial Guard, coinciding with his parents' disappearance. Although he lacked experience in life as a young man, he began to grasp, with incredulous recognition, the implications of what was being said. Yet, he felt he was only seeing flecks of the truth.

"My parents... alive, all this time?" Cane muttered, picking up his chair in slow motion, automatically sitting down, his stare vacant, unable to get his mind to catch up with the meaning of his words.

"Yes," Gerant confirmed sympathetically. "I'm sorry Cane. They're toiling in a prison camp near Gribthorpe. There, the women serve as cooks and cleaners, while the men are building a dam across the River Titan, now dubbed Titan's Vein. From it pours the prisoners' blood sweat and tears into what the locals call the Basin of Whispering

Hollows." Gerant placed his large, rough hands flat on the table. "I'm sorry, young man. This is a terrible burden to bear, but there's more you need to know."

Cane shot to his feet again, his chair scraping loudly against the floor. "More! Yesterday, I set out on a gloomy assignment. Since then, I've witnessed horrors beyond imagination, sought refuge among gentry playing at monks, and discovered that my parents—whom I've mourned—are likely still alive, enslaved by a man I once thought a benefactor, but who is instead a demonic tyrant. I'm not sure a man could take *more*."

He slumped back down again, burying his head in his hands. Almost immediately, though, he sprang up, pacing the stone floor as the six men watched him in silence, following his every step. Back and forth he went, his mind whirring like a windmill in a storm. These men seemed earnest enough, not the sort to make up wild tales or kidnap strangers. And though Cane's reason balked at the story, his instincts told him there was truth in it.

Finally, he stopped pacing and faced Gerant. "Alright," he said, his voice steadier now. "What else do I need to know?"

Chapter 4

HOLIER THAN THOU

G ERANT'S CONCERNED FACE RESEMBLED a cartographer's dream, his tone hovering somewhere between 'I hate to be the bearer of bad news' and 'Don't shoot the messenger'. "It's not exactly a pleasure to share this, but here we are." He sighed heavily before continuing. "You and the young lady are in very real danger. Something followed you here yesterday, your presence here has endangered us all."

Percy gulped audibly. "So, by that you're implying we're in very real danger too? Those 'things' could be after *us*?"

Surprisingly, Gerant smiled at Percy's panic. "Oh, yes. Hellhounds, demons, Blake's sour ex-girlfriends—take your pick. Something nasty is snapping at all our heels now, young man." Percy looked as though he might faint, which seemed to amuse rather than concern his older brother, Tristan, who gave him a reassuring pat on the back.

"Don't worry, little brother. I'll protect you." The wink he added didn't exactly scream confidence, but it was well meant.

When Gerant looked at Cane, his smile faded. "Whatever followed you here, we managed to keep them at bay last night, but we failed to kill or capture them."

"Hideous creatures," Bain added. "We don't know what they are. Though I'm certain they didn't come here for the monastery's room service."

"And they're naked!" exclaimed Percy.

This news worried Cane—not so much the lack of clothes, more the possibility of the crawlers having followed them. "Wait a moment! I know of what you speak. I killed those things back at Castle Gradunce."

Bain was not reassured. "These *things* come from the castle?"

"Yes," Cane said. "I presume we're talking about the same... *things*. Hideous, naked creatures are not exactly a common daily sight. I don't know what they are either. If we're to believe the rumours, they are the 'castle crawlers'. But I drowned them in the castle's kitchen. Flooded the place with water from the silo. Trust me, none of them could've survived. I mean, unless they were already outside." His tone turned sad. "I had to kill them; they were eating the servants." He paused for the 'yucks' and 'arghs' to pass. "As I said, not all of them might have been in the kitchen."

"So, those rumours of ghouls are true," said Bain.

"I don't think they are ghouls," said Cane. "They feed off the living. But they're not human either. I've been hunting since I could hold a bow, and they are like no beast that walks our lands in Valoria."

"We're all going to die!" young Percy wailed.

"I say let's go bash their skulls in if they dare come back," said his foolhardier brother Tristan.

"Yes, let's not hide in here like cowards," Blake agreed, looking ready to pounce.

"Calmly now," Gerant soothed, trying to temper the mounting lust for blood. "We don't know what we're up against."

"How did you keep them at bay last night?" Cane asked.

"Well, we didn't exactly fight them. We played the organ."

Cane did a double take. "Excuse me?"

"Our watchman was Felix last night. He spotted them lurking in the distance. They stayed back until Rowan here stopped playing the organ. Once the music stopped, they shook the gates like they were late for a dinner reservation—and *we* were on the menu. So, Rowan played the organ all night."

"That explains why I slept so well," said Cane.

"And why I didn't," grumbled the solemn Rowan not looking up from his book.

Cane felt a little uneasy, as though Rowan blamed him.

"Don't mind him," said Bain gruffly. "He's always a bundle of laughs."

"Why didn't you try to kill them?" Cane asked

"Do we look like soldiers?" Tristan asked, with a twinkle in his eye, clearly hoping Cane would say 'yes'.

"I've only ever wielded a quill, not a sword," said Rowan.

"And I'm far too young to be anyone's midnight snack," said Percy.

"I've got more, many more, women to woo," said Blake.

Gerant looked to Cane. "We need your help. We're not prepared for a siege. This whole mess has surpassed our expectations. It's beyond the realm of just men and politics. Cane, with your skills, you could be a great aid to us. We need to be ready for whatever comes next."

"Of course I'll help," said Cane. "What of the Baroness? I must help her too. I cannot abandon her. She cannot go back there."

"Pretty thing, too," Bain remarked, not bothering to hide his grin as he tore into some cornbread like it had personally offended him.

"One thing at a time," said Gerant. "Our attackers must be dealt with first. Come with me. We have a modest arsenal, and I think you'll find something to your liking to help fend them off, should they return."

They made their way to the monastery's cellar, which turned out to be a collection of rooms that could put even the most affluent castle pantry to shame. Enough cured meats, cheeses, pickles, and jams to rival a royal banquet stretched before him. Cane almost felt guilty for being armed with a sword instead of a fork—until they arrived at the weapons store.

An imposing collection of weaponry lined the walls: gleaming swords, their hilts intricately carved, several so old they might have been antiques; longbows crafted from yew wood, with quivers of arrows tipped in polished iron; and flails hanging menacingly from hooks, their spiked heads ready to gauge flesh. Some of the pieces were clearly for display, too elaborate to be practical, but others looked like they had seen real battle. A row of halberds stood upright in the corner, while an old but finely kept crossbow rested on a stand, its string taut and ready for action. That was Cane's weapon of choice.

Tristan proudly waved his hand at a set of small wooden catapults. "See these beauties here? I made them myself. This one's Legbreaker, the other's Endmaker, and this little fellow is Mercy Shooter."

His brother Percy snorted. "More like Peashooter."

"Oi," Tristan feigned feeling insulted. "Mercy Shooter gets the job done. Right between the eyes." He poked his brother on the forehead. "No mercy."

As the men continued through the cellar, Gerant began outlining their situation, throwing in the occasional grumble about Duke Nieman and his underhand takeover. "You see, we've expected a conflict with that scoundrel Nieman for a long time, but we're not exactly an army ourselves—just a few noblemen in monk's robes. By pretending to be monks, we've managed to keep an eye on things. The Duke? He has the people of Bellingham and the surrounding towns eating out of his hand. No one even thinks of him as an outsider anymore, which is... problematic."

"You do realise there are only seven of you?" Cane said, sounding both impressed and concerned.

"Seven of us here," Gerant corrected with a wink. "But out there? We've got an invisible army ready to strike when the time is right. All loyal men and women, prepared to do what needs to be done. Maybe two hundred strong."

"But know this," Bain's voice was crisp, "we're not instigators of war. We'll only act if it comes to that."

"And where do I fit into all of this?" A soft, frail voice asked from behind them.

The Baroness, pale and weary, appeared in the archway, with a man who must have been Felix huffing behind her, looking deeply apologetic.

"Oh, where are my manners?" Felix beamed, extending a chubby hand. "Felix, at your service! How was breakfast?"

Cane shook his hand politely. "Delicious thank you." He glanced at Agatha, noticing she swayed slightly, and he rushed forward to steady her.

"Baroness, we thought you were resting," he said gently.

"I've rested my body, but I fear my mind will never find peace again."

"Rowan," said Gerant, "please show the Baroness where she can freshen up. We'll meet you in the organ room shortly, Baroness."

"Come, my lady, this way." Rowan guided her like a chivalrous knight. She offered him a weak smile before allowing herself to be escorted away.

Gerant turned back to the others. "Now," he said after a suitable pause, "tell us more about what happened at the castle. We need to know everything."

Cane took a deep breath, uncertain if they'd even believe him. Grotesque beings, half-eaten servants, and then—well, the Baron.

"You're not going to believe this," Cane warned. "The Baron... he wasn't alone. He had somehow... merged with a woman."

Bain and Gerant exchanged puzzled glances. "Merged?" Bain asked, unconvinced. "What do you mean?"

"One body, two souls," Cane said, struggling to explain. "The woman—Arabella. They'd fused into a single being. I found them like that." Cane pressed his hands together. "As one."

"Well," Gerant muttered, shaking his head, "that's certainly a new way of putting it. You sure you didn't just catch them in the *act*?"

Tristan giggled. "Maybe the Baron was using his bagpipes to handle his problem, instead of an organ."

"Oh no, I think he was using his organ alright," Blake said, laughing.

"I may be naïve in certain matters, but I know what I saw," said Cane firmly. "There was nothing romantic or funny about it. They were... transformed. Eight limbs, two heads, one body."

"Yuck!" The brothers recoiled in disgust.

"Impossible!" Bain exclaimed. "Such a thing is impossible!"

"I would have said the same myself, sir, had I not seen it with my own eyes."

"And what, pray tell, has happened to him—or them?" asked Gerant.

"Well, that's the million-pentling question, isn't it? He... it... they must still be at the castle. It couldn't move them, and... well, I couldn't exactly help them either."

His face deep in thought, Gerant stroked his beard. "This situation is more bent than a politician's promise. Ineffable creatures, merging bodies... ghastly. And there's a whiff of forbidden magic behind it all!"

"Forgive me, sir," Cane said, trying to steer the conversation back from the brink of wild conjecture, "but magic no longer exists in Valoria."

Gerant chuckled, the way a grandfather might when amused by a child's naivety. "Oh, no, no, dear boy. How could you possibly think you live in a world without magic? Magic is alive and well, all around us. It's in the brew of a simple cup of tea, the rise of the sun each morning, the flash of fireworks on a midsummer's night. That chamomile I gave you last night—did it not calm your nerves?"

"You practice forbidden magic?" asked Cane.

"Good heavens, no! Practical magic. Herbs, roots, minerals—all tools of a subtle sorcery that's as old as the hills. Why, right outside the monastery, we've planted aconite. Wolfsbane, if you like your flora with a bit of bite. It's not the dark arts you're imagining, but rather a gardener's precaution. As for the mutants we encountered yesterday, well, that might be knocking on the door of a different school of sorcery: forbidden magic."

"More to the point, Gerant," said Bain, who had been striding in the background. "I don't trust the Baroness. She's involved in all this somehow."

Gerant turned to his friend and said good-naturedly, "Bain, you've never trusted any woman since that dazzling courtier danced you into a corner at the hunter's ball and then rode off on your prize stallion. Hardly news."

Cane was taken aback. Bain, suspicious of the Baroness? "But she's so... fragile! How could someone like her be involved in anything as ghastly as—"

"Flesh-eating, cannibalistic castle crawlers?" suggested Gerant. "Let's call them crawlers—less of a mouthful, if you pardon the pun."

Bain's expression darkened further. "Cane, she lived there! Open your eyes, boy. People don't just decide to merge with other people for fun or out of boredom. If anyone knows what's going on, it's her."

Feeling like a schoolboy being scolded for not paying attention in class, Cane shifted uncomfortably under Bain's stern gaze.

"Well, whether she knows anything or not, we'll soon find out when we ask her," Gerant interjected smoothly, as peacemaker.

In the organ room, the sun was doing its best to shine through the dark clouds outside, sending flickers of light through the tall windows as if trying to remind everyone that daylight still existed—somewhere.

Cane, now armed with a fine crossbow and a quiver of bolts, sat beside Agatha, who looked about as cheerful as a wilted flower. He wondered if she'd ever smiled in her life. Gerant, undeterred by her solemn mood, addressed her in his best fatherly tone.

"Now, my dear, I don't know what you plan to do about your father, Duke Nieman, but I must warn you—a warm welcome may not be in the cards. There's the small matter of you failing to provide the Baron with an heir, which, I understand, has put you in quite a precarious position." He paused, exchanging a glance with Cane, who suddenly found the floor very interesting. "Unless, of course, you do have a child?"

Agatha's eyes widened, her cheeks flushing as if someone had slapped her with a bouquet of brambles. "No, sir, for my sins, I do not—"

Gerant dropped the matter, giving her space to talk.

Agatha's trembling voice broke the awkward silence. "I know you must all be aware of my... unfortunate situation. I don't understand why I've become such a disappointment—to my husband, my father. The servants—oh, how they laughed behind my back. 'The barren Baroness', they called me." Her hands clenched in her lap. "I don't know what I've done to deserve this. My husband—he was kind when we first married, but over time... well, as you can imagine, his patience wore thin."

Her voice trailed off into another fit of quiet sobbing. She fiddled with her necklace, twisting it around her finger to ease her anxiety. Gerant gently patted her shoulder. "Now, now, my dear, no more tears. You've suffered more than enough for someone so young. You're a victim, that much is clear. If I were a man who believed in fate, I'd say you were brought here for a reason. Perhaps you know something that could help us stop your father from carrying out his plans."

"My father?" Agatha's face hardened, her tears drying up as if by magic. "What plans would my father have?"

Gerant's kind, grey eyes locked onto hers with an intensity that said, 'don't hold out on me now'. Agatha sighed, resigning herself to his unspoken demand. "I know very little of my father's affairs. My life was sheltered—far from his dealings. We moved when I was just a child, after my mother died. All I remember is darkness. When I came of age, my father arranged my marriage to the Baron, as custom dictates. The Baron treated me well enough, though neither of us truly chose this path. But as you can imagine, the presence of a certain woman—Arabella, the love of his life—made things... complicated."

Her lips quivered. "And now, here I am, swept up in a fiasco I can't even begin to comprehend. All I know is that I was barely holding onto my sanity when this Imperial Guard saved me."

Cane shifted uncomfortably in the role of hero.

"Rest assured, my dear Baroness, you're safe here," Gerant said. "And perhaps in time, the answers will present themselves—whether we like them or not."

Blake sauntered over to Cane, his grin wide and knowing. Leaning in like a conspirator about to reveal a golden nugget of advice. "Women, eh?" he snickered. "The prettier they are, the more likely they are to drive you absolutely mad. Ha! It's as if they come with a built-in ball-ache." He punctuated his maxim with a hearty slap on Cane's back.

Cane forced a smile. Foolish as Blake's words were, they held a grain of truth—a grain stuck in his mind, burrowing deeper with each passing thought. Meeting Agatha: a step closer to Captain of the Guard, or to one of Blake's 'ball-aches'?

Chapter 5

SHADOWS THAT FOLLOW

"B ARONESS," GERANT HAD ADOPTED a 'talking to fragile damsels' tone, "you are aware that we're not only dealing with your father's scheming but also with... those creatures... those crawlers. Perhaps, you could shed some light on this matter?" He paused tactfully, waiting for her sobs to taper off. "Any information you might have, no matter how trivial, could be vital."

Agatha hesitated, her fingers worrying the hem of her dress, her eyes fixed on her lap. "I... I'm not sure what you mean, sir," she stammered, her voice so quiet Cane wondered if she hoped her lack of volume might spare her from further questions. "The first I saw them was yesterday." She glanced shyly at Cane, like a child gauging if her confession would earn her a scolding. "Until then I'd only heard rumours, silly, unkind stories about the Baron, about how he didn't feed his servants enough, so they fed off each other."

"I knew he was short on funds but that's a tad extreme for cutting down on the grocery bills!" Felix exclaimed.

"It was all hurtful gossip, you understand," Agatha continued. "I put it down to servants being spiteful. Although..." She bit her lip, clearly uncomfortable. "We did seem to hire new staff every month, but I, being inexperienced in such things, assumed that was normal. The rumours of... cannibalism... were just that, rumours."

Gerant stroked his beard like a man who believed that stroking facial hair would awaken wisdom. "These are not rumours, Baroness. We have seen them, up close. So have you. Now, you know as well as we do, they are quite real. Any detail, no matter how small, might help us."

Agatha looked deeply troubled. "I once heard the maids talking of mysterious happenings at night that made them scared to go out alone. Shadows moving on their own, unexplained wailing. My husband dismissed it all as an overactive imagination."

"Of course he did," Bain muttered. "Men with secrets are excellent at dismissing things they don't want to talk about. Anything more specific, though?" His gaze bore into hers with a relentless intensity that seemed to say, 'I know you're hiding something'.

Agatha shook her head. "I'm sorry. I wish I could offer more. But men always keep me, um, well, sheltered from these matters."

Felix sighed, leaning back in his chair as though he'd just been told his favourite pie was off the menu. "It was worth a try."

"You must stay here for now, Baroness," Gerant said firmly. "You do understand that we're all in danger? Should your whereabouts be discovered, particularly by your father—" He let the implication speak for itself.

"My father may be strict," Agatha said defensively, "but he doesn't go around murdering people."

"Ah, but fathers like yours rarely share their business with their daughters, do they?" Felix scratched his wispy ginger beard and took a noisy bite of his apple; apparently fuelling his thought process. "Maybe the crawlers were sent by the Duke," he suggested, mouth full. "Food for thought."

Gerant gave Felix a look that suggested he could do without such pearls of wisdom. "Maybe," he said, noncommittal. "Speaking of food. Felix, why don't you take the young lady to the kitchen for some breakfast? She needs to regain her strength."

Felix brightened at the task. "Why yes, of course! Come along, dear," he said to Agatha, his tone far too cheery for the current mood. "This must all be quite distressing for you." He offered her his arm.

Once they were gone, Gerant turned to Cane. "Tell us exactly what happened in the castle with these crawlers."

Taking a deep breath, Cane began recounting his killing spree in the castle kitchens. Tension mounted with every stab and malformed limb described. The men's frowns grew longer by the second. He could practically hear the icy prickles crackling up their spines.

"We must return to the castle as soon as possible," Gerant said decisively.

"Oh yes, of course!" said Tristan. "That's what I was just about to say. Let's go back into the mouth of hell. What a fine idea. Sounds like a right hoot!"

"Don't worry, Tristan, I have other plans for you," said Gerant. "But Cane, you are the very man we need to train our men. You asked what you could do in return for our help—well, there you have it. You shall be our captain."

Captain? That wasn't quite what Cane had hoped for: Captain of the Guard yes, Captain of Undercover Gentry, not so much. "Naturally, I thank you for deeming me fit for this role, sir," Cane replied without hesitation, though inwardly, he was less than thrilled at the prospect. It was all highly irregular. "First, I must visit King Aurelius. I have obligations to the Sovereign Court, and after hearing all of this, it seems only right to confer with him. Perhaps he has a plan to defeat the Duke. And I must free my parents from the Duke's prison in Gribthorpe."

"Such impetuous action will compromise your position!" Bain almost shouted in his angry schoolmaster tone as though berating a wayward student and earning that 'e' in bane. "There are hundreds of men between you and your parents. And more to the point, you are needed *here*."

Cane sighed. "I understand. But I must resume my duties as Imperial Guard."

"Haven't you been listening?" Bain asked, tempering his rising impatience and incredulity. "There is nothing to be guard of. Nieman holds the power now. To carry on as normal is paramount to siding with him."

Gerant raised a hand to defuse the tension. "First things first. Deal with those crawlers tonight, please, Cane. You're always first at the Sovereign Games, and right now, we need those skills. We've provided the weapon, you provide the results. We can't afford to be under siege by crawlers. And you can't risk being followed by them."

Cane nodded. It seemed like he was being recruited into every job but the one he really wanted: freeing his parents. "All right," he agreed.

"That's the spirit, lad," Bain said, a grin creeping into his otherwise serious expression. "Now get ready to save Valoria, one evil creature at a time."

<hr>

Each prepared for battle in their own peculiar way: Rowan loosened his fingers at the organ, Bain methodically lit the torches, Cane checked his bow while the brothers and Felix busied themselves cooking what could either be a celebratory feast or a final meal.

The tall bushes outside the monastery's walls became a waving crowd in the moonlight, casting shadows that competed to become the longest. Nothing stirred. Even the owls, who normally flitted down like clockwork from the quarry for their evening buffet, chose to fast tonight. The wind, which had been gusting earlier, now seemed to have taken a break, as though it too was tired of fighting against the pressure of the suffocating stillness. It was the kind of night that gave gothic poets inspiration and mothers nightmares.

Positioned at the top terrace, Cane scanned the grounds with an intensity that suggested he expected trouble and was ready to meet it with bolts and an endless serving of no mercy. Taut nerves and heightened senses readied him for the inevitable confrontation.

Bain approached, his torch shone a light across the gardens. His normally heavy footsteps oddly muffled, as though even the ground was stifled to a heavy silence. "It's never like this," Bain remarked, loosening his cape in an attempt to relieve some of the tension. "Such a suffocating atmosphere usually belongs to summer."

Cane gave a curt nod. "I felt it at the castle, too. There's definitely something unnatural here." *Understatement of the century*, he thought. It wasn't every day you found yourself waiting for cannibalistic creatures to pop out from the bushes. He'd never faced such a task. Dread embraced him like a curse.

"I can hear them, but I can't see them," Cane whispered, his hawk-like gaze sweeping over the shadowed landscape. His instincts prickled. All life around him was holding its breath, not daring to inhale the toxicity.

Bain shuddered, his face scrunching up as if he'd just smelled a particularly foul egg. "I do declare I can *smell* them. Never has our clean moor air reeked so rotten." He sniffed the air with exaggerated revulsion. "It's almost unbearable."

"Their scent could work in our favour if only we had some wind," Cane said. A rustle in the undergrowth below caught his attention. "There!" he pointed. "They've heard us. They're moving around to the west side."

With practiced precision, Cane loaded a bolt and pulled the string back, tracking the rustling below. A glint caught his eye—a flash of some *thing* peeking up from the darkness. Without hesitation, he let the bolt fly. A scream, agonising and hellish, exploded from the bushes, clawing at the air like a wounded beast.

"Well done! I hear more of them moving!" Bain's wide-eyed terror betrayed the urgency behind his gruff tone. "We've got to secure the lower cloisters in case they try to sneak in."

Cane was already in motion. "Tell Rowan to get that organ playing," he said, a steadying calm taking hold. When Bain looked at him, startled by the direct command, Cane didn't falter. "Go on! Unless you fancy seeing them up close."

As Bain hurried off, the dulcet strains of the organ floated through the night. Apparently, Rowan had already heard the cries. The music drifted through the gardens, and with it came Agatha's mellifluous voice, delicate but powerful enough to lull monsters to a standstill.

The effect was immediate. Two remaining crawlers, pale parodies of humanity, rose from their hiding places, moving as though in a trance. They trembled, their ashen skin stretched taut over crooked limbs, their misshapen faces frozen in some derisory creation of life. It was almost—almost—pitiful.

"Shine your light over there!" Cane directed Bain. The gawping goons didn't even flinch when the bright torchlight hit their sunken eyes, casting their grotesque forms into sharp relief. In that brief moment, Cane felt an unexpected pang of pity for the things, as wretched as they were. But pity wouldn't save anyone tonight. He had seen what they were capable of: ripping flesh from bones, feasting on the living. There was no room for pity.

Drawing back his bow again, Cane aimed at the misshapen figures. The crawlers remained hypnotised by the organ's spell, unaware of their impending doom. As Agatha's final note rang out, Cane released his bolts. The crawlers gasped their last breaths, collapsing into the cold, frozen grass.

It was over.

"Well, that was easier than I feared," Bain said with a sigh of relief. "Let's hope there were only three."

Heading back to the courtyard, something by the well caught Cane's eye. The well, which by day was as innocent as any stone hole in the ground, now seemed ominous under the moon's pale glow. Its usual role as 'source of life' had switched to 'source of something far darker' as if danger not water lurked within.

Cane and Bain crept closer, crossbow and torch at the ready, every instinct screaming that whatever they were about to face wouldn't be pleasant. From behind the well, a dark form began to rise, limbs groping at the air, as if searching blindly for something lost. The figure stumbled forward, its movements erratic. Bain let out a low, horrified gasp.

"There must have been four."

Cane's heart sank as the bulky crawler came into view. He pulled back a bolt, his hands moving automatically, the drill of 'kill or be killed' taking over. The bolt flew straight and true—Cane never missed. But when Bain's torchlight illuminated the fallen figure, Cane's stomach turned to rock.

It was the fused form of the Baron and Arabella, their bodies together in a horrifying union. Cane's heart skipped a beat—no, several beats. A wave of guilt and revulsion crashed over him.

As the fused beings collapsed against the well, their last breath came in a chilling, synchronised warning. "Beware! No woman..." And then, they tumbled backward into the well, their fall ended in a splash that reverberated through the hollow pit.

"No!" Cane rushed forward, but it was too late. They were gone. His hands gripped the cold stone rim of the well, knuckles white. "I killed them."

Bain, sensing the weight of the moment, gently placed a hand on Cane's shoulder. "It was a mercy, Cane. They could never have lived like that. Come, there's nothing more to be done here. Let's go inside."

Cane moved with leaden feet, burdened with remorse. He had never been in a real battle scenario of taking the life of another person. Every thought waded through a swamp of guilt. This wasn't just about killing monsters anymore; this was about watching his normality, his innocence crumble before him. He'd killed two people.

He took one last look at the well. Bain was right. It was time to leave. There was nothing he could do here.

The darkness inside the cloisters felt even heavier than before.

"Let's go eat," said Bain. "I'm famished."

Cane had quite lost his appetite but followed Bain down into the dining hall, nonetheless.

Chapter 6

SNOOP AND DESTROY

F ELIX CLAPPED HIS HANDS with urgency. "Hail brave warriors! Well done! Come, come, eat while it's hot!" His enthusiasm was that of a man presenting a feast to heroes returning from slaying the dragon, though the setting left much to be desired. The stone-flagged floors, bare walls, and towering ceilings were unforgiving to graceless eaters—very clang of cutlery resonated through the air like a church bell. Still, despite the austerity, the richness of the food surprised them. Felix had proven that miracles weren't limited to divine intervention. Sometimes they came in the form of caramelised potatoes and braised pheasant.

Percy, whose small frame seemed ill-equipped for even a single potato, let alone a pheasant, asked with all the hunger of a man twice his size. "What delights do you have for us tonight, Felix? I could eat a whole cow!"

"Ha! You're always thinking with your stomach," Felix jabbed.

Percy tried to stand taller. "And you're one to talk! Maybe you should leave the serious eating to me and just hand over your plate—"

Felix let out a hearty laugh. "I'm as likely to stop eating heartily as you are to let your curly locks run wild."

Felix's retort amused Tristan. "Percy, it's like your head's trying to join the monastery by taking a vow of stillness."

"I'll have you know this fine style is in homage to our great ancestor, Sir Perceval. He wore his curls flat and he was a warlord, a true knight, and at the Great Battle, he saved—"

"—saved the horses two by two, carried them right out of the gates, blah blah," Tristan cut him off with a mock yawn, drawing chuckles from the rest of the men around the table. "Honestly, Percy, if I had a pentling for every time you told that story, I'd buy my own kingdom and call it *Percyland*, just to spare the rest of us."

After the horrors of the night, being with men who could still laugh at and with each other was something of a comfort to Cane. There was camaraderie in this band of pseudo-monks. Despite the fear waiting for them outside, the humour kept them tethered to a shared, sane reality inside.

The mood shifted slightly when Gerant stood, raising his tankard in a mock grand gesture. "I'd like to officially welcome Cane of Cromlech and Baroness Gradunce to our humble abode," he began with a dramatic flourish. "Though, to be fair, I'm not sure they *chose* to be here, but nevertheless—we're happy to play the obliging hosts!"

The others raised their tankards, echoing the sentiment with hearty gulps before digging into their pheasant. Cane noticed Agatha picked at her food. He suspected her thoughts were likely on the Duke, uncertain whether he was the tyrant Gerant painted him to be.

For now, though, the conversation thankfully stayed on light topics, avoiding anything serious. That was, until Felix clapped his hands again and called out, "Come now, you whippersnappers!" He pointed a playful finger at the drowsy duo of Tristan and Percy. "Let's make use of those young limbs of yours before they wither away!" With that, they were promptly despatched to wash the plates.

"I am a little tired myself," said Agatha quietly rising. Before Cane could escort her to her quarters, Rowan was already at her side.

Blake, who had been doing a terrible job of containing his curiosity, finally burst when they had left. "What was that out there, Cane?" he blurted out, his voice louder than intended in the echoey dining hall.

"Honestly? I don't know much more than you do. Whatever the Baron had become, it must've followed us here last night. I'm as much in the dark as anyone."

"And his final words? Bain said something about 'beware the woman'. What could that mean?"

"I thought he said, '*Take care, the woman*'," Cane corrected him. "Probably something to do with the Baroness."

"So, he used his final breath to tell us to look after his wife? Rather unlikely, don't you think?" Bain frowned.

"Or maybe 'beware' to warn us," said Cane. "Not 'take care' to look after but to be careful because she's... fragile. Oh, I don't know. Maybe his final wish was for us to look after her. He felt guilty." Cane could tell Bain wasn't convinced. "It's not her fault. Spend enough time in Castle Gradunce, and you'd be a little crazed too. Trust me, the place practically breathes madness."

Blake, who had been nervously eyeing the door, asked, "Are we sure there aren't more of those things out there?"

"At this moment, we know very little," Gerant replied, his words weren't particularly reassuring. "We'll examine the crawlers in daylight. Then we'll return to the Baron's castle to see if we can get to the root of this mystery."

Felix re-entered the room after Tristan and Percy, coughing and waving his hands theatrically through the smoke from Gerant's pipe. "If it weren't for the fact that the air outside was so foul, I'd crack a window! Honestly, Gerant, between those asphyxiating clouds and your pipe, it's a toss-up which will suffocate us first!"

"Careful now, Felix, let me assure you when it comes to foggy smells and your socks, you're in no position to complain."

Felix opened his mouth to retort, but the others heckling in unanimous agreement silenced him. He sat down with a sheepish grin and Gerant casually resumed their plans for Bellingham, the smoke swirling as he spoke.

"It's tough to convince people their benefactor is evil. Especially when they're living in comfort and apathy. But that's where our three-pronged approach comes in—my favourite tactic." He grinned. "After Cane's fiasco at the castle, it's time to act. First, we gather information on the Duke's next move. Percy, Tristan, you'll snoop around Bellingham. Second, we'll bring our hidden forces to the monastery for training. Cane, that's where you come in. Third, we'll scout Castle Gradunce for survivors, clues, anything that can help us."

"Well," Felix said, patting his portly belly, "I've never been one to turn down a three-course meal of any kind."

"Me neither," Percy said, trying to sound as brave and light-hearted as the older men.

"Just as well, brother, because it sounds like we'll be dining on risk for breakfast, peril for lunch and disaster for dinner."

"And maybe a serving of catastrophe for supper, if you get caught," Rowan added gloomily, walking back in with a candle.

"As long as we don't get *crumbled* for pudding," Felix chuckled at his own play on words, bringing laughter back to the table.

"Yes," Percy hiccupped, "they'd better not trifle with us!"

"I wouldn't say no to a tasty tart," Blake added, with a broad grin, oblivious his was a little off the mark with his pun.

"Very, good, very good gentlemen," said Gerant. "Let's get down to details."

As the night wore on, the mood gradually sobered and so did the men. Plans were made and strategies discussed. By the time they finished, the pale light of dawn had crept through the moth holes of the old curtains. Morning had come without warning, without sleep.

For all their bravado, none were eager to spring into action. After all, the first task wasn't exactly something anyone was excited about: retrieving the body from the well.

———◄○►———

Gathered around the stone rim, the frozen grass crunched under their boots.

"I'll pull him up," Blake declared, flexing his biceps like a circus strongman. "Easy."

"A pulley system would be better," Rowan said. "Wouldn't want to chafe our delicate hands, now would we?"

"Whatever we do, we'd better be quick," Felix said, glancing at the well. "This is our drinking water. Lower me down in the bucket, and I'll see what's what."

"Why don't we send Rowan down?" Bain suggested with a grin. "He's lighter."

Rowan immediately crossed his arms and glared. "You'll never get me down that dark hole."

"That's why," Felix replied cheerfully.

"And I'm certainly not pulling anyone up," Rowan added, thrusting out his limp hands. "These hands are meant for playing the organ, not lifting anything heavier than a pen or book. What if the beasties come back? Who'll serenade them away?"

"Hah! Stand aside!" Blake flexed, unable to resist. "I welcome the challenge of pulling your heavy backside up—"

"What are you trying to say?" Felix asked in mock abjection.

"I'm not *trying* to say anything. I said it. You've eaten too many of your fine apple tarts," Blake said with a roguish smile.

"Can you manage it alone?" Cane asked.

"With Thunder and Lightning," Blake said, proudly gesturing to his biceps as if they were legendary warriors. "Together, we can handle anything. Besides, I've had *loads* of coulain this morning. It tasted extra smooth. Normally, I only have one cup. So, I am *full* of energy." He stuck out his broad chest, cracking his knuckles like a circus strongman preparing to lift a grand piano.

Blake's over-the-top display of machismo was both ridiculous and painfully amusing. He was bouncing around on his toes. Far too much enthusiasm for a man about to pull a corpse from a well.

Bain rolled his eyes so hard it looked like they might stick in the back of his head. "Give it a rest, Blake. You're making me feel tired just watching you."

"Lots of coulain, you say," Felix's voice resounded from below, as they lowered him down. "Considering the water you used came from yesterday's well, you're *full* of something and it's not just hot air."

Blake froze mid-bounce. "Wait, what?"

"I think you had a nice brew of *Baron* in your cup, not coulain," Felix shouted.

Blake's hand shot to his throat. "What does that mean?!"

Before anyone could answer, Felix's voice pealed, "Pull me up! Now!"

Blake, with all the flair of a showman, flexed again. Thunder and Lightning rose to the occasion, hoisting Felix with ease. But as the bucket cleared the well, it wasn't just Felix's frizzy head emerging. Dangling beneath him were the tangled bodies of the Baron and Arabella.

Rowan, who had been watching with mild amusement, paled at the sight, then said, "You haven't even broken a sweat."

"Who?" Felix gasped. "Me from fear or Mr. Muscles over there?"

"Blake."

"What can I say?" Blake slicked back his hair with a debonair flourish. "Thunder and Lightning make short work of any challenge."

Felix, now back on solid ground, looked down at the grisly mass and grimaced. "Well... that's a messy sight."

The men untied Felix and the heap of flesh that had once been two lovers. Rowan, whose stomach was clearly not designed for such things, hastily volunteered to fetch the shovels. A task he was all too eager to escape to.

"Those crawlers are disturbing enough," Gerant said, studying the fused bodies of the Baron and Arabella. "But this... this beggars belief."

The two were so entwined, it was impossible to tell where one ended and the other began.

Bain crouched down. "Their tissue is physically bound together. How in the seven heavens is this possible? Magic's been outlawed since the Gaene Kin were banished."

"Who are the Gaene Kin?" Cane asked. "Magicians?"

"The Gaene Kin were a tribe of wise women," explained Gerant. "Every generation had a High Priestess with powers of foresight and insight. She was their seer."

"Foresight isn't exactly magic," Cane said. "Certainly not this body-melding kind of magic. Was that part of their repertoire?"

"They controlled natural forces, healing with herbs, purifying with touch and water, that sort of thing. But they never used their powers to harm. In fact, it was the last High Priestess who banned the use of magic altogether, saying it was too dangerous."

"What about these crawlers?" Cane asked, taking a shovel from Rowan. "Could they have been made by the Gaene Kin?"

"Highly unlikely. Then again, I'm not sure. It's not an area I studied up on. I only know what has been passed down by word of mouth, and most likely exaggerated in some way or another and important details forgotten. This," he pointed to the dead body, "must have been magic. Maybe some of that magic passed to Blake when he drank from our dearly departed friends. A little essence of Baron and Arabella in your morning brew. Whatever entered them might've entered you."

Blake paled. "You think that's why I was... stronger?" He flexed his biceps, now suddenly less proud of them.

"Possibly. The Baron's body might've been infused with something—a lingering spell, a curse, or... whatever magic merged him with Arabella."

Blake groaned. "I feel sick."

"Don't worry," Gerant tried to reassure him. "It doesn't seem to have had any *negative* side effects. Maybe it'll just, you know, work its way out of your system."

"I hope so," Blake muttered, feeling sorry for himself.

"We'll keep an eye on you, Blake," Gerant said. "In the meantime, try not to overdo it."

Blake lost his usual swagger and even his moustache seemed to droop.

"We'll get through this, old friend," Bain added, clapping Blake on the shoulder. "Maybe give the log lifting and hundred morning pull-ups a miss for a while though, in case you get too big."

"Thank you," Blake said, brightening up a little.

"Were there any others like the Baron?" Gerant asked Cane.

"No. Just those crawlers. Some were smaller, though."

"Child-sized?" Bain almost didn't dare ask.

"I didn't exactly have time for a detailed inspection," Cane replied in self-defence. "But wait, one of them was so small I managed to shove it into a pot of boiling soup."

Bain let out an impromptu laugh. "Ha! I like your style."

"Though, now that I think about it, that thing moved faster than any child I've seen."

"These three don't look like they did anything quickly," Gerant said, looking at the fallen bodies with their humungous eyes and undersized skulls. "They're not right. Pasty, with that thick, leathery skin and those bulging eyes. Something about them feels... stunted. It's as if their bodies never fully developed; like they're missing pieces."

He paused, considering his next words carefully. "They seem... deranged, like their minds are trapped between evolutionary madness and interrupted nature. Whatever they were meant to be, they're not human."

"Talking's good, Gerant," Bain interrupted, sleeves rolled up as he dug one of the four graves. "But it works better when combined with shovelling."

Gerant took the hint, and a shovel, before continuing. "Anyway, the Gaene Kin were banished. Yet... it seems someone's either broken that law or found new kind of magic."

"What happened to the Baron and Arabella isn't healing or insight. This is pure hatred," Cane said. "It's revenge, no question."

Bain straightened up, an 'I told you so' grin on his face. "And who do we know that might want revenge? Who hates the Baron for loving another?"

"Could she be one of these Gaene Kin?" Cane asked.

"I doubt it," Gerant said. "She's an outsider. The Gaene Kin are Valorian-born. More likely, it was the Duke's doing. He's tired of waiting. Turning the Baron and Arabella into this lump seems right up his alley, to get rid of his problem."

"But how?" Cane felt frustrated. "We're going in circles."

Bain stabbed his shovel into the dirt. "Find comfort in the fact that we're digging graves for them and not ourselves."

"The events at the castle are part of a much bigger picture we cannot yet see," Gerant said, wiping his brow with a dirt-streaked hand. "Things are in motion now that weren't before. We're not going to be in the dark much longer. More unexpected sights will come to light now, and faster. Whoever is behind this has started on their course. They'll make themselves known to us before long."

Chapter 7

BETTER THAN YOU

Dagma entered Duke Nieman's lavish study with the poise of a predator surveying her prey. Her voice practically rolled out before her like a velvet carpet, matching the dramatic sweep of her robe's train, which flowed behind her as if upheld by tiny fire sprites. Khyro and Galcion, her striking white huskies, flanked her like bodyguards.

"I must speak with you, Father."

She noted with amusement how the Duke's eyes, set in his weasel-like face, darted over her, caught between awe and terror. She knew she was breathtaking—blazing red hair to her waist, skin pale and flawless like porcelain, and eyes that seemed to promise hellfire with every blink. How could she be anything less than awe-inspiring? The Duke's brilliant blue eyes, which he liked to think suggested a sharp and insightful mind, paled in comparison. And unfortunately for him, they lied. His mind and thoughts were shallower than most puddles she'd walked through.

Locked in a state of deep but entirely vacuous contemplation, the Duke stared down at the mess of papers cluttering his grand desk. In front of it, an impressive fire roared in the hearth, valiantly battling the frozen fingers of the winter morning, which had no business invading this sanctuary of opulence. The study itself was an almost comical display of luxury: a regal array of polished gems, enormous bronze vases stuffed with outlandish crystal grasses, and decanters that appeared to outnumber the books. Plush rugs and antique maps did their best to suggest an aura of intelligence and comfort, though in reality, only one of those things could be said to exist there.

He gestured for her to sit in one of the sumptuous leather armchairs by the fire, as though he had any power to command her. Dagma seated herself with the elegance of a queen, her long cloak folding perfectly over her knees as she did so. She regarded him with that same composed, almost serene expression she always wore, masking her true look of attack—sharp, savage—that lurked just beneath the surface.

"Ah, Dagma! Glad you've come!" The Duke's voice stumbled through his teeth as if he hadn't quite rehearsed this conversation enough. "There is something I, um, we, must discuss." He nodded, as though pleased with himself for recovering so quickly.

"I'm glad to hear that, Father, dearest," she said, her tone carrying all the warmth of permafrost. The Duke shivered, despite the roaring fire.

They always kept up the charade of father and daughter for the benefit of prying ears, but the pretence was as thin as the lace on Duke Nieman's overly flamboyant sleeves. With a nervous laugh, he closed the door to the study and made a beeline for the drinks cabinet, his movements, betraying an anxiety, had all the grace of a clumsy peacock fluffing its feathers. The man was clearly out of his depth, his fine silks, oversized ruby ring, and brooches doing little to disguise it. He liked to think he moved with the elegance of a dancer, though in truth, 'average' was probably the kindest word anyone could use to describe his stature. His wardrobe, however, was anything but. He wore only the best, darkest silks adorned with silver embroidery and jewels that sparkled far more than his wit ever could. Hours not invested in reading or strategising were evidently spent on his neatly trimmed black goatee and perfectly groomed eyebrows.

Pouring himself a large drink, he took a swig for fortitude before turning back to Dagma. "As you can see, everything is working according to plan." He conveniently ignored the look Dagma gave him. A look that said she was bored by his words before they even left his mouth. "Apart from your sister, Agatha," he added, his voice dropping. "She's failed us. Badly."

Though the Duke was not Dagma's real father, Agatha *was* her real sister, and her enjoyment of Agatha's failures bordered on gleeful. She bowed her head demurely to mask her sly smile.

"Yes, I know," he continued, now visibly vexed, "I should have listened to you and put you in her place. But, you know, I was only following your mother's instructions. Atropa wanted Agatha to be the one because of her, well, her fair beauty. Perfect for blending in. Whereas you, uh... are less..."

He floundered for the right word.

"Less innocuous?" Dagma offered with a raised brow.

"Precisely!" The Duke latched onto the word, though he certainly had no idea what it meant. "Less innoc—uh—less innocent," he corrected, covering up the blunder. "Because your eyes, they, um... well, they have this, uh... thing about them."

"A nefarious darkness?" Dagma enjoyed his struggle.

"Yes! Yes, exactly. Dark, like, uh, deep, you know. Like they've seen things—terrible things, probably."

"Wickedness, perhaps?" Dagma suggested dryly.

Sweat glistened under the Duke's frilly collar. Her interest waned. The thrill of intimidation had faded quickly, leaving only a dull sense of superiority. It was too easy.

"Talking to you is like being in a house with only one dimly lit room, and if you don't get to the point quick, I'd be happy to turn off that light." The metaphor, she knew, was wasted on him.

"But it's midday."

Really? Could Mother have chosen anyone more witless to lead her plan?

It was almost laughable, how Atropa expected this pitiful man to play a pivotal role in her grand design. Dagma's mind wandered, her thoughts slipping to her mother's true intentions. She had seen the patterns, the way Atropa maneuvered her pawns into place. She played the long game: metamorphosing into the ultimate sorceress and breeding her own indefatigable legion of followers. She was out for blood, and the Duke was just another piece on the board—disposable, easily replaced. Perhaps that was the point. He was a diversion, a bumbling fool meant to occupy the attention of their enemies in Valoria—at least those with brains enough to resist the Duke's bribes—while the real plan of revenge played out.

But was her mother's endgame really just revenge? Atropa's scheme was layered, intricate, and Dagma knew better than to underestimate her. She'd already mastered the four powers. A level Dagma herself aspired to attain. Whatever the Duke's role was, it remained insignificant in the grand scheme. A necessary annoyance.

She allowed herself a moment of satisfaction. *At least she put me in charge of this dimwit,* she mused. But the thought quickly turned cold. If her mother could manipulate Duke Nieman so easily, who was to say she hadn't manipulated her? Was she just another pawn in Atropa's game? Were her ambitions and desires merely orchestrated from afar? Had she been given this role to keep her in check?

Dagma's calculating thoughts picked apart the possible intentions behind Atropa's decisions.

The Duke's incessant rattling and glass against glass, the clinking of a decanter unsteadily handled, brought her back to the present.

He fumbled with the bottle, his hands trembling as he poured another drink. The golden liquid sloshed over the rim, rambling words spilling out of his mouth—a jumble of meaningless drivel. Dagma had to fight the urge to draw on the flames in the fire and incinerate him on the spot.

If I am lucky, he'll rattle himself into his own meltdown. For now I must play my part. Later I'll dismantle Mother's true plans.

"Yes, yes, and your sister, Agatha, she's fair—inside and out," he prattled on, oblivious to Dagma's cold stare. "People like her, you know? She's, well, like the meek." He paused, probably realising he had no idea where he was going with this. "Anyway! Things there are *not* going to plan. Not *one* child. You'd think after a year they'd have—well, you know…"

He made a vague, juvenile gesture with his hands, forming a circle with one and poking a finger through it. A bawdy expression unfitting for a man of his station.

"What? I know what?" Dagma asked, staring at his lewd hand gesture in all seriousness. "What are you doing with your hands? I wish you'd stop it."

"They haven't, you know, done the baby thing! No jiggy-jiggy. No baby. And Atropa needs one for the future, or we're in trouble." He took another swig from his glass. "I've even heard talk of things, uh, cannibalistic castle crawlers," he added, emphasising 'cannibalistic' proudly, as though he'd just invented the word himself. "You're not up to something, are you, D-Dagma?"

"Me? Why, no. I don't take kindly to your insinuation." Looking innocent was not her strong suit, but it hardly mattered. What could he do about it, anyway?

As the Duke nervously tugged at his loose collar, as if it had suddenly tightened around his neck, Dagma's smile coiled like a viper preparing to strike. The Duke gulped, once again unsure if he would survive this conversation with all his feathers intact.

"And when I came in here this morning this blasted window open," he said, changing subject, unable to hide his irritation. "That stableman out there could've been spying on me," he grumbled.

"Khyro peed on your chair last night," Dagma drawled. "I thought it best to aerate."

"Ah, well, yes, I see… of course. That's best." He mumbled, clearly deflated. On the ladder of importance, he ranked below 'dog'—and was barely hanging onto that rung.

Dagma knew he only tolerated the insults because of the substantial payments he was receiving. The money was enough to make him swallow every one of her demeaning comments. After all, the opulence of Malcrov Court was a far cry from the dingy, rat-infested alleys of Illminster, where his past as a lowly trickster had left him hungry and desperate. Here, he had a fortune large enough to rival the coffers of Valoria, plus—the illusion of—power.

The Duke dabbed at his increasingly clammy forehead with his lace-edged handkerchief. "So, ah, where was I? Yes! A few days ago, a certain Cane of Cromlech, an Imperial Guard, no less, was sent to check on our Baron Gradunce. The Baron, as you know, has been neglecting his duties at the Sovereign Court. Well, Cane hasn't returned. Something's gone wrong. The assignment shouldn't have taken more than a day or two, at most. I've sent out a few men to investigate, naturally, but as soon as this is sorted, I have splendid news!"

Dagma's eyes flicked upward in disinterested acknowledgment, her perfectly arched brow implied that this 'splendid news' had better be worth the time she was wasting listening to it.

"Splendid, yes!" The Duke puffed out his chest, momentarily emboldened by the sound of his own voice. "I have grand plans to arrange your marriage to this Cane. He is of excellent stock, you know. Quite the star with a bow and arrow. He can shoot the wings off a fly, they say! Tall enough for you, I think, though not too tall. But most importantly, he comes from the Cromlech family, an old and respected name in the Sovereign Court. His parents, well, they're currently locked up in Gribthorpe, slaving away on the reservoir your mother wants built." He smiled, clearly pleased with his own ingenuity. "It's perfect for our plan to seize control of South Valoria. Cane is bound to fall head over heels for you, after all, you're quite, er, quite the beauty."

Dagma's enthusiasm was as stale as year-old bread. "Your words please me, Father."

Nieman, undeterred, continued, now hitting his stride. "And as your mother so wisely ordered, I'll soon be in charge of Bellingham! Yes, Bellingham, Valoria's mighty capital. I already control all the surrounding towns and villages on this side of the Valorian continent, and Aurelius, the old fool, he can't do a blasted thing about it!" He snorted triumphantly.

What an insufferable, self-loving bore!

"I don't see why we couldn't just get rid of the *old fool* in the first place," she scoffed, the disdain in her voice as sharp as the edge of her withered patience.

The Duke, still riding high on his imagined genius, wagged his finger at her like an owner correcting a naughty pet. "Ah, but your mother insists on savouring the moment. She wants to gloat, you see! As my mother always said, 'Nothing done in haste lasts!'" He puffed up again, convinced he was imparting valuable wisdom. "You see, by following Atropa's plan, I've won over the hearts and minds of the people. I've removed people with influence one by one, replaced them with loyal followers who respect me as their leader. The people of Valoria have never had it so good, and all for doing so little! Why, they've practically fallen at my feet! Meanwhile, Aurelius, the old codger, has done nothing. Maybe because he has no seer to advise him like the kings of old, as it was with the Gaene Kin. He's blind to what's happening!"

"Gaene Kin? Who are they? You mentioned seers. Explain!"

"Oh, some witchy lot. Not important, they're all dead and gone now."

"Okay, who *were* they?" insisted Dagma.

Nieman swallowed an involuntary but habitual lump of fear-of-Dagma fear. "Really, I don't know. Some witchy lot into herbs and stuff. Women. But all sent off to die somewhere. That's why the king no longer has a seer to advise him. It was all before my time. And well, I am not big on reading." He paused. Beads of sweat bulged along his receding black hairline. The lacey handkerchief was soaked—expensive ones had more holes than fabric.

Dagma did not see the point in bombarding him with more questions he could not answer. But this omission of the Gaene Kin, on the part of her mother, was just another reason not to fully trust her plans.

The imbecile in the room clapped his hands together, clearly enjoying his own oratory performance. "This is what Atropa wants: her heir in the Sovereign Courts, a dummy king, Aurelius hostage, and the circle's watchtowers!"

"It's not a shopping list," Dagma scolded.

"Well, no. It's a fine plan! No one will suspect a thing!"

Dagma sighed deeply, her voice contained all the keenness of someone forced to watch a damp log dry. "Of course no one is going to suspect Atropa of returning and making Valoria her bitch, because it's never been done before. And please, for the love of all that's dead, spare me another progress report. We just went over this yesterday." At the snap of her fingers, her two large huskies padded silently across the room and sat obediently at her feet. She stroked their thick white fur, not just to calm down but because they were more deserving of her attention than the Duke.

"Oh, well, yes, right. In any case, we're nearly there, Dagma! Soon, it'll all come together! South Valoria will be ours, and no one—least of all Aurelius—will be the wiser!" He ended with a triumphant swig of his drink, the liquid splashing down his chin as his self-aggrandisement once again overtook his coordination.

As the Duke blundered on, his monologue spiralling into repetition, Dagma dipped into her own thoughts. Her fingers absently stroked her huskies. This moron... well, he was tolerable for now, until his usefulness dried up.

Oblivious to her waning interest, the Duke's voice grew more grandiose with every word, utterly engrossed in his own borrowed brilliance. She could feel his eyes flicking toward her, but she barely registered his presence. One of her many talents: tuning out incessant drivel while maintaining just enough attention to avoid suspicion. Her fingers slid through the soft, cool fur of her huskies.

As he floundered on, her gaze settled on the ridiculous crest on his cuffs and waistcoat: a dragonfly. "I'm mighty like a dragon," he had once explained, "but since most family crests in Valoria are either lions or dragons, I settled for the dragonfly. It is implied. Clever, aren't I?" *Pathetic*, had been her silent reply. If he was a dragon, he was the kind to accidentally set his own tail on fire. The thought brought a rare, genuine smile to her lips. She enjoyed picturing him in self-induced catastrophe and pain.

But the entertainment was short-lived. She resumed her roleplaying of listener to his grandstanding, rattling off Atropa's plans. Dagma knew she had to be patient. The Duke was her puppet, after all, and a puppet was no fun if you snapped its strings too early. She tuned back into his droning.

"—the reservoir at Gribthorpe is almost complete. The citadel of Falconberg in North Valoria is ours, since King Dunwood has been turned, so that just leaves the Syphilis Sanctum to the east—"

"*Sylphic* Sanctum," Dagma seethed. "It's not a hotspot for venereal diseases, but for the air spirits, fool. Get it right! The Sanctum is built on a sacred site hidden to the human eye by the Veil of Whispers—a powerful enchantment cast by the sylphs to conceal their sacred *Sylphic* energy. And my unreliable sister has the key!" She was ready to unload a slew of insults but decided she wasn't interested in him enough to think of him for longer than a second. And even that was too long.

"Right, yes. That's that. So, where were we? Back to business. I'm sure Agatha won't lose the key. I believe Atropa will be pleased with my progress. I mean *our* progress. The stage is, er, ripe. If Agatha can't make an heir, well it'll be up to you to make one."

"Marvellous." When said in a completely sardonic tone, 'marvellous' is anything but.

"Well, yes. Um, well, so, everything is falling into place." He reached for the decanter again. There was a knock at the door. "Come in!" he ordered, visibly relieved.

<hr />

Five of his men marched in, wearing thigh-high brown leather riding boots thudding on the floor. Each wore the same black uniform emblazoned with the Duke's feeble white dragonfly insignia. Dagma cringed as she noticed they all sported goatees. *Did he order their copycat facial hair?*

The guards stopped in front of him and bowed. "My lord," the first man spoke, slightly out of breath. "We bring news from Castle Gradunce."

"Good, good. Has the Imperial Guard returned? Tell me everything." The Duke moved to stand behind Dagma's chair.

"It is not quite what we expected, my lord. We found the castle empty."

The Duke choked slightly on his drink. "Empty? What? Completely empty?"

"Yes, my lord."

"No, that can't be," he muttered, clenching his jewelled fist near his mouth. "Anything else?"

"Yes, my lord. We noticed a lot of, er, deformed bodies in the kitchen, and a very large oval object in another room."

"Oval object? What was it, man?" the Duke demanded, ignoring in his cowardly way the more pressing matter of dead people.

"Not sure, my lord, like a big, oval, round thing, reaching right up to the ceiling, but it was empty inside," stammered the guard not knowing what he had seen and so not knowing how to describe it.

"Curious," the Duke mused. "Tell no one of this. What other buildings are near the castle? What did you pass on your return journey?"

"There's very little out there, my lord. Mostly the Baron's hunting woodlands. On the moors, there are some disused mills, old Rudston Monastery, and a few hamlets within the Baron's fief. The village of Inglebruk is near the castle, about a mile away. We asked at the inn if they'd had any new guests. Just an Imperial Guard the evening before last, but since then, no one."

The Duke rubbed his trim little goatee and then looked up abruptly at his men. "That will be all, thank you. Out, out!"

The men bowed again before making their way back out of the heavy oak doors. Dagma paced beside the oversized desk. Its thick bombe shaped legs, gold leaf accents and floral motifs suggested it would have been more at home in a royal palace.

The Duke blurted out his thoughts in rapid succession: "What does it all mean? Were they driven out? Did anyone else see the bodies? Is Agatha still alive? Was that a giant egg? Why so big? Were they after the syphilis key? Did they find it and take it? Is our mission at risk? Do you think they found out the truth?" He was going to continue his frantic soliloquy when Dagma raised her pale hand to silence him. He stopped dead.

"We'll visit the scene ourselves tomorrow. Perhaps we can still find the key or some clue left behind by Agatha." Dagma didn't care what had happened to her sister, but she did care about the Sylphic key. Losing it would set everything back, and she had no interest in cleaning up Agatha's mess. If her sister had botched things, Dagma would see to it personally that she didn't live long enough to make another mistake.

The Duke resumed buzzing around her like an irritating fly. "Oh, and then there's that matter you wanted to talk about, too. You never say things unless they're important, Dagma—now out with it, what did you want?" He pressed, his voice wobbling with false authority. "I demand to know what you wanted to tell me."

"Demand?"

"Um, er, yes, I'd very much like to know."

Ah, there it was—the squirming. He knew better than to cross her, yet he still felt a need to pretend he was in control. Poor, deluded fool.

Her lie slipped from her lips with practiced ease. "I need to commandeer the cattle barn for my herbal experiments. My lady-in-waiting is getting too curious about my bottles and collections of plants, powders, and curios." Her actual plans for the barn would ensure that, if she was a pawn in her mother's game of chess, she'd soon crossover and promote herself to queen. If her mother thought she'd settle for playing nursemaid to this moron, she was sorely mistaken. "Since you hold authority at Malcrov Court, assign it to me alone. You know my divinations are crucial to your success. Think of me as the Gaene Kin seer advising a king." She infused her words with charm.

The Duke straightened, visibly flattered. "Why, of course."

As Dagma swept from the study, her gown trailing behind like a bloodstained shadow, she heard him murmur, almost to himself, "What have I just agreed to?"

He must have caught her small smile of satisfaction.

Chapter 8

SOME KIND OF MAGIC

T HE CASTLE JUTTED OUT of the hill, a giant's tombstone marking a forsaken graveyard. Cane eyed it warily as their horses trotted over the dry moat. It *looked* deserted, but Cane knew better than to trust appearances. Just because the place looked like a hotel for the dead didn't mean it wasn't crawling with trouble.

The black clouds overhead had thinned into a misty haze, casting the morning in a washed-out pallor. Cane exchanged a look with Bain and Gerant, their unspoken thoughts the same.

"Might as well get on with it," Bain said nudging his horse forward through the open portcullis. Their horses' hooves clattered through the empty courtyard as loud as a cavalry parade. If anyone *was* lurking, they certainly weren't sneaking up on them now.

The horses were jittery, their ears twitching at shadows. Cane dismounted and tied them up near the stables where they could chew on some hay instead of bolting the first chance they got. He gave them a firm pat on the nose. "Stay put, we'll be back soon."

"First stop: the kitchen," Gerant said, striding ahead. They weren't only searching for clues—they needed to be sure nothing was laying in wait for them.

"Someone's been here," Cane muttered, eyeing the front door that hung slightly ajar.

Gerant stopped mid-stride. "Or maybe something's crawled *out*," he said with a shiver.

"More likely those sloppy scouts of the Duke," Bain said, "unable to close doors when they leave."

Cane tightened his grip around his sword as he nudged the door fully open, his pulse quickening. Bain and Gerant, their only swordsman skills forced on them as adolescents, stayed behind him as they stepped inside.

Advancing toward the kitchen, Cane drew his sword. Rot, wet decay, and blood assaulted their senses before they even entered. Then they saw it. Piles of wet, mutilated bodies lay slumped under the kitchen door jamb.

Nothing could have prepared Gerant and Bain for the slaughter scene. The air reeked of death. They recoiled at the horrific sight of gungy bodies, some half-eaten, some completely mutilated. Bulbous eyes, wide open with the look of fear indelibly printed on their faces, stared back at them.

Many had died with their teeth and talons rooted firmly in the back of what was probably the cook—the largest of the human items under the main course menu.

The three men frowned down at the contorted carnage.

"Lovely," Bain said grimly, stepping over a particularly gloopy appendage.

Gerant wrinkled his big nose, clearly suffering under the awful stench. "It looks more like the condemned meat room of a human abattoir than a kitchen."

Bain grimaced. "Definitely nothing human about them," Bain said, prodding one of the misshapen corpses with the tip of his boot. "They've got that 'started-as-a-human' look, but then something went wrong."

"Wrong how?" Cane asked.

"Like someone started sculpting a human but got bored halfway through," Bain said, tapping a lopsided head with the flat of his sword. "They've got two arms, two legs—more or less. But look at those heads—huge, bulbous things. Eyes like full moons. And don't get me started on the genitalia situation. I mean, I think they're all female, but... well, it's hard to say."

Gerant, who had been silently frowning, crossed his arms. "I don't like it. Not one bit. This whole place smacks of something foul."

"That's just the bodies," Bain said, waving a hand in front of his nose. "Death always has a way of being... odorous."

Gerant gave one last look at the revolting scene and gestured to the door. "Right, enough of this. Let's see what else this place is hiding."

While Bain and Gerant made their way up the wide central staircase, Cane quietly headed for the cellars, torch in hand. The iron bars he had glimpsed during his last visit were real enough—no figment of his imagination. But the cells stood empty. No writhing figures, no overpowering stench. It seemed the bodies had migrated to the kitchen.

At least they had all conveniently gathered in one place, he thought.

Next, he had to check the room he least wanted to enter: the dead animal room. When he pulled back one of the heavy velvet curtains, his eyes took in a new sight, thankfully one not as awful as that of the merged lovers.

He bolted upstairs to find Gerant and Bain, who were creeping through the rooms like a couple of overgrown burglars. They were in what he assumed had once been Agatha's chambers. It bore a woman's touch: pretty bottles lined a dressing table, the faded scent of Agatha's sweet scent lingered in the air. Bain was rummaging through a chest at the foot of the messy four-poster bed, while Gerant was cursing from across the room, tangled in a mass of ribbons and dresses.

They froze at the sound of Cane's sharp shout.

"Come quick! I think I've found something!"

Gerant and Bain hurried down the stairs, following Cane's voice.

"In here!" Cane was staring at something massive and glistening in the corner of the room. They skidded to a halt beside him.

"What in the blazes is that?" Bain asked, eyes wide.

Gerant stood there, mouth half-open. "Magic, if I'm not mistaken. Unless the Baron had some outlandish taste in decoration, I'd say it's magic."

"Whatever it is," Cane said, "I'm not going near it."

The ceiling-high oval ball sparkled like something out of an overzealous jeweller's wildest dreams—massive, glittering, and more than a little mysterious. It reminded Cane of some insect's lair, spun from shattered glass and sparkling gems. If it hadn't been so peculiar, it would've been beautiful.

Gerant cautiously circled the large crystalline structure. "I've never seen anything like this." His voice trailed off as he reached toward the jagged, broken edge.

Bain moved closer but kept his distance. "Careful! Don't touch it. We don't know what insanity this is." His usual composed expression gave way to bewilderment. He looked closer, grimacing as though he expected the thing to grow legs and run. "Looks like something ripped its way out." He flinched back as though burned, glancing at Cane, whose face was a picture of awe. "Why did you not mention this before?"

Cane, embarrassed, cleared his throat. "Because I didn't see it before."

Bain gave him a sideways look. "Sky-high crystal seed pod," Bain said sarcastically. "Oh yes, I can see how that would escape your attention. A trifle of a thing, easy to miss."

"The curtains were drawn then and, well, I know it sounds unthinkable, but my attention was so caught up by the Baron's pained face merged with Arabella." An uneasy shudder ran through him at the memory. "Maybe they came out of this. But who—or what—made it? And why?"

The crystalline surface shimmered in the light, each facet throwing off a dazzling prism of colours, blinding him momentarily. Gerant squinted. "It's almost like... it grew here. Like the castle birthed it."

Bain shook his head slowly. "You don't normally say daft things, Gerant. This isn't the castle's doing. It's an obvious act of hate and revenge. That's what this is. So, stop spouting nonsense."

"What I mean is, Bain with an 'e'," Gerant scowled at his old friend, "is it's too big to fit through the door." Bain could not counter that logic and responded with a conceding I-see-what-you-mean 'Ah'.

Cane knelt, brushing his hand against a small shard of the crystalline shell on the floor. He picked it up gingerly, holding it to the light. It glowed faintly in his palm, as if it were still alive. "It's hard... but warm. As if it's feeding on something. Alive."

"Put it down!" Gerant ordered. "Before it starts feeding on you."

Cane dropped the shard quickly. "Whatever was inside... it wasn't meant to stay contained. It broke free. Yes, it was trying to escape."

They all fell silent, their eyes fixed on the fractured cocoon. It felt as though they were standing in the middle of a riveting story, half read—its ending missing, the pages nowhere to be found.

"This thing... it's like a chrysalis," Gerant said. "And whatever emerged from it—whether it was the Baron and Arabella or something else—it's not natural."

"What if there are more of them? What if this is how the crawlers are born?" Bain said.

They exchanged uneasy glances. No one spoke the ludicrously possible thoughts growing in their worried minds.

"I hate to mention this now," Cane began.

"What?" Bain asked unforgivingly. "Did you forget you saw an army of weaponised crawlers skulking in the cellars?"

"Well..." Cane paused, hoping he hid his surprise at Bain's accurate accusation. "I think I did see some creatures locked up in the cellars." He cleared his throat uneasily. "But now the cells are unlocked. Empty."

"What's wrong with your eyes boy!?" Bain shouted. "You're a master archer, yet in this castle you fail to notice mountain-sized eggs and confuse a cell full of rabid, flesh-eating crawlers for an empty one."

Cane winced. "I'm fairly certain the things I saw in the cells are dead now. In the kitchen."

"*Fairly* certain?" Bain growled, looking ready to throttle him. "Let's hope you're more than just *fairly* certain when they come for us. If anything came out of this thing and it's still alive, we're in serious trouble."

"Go easy on the lad, Bain," Gerant soothed. "This place plays havoc with the mind."

Cane was about to volunteer to check more rooms when something caught his eye. No, not caught, more like pulled him full circle. His senses buzzed, he could feel the air vibrating around him. There was no sound, just a ripple in the atmosphere, pulling him toward the wall. His gaze locked onto a mounted bear's head, its glassy eyes frozen in perpetual fear.

He hesitated. The pull felt too specific, too deliberate. His hand, moving of its own volition, reached toward the bear's open mouth.

"What are you doing Cane?" Bain's words came to him through a muffling of clouds. His fingers brushed the inside of the jaw and froze on something smooth and cold beneath the taxidermized flesh. With a sharp tug, he pulled free the object, stepping back as he stared down at what had been entombed inside the skull.

It was a key. An impossibly light, weightless key made of intricately carved bronze. Three filigree spirals looped like delicate strands of silk around the bow.

Cane held it up to the dim light filtering in through the window, and the key caught the sun rays in a peculiar, almost hypnotic way, reflecting thin beams of pale blue and green across the room. Gerant and Bain stepped closer, drawn by Cane's quiet intensity.

"What is it?" Bain asked. "A key?"

The key was larger than any ordinary key, its oxidised bronze surface transformed into a rich teal patina that glinted in the light. Though it appeared solid and heavy, it was more like the fragment of a deep ocean.

"I—I don't know," Cane said. "If this is a key, it's for a very big door. Or a very big person."

Gerant studied the swirling design. "Yes. It's no ordinary key. It's... it's like the wind itself shaped it."

Cane turned it over in his hand. The key slipped from his leather glove, missing the fur rug, and clattered onto the stone floor. A unified "Oh no!" escaped their lips.

"You're not usually a clumsy sort, Cane," Gerant tutted.

"Or blind," Bain muttered under his breath.

"No," Cane replied, slowly realising how off-kilter his senses had been these past days. Removing his gloves, he picked up the key. "These spirals and lines... I've seen carvings like this before, in works by the Octules. My father's library did not have much on them, but legend says they were master engineers. Capable of flight, like birds. And... they were taller than—" Cane looked out the window. "Horses."

"Horses? It's not that hard to be taller than a horse," said Gerant.

"No," Cane said quietly. "There are horses coming."

"Oh!" Bain said in a hushed voice. "At least your ears work. Even if your eyes and hands don't."

"How the devil did you hear that?" Gerant asked in a whisper, as the three of them took refuge behind an enormous hunting tapestry.

"Shh," Cane hushed him. He heard footsteps in the hall.

"They must be here somewhere," came a man's voice.

"Obviously!" a woman replied disrespectfully. "Their horses are still here, and one is definitely from the Sovereign Court."

They were moving away. Cane strained to hear.

"Check upstairs!" the woman commanded. Thunderous boots marched upstairs, then silence. "Father dearest," she then said aloofly, "you might find the kitchen... particularly enlightening."

"Now is our chance," Cane whispered, moving to the window. Silently, he eased it open. Keeping low, they headed toward their skittish horses in the courtyard. The Duke's men stood guard.

"We can't even steal *their* horses," Bain whispered. "There's no cover out in the moorlands."

"I have an idea," Cane said.

He crouched low in the shadow of the stables, his sharp eyes trained on the three guards standing by their horses. The task felt completely natural to him, he knew exactly what to do. Glancing back at Gerant and Bain, who were hidden just beyond the stable doors, he saw them nod. They were placing their trust in him—well, what other choice did they have?

Without a sound, Cane moved swiftly towards the guards, melding into the background, his steps softly falling feathers. One by one, the guards fell victim to his blade.

The first never saw him coming. Cane struck from behind, slipping his blade between the man's ribs, pulling him back into the stables before he could cry out. The second guard turned at the last moment, catching sight of movement from the corner of his eye, but it was already too late. Cane's arm wrapped around his throat, cutting off his air as his dagger found the soft flesh of the guard's neck. He slumped silently to the ground. When the third guard opened his mouth to cry out, Cane's fist collided with his jaw, shattering bone and sending him sprawling. A swift stab to the heart ensured he wouldn't rise again.

Panting slightly, Cane gave a quick hand signal to Gerant and Bain. They emerged from their cover, rushing to his side. Together, moving quickly and quietly, they hoisted the limp bodies of the unconscious guards onto their own horses and tied them securely to the saddles. A slap to the horses' flanks sent them galloping over the moors with their decoy passengers.

As expected, the sound of hooves drew the immediate attention of the other visitors. Duke Nieman and a grand lady in crimson come rushing outside with their entourage of guards. Shouts rang out as they caught sight of the galloping horses. Without hesitation, the Duke barked orders, sending his men scrambling to give chase. They mounted their remaining horses, determined to catch the fleeing men.

The lady remained still. Her eyes searching every inch of the courtyard.

Hidden by the commotion, the trio made a dash for the Duke's horses, left unattended. Cane grinned. "Time to ride hard," he said quietly and confidently.

They urged their horses forward, heading unnoticed toward the monastery, while the Duke's guards rode in the opposite direction, in pursuit of their own men.

Chapter 9

SLEUTHING AND REDEMPTION

Tristan wished for eyes in the back of his head as he and his brother crossed the open moor. Once they reached the dusty, rock-strewn plains near Bellingham, the feeling of being easy targets began to fade. Finally, the city appeared—carved from a limestone quarry and surrounded by towering cyclopean walls. Normally, those walls promised safety, but today they screamed 'Keep Out'. Ever since that sodding Duke had shown up, nothing about Bellingham felt welcoming.

The usual thrill of wandering market stalls and tricking old friends with their card games had vanished. Today, they had a far more serious task—one more likely to get them killed than earn free ale from their playful ruses.

"I still think it's a bad idea for us to split up," Tristan said, trying to sound optimistic but certain he came across as mildly terrified. "I mean, if something goes wrong, we're both still at risk."

"It's precisely in case something *does* go wrong that we must split up. Then we'll only lose one of us."

Tristan forced a laugh that came out as more of a strangled wheeze. "You always were the pragmatic one."

The Arc Tree, a weeping willow with droopy branches that seemed genuinely sad, stood at the base of a small hill before the city gates. They paused under its forlorn canopy, seeking a moment's respite before continuing their covert mission.

"If we're both dressed as monks, they might think we're just a couple of lost clergymen," Tristan said hopeful his brother would change his mind. Although known as the brother of action and Percy the thinker, Tristan's courage was firmly rooted in having his brother by his side. "I'm sure they won't suspect anything."

"No. You'll go to the cathedral, and I'll mingle with the townsfolk. We'll meet back here before sunset. And don't forget to hand out the messages." Percy wiped his clammy brow, despite the cold being sharp enough to turn his breath into mist. He took off his monk's habit, carefully tucking it into his saddlebag. Tristan saw his brother shared his fear and made an effort to act as if everything was normal.

"Aren't you going to take off that bulky pouch, too?" he asked, helpfully pointing to a green pouch tied to Percy's waist.

Percy clutched it defensively. "Don't touch that. It's important."

"Alright, alright, easy," Tristan said, pulling his hand back with exaggerated caution. "I won't touch the mystical pouch. I'm sure it contains your secret diary or, at the very least, your emergency supply of... what, exactly? You have no vices."

"Just go, you silly bugger! Don't draw attention to us. We're not exactly the world's best spies, so don't get me all riled up before we've even started."

"Sorry, you're right." They shared a nervous laugh, followed by some manly throat-clearing. "Good luck, brother," Tristan said, trying to sound more confident than he felt.

He turned his horse towards the city gates. Once inside, Tristan tethered his mount by a trough of water next to several others under a purpose-built shelter. Thieves rarely troubled Bellingham; its people lived in harmony, earning their daily bread and wanting for nothing. At least, they had under Aurelius's rule. His reign, and that of his forefathers before him, had provided all its residents with a peaceful life: a roof over their heads, land to grow crops and keep livestock, imports of fabrics and materials to sustain their trades. It was in this atmosphere of trust and companionship that Tristan passed an unmanned watchtower.

As he made his way deeper into the city, he walked beneath lines of colourful banners draped across the sand-coloured walls of the rambling houses and shops. Children played in the streets, men bartered in the square, and market stalls—sheltered under wooden canopies that would be dismantled by nightfall—bustled with activity. Hanging herbs, onions, and rows of preserves gave the scene a festive air, an ambiance of abundance and cheer enveloping him. Other stalls, selling furnishings and handcrafted oddities, were quieter, with merchants huddled around fires, warming their hands and sharing stories. Tristan moved in and out of these circles, slipping messages where needed.

A commotion by the leather stall caught his eye. He smirked as he watched the stallholder, an acquaintance, try to swindle a customer into overpaying for a pair of boots. What the seller didn't know was that the man had crafted the boots himself, sold them to traders from Stoketon, and now faced the irony of buying back his own handiwork.

Seizing the moment, Tristan joined in the bartering, using the distraction to discreetly hand over training instructions to the stallholder. The message detailed alternating routes and dates for secret sessions at Rudston Monastery. Nervous, Tristan paused more than once to steady his shaking hands. Cold sweat trickled down his clean-shaven face, betraying his anxiety. With the Duke's spies everywhere, even the most ordinary citizen could sell him out. The reward for turning in a neighbour was temptation enough for men without scruples.

Families bustled indoors, cooking stews and baking bread. Lunchtime aromas filled the air with delicious scents. Imperial guards dressed in perfect white uniforms—topped with brimmed hats, gold braiding, and pristine white gloves—mingled with the crowds, clearly enjoying the market's antics. But it wasn't them Tristan worried about; it was the shifty figures in darker clothing, loitering aimlessly in small groups as though auditioning for jobs with an undertaker.

He was relieved when he'd finally delivered all his messages. Now it was time to listen in—to hear the city's secrets. He strolled through the old town, not far from Aurelius's palace. Looking out for potential spies spying on him spying, his eyes rested on the cathedral overlooking the square. Quickening his pace, Tristan kept his head low as he stole through the throngs of people.

Inside, the cathedral was relatively quiet, save for the murmured prayers of a few old women dotted among the pews at the front of the nave. Despite its simplicity, the building evoked the sense that the hand of God hovered above and His eyes were always upon you. The moment he crossed the threshold, energy rushed over Tristan—overwhelming, wordless, even beyond Rowan's poetic grasp.

Taking a moment to recompose himself, he moved over to the Table of Light, where people lit candles, hoping their prayers would be answered. Pretending to tidy away spent flax and burnt-out candles, he scanned the area from beneath his cowl. No sign of any clergy—just the eyes of a docile yet fearful-looking woman depicted in a large mosaic on the wall. Her gaze too seemed to follow his every move. *I guess you feel like everybody is watching you when you're a novice spy.*

There were no other decorations in the building, only practical items like candlesticks, hymn boards, and an octagonal altar fashioned from oak in a simple style—except for a large processional crucifix, metal and weathered, corroded around the base, resting beside the missal stand.

Convinced no human eyes were watching him, Tristan edged into the confession booth. He pulled the black curtain across, setting out the sign that indicated he was 'open for business' before retreating into the shadows. There he sat on a cushioned seat, dwarfed by the silence, waiting. Perhaps someone in Bellingham with something worth telling would appear on the other side of the screen and confess their secrets.

Time crawled, the stillness growing almost unbearable as he waited. He wished he'd brought a pack of cards or a book to pass the time. But after what felt like an age—though in reality, it was probably no more than an hour—he finally had a visitor. A middle-aged man who rambled about how he had pulled down his neighbour's washing line last summer to steal some much-coveted undergarments, and had since been wracked with guilt, unable to even bring himself to wear the ill-gotten pants. His second visitor hadn't prayed for over a month, so that was a quick job of three hail Mary's.

Tristan's hopes perked up with the arrival of his third confessor. A young woman. *Third one's a charm!* he thought.

Peeking through the latticed screen, he could tell she was anxious about sharing her sin—or rather, her secret. Tristan soon realised she hadn't sinned but carried a far more intriguing burden. A burden Tristan was all too eager hear about, since it revolved around the secrets of Malcrov Court and its mysterious inhabitants. The details she shared sounded like they belonged in a thriller, complete with hidden chambers and a wicked sister.

"Well, right... I haven't exactly sinned, you see. More like I've been having bad thoughts about people—suspecting them of things. And being a trusted member of Malcrov Court, with all the power it holds these days, I couldn't very well go telling just anybody about the suspicions that've been weighing on me."

"Quite, quite," Tristan replied, doing his best to sound priestly.

"Oh! Where are my manners? Father, bless me for I have... sort of sinned. And, well, it's been donkey's years since my last confession."

A long, awkward silence followed. Tristan figured he should probably say something, he didn't want to let this golden opportunity slip through his fingers. "Place your trust in God. He will, um, sort it out."

That seemed to be all the encouragement she needed.

"Right, so, here's the thing. I was offered the position of lady-in-waiting at Malcrov Court. I fit the criteria perfectly: no family, aside from my ailing father—but I didn't mention him, of course. That would've cost me the job. I presented myself as someone with sound experience in service, and when they accepted me... I was overjoyed. More than I could have ever hoped for.

But from the moment I set foot in Malcrov Court, something didn't sit right with me. The house itself—oh, it's unlike anything I've ever seen. It's not made of any stone I can name—neither limestone, nor granite. The walls have this smooth, almost metallic finish, with a faint glow to them. It's beautiful. And the features inside... they're beyond anything I could have imagined. But somehow, not quite natural, you know?" She didn't wait for an answer. "No one around the estate knew a thing about the court's origins. It was as if it simply... appeared. The locals said the building had been empty for decades, yet the inside was spotless, like someone had been caring for it all along.

Soon after arriving, I stumbled across something peculiar. Behind the main staircase, hidden in plain sight, is a small door that opens onto a narrow wooden passage. This passage runs parallel to the kitchens and leads to a rectangular stone pool in the middle of an inner courtyard. More like a secret garden, really, with shimmering lights and leafy plants—an indoor paradise hidden from the outside world. I told no one I went there. Only two bedrooms on the first floor have access to this hidden courtyard, through a secret panel that leads to a spiral staircase, ending in the hidden pool room.

Lady Dagma never spoke of it, never let on that she knew of its existence, but I noticed how she'd disappear for hours, always returning from the hidden courtyard with a strange look on her face. It got me wondering.

But that was just the beginning. The longer I worked for her, the more I realised how devious she was. I started having... misgivings. Something wasn't right about the place—or about her. There was this feeling hanging over the household—unnerving, unnatural. Something... disturbing.

And then it became more than a feeling. One afternoon, Baroness Gradunce came for lunch. Since it was such a rare event, I was very attentive. At the table, I saw with my own eyes, Lady Dagma slipping something into her sister's food. She did it so casually, like she'd done it a hundred times before. I stood there, frozen. I remembered seeing her gathering plants from the garden earlier that day—hogweed and nightshade, I think. Then I thought of the vials she kept on her dressing table, the ones she claimed were filled with ointments to preserve her beauty.

I should have known then. I should've trusted my instincts. But I am not versed in poisons and evil. All I knew was that whatever Lady Dagma was up to, it wasn't for her sister's benefit. No one could call that *right*, could they? Slipping something into her own sister's food without her knowing. I can't even imagine what purpose she had in mind. Not until last week, when I found out what hogweed can do to a person's skin. And that's when it clicked. As soon as I had thought the words out loud in my mind, I knew I couldn't stay silent any longer. I had to tell someone. I had to tell someone before it was too late. So, I came to tell you, Father."

"Well," Tristan said, trying to sound authoritative in his most convincing 'confessor' voice, "You've done well to bring these matters to light." Another awkward silence followed.

"Yes, and for delaying this truth, and thinking ill of others and prying, what is my penance, Father?"

"Ah, yes. As for your penance... um... let's see. Three Hail Glories, a couple of Your Fathers, and... throw in a Holy Ghost once a week."

The woman did not reply for a while. Since Tristan had no idea what he was supposed to say, he said nothing.

"Um... Okay, thank you, Father."

As she left, Tristan wondered if he'd botched any theological nuances in his impromptu penance. But it was done. Now, it was time to meet up with Percy and see how his day had gone.

⸻⸻◆⸻⸻

The moment Tristan stepped outside, all pretence fell away. He tore out of the cathedral's vestibule with all the grace of a schoolboy hearing the end-of-day bell. He slowed to a casual swagger as he passed the lady who must have been in the confessional—she was the only one young enough. It was no wonder she gave him a puzzled look. If there were an award for 'Most Suspiciously Dishevelled Monk', Tristan would have won it hands down. Then he bolted towards the Arc Tree.

"Percy!" Tristan shouted, his relief evident. "You're a sight for sore eyes! I'm glad you're alive. I've got exciting news! What about you?"

"Definitely not exciting."

"Well, at least we both survived," Tristan said, trying to cheer his brother up. "What happened?"

Percy looked like he'd been through a different kind of adventure. He gave a weak but genuine smile. "After we split up, I went through the east gate and headed for the lower town square. It's the perfect place to blend in and overhear gossip. I went undercover as a foot masseur. I know, but it was all I could think of off the cuff that didn't require a toolkit or a lot of explaining. Plus, people tend to talk freely when they're getting pampered."

"Foot masseur, huh? That's... original. How'd it go?"

Percy grimaced. "Let's just say I regretted my choice when my first customer rolled up. Picture a mountain with feet. He takes off his boots, revealing feet so calloused and pungent they could have their own weather system. The stench was something between old cheese and boiled cabbage. And the worst part? The man enjoyed it. A bit too much. He moaned like I was performing some kind of miracle. Made me wish I had earplugs as well as nose plugs."

"Oh dear! I thought you'd end up as a spy in some bookstore or the library."

"I would have, but they're shut on market days. Instead, I spent the afternoon as the town's unofficial therapist for smelly feet. I didn't learn anything Duke-related, but

I got a detailed history of their children, their cooking, and their dreams of becoming professional cowherds, and—"

"—did you find out *anything* about the Duke?" Tristan asked.

"Nothing, but I guess that says a lot in a roundabout way. The townsfolk seem blissfully unaware. If the Duke's up to something, he's blended in perfectly. It's like he's a snake in the grass, except without any noticeable hissing and slithering."

Just as they prepared to mount their horses, a voice called out from behind them.

"Hey! Hey, you!"

Tristan turned to see a portly, middle-aged man, breathless and wheezing, clearly winded from his sprint.

He felt the man gave him a good look up and down before speaking. "Ah, I've not seen a Cretyne monk in the south for an age. Good day to you, sir."

Tristan gave a reverent nod, slipping into his most priestly tone. "We come to assist our brother healers and share our knowledge of sacred remedies."

"Ah yes very good." The man's face, red enough to rival a tomato, then zeroed in on Percy. "Are you the foot masseur from the square?"

"Yes, that's me," Percy said, trying to maintain his composure. "What can I do for you?"

"I am Gwaine, groom at Malcrov Court." He paused as if expecting a reaction.

Hearing his name triggered a distant memory in Tristan, but he couldn't place it. Though the name was unusual in those parts, it sounded familiar. Before he could think further, Gwaine continued.

"I was wondering if you'd be back tomorrow. My feet are killing me, and I've got these sore bumps. Could really use some of your expert touch."

Tristan had to hide his chuckle.

"I'm afraid I've got a full schedule in Ironholme tomorrow," Percy improvised. "But if you soak your feet every night in a bucket of warm water with comfrey leaf or all-heal, it should do wonders."

Gwaine looked disappointed but thanked Percy for the advice. "I'll be sure to try that. Hope to see you again soon!" he said, before waddling off.

Percy and Tristan exchanged a look of relief. With a light kick, they urged their horses into a canter, Tristan eager to share his confession tale, and Percy more than ready to leave the smells of the day far behind.

Chapter 10

AGATHA'S APOCALYPSE

C ANE, GERANT, AND BAIN hurried back to the monastery, their minds reeling from the frightening sights contained in Castle Gradunce and relieved they had escaped with their lives. Entering the organ room, Cane immediately took in the scene. Rowan and Blake were hunched over a detailed map of Southern Valoria, their faces set in concentration. Agatha sat at the organ, her fingers moving across the keys, playing a melancholic tune that mirrored her sorrow. Felix, oblivious to it all, devoured an apple tart, letting crumbs collect in his beard.

"Felix, your beard's getting more pie than your mouth," Gerant said laughing.

"No, no, I assure you it's deliberate. I'm feeding it." Felix grinned, unbothered. His beady blue eyes spotted the large key gleaming in Cane's hand. "Oooh! Tell us everything! And I mean *everything*—don't leave out any juicy details!"

Cane hesitated, glancing at Agatha. She seemed lost in her own world, using the music as a shield. Discussing their findings in her presence didn't feel right, but Gerant took the reins, recounting their venture into the castle with his usual air of authority and theatrics.

"It was just as Cane described. The castle was, well, it was like a haunted cemetery. Waste everywhere, a stench that could put a skunk to shame, and beasts that looked like creations of a deranged potter."

"And a crystalline pod or cocoon the size of a small house," Bain interjected with an enthusiasm he usually reserved for discussing rare coins and clockwork mechanics. "We're assuming that's where the Baron and Arabella came from."

Felix shuddered. "By Jove! What's going on? Have the ancient gods returned?"

"Was there just one poc?" Blake asked hopefully. "Please tell me there was just one."

"Yes, as far as we could tell," Gerant said. "Unfortunately, this morning's session for poking around at the castle was double-booked. That brigand of a Duke turned up with some terrifying woman and a handful of his guard chums. We barely made it out alive, but thanks to Cane, and some very deft blade work, we gave them the slip."

Cane noticed Agatha's fingers falter on the keys for a moment, though she gave no sign of listening.

"The Duke's alarm bells are probably ringing louder than a church on Sunday," Gerant said, packing his pipe with a worried look. "He'll come after us, mark my words. Time's running out. We need to move things up a notch."

"Did you find any answers, or just more questions?" Rowan asked.

Cane handed the key to Gerant, who held it up with the reverence of a bishop presenting a holy relic. "We found *this*." The key inspired many 'oohs' and 'ahs'. "Baroness, we could really use your help." The music stopped abruptly. "We found this key in your home, along with all the other inexplicable... things. Surely you must have had some idea... one would hazard a guess that you would have some notion of—"

"Do you want to help or not?" Bain interrupted bluntly.

Agatha turned to face them, her expression unreadable. Cane studied her, but she revealed nothing. "Of course, I'll help. You've all been so kind to me. But I don't think I know anything you want to know."

"Baroness, surely you must have noticed *something* during your time at the castle that was odd?" Gerant tried to coax out an answer.

Bain paced like a caged lion, his patience clearly fraying. "We know it's the woman. The Baron warned us to be wary of her—'Beware the woman' he said. "Plus, we found this key hidden." He snatched the key and thrust it under Agatha's eyes where she could not fail to see it. "Nothing is deliberately hidden unless it's important. If you won't talk, it means you're hiding something. Maybe you're protecting someone. For all we know, we're harbouring one of the Duke's spies—giving you information before you run back to tell him all."

Agatha froze like a deer in a hunter's sight, then tried to protest. "No, no, I—"

"Your sweet, innocent façade might be hiding something more sinister!" Bain roared, slamming his fist on the table, sending Felix's discarded apple cores bouncing.

Just as the tension hit breaking point, Tristan and Percy burst into the room. The loaded atmosphere wiped the smiles from their cheerful faces.

"Ah, perfect timing, gentlemen," Bain said, with forced calmness. "The Baroness was just about to clarify a few things for us."

Gerant guided Agatha to an oversized armchair that accentuated how she looked: diminished. "There, now, dear lady. Tell us what you know. We only want to help you—and the people of Bellingham."

Agatha, engulfed in a sea of fabric, looked around at the expectant faces. All hopeful she'd start spilling secrets—or at least try to.

Her eyes darted nervously around the room. "I understand you're desperate for answers. If the Baron were alive, I'm sure you'd hurl these accusations at him. But now that I'm the sole survivor of the castle's melodrama, it's only natural that I'm in the firing line."

Bain's shoulders, which had been as tense as a drawn trebuchet ready to fire, relaxed ever so slightly.

"It's all too dreadful," Agatha continued, shaking her head as if to clear out the bad parts of her memory. "Until Cane came into my home, music was my only saviour." Cane watched as she stood, poised like an actress preparing for a dramatic stage entrance, and moved towards the full-length windows. Perhaps she sought inspiration from the outside world.

"For the first time in my life, I feel safe," she said, turning to face them with a look that could only be described as heart-wrenchingly earnest. "So, it's only fair I be truthful with you."

Cane thought Agatha struggled with her next words as if they resisted her attempts to pry them loose. "Since being at the castle, I've changed in ways I can't fully explain. It started after a few months. I tried to hide it from the Baron, but when I began feeling ill... and, let's just say, no future barons or baronesses were on the horizon. I knew something was seriously wrong. I—" Her voice cracked, tears welling in her eyes. "I am either a freak of nature, gravely ill, or someone poisoned me to get me out of the way. The physician was the first to suggest poison. I never suspected my husband—after all, that's the stuff of tragic plays, not real life. But who else could it have been?" She placed a hand on her stomach. "It was too horrid to think, but I had no other explanation. The physician confirmed I have no womb. I already told you I have no child," she looked straight at Cane. "So please, desist with your misconception that I am a mother."

Rowan looked inspired by a sudden revelation dawning in his mind, "*Beware, no womb, man*. Perhaps that *was* what the Baron's last words were. The Baroness has no womb. And it was a man's doing."

"Yes, perhaps," Gerant agreed. "Odd for his last words though. I don't think we can hold much stock in our hypothesising. For all we know he could have said, 'Beware, gnome man' or even 'Be there, go mad'. Let's stick to facts. Baroness, can you go on?"

Agatha broke her sobbing with a shaky attempt to control her emotions. "Yes." She cleared her throat, but her words came out ricketier than a fly struggling in a spider's web. "As for my father, the Duke, I only know that I was meant to provide an heir to continue the family line."

She looked imploringly at the serious faces around her. "I did not lie when I said I could not remember my childhood. In truth, I can't remember *anything* before coming to Malcrov Court. Sometimes, I think I invent memories just to comfort myself, because having no past makes me feel estranged from my own life, as though I have no place or purpose here."

"You know, it's quite possible you're trying to forget something bad from your childhood," Felix suggested. "A sort of mental blackout. Classic case of 'I'll remember the good stuff and pretend the bad bits never happened'." He then pounced on his next victim in the fruit bowl.

"Thank you, Professor Felix," Gerant said dryly.

Cane tried to steer the conversation back to something more useful. "But you have a sister. Did you not reminisce with her while you were at Malcrov Court?"

Agatha looked as though Cane had asked her to solve an impossible algebra problem. "My sister, Dagma, has always been jealous of me. We have never bonded as siblings. As her older sister, I tried to guide her, to help her. In return she has shown me nothing but ingratitude and bitterness. And I have this awful feeling, this persistent conviction, that Dagma isn't really my sister. Or that the Duke is even my real father. I feel like a perpetual outsider in my own family, and the whole mess with my husband just intensified that feeling."

She paused, the room filled with the kind of silence that reigns when the executioner raises the guillotine. Cane noticed he wasn't the only one holding his breath. They were all watching a tragic opera unfold in real time and were relieved when Agatha broke the tense silence.

"I was seventeen when I first remember being at my father's estate in Malcrov. They threw a birthday party so extravagant it would put a royal celebration to shame. For nearly a year, I was taught all the 'essential' skills—sewing, cooking, flower arranging. Then, just after my eighteenth birthday, I was betrothed to the Baron, a man twice my age. I was assured that such arrangements were quite normal. I had met him before, and he seemed kind, considerate even. I spent a few happy months as mistress of his castle, though honestly, I wasn't fully prepared for what that entailed."

She managed a small, wistful smile, but it faded quickly. "Then darkness descended. My husband stopped visiting my chambers. I found out he had another woman. Abandoned, I was left to endure the slanders of the servants. They called me the 'barren Baroness' behind my back. I was alone, in pain, and felt such anguish."

She forcibly recomposed herself and continued, her voice trembling, "I was at my wits' end. The Baron wanted me to go back to my father, but I turned to my sister for help. I visited her for lunch one day. She seemed unusually happy to see me. Only too happy to help. I should have known better—I couldn't rely on her. She offered no real help; no one did. I felt utterly alone. It was during this time of malcontent that you arrived. If you hadn't come, I'd still be trapped in that miserable existence without hope. I am eternally grateful."

No one spoke. Even Bain did not have it in him to add to his succession of accusations. The image of a young lady, abandoned by her own sister, mocked by her servants, and possibly poisoned by her husband, filled their thoughts.

"What do you know about the key?" Gerant asked, changing the subject. "Have you seen it before?"

Agatha lowered her eyes, as though she were about to confess to stealing the king's jewels. "Yes, I have."

"What is it for? Why didn't you mention it before?" Bain asked, his tone less harsh but still accusatory. "If you're truly innocent, help us. The key has markings that don't appear Valorian."

"The Duke gave it to me on my wedding day. He said, word for word, it would one day 'help unlock the doors to a more powerful world'. I thought it was a poetic metaphor for my transition from childhood to married life. My husband kept it safe, as requested. Its hiding place was not known to me. That's all I know."

"Well, you're either an extremely good liar, or there is something larger at work here. I don't like it though. I don't like it one bit." Gerant paced up and down in front of the silent organ. "You seem to be caught up in a much grander scheme. We need to find out what that is, and fast. I suspect the Duke has plans, big ones, and I doubt it is to the advantage of his fellow man, but to his advantage alone." He stopped mid-pace to face Agatha. "You must stay here with us for now. I don't want you leaving the monastery. Is that clear?" Agatha gave a quiet nod. "It's for your safety, and ours. We need to uncover what the Duke is plotting. Staying put keeps you out of his reach. There's always the risk your sister might try to find you, and who knows what the Duke might do then? He might toss you into the dungeons at Gribthorpe, along with his other political prisoners he no longer has use for."

With a meek tilt of her head, Agatha agreed silently. Bain seemed somewhat mollified by the arrangement. With Agatha under their watch, the immediate risk of her running off to the Duke—or worse, informing him of their hideout—seemed handled, at least temporarily.

"Perhaps Tristan and Percy have had some luck today," Felix chirped with the optimism of someone who'd just been told his bottle of port wasn't empty after all. He patted Percy on the back. "It's been a day of snooping and sleuthing, I hear! Did you enjoy your little adventure?" Felix stood back a little wrinkling his nose. "What's that smell? Did you buy cheese at the market?"

"Don't ask," Percy grumbled, wiping his hands on a rag with the kind of vigour usually reserved for greasy tools and overripe fruit. "I really need to wash my hands."

"Did you manage to contact our men?" Gerant asked.

"Yes," Percy said with pride. "We spread the word among our allies as planned. I don't think we were spotted, but the Duke's got eyes everywhere. I swear he's got more spies than a beehive has bees. You can spot them a mile off though. As for the people, well, they're going about their business as usual, though I've never seen so many sore feet. But I'll explain that later. The real news is that Tristan struck gold." Percy gave a nod toward Tristan, who looked as pleased as a cat in a sunbeam.

Tristan, basking in his moment of glory, relayed his information with the enthusiasm of a magician revealing his latest trick. The news of the confession story was a much-needed lift.

"Oh, bravo Tristan!" Gerant said, shaking his hand energetically. "That clears up a great deal for us."

Cane noted both Bain and Agatha were turning various shades of red—Bain from embarrassment, Agatha from simmering anger.

"Dagma poisoned me!" Agatha shook her head slowly, as though trying to make sense of a particularly baffling riddle. "Dagma poisoned me!" Her small hand came down on the table with a decisive thump. No apple cores bounced. "So, why am I not dead?"

"All I know is that the lady-in-waiting saw Dagma collecting plants and put them into your meal," Tristan explained. "She was too afraid to speak up—afraid of losing her position, I suppose. But eventually, she needed to unload that guilt, and I just happened to be in the right place at the right time when she spilled the beans."

"Yes, it seems providence is on our side," Gerant remarked. "Good work, lads, good work."

The room broke out into a lively discussion full of theories and conjectures, tossed about like hot potatoes at a circus. "Did they plot to kill Agatha because she didn't bear an heir?" "Was the Duke involved in the poisoning too?" "What would they gain?" "What was Dagma hoping to achieve?" "Maybe she wasn't even Agatha's real sister?" "Was she working under the Duke's orders?" "Why didn't the poison kill Agatha?" "Maybe it wasn't meant to kill her, just to incapacitate her?"

Blake, who had been sitting quietly, suddenly stood up with the air of someone who had just cracked a long-standing mystery. "I've got it!"

"Oh no, here we go," Felix tutted. "Prepare yourselves for Blake the braggart, sorry I mean Blake the laggard. He's solved the mystery all on his own."

Blake smoothed his large moustache with the care of a tailor pressing out the last wrinkle from a silk suit. "You said she was always jealous, right?"

"Yes, always, and she was especially jealous that I married before her. I saw it in her eyes, but I thought it was just my imagination or paranoia."

"That's why she did it!" Blake's smile stretched from ear to ear, revealing his impressive set of perfect white teeth. "Because she was jealous."

"Well, of course, that's why she did it, super sleuth," shouted Felix. "What else did you deduce while you were at it? That the sun rises in the east?"

"What I think, or at least I hope, Blake meant to say," intervened Gerant calmly, "is that Dagma's cruelty ran deeper than just envy. The poison was likely designed not to kill Agatha outright but to make her barren, prolonging her suffering. Death would have been too merciful. Dagma wanted her sister's life to be a living hell. We know how powerful some herbs can be."

As awful and unkind as the theory was, it seemed to fit the facts. Agatha visibly relaxed, as though the explanation had finally given some structure to the torture she'd been enduring. No longer just a victim—she knew the identity of her torturer.

Agatha, evidently feeling somewhat vindicated, was emboldened by this revelation. "The lady's voice you heard at the castle with the Duke... that was most likely my sister." Her observation was more than just a helpful contribution; it was her claiming her place within the group—a statement of belonging.

Cane exchanged a glance with Gerant. In that moment, he knew what they had begun as seven had become eight, and now, with Agatha, they were nine.

Chapter 11

TENSION RISING

T HE DUKE KNOCKED ON Dagma's door with the subtlety of a bull in a China shop. "Are you ready?" he whispered so loudly he may as well have shouted.

"I've been ready for hours," Dagma whispered back, checking the hallway left and right; it was as empty as the Duke's head. "Why are we whispering? It's just the two of us."

Nieman's eyes slid back and forth shiftily, a picture of exaggerated caution. "Best to be as careful as possible. As my mother always said, 'Wolves have ears', and I trust no one."

"A fine comment coming from you. And stop quoting your dead mother. She died by accidentally drinking the poison she intended for your father, so I think I can live better without her advice. And it's '*Walls* have ears'—it's quite obvious that wolves do."

She didn't bother to explain away the Duke's confusion. He looked as though he'd sucked on a sour lemon as he mulled it over. *Good, that'll keep his pea brain busy for a while.*

The pair made their way down the spiral iron staircase, their boots clinking underfoot in the early morning quiet. They crossed the deserted courtyard, passing tools left lazily beneath an ancient elder tree, and saddled their horses.

Trotting out of the grounds, they met up with a small entourage of the Duke's men at the edge of the woods. Only empty windows watched them gee their rides.

Galloping over the still-dormant moors, the pounding hooves startled rabbits and voles in the undergrowth—or perhaps it was the ferocious energy Dagma gave off that made all living things clear out of their way in haste. With the command of an empress directing her soldiers, she gestured toward the mill and monastery. "We'll check them on our return."

When they finally arrived at the castle the following day, the Duke dismounted with all the grace of a sack of flour. His thigh-high boots crunched against the gravel, his eyes poked about the perimeter. He was used to snooping in his past life, but he still looked like a ferret that just noticed a rabbit when he spotted three horses tied by the stables.

"Aha! We're not alone. Perhaps the missing Cane of Cromlech. Perhaps three traitors. They must be here somewhere."

"Obviously! Their horses are still here, and one is definitely from the Sovereign Court." Dagma strode past him as though he weren't there. "The more pertinent line of thought would be whether they're here breathing or decomposing."

The Duke bit back a curse, his face a picture of a sulky child. "I was thinking that."

"Check upstairs!" Dagma commanded, as further proof that she was in charge. She swept her way toward the castle kitchens, leaving him to stew like a lame duck.

Moments later she popped her head out. "Father dearest," she called out with casual aloofness, "you might find the kitchen… particularly enlightening."

With a huff, the Duke followed her lead, stomping into the darkened interior like the child that had been told he could leave the naughty step, or in his case, the stupidity step.

"Eew," was all the Duke could say at the barbaric kitchen scene.

Idly prodding the limbs of the dead pasty figures with her riding boots, Dagma smiled quietly to herself. She was glad she had poisoned her sister and that Agatha had given birth to monsters, not the future queen. If she was lucky, the poison might have ruined all of Agatha's chances of bearing children.

"Why do you think all the bodies are piled here in one place?" The Duke stood behind her, holding an ineffective lace hanky over his nose.

"They're not *piled*. They *died* here," Dagma said, pointing up at the empty water silo. *He can figure the rest out himself, or not.*

Suddenly, Dagma's instincts pricked up. She could sense a presence nearby. Without warning, she rushed back to the courtyard, the Duke scampering at her heels. Outside, a new sound filled the air—a rhythmic rumble announcing the departure of horses.

Nieman followed her gaze to see three horses charging over the open country. "After them!" he ordered.

His men scrambled into action, their movements a clumsy clattering of metal and hoofbeats. Dagma clenched her teeth. These elite soldiers, trained for precisely this kind of situation, were making a complete farce of it.

But then, something else caught her attention—a faint shift in the shadows. Rage flared inside her as she realised they'd been too late—again. Three of their own horses had vanished as well.

A dark growl rumbled in her throat as she watched the Duke's men gallop off in the wrong direction. They were chasing nothing but the wind, while the real targets had stole away under their very noses.

"Bastards! Seems they were smarter than I gave them credit for. I'll catch them one day, and when I do, they'll regret ever crossing me. For now, let's find that key. It's more important."

The Duke pulled out his black, richly decorated walking cane, which matched his equally ornate waistcoat, and began to push and poke ornaments, books and furnishings in an unproductive attempt to find the Sylphic key.

"What do we do if we can't find it?" he asked.

"Just hope that whoever has it does not find out what it is," Dagma said, looking around the room. "Because then suspicions will be raised. But I doubt anyone in Valoria will ever discover its actual origin and purpose."

Dagma, looking keenly around the Baron's study, moved through the rooms on the lower floor until she saw the large 'oval thing'.

"Curious," Dagma said, genuinely intrigued by the broken shell. "Earth magic has been used here."

"What is it?" asked the Duke.

"I don't know," Dagma admitted. "I've never seen one before."

"Maybe the Gaene Kin have returned," the Duke ventured. "They did stuff with nature and earth."

"You said they were only herbal witches," Dagma snapped. "This requires proper elemental magic—earth magic. Or are you telling me they were capable of this too?"

The Duke shifted nervously from one shiny, pointy boot to the other, most likely wishing some earth magic would swallow him whole right then. "I don't know much about them. I only said it because they're the only magicky thing I've heard about," he spluttered in his defence.

"Well, next time think before you squeak, if that's possible. I want facts, not unfounded machinations and hypotheses."

Hit by a wall of big words, Nieman shut up.

After a thorough inspection of the shiny casing, Dagma placed her hand on it and watched with satisfaction as it shattered into a pile of sand.

"We can't leave things like this lying around for curious eyes to see. Our unwanted visitors must've seen it. Maybe they saw more than they bargained for. Let's get on with it, *Father*. Things are moving, and we need to stay ahead."

Dagma marched into the gloomy entrance hall, brushing dust off her sleeve with a mild look of disgust. "Alright, let's see if this place has anything interesting to offer other than mildew and disappointment." She sent the men off in different directions to search and then tuned into her senses.

Nothing. Not a trace, not even a faint hint of that key.

"We're going," she yelled at the Duke. "Come, now! It's not here."

"How do you know?" he asked, trailing behind like a chastised puppy.

Dagma shot him an exasperated look. "Because it's not in my hand. Sometimes you really earn the title of moron without even trying." She walked brusquely to her horse. "We'll head to the hamlets and Inglebruk. Discreet enquiries might turn up something useful."

"What about my three men without horses?"

"They can walk back!"

"What about the big egg thing? Why do you think they didn't take that?"

"And slip it in their pocket? Enough with the hundred-and-one idiotic questions!"

"Sorry, I—"

"You can ask as many as you like when we're in Inglebruk. Now, Come! We're wasting time."

The Duke was allowed to ask questions to his heart's content all the next morning in Inglebruk and the surrounding hamlets, but to little effect. Only the innkeeper confirmed having accommodated an Imperial Guard several days before.

Rudston Monastery was a destination on their return route.

"I don't think there are any monks in the monastery," Nieman said. "My butler says it's been empty for years. We've been riding for hours, days, and it's getting late."

"This is the last place in the area we still need to check. When I said I'd hunt them down, I didn't mean a half-cocked effort. And it's not getting late; it's getting dark," Dagma retorted, her tone firmly planted in the realm of 'do as you're told'.

Nieman swallowed his next objection in compliant silence.

A chubby, ginger-bearded monk greeted them, taking an unreasonably long time to tie up their horses at the furthest point by the stables before leading them inside, while their guards—the ones *with* horses, the whereabouts of the other three on foot were unknown—waited by the iron gates. Dagma glanced around with feigned disinterest.

Her dismay grew upon realising the monk didn't speak. She was also perplexed to find five dormitory rooms locked. The absence of an explanation from the monk heightened her suspicion.

After being shown around the inside of the cloisters, she ventured outside and strolled through the gardens. There, she noticed fresh mounds of soil that looked disturbingly like graves. Three normal-sized graves and one rather large mound. The orchard was the burial ground, not the small cemetery. *Interesting*. She returned to the Duke, who was now standing in the enclosed cloister.

"So, it appears I was right," the Duke said smugly. "These monks are useless. We need to look elsewhere. There's not much we can learn from a monk who doesn't speak."

"I wouldn't be so sure. There are some freshly dug graves in the orchard. Those dead bodies are even quieter than these monks, but they tell us a lot." Perhaps one of the graves was Agatha's. The thought both amused and pleased her. If Agatha wasn't buried there, she was likely a captive. Either way, Dagma's priority was to find out if they had the key.

"Dagma, it's dark, we can't see a thing, we should get going. I'm not scared of the dark or anything, but the horses won't be able to see soon."

Oh, blast, the monk had locked the door. She could always return later. "Whinge, whinge, whinge. Fine. We'll stay at a guesthouse for the night."

They hired rooms in the modest Avonlea guesthouse, typically frequented by traders and the post coach. Once alone in her room, Dagma got to work.

She rinsed her hands in a porcelain bowl decorated with blue cornflowers, massaging the water into her hands and neck. She then lit a small fire in an iron chalice, adding the sage she'd picked from the monastery's herb garden. "Sage to clear the mind," she whispered, inhaling the smoke deeply. "To open the way." She passed her hands through the smoke, focusing on her intent.

Finally, she opened a small bottle of yellowish liquid hanging like a pendant around her neck, dabbing it on her temples and forehead. Closing her eyes, she repeated the action, breathing in deeply. "Let me see! Open the way!"

After sitting motionless for a while, surrounded by swirling smoke, she opened her eyes and smiled. "The monks are not monks."

Resolved to revisit the monastery the next day, Dagma concentrated on finding the key. Her thoughts were interrupted by the Duke, who barged into her room without knocking. Ill-bred! He was always the one keeping her from seeing the obvious, constantly distracting her with moronic questions and his incessant whining.

"You knock before entering my room!" she snapped.

The Duke muttered a grudging apology before asking, "Coming for dinner?" He rubbed the back of his neck and stroking his meticulously trimmed black goatee—his usual tics when frustrated.

Dagma followed him into the low-ceilinged private dining room, its oversized fire blazing far too hot for such a small space. Unable to stand upright due to the sagging ceiling, she sat down, flinging open a window to relieve the stifling atmosphere.

The Duke entered, decanter in hand. "I can't make head nor tail of what's going on," he complained, pouring himself a large glass of wine and downing it in one gulp. "There've been no sightings of any groups travelling through the area. I've instructed my scouts to be on the lookout for any Imperial Guards. It must have been Cane. But I'm wasting no more time on this. There's no need to wait. It's time to move forward. That Cane is irrelevant now. We'll sort out finding you a new partner later. By the end of the week, I'll have the king in hand, and we'll put our dummy in his place. At least that part of Atropa's plan will be secured."

Finally, real action was about to begin.

"Why wait?"

"Atropa wants to take over the land, not trample over it," the Duke said. "The people must be hers. She made that perfectly clear. To do this, I need a few days for word of Aurelius's bad reputation to spread. He's had decades of admiration, but within hours, I'll have the people believing he's greedy and self-serving. I'll start the wheels turning in the morning."

"How will you do that?" asked Dagma, looking at her nails.

"Quite simply," the Duke said, his eyes gleaming with malicious glee. "I'll start a rumour that Aurelius plans to introduce a new system for his own gain, disguised as being for the public good. He'll claim the money collected from the people will be used for improvement to roads and drains, but in reality, it's to make himself rich. You get the idea."

Dagma smiled wryly. "And how does that benefit you? If you're substituting the king, you need his reputation intact because you can control him, dummy."

"No we're using a real person, not a dummy."

Blethering idiot, he'd missed the point again.

"You're the dummy. Replace the king and control the substitute."

"Oh yes, I see, quite right," the Duke said, pouring another glass of wine.

Plop. There we go, the penny has dropped.

"Right. We'll keep Aurelius alive, hold him prisoner. Maybe he'll serve us until Atropa arrives. Like a servant, ha, ha—what fun! Or maybe not..." He coughed awkwardly, noticing Dagma's unamused expression. "He needs to be alive to witness Atropa's return. So does King Dunwood."

"Good. Seems like you've got it all under control. You don't need me, do you?" Dagma asked, without waiting for an answer. "I'm going back to the monastery tomorrow. Something's not right there. Those monks aren't real monks. They may know something about the key." It would be a godsend to be able to leave without this idiot.

"Oh, well of course, maybe I was wrong and certainly, if, er, you feel it is *key* to our investigations?" The Duke laughed at his own joke but immediately regretted it. He could've sworn the flames from the fireplace were reaching out toward Dagma.

"As a matter of fact, yes," Dagma said.

"Oh, that is good news. Well then, I'll get on with substituting the king," the Duke said turning to the open window. "Who left this blasted window open? It's freezing!"

"That was me," drawled Dagma. "Your 'man perfume' gets a little pungent in hot, enclosed spaces.

"Oh, right... Well, I'll just leave it open, then." He pulled his frilly sleeve down ineffectively. "Let's eat."

Outside, in the cover of darkness, a figure crouched behind a bush near the window. It moved carefully into the shadows before creeping back to the safety of its small room. Gwaine, his heart pounding with both fear and excitement, now had *real* information to tell the men when he visited the monastery tomorrow.

Chapter 12

THE DARK SIDE OF REVERENCE

C ANE'S MORNING HAD GOTTEN off to a bumpy start, and it wasn't just the lumpy mattress. Hellish visions jumbled his dreams, leaving him more than a little on edge. So, perhaps not in the best frame of mind, and against Gerant's advice, he decided it was time to visit King Aurelius. He left before the sun or anyone else had risen.

Nostalgia surged through him as he rode onto the palace grounds at Bellingham. Each sovereign leader had tried to outdo the last in making the palace a symbol of affluence and power. The grounds, in his opinion, were as over-the-top as they could get, with palm trees that looked as though they'd been plucked from some far-off land, and a building so golden it made the sunrise look dull by comparison. The tulip-shaped towers, marble columns, and elaborate gardens stood out, eccentric yet strangely comforting, just as always.

One of the palace's day guards—a man dressed head to toe in blinding white—came out to tend to his horse. Cane thanked him, recalling the long hours he'd spent in the same role, determined to be a real soldier and see real action. Well, that day had come, but not in the way he had imagined. All the more reason to restore a sense of balance in his mind. The steady hand of King Aurelius was sure to help him.

He strolled through the entrance hall, lined with portraits of Aurelius's ancestors, all looking stern and important. They shared the same signature rampage of golden hair they swore was natural, along with blue eyes and smooth—some might say weak—chins. But Cane didn't linger. He had walked these halls a hundred times, so he breezed past the endless dining hall and several other equally grand, yet empty, rooms.

He knew where to find Aurelius. It was always the same place: the botanical garden, a lush, green jungle contained within an enormous glass conservatory. The air was thick with the scent of flowers and damp earth, and the sound of a waterfall splashed through the foliage. Cane pushed through a curtain of vines, and there was Aurelius, sitting on his usual stone bench, looking like a man who had seen better days. The king watched the water with a deep, brooding expression, his once-bright blue eyes now clouded with age and regret. The golden whiskers of his moustache twitched as Cane approached.

"It's been a while, young Cane. I thought you'd been eaten up by the mysteries of Castle Graduce," Aurelius said, his voice serious but without judgement.

Before Cane could launch into his report, Aurelius cut him off with a weak wave of his hand, the many rings on his fingers glinting in the dappled light.

"You don't need to explain. Sending you to speak with the Baron was but a fool's hope. I'm grasping at straws to win back my loyal subjects. I can feel my kingdom slipping away, and now... it's too late. The Duke has won. He has imprisoned or bribed my best men and the people see him as some kind of hero—like these pond skaters, he seems to walk on water."

It was the first time Cane had heard him speak so openly—and against Duke Nieman. He felt it gave him permission to be equally candid. "My assignment was enlightening but not fruitful in the way you had hoped. I discovered that many of our people are still loyal to you. All is not lost," Cane protested, and as the words left his mouth, he felt their inadequacy.

Aurelius shook with laughter, though it was more of a resigned chuckle than anything joyful. "Ah, but it is. This Duke, this cuckoo, understands people all too well. In just a few years, he's turned them against me with empty promises and a few extra pentlings. Soon enough, he'll have them believing I'm the enemy or my head on a stake."

"We have around two hundred men," Cane offered. "A hidden army within Bellingham, loyal to you."

Aurelius gave him a sad smile, one that spoke volumes of his resignation. "Two hundred men against a battalion of snakes? It's like pitting a puppy against a pack of wolves. It would be a massacre. I can't ask them to risk their lives for me, not when the fight is already lost."

A heavy weight pulled at Cane's heart. He had come here seeking help, only to feel the burden of rallying the king himself. Aurelius looked more like a man ready for bed than one ready for battle. Was this the man Cane had admired since childhood? A man who had embodied everything he believed in: honour, loyalty, strength? All Cane saw now was an old man hiding in a garden, watching as his kingdom crumbled around him. He had known all along what was happening, but did nothing. There was playing it on the safe side and then there was mastering the ancient art of 'it'll fix itself if I don't look at it'.

Aurelius had always seemed larger than life, but now, Cane saw him for what he was: just a man—flawed, isolated, and perhaps a little lost in his own regrets. The king had never married, never had children, all because of some tragic, forbidden love in his youth—if the gossips were to be believed. But was that any excuse to retreat from the world?

Now, when Cane looked at his leader, he felt a burning sting of disappointment.

And yet, instead of the sense of loss he expected after this realisation, something else entirely rose within him: freedom. It was as if the invisible strings tying him to Aurelius's ideals had been cut, allowing his own thoughts to come to the fore and take root. In that instant, the king, once a towering figure in his mind, had shrunk to the size of a mere symbol. The symbol of a figurehead that the loyal people of Valoria still needed. Without Aurelius, they'd be like a ship without a compass, lost in a sea of uncertainty. But with him? Aurelius still represented all the glory of his long lineage, and that mattered.

A newfound confidence welled up within him as he deigned to present his plan to the king, who all the while had been silent; no doubt still brooding over his melancholic thoughts.

"Your Majesty," Cane began, trying to control his eagerness, "if you won't let our men fight, then at least let them protect *you*. Your safety as the leader of Southern Valoria is vital. If anything were to happen to you, it would be like breaking a sword's point, making it more difficult to slay the enemy."

"But if that sword is wielded by the hand of evil, what does it make it then?" Evidently his king was a 'glass half empty' kind of character. Refusing to allow Aurelius's pessimism to dampen his spirit, Cane dropped the metaphorical sword approach and went straight for the practical approach—one that didn't mention merged bodies or crawlers, as that would most likely tip his king over the edge into complete despair, and maybe his pond.

"My plan is this: We move you to safety. We've already sent a small, elite team to free the prisoners in Gribthorpe. Once the people see what's happened, they'll know the truth. We'll expose the Duke for what he really is—an usurper under the lace and fanfare."

Aurelius raised a bushy golden eyebrow, as if Cane had just suggested they all take up knitting instead of freeing prisoners and preparing for war. "How will you manage this with so few men? You're fighting a battle that cannot be won with swords and arrows, Cane. You'll need a miracle."

Cane, who was not one to believe in miracles let alone wait around for one, squared his shoulders. "The alternative is far worse. We either surrender like frightened rabbits caught in a snare, abandoning everything we stand for—fidelity, free-thought, free will—or we fight. I, for one, cannot abandon such values. And you cannot abandon those loyal to you. I intend to fight until my last breath."

For a moment, Aurelius simply stared at Cane, his old eyes crinkled. Then, something seemed to spark alive within them, and a slow smile spread across his face—a smile that was far too mischievous for a man of his age and station. "Maybe," he said, like a boy with a new toy, "it's time we made use of my hidden army."

Cane blinked, caught off guard. Had the old man gone mad? "*Your* hidden army? No, *we* have the hidden army."

"Yes, yes," Aurelius said, nodding eagerly. "But follow me, and I'll show you mine."

Cane followed the king across the palace grounds to the palace museum. The bright sunshine and the sweet sounds of songbirds made it feel like a typical peaceful day. But to Cane, everything felt oddly detached, as though the world around him had become a stage. And Aurelius was narrating the story.

"Many years ago, my great-grandfather received a gift from the Tunderian king. A rather impressive, though somewhat impractical, gift. A life-sized woven replica of my royal troop. It's quite the sight to behold, though I must say they take up far too much space to keep on display."

Cane wasn't entirely sure where this was going, but he decided to play along. "A unique gift, indeed."

"The Tunderians are skilled weavers," Aurelius continued, relishing his trip down memory lane. "Their ancestors built houses out of reeds that still stand today. They have a rich culture and honour it by keeping this craft alive. When a leader dies, they weave life-size figures of their closest guards to accompany them in the afterlife. As a symbol of our alliance, they gifted these to my great-grandfather, King Valkarse. Come, let me show you."

When Aurelius opened the museum storeroom, its contents momentarily stunned Cane. Before him stood a stack of life-sized, woven figures, each one a colourful replica of Valorian soldiers in full regalia. They stood there, gathering dust like a forgotten brigade waiting for orders they would never hear.

"Well, what do you think?" Aurelius spread his arms wide, as if unveiling a grand masterpiece. "My hidden army. Dormant soldiers, just like the loyal men and women hiding in Bellingham."

He hasn't completely lost it after all, Cane thought, staring at the woven warriors. While he doubted these straw soldiers would intimidate anyone over the age of five, an idea was already forming. Maybe, just maybe, there was a way to turn this odd gift to their advantage.

He looked at Aurelius with a grin that matched the old man's earlier mischievous smile. "I think we can work with this, Your Majesty. We might just give the Duke the surprise of his life."

Cane's plan crystallised with the clarity of a sparkling diamond. "What if we positioned these woven soldiers along the palace's ramparts and outer wall?" he suggested. "That way, no matter when the Duke strikes—"

"*If* he strikes."

"Yes, well, *if* he does, he'll be met with what appears to be a full garrison. They may need a change of uniform, though—something not quite so... colourful."

The king, now looking less like a wilted fern, nodded in agreement.

"We'll set them up before nightfall, when he's most likely to come. In the dark, shadows from the palm trees will sway across the ramparts, making it seem like the figures are moving. The moonlight will play tricks on the eye, making the whole setup appear lifelike. We might just fool the Duke's men."

"Ah, that it should come to this," the king sighed. "Those men are Valorians. To think I must defend myself against the very people I've served and cared for... it breaks my heart."

Has he always been this melodramatic? Cane wondered. "Your Majesty," he said as gently as he could manage, "with respect, we must steel ourselves to fight for what we hold dear." He cringed inwardly, hoping he hadn't overstepped.

Aurelius tilted his head, his gaze turning misty. "A juxtaposition of sentiments... our paths are sometimes already paved for us," he intoned, clearly drifting off into one of his poetic reveries.

Normally, Cane would have listened patiently in silence and let the king finish his waxing lyrical. But now, there was no time for such indulgences. "If an attack were to take place, we have enough men to take positions at the top of the quarry to throw down boiling tar, stones, arrows—anything we can use. Though we've sent our best men, a small specialist unit, to Gribthorpe, I believe we can hold them back."

Aurelius finally seemed to focus again. "Thank you, Cane. You've reinvigorated my faith in hope. Your father would be proud of you." He took Cane's hand, squeezing it with a warmth that caught Cane off guard. "*I* am proud of you."

The handshake lasted just a fraction too long, but Cane didn't dwell on it. "Time is our enemy now; I must take my leave," he said, bowing respectfully before swiftly heading for the door.

Once outside, he delivered his orders to the guards with a newfound authority that surprised even him. He could not rely on the king to take action. There was no time to waste. Mounting his horse, he spurred it toward the monastery.

Oddly enough, instead of feeling burdened by the king's atrophy, Cane felt invigorated. Seeing Aurelius so diminished and yet managing to incite him into action had lit a fire in him. For so long, Cane had been the diligent student, the obedient follower, mimicking every move of his instructors with dedicated precision. Now, he was no longer the student. He was the one designing the plans and, thanks to Gerant, the one teaching.

Training, Cane realised, was going to be a different challenge altogether. It wasn't just about repeating what he'd learned—it was about breaking it down so that others, older and gruffer than him, could grasp it quickly and effectively. The thought of leading these men and women, who, for the most part, already had excellent fighting skills, was enough to make his stomach flip with self-doubt.

What if he couldn't do it? What if he was only good at following orders, but hopeless at giving them? He tried to push these worries aside, but they stuck to him like burrs. Too many people were counting on him, and too much was at stake for him to get cold feet. *Blast it!* Now the doubt had opened the floodgates. He struggled to stay focused, his mind kept drifting back to his dreams.

Those blasted dreams! They were a chaotic jumble of childhood memories, mostly about the day his parents had left for their excavation mission in North Valoria. Had they been afraid? Where was the letter they'd left him? He couldn't remember the details. He couldn't even recall if he'd waved them off. He had been so consumed with preparing for the Sovereign Games and winning that he hadn't given their sudden departure due thought.

And then, there was Agatha. Ever since he'd met her, he couldn't get her out of his head. Her face, her voice—she was like a spectre haunting his thoughts, pulling him into her pain and loneliness. Whenever he pictured her, it was always in darkness, as if she were trapped in a void, utterly alone. No matter how hard he tried, he couldn't rid her from his mind.

Frustrated, Cane stormed into the monastery gardens, his stride quick and irritated. He'd have given anything for a good, long run across the moors to shake this off, but thanks to the Duke's scouts lurking about, that was out of the question. Instead, he sucked in a deep breath of the crisp, fresh air, hoping to blow out all the confusion and anxiety along with it.

Even as he tried to clear his mind, Cane knew one thing for certain: there was no going back to the simpler days. This mess, unwanted and uninvited, had landed squarely at his feet, and no amount of wishing would make it disappear. The only thing to do now was to face it head-on, no matter how uncertain or overwhelming it seemed.

By the time the volunteers from Bellingham began trickling into the monastery, Cane's head was clear again. His plan rolled out in his mind like a mapmaker's masterpiece. The men and women arrived in staggered groups, taking care not to draw attention. With his focus restored, he stepped into the role of teacher as though it was his natural calling. He enjoyed the command, instructing with ease and good humour. They responded to his straightforward manner, their eagerness to learn making the training sessions a pleasure. Even as the drills pushed their basic skills to the limit, their determination to master them fuelled Cane's own energy.

High above in the monastery's balconies, Agatha watched him with an intensity that would have made a lesser man stumble over his words. But Cane was in his element. He ignored her. The men and women hung on his every word as he laid out the tactics they would use.

"There's no sense in hoping for an easy victory," Cane began, pacing the courtyard like a wolf before a hunt. "While I've shown you a few simple ways to maximise the effectiveness of your weapons in hand-to-hand combat, it's our coordination as a unit that will give us the greatest advantage. Surprise and speed will be our allies."

He explained the plan with razor-sharp clarity, his sword carving out the strategy in the soil. The men and women nodded, they were determined and their optimism grew. Cane felt a swell of pride—they were ready to follow him into the very jaws of death if need be. He could feel it.

He could also feel Agatha. Above him, she remained transfixed, her eyes never leaving him. As he wrapped up the day's lesson, Cane suddenly felt an invasive fog cloud his mind. The words on the tip of his tongue evaporated, leaving him momentarily adrift. What had he been saying? What was he supposed to say next?

"Well, I think you've got the gist of it," he improvised, waving a hand as if shooing away an invisible fly. "That'll do for today. Well done, everyone." He dismissed the fighters with a quick nod, his feet carrying him briskly to the inner cloister, away from prying eyes. As he entered the shadowed corridor, a voice, soft and familiar, purred in his mind.

You were watching me. I am here. I need your help. I need you, Cane. I want you.

His heart skipped a beat. He knew that voice. *This isn't the first time you've visited my mind,* he responded, his thoughts clear yet disoriented. *You came into my dreams.*

I hope I didn't disturb you, came the reply, with a seductive sweetness that sent a shiver down his spine and into his trousers.

What kind of trickery is this? he thought, his mind whirling. He felt violated. *I can see you. Your lips aren't moving, but I can hear you as if you're right next to me.*

You're thinking this all by yourself, she purred. *I'm not tricking you. This is what you want. Think about what you want.*

Suddenly, the cool stone walls of the cloister blurred, and he found himself standing in his own quarters. The shift was seamless, but entirely impossible. Agatha was there, sitting on the edge of his bed, her gown slipping off one shoulder in a way that was far too deliberate to be accidental. *I didn't force you to come,* she said, her voice smooth as velvet. She removed the gown, baring herself to him. *Come closer.*

A surge of heat seared through Cane, desire rising like a tide he couldn't control. Oh, God, he wanted her. His feet moved of their own accord, drawing him closer to her, closer to that intoxicating invitation. But just as he was about to reach out, a dark, cold thought sliced through her irresistible pull.

No! His mind screamed. *I do not want this.*

With tremendous effort, he forced his eyes open. The scene vanished as abruptly as it had come. He was back in the courtyard, the harsh winter light a stark contrast to the seductive darkness that had clouded his thoughts. Some of the men he'd been training were looking at him with concern. Gerant was kneeling beside him, trying to lift him up.

"I think you must've eaten something off," Gerant said, frowning. "You collapsed."

"Definitely something off," Cane muttered, his face flushed with embarrassment. Agatha's voice echoed in his mind, her imagined touch still pressed on his skin. He felt hot all over, a deep, uncomfortable heat that refused to dissipate. He allowed Gerant to help him to a low wall, needing a moment to collect himself. "I was hoping to talk with you about your visit to Aurelius." He paused. "Yes, we know you went. But perhaps we'll talk some other time as I see you're not well. Fatigued?"

"I'm alright, Gerant," he said, brushing off the man's concern with a forced smile. "Really, thank you."

"If you're sure," Gerant replied, hesitating as he studied Cane's flushed face. But seeing that Cane was eager to be left alone, he reluctantly conceded and made his way to the library, casting one last glance over his shoulder.

As soon as Gerant was gone, Cane buried his face in his hands. His pulse was still racing, his thoughts a tangled mess of confusion and desire. What in the world had just happened? Whatever it was, he wouldn't let it distract him again. He had to be ready to lead, not be lead astray.

Chapter 13

MY KINGDOM FOR A KEY

Cane's smooth transition into the role of commander quietly impressed Gerant, directing the men with an ease that belied his young age. He thought he'd discerned a natural leader in him, but seeing him in action now, Gerant couldn't help but feel a certain pride in the young man's progress. He hoped his reverence for the king and the golden days wouldn't blind him.

Though hearing about Cane's visit to Aurelius didn't sit well with him, it was the fact that he'd gone alone that really bothered him. If they were to defeat the Duke, there could be no solo players, no secrets. *Well, he's young, and with youth comes the impulse to be rash. I can't expect him to be perfect.*

As he took a moment to assess the sky, trying to predict the weather for the following day, he noticed Agatha standing on the upper balcony. Her eyes firmly locked on Cane, her expression one of intense focus.

Ah, the saviour becomes the lover—it's only a matter of time. Gerant chuckled, biting down on his pipe as he noticed Agatha's gaze practically glued to Cane.

But then something odd caught his attention—Cane, usually so steady on his feet, seemed to waver. His commanding tone faltered, and his words tangled together as if he'd forgotten what he was saying. Then, some invisible force swept under him and Cane's legs gave way.

Gerant rushed to his side in an instant, helping him over to a stone bench. Cane looked shaken, though he tried to put on a brave face.

"I think you must've eaten something off. You collapsed."

"Definitely something off." Cane did not look himself at all. Quite sick, perhaps a fever, thought Gerant. "I was hoping to talk with you about your visit to Aurelius." He paused trying to hide any trace of disappointment. "Yes, we know you went. But perhaps some other time as I see you're not well. Fatigued?"

"I'm alright, Gerant. Really, thank you."

"If you're sure," Gerant replied, lingering for a moment. Cane's discomfort at having him so close was unmistakable. With a nod, Gerant reluctantly took his leave, heading toward the library. As he walked away, he couldn't help but wonder what had caused Cane's sudden weakness. *Probably just exhaustion. Or maybe Agatha's gaze was more powerful than I realised—left the poor lad weak in the knees,* he thought smiling. He'd see how he was later. No point in smothering the young man.

Gerant entered the monastic library—if it could still be called that. The shelves, once overflowing with knowledge, now stood mostly bare, the Cretyne monks had already taken the important texts, leaving only the trivial and fantastical. Thankfully that was exactly what he needed. If he was going to find anything about the Octules and the old lores of the Gaene Kin, it would be buried in these remnants.

Gerant wasn't much of a bookworm—that was more Rowan's territory—but the legends of the Octules intrigued him. He scanned the dusty tomes, searching for any reference that might be of use. Their fight wouldn't just be waged on a battlefield with swords; an older war simmered beneath the surface, and the secrets of the Gaene Kin and the Octules played a part.

His thoughts were interrupted by the sound of rustling paper. Gerant turned to see Bain, also an unlikely scholar, hunched over a pile of old manuscripts behind one of the bookcases.

"What are you doing here, Bain?" Gerant asked, surprised to find him among the books.

"I thought I'd dig into the Cretyne monks' scriptures," Bain replied, without looking up. "See if there's any mention of the Gaene Kin."

"Great minds think alike!"

"They were wiped from most records, but the monks were meticulous. Didn't leave much behind when they relocated up north, though. What little there is around the time of the Gaene Kin's banishment is full of warnings. They were seen as freaks of nature, against God's will, and so on."

"Yes, that's what I have heard too."

"The monks believed the Gaene Kin's powers would come at a price. Only God was meant to have such power, not people. So, naturally, they were branded as evil doers, no mention at all of them using their magic for good. What I have found so far insinuates that they, the monks, were the ones to rid the populace of these heretic women."

Gerant pulled up a chair beside his friend.

Bain shared his findings. "Here it says they even spread rumours that the Gaene Kin never existed, dismissing them as figments of a fanciful author's imagination. That way, they could condemn the whole idea as mere fiction."

"They fuelled those superstitions too," Bain continued. "Like the tale of the Devil's Needle—allegedly a Gaene Kin who tried to use dark magic but was turned into a standing stone. As the tale goes, the stone will return to human form when the Devil decides to use her as his messenger."

Gerant nodded, leaning over Bain's shoulder to peer at the yellowed pages. "Very inspired," Gerant said, looking at the chilling images. "People do love their stories."

"And look at this," Bain pointed to a blood-curdling drawing, "the monks weren't content with just stories, they had to turn the Gaene Kin into actual demons. This one here, the first High Priestess, she's got a forked tongue, fiery eyes, a scaled tail, and enormous hands."

Bain's finger traced the symbols around the demonic figure. "These symbols represent the four elements she's meant to control: air, earth, fire, and water. But there's nothing benevolent about how they've depicted her."

"Powerful, though. Maybe that's why they feared them so much. Fear can make men do extraordinary things. Still, I can't help but think—these other Gaene Kin, they were normal-looking women. They can't have all died out."

"Well, they were banished back in King Valkarse's time. That's three generations ago. Still, I was told they'd set up their own society, isolated from the rest of us."

"That's one of the stories," Gerant said with a shrug. "But who knows what's true and what's just hyped up hearsay."

"Quite. Supposedly, they live on some secluded island now, just women. All beautiful, all trained warriors. Sounds incredible, doesn't it?"

"That sounds like a version Blake would have dreamt up!" Gerant laughed.

"Not if they're all pissed-off warrior women with demonic powers." The two men shared a chuckle at the thought of a Blake being chased by a tribe of warrior women.

Their laughter faded, replaced by the rustle of parchment. Gerant's thoughts, however, turned to darker matters.

Had the Gaene Kin truly returned? Was the Baroness trustworthy? Bain had been his friend since childhood—a man of sound judgement. He didn't trust her, yet she seemed more victim than villain in Gerant's eyes. The questions weighed heavily as he rose, leaving the library behind and his friend to read the dubiously recorded histories by dim candlelight.

Making his way through the quiet halls, Gerant retreated to his quarters, but sleep wouldn't come easy. Not with so much to think about.

A few hours of fitful sleep were all he managed before waking, well before dawn.

Rising quietly, Gerant made his way to the kitchen. The chill of the stone floors was sobering as he filled a pot and set the water to boil, his thoughts still distant. As the gentle hiss of the rising steam filled the room, something stirred outside—a faint noise, barely noticeable at first. Was it Cane, slipping off again to visit Aurelius? Or had some flesh-eating monster made its way from Castle Gradunce?

Peering through the small, warped window, Gerant spotted a stout, portly man huffing and puffing at the monastery gates, his round face flushed with effort. The man's eyes darted nervously behind and above him, as though he expected the full moon to fall on him at any moment.

Great! Just what we need, Gerant thought. *Another mystery guest to add to our troubles.*

Noticing Gerant's approach, the man straightened . "Apologies for arriving at this early hour," he wheezed. "I had to make sure I got here before Lady Dagma did." Gerant looked at him with suspicion. "I know my appearance may not suggest it," the man continued, "but I believe I may be of use to you. I have some information."

Gerant, who had long learned that the best way to handle situations like this was to keep a straight face and let the other person either dig themselves into or out of their own hole, maintained a steadfast silence. He gestured for the man to follow him into the monastery. The two walked down the dark, torch-lit corridor, the visitor's heavy breathing echoed loudly within the vacuous stone corridor.

Halfway down the passage, they met Tristan and Percy sleepily heading for the kitchen. The visitor's face lit up in recognition. "It's you!" he exclaimed, pointing an accusatory finger at the brothers.

Percy's attempt at nonchalance failed miserably. The man, however, was undeterred. "It's me, Gwaine the groom, at your service," he said excitedly, bowing with all the grace of a man who had never bowed in his life. "Don't worry, your secret's safe with me."

Percy, looking as if he'd just swallowed a particularly large conker, exchanged a brief, tense glance with Tristan. Gwaine, either deliberately ignoring or oblivious to the tension, launched into a hurried explanation, detailing how he had pieced things together: their irregular but frequent trips to Bellingham, the monk's habit worn by Tristan, and even the suspicious foot-massaging ruse.

Gerant's initial mistrust of Gwaine began to fade. There was something very familiar about him. He tried to place him as he listened.

"So, there I was in Bellingham, doing a spot of shopping for the missus, minding my own business," Gwaine began, with a grin that suggested anything but happenstance, "and what do I see but this young man strolling past in a monk's habit, of the Cretyne order no less. But those feathers there on your rope, well, they're only worn by senior members of the order, not the younger lot. I know that because my grandma's brother used to be a monk, back when they were still in the south. Now, I'm not one to jump to conclusions, but I definitely jump at gaping inconsistencies like that. Especially with everything so *off* in Bellingham these days."

Gwaine lowered his voice, as though preparing to share a top-level secret. "That little detail tickled my brain all day, so I decided to come check out my theory for myself. A band of rebels tucked away in a monastery somewhere. There's only one monastery within a day's ride of Bellingham—this one. So, after work, I rode out and stopped at the Avonlea Inn, where, by pure chance, I happened to overhear some rather interesting chatter. None other than Duke Nieman and his daughter, Lady Dagma, having a cosy little chat. And let me tell you, it wasn't about the weather."

The man was so keen to share his story, he didn't seem to need to breathe.

"I've had my suspicions about that Duke ever since I started working on his estate. I mean, come on, everything there was just a bit too perfect. And when I tried to bring it up with the other lads? They just waved me off like I was raving mad. Said I was overthinking it—me! Overthinking! I'm a simple man, that's not possible for me."

Gerant, thinking he was anything but simple, crossed his arms and remained silent.

Gwaine made a visible effort to get to the point. "Well, I'm not one to give up that easily. So, I asked for a little switcheroo in duties—I added gardening and fertilising to my roster, since I used to be head gardener at the Palace of Bellingham before things started to... change. Figured it'd give me the perfect excuse to mosey around unnoticed, eavesdrop on the odd conversation, maybe dig up more than just weeds, you know. And guess what? Worked like a charm."

A lightbulb went on in Gerant's mind. "You used to be one of the head gardeners for the king. Didn't you design the last labyrinth for the Trial of Unity at the Sovereign Games?"

Gwaine's grin stretched to fit his wide face. "Yes, that was me. They even named it after me: Gwaine's Gambit. My finest moment." He beamed. "Anyway, enough reminiscing. I put those skills to good use at my current employment. Turns out, being a mucker and gardener is the best way to become invisible. No one looks twice at the bloke shovelling poop, which suited me just fine. I heard enough in those flower beds and stables to know that something shady is definitely going down. So, here I am, laying it all out for you."

Gerant found himself both amused and intrigued. *Who would have thought the Duke's downfall might begin with a brave horse mucker?* He led Gwaine to the warm kitchen.

Once he was settled with a bowl of steaming porridge and a cup of hot coulain in hand, Gwaine shared the rest of his tale.

"They mean to take King Aurelius hostage this week," Gwaine declared between mouthfuls of porridge. "They've found a double to replace him."

Gerant exchanged a worried glance with the brothers, his earlier amusement replaced by unease.

Gwaine, seemingly unaware of the worry he had caused, continued in an almost casual tone. "Other powerful men of the Sovereign Court are being held captive in Gribthorpe. Apparently, King Dunwood in the north has already been turned. And Lady Dagma thinks some important key might be here." He rattled off these vital details with the ease of someone recounting the latest village gossip.

He was far from an idle gossip, though. Gerant couldn't help but admire the man's nerve. Here he was, spilling secrets that could get him killed, while munching on porridge as if it were just another day at the stables.

When Gwaine paused to take another swig of coulain, Gerant finally spoke. "Thank you for being so brave in coming here. Is there anything else we should know, no matter how insignificant it may seem?"

Gwaine frowned, as though trying to recall a forgotten detail. "Now that you mention it, yes, quite unforgivable of me to forget. Lady Dagma spoke of you. Well, I think it was you—she mentioned monks. She's planning to come here, to get that key. And it all has to be done before someone called Atropa arrives and takes over Valoria. That's why I had to get here quick smart."

Gerant's heart sank. Who is this Atropa? More pressingly... Lady Dagma, here? That was the last thing they needed. He shot a glance at the brothers. Percy looked like an over-used blood donor.

Gwaine, satisfied with having passed on the information, drained his cup. "I'd best be off before I'm missed. Already been gone two days. Can't have the missus worrying. And don't you worry neither. Your secret is safe with me."

Gerant thanked the beaming Gwaine, his gratitude hiding the sense of dread settling over him. "My pleasure, to be of service, sir." Bidding him farewell, Gerant knew that their most informative guest had just unveiled a very dangerous game already in motion.

And it's us who'll be playing it, he thought as he closed the door behind Gwaine.

Gerant was just starting to reflect over Gwaine's revelations when Percy abruptly stopped clearing away the bowls and looked out the warped window. "There's another bunch of people by the gates."

The morning had been abnormal enough, but it seemed the day had more in store for them. Going to the window, Gerant saw a decidedly more ominous visitor: Lady Dagma. She was on horseback, flanked by four guards, and looked as though she was about to personally evict them from the monastery—and their own bodies given the chance.

Just perfect. He watched Dagma closely. She was already smiling a victorious smile, clearly filing away some information or decision. *Gwaine!* Gerant cursed silently. *She must have seen him leave. Was she smiling because she spotted him? Or worse, had he led her here? I thought we could trust him.* He sent Tristan to warn the others of Dagma's arrival, then turned his attention back to the gate.

Dagma rode through with slow, deliberate grace, her hard eyes fixed on them. Gerant and Percy stood paralysed. Fear gripped them in it is invisible, iron shackles. There was something particularly unsettling about Dagma's hard smile—like the moment before a trap springs shut.

"Vows of silence are not part of the Cretyne monk doctrine," Dagma declared with the air of someone accustomed to presiding over others. She lowered the hood of her cape with the commanding air of a queen. "I care little for your intentions. I'm here for what's mine. Retrieve it, and I'll be on my way."

Gerant exchanged a quick, desperate glance with Percy, hoping the younger man might miraculously find a convincing response. But Percy's face was as blank as his mind appeared to be. Realising he was on his own, Gerant forced a smile.

"I apologise, my lady, for any appearance of deceit," he began, doing his best to sound contrite while internally cursing every deity he could think of for putting him in this predicament. "We've heard of raiders in these parts and decided to stay silent, perhaps overstepping our bounds as humble monks. It was not meant to deceive one as esteemed as yourself, but one must be cautious these days."

He bowed modestly, though he doubted it would earn him any favour. Dagma, looking down at him, merely arched a perfect eyebrow, clearly unimpressed. She began circling them on her horse, each hoofbeat like a ticking clock reminding him how little time he had to turn this around.

"Baron Gradunce's castle was recently burgled," she said, her tone as sharp as a needle piercing its way into Gerant's mind. "It's my belief that you and your merry men took my key. Hiding behind your pious lies, don't think talk of raiders will fool me."

Well, this is going splendidly. Gerant fought to maintain his composure, knowing Dagma was playing with them, and thoroughly enjoying it. He felt more like a cornered animal, unable to escape, with an eagle circling in for the kill.

"I have come to reclaim the key. You know of what I speak. It is unmistakable—there's none like it. You are hiding it here, but it belongs to me. You've stolen it, and it's of no use to the likes of you."

Gerant's safety rope was fraying fast. "I'm not at all enamoured with the tone you take with us, my lady," he said, doing his best to keep his voice steady. "We may be many things, but we are not thieves."

Percy, who had been struck dumb until then, suddenly found his voice. "And how do we know *you're* the rightful owner of the key?" he asked, sounding far too pleased with himself.

Gerant scowled, feeling the urge to throttle Percy on the spot. The last thing they needed was to confirm anything about the key, and Percy had just blurted out exactly that, albeit unintentionally. Sure enough, Dagma exuded with triumph.

"Ha! You've confirmed my suspicions." Her voice took on a cruel edge. "Hand it over, gentlemen, and quickly."

Just when Gerant thought things couldn't get worse, the ground seemed to tremble beneath them, as if the earth itself was shifting in deference to Dagma's demands.

Bain and Felix arrived, looking utterly bewildered.

"What's happening," yelped Felix before slapping his chubby hand over his mouth.

"It's alright Felix," said Gerant. "The game's up. The lady here knows we speak."

"Which of you wants to give me the key?" All eyes dropped to the ground. "No takers? Then let me rephrase the question: Which of you wants to die first?" She cackled at her own joke. The earth trembled again, and a gust of wind howled through the courtyard.

"None of them," said a calm female voice. Felix nearly jumped out of his skin as Agatha appeared beside him.

"Where did you come from?" he stammered.

"The crypt," she replied, pointing her lit torch toward the shut crypt behind them.

Gerant's heart plummeted past the 'Oh bugger' level straight down to 'We're in for it'. Things had officially spiralled out of control. Any hope of escaping this without capture—or worse—was quickly fading.

For the briefest of moments, Dagma's poised look wavered as she locked eyes with Agatha, but she quickly recovered, her smile turning icy. "Glad to see you're alive, big sister," she hissed.

"I'm sorry I can't say the same," Agatha replied, her voice firm despite the tremor in her hands.

Dagma's tone turned sardonic. "Father and I were starting to worry about you in that grisly castle. Such bad luck. You were trying so hard. You would've made the perfect mother."

Her cruel barb hit the mark. Gerant saw Agatha's eyes flutter shut, he feared she might collapse. Then, with a speed that startled all of them, Agatha hurled her flaming torch at Dagma, letting out a scream that would freeze a volcano.

The torch flew through the air in a blazing arc, embers scattering like sparks from a dragon's jaws. As soon as it left Agatha's hand, the flame seemed to take on a life of its own, growing brighter, fiercer, as if fuelled by Agatha's rage. The fiery arc coiled like a living serpent, hissing and crackling as it hurtled toward Dagma.

When the torch struck, it didn't just ignite—it exploded. Flames spewed in a violent cascade, racing up Dagma's body with terrifying speed. This was no ordinary fire. The blaze burned in deep reds and purples dancing like fire spirits.

Dagma's eyes widened in shock as the fire engulfed her, the heat so intense it warped the air around her. The flames licked at her skin, but instead of burning away like normal fire, they seemed to dig in, tunnelling into her. The stench of burning flesh filled the courtyard, mixing with the acrid tang of death. Any normal person *would* have been dead.

But something extraordinary happened. From deep within Dagma, a pale blue light began to glow, weak at first, but growing stronger each second. The flames recoiled from this light, as though repelled by it, but they were relentless, fighting against the light in a vicious tug-of-war. The blue glow pulsed, and with every pulse, it absorbed more of the flames, drawing them in until they disappeared entirely, leaving Dagma sitting there, her body smoking charred beyond recognition—but still upright.

Gerant felt his stomach churn at the sight. Dagma's skin was blackened, cracked, and oozing, her eyes burning with such pure hatred it made him shiver. The blue light still enveloped her, a ghostly aura that refused to fade.

"You wretch!" Dagma spat, her voice raw with pain, yet filled with hatred. "Damn your eyes!"

Agatha, now disconcertingly composed, stared back at her sister. "You'd better tend to those wounds, Dagma. No one here will help you. And in your weakened state, you make for easy prey."

Though fury blazed in Dagma's eyes, she looked beaten. "This isn't over, sister. I know where to find you now."

With that, she spurred her scorched horse, but the animal collapsed beneath her. She angrily dragged one of her guards off his saddle and took his horse instead. For all her haughtiness, the earlier confidence had burned away with her flesh.

Gerant moved toward the gates, watching as Dagma and her guards rode off—well, three riding, one running.

The time to act had come. They were no longer safe there. That morning's visitors had left a behind more than chaos and a dead horse; an unsettling tension pervaded them, along with the stench of charred flesh. Rudston Monastery was no longer safe.

Chapter 14

HARVESTER OF PAIN

D AGMA RODE LIKE A shadow-being fleeing the dawn, her cape still smouldering as she sped back to Malcrov Court. The sooner she submerged herself in the healing waters of the pool, the better her chances of salvaging what remained of her once-beautiful body. It was over a day's ride away, but she had no choice. There were other sacred springs and mystical rivers in Valoria, but she hadn't the faintest idea where they were. Her mother had promised to bond her with the water spirits, but that luxury was currently out of reach. Instead, as a girl, she had chosen earth magic as her secondary power. Fire had always come naturally—she needed no help with that. Though the earth's affinity with herbs and minerals had its uses, they were of no help now. Only water could mend this disaster.

I must reach that water, she thought, the agony of her burns intensifying with each jarring movement of the horse. Her guards had long fallen behind. Tears of loathing and pain streamed down what was left of her face, each one a silent curse aimed at Agatha. *I'll make her pay for this, even if it's the last thing I do.*

By the time she arrived at the front gates of Malcrov Court, she resembled a week-old corpse dragged from its grave. The doormen, accustomed to her imperiousness, scarcely glanced at her before she waved them off, her charred face hidden beneath her hood. If she'd had the strength, she'd have turned them all to stone for daring to look.

She hurried through the polished corridors, praying not to encounter anyone. The spiral staircase leading to the pool courtyard seemed endless, every ragged breath a tormenting reminder of how much she had lost. What remained of her skin hung off her body like a tattered cloak, peeling with the slightest motion. Normally, shedding was an annual, controlled process—now it was an exercise in sheer misery.

Finally, she reached the inner courtyard, where the sacred water, transported specially from Gribthorpe Reservoir, shimmered invitingly. The water nymphs had better not fail her now. She was halfway into the pool when the door creaked open behind her.

"What do you want, you moron? Don't you ever knock!" Dagma snapped abrasively.

Nieman, standing in the doorway, recoiled at the sight of her, his face turning sallow green. He clutched his mouth, clearly fighting back the urge to vomit.

"I—I'm sorry," he stammered, barely able to repress his reflux reaction. "The servants said you came back... smouldering... glowing blue... and that sparks were flying off you..." His voice trailed off as he stole another glance at her, wincing. "What happened to your face?"

"What do you think happened, you imbecile? I was burned!" Dagma shouted, but the Duke's expression didn't change.

"No, I mean your face—most of it... isn't there anymore."

Dagma turned toward the pool, catching a glimpse of her reflection in the water. What stared back was a hideous ruin.

"Oh, bloody hell, Agatha. I can't fix this. You infernal wretch! My face is gone. Damnation!"

"You saw Agatha?" Nieman asked, tentatively.

"Of course I did, you sodding moron! Who else do you think hates me enough to do this to me? Luckily, I drew off the blue flame."

"I thought... you weren't supposed to use your powers. It draws attention to us."

"Don't you dare tell me what I can and can't do!" The water around her began to boil.

"Sorry, I—I didn't mean—"

"What did you expect me to do, you blethering fool! She threw a torch at me, the witch! I had to use my inner fire to shield myself until I could get back to the pool to heal. Now everything's changed. I'm going to make her suffer even more this time."

"Even more? *This time*?" Nieman was uncharacteristically on the ball. "So it *was* you! What did you do, Dagma? Are behind those castle crawlers?"

"I'm supposed to be the heiress, not Agatha. *I* am the better leader. I have the power of fire. She's ordinary, weak—just pretty. She doesn't deserve to be queen. I've always been in her shadow. But soon, Mother will see who's truly worthy. *I* know what needs to be done."

"You know Atropa's plans would have gone much smoother if you'd just let Agatha fulfil her duty with the Baron. Instead—" He stopped abruptly and took a few paces back. "I'm sorry." He raised his hands in a placating gesture.

"You dare question me?" she snarled.

"So sorry. Forget I ever said it." A tense, deathly silence. "So, what happened, then?"

"Dey are not who dey say dey are—" Dagma's speech was garbled, her lips having slipped off into the pool during her tirade. She could see the Duke straining to comprehend. "Dey must de stopped. She has sided wit dem—"

"I understand, she's sided with them. Rest now." He tried to help her out of the pool, but his extended hand made no contact. He flinched away from her scorched fingers. "It'll be alright, Dagma."

She didn't believe him. The pool's magical waters might have been restoring her body—first blue, then returning to its normal pale hue—but her face was beyond saving. Most of the flesh was gone, her once-luscious red hair reduced to a patchwork of bald spots, her eyelashes and eyebrows now nothing but ash. She was a grisly, unpleasant sight to behold.

The Duke, trying not to gag, threw his cloak around her shoulders. As they walked toward his study, he signalled to a guard to fetch a nurse and open a window. The smell of charred flesh was too much for his lace handkerchief to block.

When the nurse entered, bearing a tray of bandages, instruments, and steaming hot water, she looked like a child encountering the boogieman for the first time. The tray clattered to the floor as she caught sight of Dagma, who now resembled the stuff of nightmares. The poor nurse, wide-eyed and as pale as a sheet, made a hasty exit, leaving behind her dignity and, unfortunately for the scullery maid that day, her lunch.

As Dagma bent to pick up the fallen tray to fling at the nurse, she caught her reflection in its shiny surface. The piercing shriek she let out would have put a banshee to shame, sending the Duke leaping out of his skin. Her wails, loud enough to shake the mansion's foundations, went on for what felt like an eternity. Desperate to stop the cacophony, the Duke grasped her shoulders. In the process, a piece of charred flesh stuck to his palm—what appeared to be a fragment of her crumbling ear. Repulsed, he quickly flicked it toward the open window, exclaiming, "Yuck!"

Outside, Gwaine the groom was pretending to check a horse's shoe, hoping to gather more information from the enlightening show unfolding inside. The offending piece of Dagma's ear landed squarely on his cheek. He stood up, peeling it off with a mix of confusion and disgust. After examining the charred morsel, he glanced suspiciously at the sky, as if the heavens themselves had rained down this gooey gift.

In the study, Dagma's sharp eyes spotted Gwaine standing at the window. Her rage reignited, she pointed a skeletal finger at him. "You! It's him!" she sputtered, half mad and entirely furious. "It was you I saw der! Get him! He's a pie!"

Nieman, quick to decipher her burnt-lip speech, sprang into action. "She means 'spy', not 'pie'," he explained to the guards, who had hesitated, unsure if they should arrest someone for being, or simply having, a pastry dish. The Duke rushed into the hall, giving out orders. Realising the jig was up, the groom made a valiant but ultimately futile attempt to escape. His short legs and stout physique didn't exactly scream 'fleet-footed', and the guards soon had him cornered, panting and trembling.

"Well done," the Duke praised them. "Put him in my study. Have four men guard him, restrain him, gag him—whatever it takes. Just don't let him get away."

Turning to Dagma, he suggested, "Now, my dear, perhaps you should, um, freshen up? I'll call for the medic."

Dagma waved him off with a charred hand, her pride as blistered as her skin. "Thank you, 'ut I do not 'ish to 'e seen 'y anyone. I shall attend to 'y own 'oonds. I 'ant to interrogate the pie."

Dagma pulled her tattered cloak over her head to hide her face from any servants on the way to her chamber. Once safely behind her locked door, she wiped down her burnt skin with a damp cloth from the large porcelain bowl filled with rose-petal water. She then mixed a pomade made from her own blend of herbs and oils, applying it carefully before bandaging her scarred limbs with strips torn from a purple satin sheet.

By the time she finished, Dagma's face was completely obscured, save for her dark eyes. She pulled a large black silk scarf over her head and across the lower part of her face to conceal her hair and bandages, tying it neatly at the back of her neck.

I shall have my revenge, sweet sister, she thought.

Upon re-entering the study, Dagma sensed the thrill of anticipation. After the week she'd had—rising from triumph one morning to becoming a scorched wreck the next—she was ready to take her frustrations out on someone, and the eavesdropping groom would do nicely. Her pomade had restored just enough mobility to her non-existent lips that she could speak without sounding like she had a mouth full of gravel. Despite her gruesome appearance, she held her head high, an air of authority clinging to her like the last vestiges of a ruined empire. The Duke, for all his cowardliness, couldn't help but admire the sheer force of her will. Dagma knew she looked even more imposing now, her injuries giving her an even greater air of gravitas.

"You cannot deny," she began, circling behind the chair where the quivering Gwaine was bound, "that it was you I saw departing from the monastery. And judging by your loitering at the window a moment ago, I'd wager you had some information to pass along to your disloyal friends. My question to you is: What did you tell them?"

The portly man shook in the chair, his silence a testament to either his loyalty or his terror. Dagma picked up the small blade the nurse had dropped earlier and pressed it gently against his ear.

"Ears are such useful things, aren't they, Gwaine?" she mused, her tone almost conversational. "Yours seem to have overheard something they shouldn't have. Oh yes, I know who you are, Gwaine. And I see from your ring you're married." She clicked her fingers. "Fetch the wife!" The blood drained from Gwaine's usually tanned and jovial face, like a candle snuffed out by a wicked wind. "Now, for her sake, let's start again with that simple question. What did you tell them?"

Still, Gwaine remained mute, his trembling the only answer he offered. Dagma's voice grew harder. "I see you're not quite at ease with the situation. Well, I sympathise—no one likes to be caught meddling where they don't belong. Usurping their station." Her voice rose to a sharp pitch. "If you won't reply, perhaps I should simply remove your ears so you can't commit the crime again."

With a flourish, she pulled a strip of bandage off her arm, revealing the raw, ravaged flesh beneath. "See, pain is so easy to bear." She wrapped the bandage around her hands pulling it taught and advanced on him. But instead of strangling him, she tied it around his eyes, plunging him into darkness. He was left to panic in the void. She placed the cold edge of the blade behind his right ear, the sting of it drawing blood. Her sickening scent of rose water and charred flesh filled the room.

"Now, you can focus, Gwaine. No distractions. It's an easy question, so I'll ask it again: What did you tell them?"

When he still refused to answer, Dagma whispered something to a guard, who then left the room. As they waited, Dagma nonchalantly picked up a crisp red apple from a fruit bowl, took a bite, and then rammed the rest into Gwaine's mouth. He choked and spluttered, struggling for air as she wrapped the remainder of his face in her foul-smelling bandages.

"Will you talk now, you imbecile! Who are they, and what did you tell them?" Dagma pressed, her tone gleefully sadistic.

Shaking his head, Gwaine clung to his silence with the stubbornness of a man who had nothing left to lose.

As the minutes dragged on, her prisoner became faint, the lack of air making him dizzy. Saliva mixed with apple juice dribbled down his chin, and tears rolled down his cheeks.

"Fidelia, how lovely of you to join us. Your husband is already here." Gwaine bolted upright at the sound of his wife's gasp and cries.

"Say hello, Fidelia," Dagma drawled. Gwaine began to convulse, the tight rope of his restraints cutting into his wrists and ankles.

"Shall we enter into dialogue now, Gwaine? Or do you need further encouragement?" Dagma's voice was dark yet amused. Fidelia continued to sob and implore for her husband's release.

Dagma's voice was cruel and languid. "I do find that the imagination runs far wilder when one cannot see what is happening."

She removed the apple. Still he refused to tell her anything. And so it continued, minute after agonising minute, the room filled with Fidelia's cries and Gwaine's laboured breathing.

"Damn it, man, tell us who they are and what they know!" the Duke shouted, but Gwaine held his silence—a silence that was soon matched by that of his wife.

"Take her away," Dagma ordered with disappointment. "Dump her body in Traitor's Square."

Gwaine fought hopelessly against the ropes that bound him. Tears ran rivers down his face. Now he really was a man with nothing to lose.

"No point struggling now, Mr. Groom-Come-Spy. What a naive man you are. Even after hearing your wife's painful anguish, you still would not comply. Did you think I valued her life more than my mission? Fool! The people of Valoria have much to learn about my ways. Lock him up in the cellars!"

The shocked Duke stood, mouth gaping in the corner, staring at the door where the guards had dragged Fidelia's slumped body out of the study.

"Father, perhaps you'd like to work on breaking his tenacity? Humans are so full of surprises. You might learn something." She tapped her charred skeletal finger on the table beside her prisoner.

<hr />

Gwaine didn't hear the Duke's response. His head was filled with the pumping and thumping of his heart. All he could hear was the sharp tapping of that murderess's finger on the table, like a raven pecking at his gravestone—a metronome counting out the end of his days as a happily married man. He wasn't sure if anyone was still in the room. Then some men grabbed him and dragged him unceremoniously down some stairs and threw him into what smelled like a sewer, his body hitting the damp stone floor with a thud. He heard the bang of metal and the turn of a key. He was locked in.

He lay there, motionless. He couldn't tell where his grief ended and his disorientation began. His world had folded in on itself. Vivid images of his happy wife curdled and twisted into a sinister vow of revenge.

Chapter 15

INSURRECTION

UNABLE TO SLEEP, CANE moved to his desk to go over his plans. His modest chamber, like every other room in the monastery, was as empty as a monk's diary on romantic conquests. The furniture was limited to a single bed and a writing desk cluttered with parchment and ink pots. A small window offered a view of the herb garden, but it was the primroses in a tiny vase—Agatha's thoughtful touch from days ago—that caught his eye, their colour a defiance to the room's austerity. The sight of those flowers brought a flood of thoughts crashing into his mind, all centring on Agatha, crowding his brain like an uninvited mob of crows in a peaceful garden.

He tried to focus on the papers in front of him—plans for defending the monastery and strategies for saving the king in case the Duke made a daring grab. Fortunately, he'd already devised a way to get the prisoners, including his parents, out of Gribthorpe before this cerebral storm hit. That small unit's mission was well underway, guided by Captain Almfred's capable leadership. His mind, usually sharp as a reaper's scythe, dulled to the sluggish scrape of an antique butter knife. Clear thoughts barely had time to form before evaporating like morning mist chased by the sun.

Is this what they call love? he wondered. *They say love takes over your mind so you can't think clearly. Well, if this is love, I'd rather do without it. I'd rather have my wits about me.*

He tried once again to shove Agatha out of his mind, but she stuck like a stubborn stain. A brilliant strategy began to form in his head—something about using the terrain to their advantage, perhaps—but just as quickly, the thought muddied, as though Agatha were splashing about in his mind like a child jumping in puddles.

"Damn it," he cursed under his breath. "I will beat this affliction."

Determined to regain control, he opened the window to let in some fresh air and snatched up his quill. Every time a clear thought emerged, he scribbled it down quickly before Agatha's image could dissolve it into nothingness. This painstaking process consumed most of the morning—what should have taken him minutes stretched into hours. Finally, he managed to outline a few strategic positions around the palace that might offer them a natural advantage—sure his former commander would not have been too impressed with the results.

His gaze drifted back to the primroses, their bright yellows and oranges catching the light. Despite everything, thoughts of Agatha still nagged him. She was unlike any woman he'd known—frail and strong in equal measure, beautiful and mysterious, like some enigmatic flower herself.

"Is she a curse or a blessing?" he wondered, lost in thought. The smell of burning wafted through his window. *Why on earth are they cooking outside?* Perhaps they were burning garden waste. Either way, they shouldn't be drawing attention to themselves for a spit roast or yard work.

He rose to investigate but was halted by a sharp knock at his door—Bain's knock. It was brisk, no-nonsense, and from its rapidity, clearly not the bearer of good news.

"What is it, Bain?"

Bain entered, his face a perfect portrait of disbelief. "It's Agatha," he said, his tone matching his expression.

Cane's heart did an uncomfortable flip, landing somewhere south of his stomach as Bain filled him in while they walked.

⸻ ◈ ⸻

At the entrance, he saw the others still gathered around the spot where the horse had become a real-life bonfire effigy. The acrid smell of burnt flesh and singed hair lingered. The scene felt surreal, like something out of a bad dream, only this was a terrifyingly real daytime terror, with Agatha playing the star role. She sat on a low cloister wall, looking hypnotised, staring blankly into space.

"You did this?" Cane asked in shock.

Agatha nodded quietly, her eyes downcast.

"Was that your sister?"

"She claims to be," Agatha muttered, visibly shuddering. "She's a monster. I hate her."

"You almost burnt her alive!" Bain screeched, his voice rising an octave in shock.

"I didn't mean to," Agatha whimpered. "I just—I threw the torch. I just wanted her gone!"

Bain resumed his role as interrogator. "Well, how do you explain the towering inferno of a human we just saw atop that horse?"

Agatha looked up, her eyes big and innocent. "I don't know. Maybe her cloak was made of something... or she had something in her pockets... I really don't know." Her voice wavered as tears welled in her eyes. "Why am I to blame? I don't know."

"She's gone," Felix said. "We should be happy about that, not attacking the poor girl. It's a good thing, no matter how it happened. The Baroness might've saved us all from that evil woman. I've seen enough trouble to know that witch had it written all over her. If it wasn't Agatha, it would have been one of us."

"Unfortunately, she's probably still alive," said Gerant.

"What happened exactly?" Cane asked, his tone gentler now as he turned to Agatha. "Why did Dagma come here? Are you hurt?"

"No, I'm not hurt," Agatha replied, in a small voice. "Thank you, Cane. I just... I feel tired. It was a nasty shock seeing her. I'm glad I had all of you to protect me."

Felix let out a hearty laugh. "You were the one doing the protecting!"

Gerant stepped in. "Dagma caught us off guard," he said. "She came back for the key, just as Gwaine said."

"Gwaine?" Cane frowned. "Why does that name sound familiar?"

"You'd remember him," Gerant replied. "You won the Trials of Unity in the labyrinth he designed for the Sovereign Games—Gwaine's Gambit. These days, he works at Malcrov Court. He arrived just before all... *this*. He warned us. I should have acted instantly. We should have been prepared. I didn't think she'd come so quickly. We've waited so long here that I didn't react fast enough. I feel to blame."

"Don't shoulder the blame for an evil sorceress's intentions, Gerant," Bain said, trying to console his friend. "We're not exactly trained to deal with the likes of her."

Cane turned back to Agatha. "Can you not think why this key so important to your sister?"

Agatha shrugged. "I don't know. Maybe because it symbolised my getting married before her."

"Well, regardless of the key, she now knows about us," said Bain. "Dagma knows we're disguised. She'll take her revenge soon, no doubt. The king's kidnapping will go ahead as planned, but now the monastery is on their list of targets as well."

"Agatha," Gerant said, giving her his most serious look, "you throw as many torches as you like if she returns. The rest of us need to get the king to safety and alert our people."

"I've drawn up our strategy," Cane said.

"Excellent," Gerant replied. "You're both a great asset to our side. Thank goodness fate brought you to us."

Agatha touched her forehead. "I feel faint," she said weakly. "I think I'll lie down for a moment." Rowan came to her aid.

As soon as they left, the men hurried to fortify the monastery—setting traps, digging ditches, barricading doors, and concealing the escape route. Dozens of white-collared pigeons were released from the dovecote at the rear of the monastery to signal their fighters that the time had come to make a stand. With Agatha's influence gone, Cane's mind mercifully cleared, focused entirely on rolling out orders.

———◄◇►———

Riding to Bellingham with Blake and Felix, Cane thought of his fellow rebels, likely spending the day battling fear while reassuring loved ones all would be well. *The plan had to work.*

Hours later, they were in position, there was nothing left but to wait and steady their nerves.

Night crept up on them swallowing the townscape in a dark, velvety blue. Hidden in the palace archway, Cane strained to hear beyond the pounding of his own heart. The steady march of hundreds filled the air, a thunderous beat so loud it seemed to drown out even the wind. *Far too many men for one kidnapping,* he thought, adrenaline flooding his veins with hot, false courage. Silence followed, a hush so complete that even the palm tree leaves seemed to still.

They waited in that silence, the kind of waiting that picked at nerves, making patience seem more like a cruel joke than a virtue.

Fifty reliable men split off towards the cliffs, vanishing into the night. The rest flowed from different parts of the city like streams feeding into a river. Approaching the palace in smaller groups, they quickly encircled the Duke's troops, ready to lay siege.

Moonlight stretched their shadows, transforming the ragtag soldiers into a live army. Across the court, the Duke's white dragonfly motifs glinted under the same silvery beams, turning his troops into a horde of skeletal horsemen.

"Don't be afraid," Cane whispered to his unit. "It makes them easier to see and target."

Flaming arrows arched overhead, crashing into the palace walls and igniting parts of it. The fire's greedy advance quickly spread, and within moments, the woven soldiers caught alight. Panic flickered in Cane's mind. "Blast!" he cursed silently, watching as flames consumed the dummy soldiers, threatening to unravel the illusion they'd crafted so carefully. The woven dummies blazed into burning figures, flames licking at their twisted forms until they thrashed and lurched like the possessed. Cane watched the terror ripple through the enemy ranks, the unnatural spectacle doing its work far better than he'd hoped.

For a moment, the Duke's men hesitated, eyes wide as the fiery dummies staggered forward. The flames danced in the wind, giving the woven soldiers a hellish animation. Unnerved by the sight of burning figures that seemed impervious to pain or death, the enemy ranks began to break.

When a gust of wind blew through the burning dummies forward like lurching zombies, the Duke's soldiers were convinced they were the work of evil. Several men, caught in the heat of panic, turned and fled, their disciplined formation collapsing under the weight of fear. Seeing their hesitation, Cane seized the opportunity.

"Now!" he shouted, and the rebel fighters surged forward. The burning dummies, still crackling with fire, were left to fall where they stood.

What had begun as a daunting siege quickly turned to a frantic rout, with the Duke's men more terrified of the supernatural spectacle than the actual threat. Watching the chaos, Cane smiled. The Tunderian king's woven soldiers had done their job far better than anyone expected. But his moment of triumph was cut short.

"Save yourselves!" Aurelius's voice rang out. The king had been taken by the Duke, who sat smugly atop his horse, basking in his supposed victory. Cane's victory smile darkened. Instantly, he and a small group of fighters moved toward Aurelius, swords drawn.

"Charge!" Cane's roar startled the Duke, who turned to see him closing in. His eyes growing in panic. Not expecting resistance, especially in such numbers, the Duke frantically gave the order to sound the horn. Within moments, hundreds more of his men, hidden in the surrounding area, emerged to join the fight.

The Duke retreated behind two of his guards, clearly deciding that courage was best demonstrated behind human shields and on the sidelines. But Cane's forces pressed forward, encircling the new wave of attackers and driving them toward the base of the cliff, just as planned.

Arrows from the archers, stationed at the top of the cliffs, raining down with deadly precision, weren't the only ones helping to turn the battle in their favour. Blake was proving himself very useful. Grabbing a fist-sized rock, he hurled it in the direction of the Duke's men advancing up the ridge.

The rock flew with tremendous force, not just striking one man, but ploughing through three before ricocheting off the ridge. The impact sent four more soldiers tumbling like skittles, and a section of the ridge crumbled from the reverberations, taking down even more of the Duke's men in the process.

"Well that went better than expected," he said, enjoying the perks of his newfound superstrength. Cane, catching sight of the scene, gave him a congratulatory smile.

"Blake!" Felix called out, still bewildered by what had just happened. "How did you—?"

Blake shrugged, trying to look nonchalant. "Must be all the *coulain* I had the other day." He flexed his arm and gave him a wink.

Felix laughed. "I'm glad you're on our side."

Cane allowed himself a moment of satisfaction. Things were going well—until they weren't.

He spotted a figure on horseback at the top of the ridge. Agatha? What in the devil's name was she doing here? She was supposed to stay at the monastery! For a split second, he wondered if it was another trick of his mind—a love-struck hallucination conjured up by his treacherous brain right in the heat of battle. But no, she was real—or at least, someone who looked very much like her. Panic twisted in his gut. "Take over!" he shouted to one of his men, then spurred his horse up the side of the battlefield toward the ridge.

By the time he reached the top, the figure had vanished, along with his archers. Cane cursed under his breath. Looking down at the battle below, he saw the Bellingham loyalists splitting into two formations. Half remained to fight, but the other half was riding off.

"Where the hell are they going?" Cane muttered, disbelief washing over him like a cold wave.

He raced back into the thick of the fight, his sword clashing against the weapons of the Duke's men. It was a frenzied melee of steel and sweat, and Cane fought with the energy of ten men. Through the chaos, he spotted the cloaked figure again. But as he drew closer, he realised it wasn't Agatha after all. The rider turned, revealing not a face but a black, expressionless mask—smooth and sinister, like something that crawled out of the dark places you tell children never to go.

The masked figure stared at him, the blank face unnervingly calm amidst the turmoil. She—he was sure it was a 'she' now—pulled a vial from her belt pouch and turned to the man Cane had left in charge. She poured a shimmering powder into her hand and blew it into his face. He blinked, dazed, as she whispered something in his ear.

Without hesitation, the man gave the order that shattered Cane's last hope. "The Duke has taken our sovereign leader to the monastery! We must kill all who are there and save him!"

The masked woman turned to Cane, and he could almost swear the mask curved into a gloating grin. Damn it, it's Dagma, he realised with a sinking heart. She had outfoxed them all. The battle was lost. The men of Bellingham now divided and misled. The archers and a large contingent were heading straight for the monastery. With them went any chance of victory.

He searched in vain for the king, with the frightening awareness that time was running out pressing all too keenly on his mind.

"We must return to the monastery!" he yelled, racing forward like wildfire, not waiting for Blake and Felix to catch up. The cold air stung Cane's eyes, he could barely breathe the air he ploughed through. Faster, he urged his steed, faster still. There was no time to lose; his troop had already left for the monastery, and he had to get there before it was too late.

Spurring his horse, Cane galloped after those who had left the battlefield, his mind racing. He could only hope Aurelius had somehow escaped and that the prisoners, his parents, in Gribthorpe were freed. But those hopes felt like feathers in the wind as he charged toward the monastery, where the killing of innocents awaited. His meticulously crafted plan that even overcame the unexpectedly high number of enemy soldiers, had been flattened like a house of cards. Now, he was racing to stop his friends being attacked by their own allies.

Such trickery, Cane mused, was the sort of thing you'd expect from a vengeful, egomaniac. And nothing was more dangerous than a woman scorned, especially one like Dagma, who'd probably trade her soul for a chance at revenge. Agatha was next on her hit list, no doubt. After all, it was Agatha who had reduced Dagma to a crispy reminder of her former self. Each beat of his horse's hooves pounded images of Dagma's demonic mask into his mind's eye. *She isn't human*, he thought. *She has the look of some unvanquishable force.*

As he reached the monastery's perimeter, Cane spread the word to his men: they'd been duped, double-crossed like naive fools in a wicked comedy.

"But sir," one man started, "we're under orders to attack the monastery. The Duke's special squad is supposed to be here with the king. They've already infiltrated the walls. Gerant and the others need our help."

"There is no special squad!" Cane shouted. "We've been sent on a wild goose chase—a mission that'll have us killing our own in the dark! Gerant will think you're the Duke's men and fire on you! Go, tell the others—quickly! And for the love of all that's holy, don't trust anyone in a mask!" The young man took off at a gallop.

Cane rode on, relaying the message to those already at the monastery. His worst fears were confirmed when he arrived on scene. Bain and his group were firing a flurry of flaming arrows, turning the monastery gardens into an inferno. The men, blinded by the light and deafened by the roar of flames, were attacking anything that moved. It was a disaster—a fatal flop that left Cane terrorised.

"Stop!" he shouted, but his voice was lost in the clashes of battle. He had to get inside the monastery—his only hope of stopping the madness. Dodging arrows and burning debris, he sprinted to the side of the building, weaving through the orchard, past the dovecote, and into the kitchens. He raced up the stairs to the rooftop.

"Bain, stop! They're our men!" Cane cried out, leaning over the edge of the turreted wall.

"What?" Bain fuelled by kill-or-be-killed adrenaline, didn't stop immediately. "What are you doing here?"

"It's all gone wrong," Cane explained urgently. "Dagma tricked them into thinking you've been overrun by the Duke's men. They believe Aurelius is here, being held hostage."

Bain's face paled as the realisation hit him like a slap from a whale. "Oh no, no, no! Stop firing! Everyone, stop firing! Get behind the walls!"

The men, dazed and battered, ducked behind the walls. Cane ripped his sky-blue tunic off and waved it desperately as a of surrender. Cheers of victory echoed from below as they rushed to the open the gates to let their own people in.

One bewildered man staggered through the gates, one of the many who hadn't gotten the message. "How is it you're well, Bain, and opening the gates to us? Where is our king?"

"Get your men in," Bain said, ushering him inside. "Quickly!"

The riders, what few of them remained—perhaps forty or so at a quick headcount—assembled in the courtyard. The men on foot arrived shortly after, though their numbers were even more diminished. With the gates secured, Cane addressed them all.

"We've been outsmarted, and soon they'll be upon us. We were outnumbered from the start, but now we stand no chance. They'll come for us because we're the last loyal men and women of Bellingham, and we'll be slaughtered like rats in a trap. Our only hope is to escape through the monks' underground tunnels. Arm yourselves with whatever you can, set your horses free, and head to the kitchens. Felix, ration out the food and equipment as they come through. Move quickly!"

There was no time for questions or doubt. They sprang into action, their movements swift and efficient. Cane, meanwhile, went in search of Agatha. He found her in her room, locked in as instructed and, to his surprise, remarkably calm.

"I knew you'd come for me," she said sweetly, opening the door.

Cane rushed forward, pulling her to him. "I'll not let them hurt you." Suddenly remembering he wasn't wearing a shirt, he quickly stepped back, aware of the intimacy of the moment. "Forgive me, Baroness, but we must hurry. Your sister may be here soon, and we need to make our escape."

There came a frantic banging on the gates. "Let us in! We've freed what prisoners we could!" Recognising Captain Almfred's voice, Cane rushed outside to unbar the gates, letting the men in before slamming them shut again. Only a handful had made it. "Many were too frail to escape, let alone make the journey."

All the survivors hurried down toward the monastery's cellar, passing dusty artefacts and forgotten heirlooms on the way to the hidden passage. Felix was already at work, hastily directing the survivors as they packed supplies. In need of a shirt, Cane grabbed the nearest garment from a pile, which just happened to be a velvet jacket—Gerant's grandfather's purple smoking jacket, complete with frills, gold stitching, and an embroidered crest of a leaping deer.

Gerant, catching sight of Cane's new attire, couldn't resist. "Well, if it isn't the Marquis of Mayhem himself!" he grinned, giving a low bow.

Cane scowled, tugging at the over-the-top lapels. "I think this will be more effective on our enemy than my plan—it'll kill them through laughter."

Despite their urgency to flee, Agatha raised an eyebrow at Cane's absurd getup as she passed.

Blake exploded with laughter. "Planning to distract them with your daring sense of fashion, are we?"

"Stop staring all of you and get into the passage!" Cane shouted.

"Hurry, Felix, hurry!" Gerant urged, guiding Agatha and Felix through.

Cane dragged an oak chair in front of the small hidden door, bolting it securely from the inside.

How could this be happening? thought Cane. Hours ago, when they stood a chance, he was leading them to victory. Now, reduced to fugitive status once more, he was leading them to nowhere—in a purple smoking jacket, in a dark tunnel, in a country without a k ing.

Chapter 16

AN EMPTY CROWN

Outside the Palace of Bellingham, Dagma steered her horse through the fallen bodies of the Duke's soldiers, indifferent to the dead and dying forms beneath her. Some still moaned the sounds of a pained life source that prolonged their agonising existence—the slow hand of time, not the compassionate hand of mercy, would extinguish their light. No pity for the dead, whose realisation and understanding of Aurelius's peaceful reign had come too late.

The Duke came clattering up behind her on his horse, looking every bit as inappropriate as a jester at a funeral. His military regalia, topped off with a ridiculous peacock feather in his shiny helmet, completed the absurd image. *Pea-cock indeed,* thought Dagma.

"We've got Aurelius," he announced with a flourish. "The other men are dead. A victory to be celebrated, wouldn't you say?" His men dragged a sad-looking king beside him, tying him with rope to the Duke's saddle. His golden whiskers now drooping, jaundiced and lifeless.

Dagma turned her masked face toward the feathered buffoon, not bothering to hide her irritation. "Why are you dragging the king around like an old laundry sack?"

"Um, er, because he is our prisoner?" Even in his moment of triumph, the Duke was reduced to an insecure fool when facing Dagma's questioning.

"Moron! Get him on a horse or put a bag on big head. We can't have him seen in public as our prisoner, otherwise it'll put in question the identity of our stooge king." She looked exasperated. "Really! It's so simple. The people of Bellingham must be told that last night put a stop to the rebellions against the king. Get with the plan, *Father*!"

"Ah, yes of course, of course. But otherwise a great victory, wouldn't you say?"

"A shit-show is more the term I'd use to describe it. A victory without the spoils. Prisoners broken out of Gribthorpe, hundreds of our men dead, and, worse still, Agatha and her merry band of men have vanished—most likely taking the key with them."

The Duke's smile wavered, the confidence slipped off his face. "B-but we've got Aurelius."

"We never really *didn't* have him. Swapping him was just an added precaution. Because you and your men failed, those rebel leaders, Agatha and the Sylphic key are now moving further away from us. We must head to Rudston Monastery to see if we can pick up their trail or if by some miracle they left the key behind." She fixed her menacing eyes on Aurelius. "How lovely to finally meet you in person, your Majesty. I look forward to deepening our acquaintance." She drawled. "Mother will be so pleased to see you when she comes."

Aurelius's tired eyes met her mocking look with silence.

"What? No defiant retort about how we'll pay for our misdeeds or how you'll make sure we don't get away with this?" Aurelius looked away. "Oh, brilliant, we've got ourselves a wet rag. You're as spineless as this moron, aren't you? No wonder the Valorians were so easy to turn against you. Greedy little beggars, the lot of them. No moral standards—you made life far too easy for them, old man. I bet you weren't even behind this little masquerade of dummy soldiers; it would take a man with imagination and passion to create such an unusual plan. No, you're all dried up, aren't you, *kingsey*." Still no reply. "He's boring me. Get him out of my sight—on a horse or in a bag, I don't care which!" She barked the orders to the men. "Clear this mess up, install the new king, get this wet rag to Malcrov Court, and you," she pointed to Nieman, "you're coming with me to the monastery."

Her obedient dog obeyed.

⸺ ◆ ⸺

After a gruelling ride through the sleet, Dagma was pleased to see the Duke's men scouring the monastery grounds like overzealous housekeepers—but the guests were long gone. Not a living soul to be found.

Dagma rode slowly into the cloister, her black mask as reflective of her mood as a mirror in a dark room. The mask may have concealed her expression, but her voice betrayed her fury. "What happened here?" she hissed at a soldier, her tone sharp enough to shave the stubble off his chin. "Where are our prisoners?"

"We caught none, my lady," the soldier stammered. "They... they disappeared."

"Disappeared?" Dagma snapped. "You didn't even capture one? How tiresome. Get in there!" she shouted, her tone turning scathingly patient, like a teacher explaining something to a particularly slow pupil. "All of you, get in there and find the tunnel. Monasteries always have a secret passage somewhere."

Footprints in the muddied grass revealed that hundreds of men, not just dozens, had been there. How could these imbeciles have let them slip through their incompetent fingers?

Inside the monastery, she sifted through the scattered plans and maps left behind in the rebels' hasty retreat. She noticed a side note on a battle plan: 'Baroness to stay in monastery'.

So, they're protecting you. You really are part of that insipid bunch. Dearest Agatha, you may have won this round, but the game isn't over. I will hunt you down, and I promise, the pain of my revenge will be eternal.

"My lady," a soldier entered, beaming at her. "We found it."

"The key?" asked the Duke, joining Dagma.

"Always late to the party, aren't you, Father." His peacock feather looked deflated. "They found the secret tunnel. Have your men get down it and start looking."

"I see." He turned to the few dozen men still standing by. "I want men down that tunnel. Call back to Bellingham for more. Carry out a full search of this area as well. Just in case the tunnel was a decoy." He winked at Dagma. No recognition of his cleverness forthcoming, he resumed. "They can't have gone far. Scout in small groups so you cover more ground, cover all directions. Search only—do not kill. Report back daily."

The men nodded briefly and rode off to fulfil their assignment.

"What about the Gribthorpe escapees?" Dagma asked the Duke who was looking more like the puffed-up peacock version of himself strutting about giving orders.

"There weren't many left alive. My men enjoyed beating those rich toffs within an inch of their lives. Besides, the reservoir is built. So, no great loss. Those who escaped must hide like the rats they are; no one will believe their story. Anyway, Aurelius is ours. South Valoria is ours!" He threw his head back and let out a laugh that was supposed to sound victorious but ended up resembling a squeaky door hinge in need of oil.

Dagma did not share his amusement. Even his laugh grated on her nerves—too shallow to inspire any awe. "I'm curious to explore their hideaway more," she said, her voice smooth but peppered with impatience. "They are sure to have left some clues behind. Care to join me?" The mask tilted slightly as she spoke, giving the impression of a raised eyebrow, even though she didn't have any.

The Duke, oblivious to Dagma's disdain, nodded. "Lead the way, my dear."

She glided ahead with a regal air despite the disappointment boiling within her. The Duke struggled to keep up with her. They upturned every chair, sifted through every book, rummaged through every pile of clothing, and even knocked on walls for secret compartments. But alas, there was no key. He called for his men to join the search, hoping that more hands might uncover what they could not. They prowled through the rest of the empty monastery like thieves in a shop full of jewels, only to find quicker thieves had already made off with the real loot.

The organ room exuded quiet grandeur, with regal furnishings and a grand pipe organ sighing with each draft of air. The dining hall, once the setting of pleasant meals among friends, was now a graveyard of spent candelabras, their waxy remains drooping like sleeping night watchmen. Cold ashes in the hearth replaced the kitchen's bygone smells of hearty meals. And the vaults below? The vaults brimmed with treasures from better times, but no key in sight. "An impressive collection of expensive furnishings," Dagma ran her gloved finger along a gold-gilded frame. "These men were of nobility."

"What do we do next?" sulked the Duke.

"Dig up the graves!" Dagma commanded. There were no limits to her doggedness. Not even sacrilegious ones. As she watched the men tear the place apart, she couldn't help but reflect on how naive she had been a year ago when they'd ordered the imprisonment of the wealthy landowners and traders. She had assumed the ones who escaped had fled north, where they would have run straight into the hands of King Dunwood—that pawn was firmly in her mother's grip. But no, it seemed they had holed up here, right under her nose, living their secret little lives in this monastery like some sort of underground society. She should have seen it coming. But then again, hindsight was a luxury she didn't have—and foresight was a skill she'd kill to have.

What is that noise? An incessant whirring. Too cold for insects, wrong place for children's grating laughter. Ah! It was the Duke droning on behind her as she walked to the orchard.

"—and of course Agatha. Normally, I pride myself on my ability to read people, to see their true nature. That's what made me such a good swindler. But Agatha has surprised me. Her switch in allegiances, her cold-hearted resolve—it seems she is even more ruthless than you, and that's saying something."

"What was that?" Dagma spun on him. "You dare to say Agatha surpasses *me* at ruthlessness?" Nieman froze and squeezed his eyes shut. "I could teach that girl ruthlessness in my sleep."

"N-No, my lady, I only meant—no one could ever truly rival your, ah, knack for the cruel. Agatha's just... following in your footsteps, but clumsily. A poor imitation, really."

Disinterested in his grovelling, she wheeled around to see the Baron and Arabella's disinterred body.

"Aha!" Dagma's screech was so sudden, the Duke ducked, hands half-raised in instinctive self-defence. "It was the Baron and some wench in that giant egg at the castle. That's that mystery cleared up, at least."

"It is?" No reply. "Oh, yes, if you say so. And the other three graves?" asked the Duke, his nerves still on edge. "Those crawlers."

She knew that although deep in his spineless depths the Duke was fully aware she had been behind Agatha's miscreant children, he dare not say anything. He had to stay on her good side.

He moved toward Dagma, trying to badly to smile genuinely. "You will get your chance to balance the scales with Agatha, I'm sure. And, all's not lost, well hopefully *they* are lost. Even if they do find the Sanctum, which is highly doubtful since no one really knows where it is, they cannot enter, even if they have the key. The wolves of Malair will see to that." Dagma turned her black, expressionless mask slowly toward him. "Or are they just a made-up part of the tale?"

"You blethering idiot, the wolves of Malair will only guard the Sanctum against those *without* the key. For the love of hell, why do I have to work with this moron!"

The Duke swallowed hard, his earlier self-confidence now slipping away like sand through his fingers. Dagma liked having that effect on people.

Chapter 17

FREEDOM OF CHOICE

C ANE TRUDGED ALONG THE tunnel, shoulders hunched beneath the low ceiling—Cretyne monks were not known for their height—and the pitch black stretched on endlessly. Each step decoupled him from the life he could never return to. The tunnel meandered for miles, as if deliberately trying to confuse them. Its air impregnated with the smell of damp earth, made the walls close in tighter with every heavy inhale.

Finally, the tunnel came to an end, but not in a convenient door to freedom. They faced a wall of stubborn vines, thick and tangled like a neglected sheep's behind. Somewhere in the matted mess was a hole leading outside. Cane watched as the men at the front hacked at the vines, their fury suggesting they were venting memories of too many forced Christmases with the in-laws. Each swing sent crumbling stones from the tunnel ceiling raining down, narrowly missing heads and adding yet another layer of danger to their already precarious situation. New to the life of a fugitive, Cane wondered if all escapes were this chaotic, or if they were just particularly unlucky. They'd saved neither the king nor his parents and now they were without a home.

Blake paced back and forth like an overexcited hunting dog, practically vibrating with pent-up energy. He flexed his fingers, eyes locked on the iron grating as if it had personally insulted him. Cane could see where this was headed and almost felt bad for the grating.

Blake cracked his knuckles. "Step back, lads," he announced, with the sort of bombast that usually accompanied terrible ideas. "I've got this."

Taking a deep breath, he reached out and grabbed the grating. His fingers closed around the rusty bars, and for a second, it looked like nothing would happen—just a big man making a fool of himself. But then, with a groan of metal and a sudden burst of dirt and debris, he ripped the entire grating from the stone as if it were made of wet paper.

For a moment, the group stood in stunned silence before the grating clattered to the ground.

"Well," Blake said, dusting off his hands and grinning like a man who'd just performed a party trick, "that was easy."

"I think we should have all had some of that Baron water," Tristan said enviously.

Blake, clearly pleased with himself, clapped his hands together. "I could have done it without of course!"

"Right, sure you could," said Tristan.

Cane squinted as they stumbled out into the open. The moon hung low in the sky, bathing everything in a cold, silvery glow. The landscape ahead was vast—a large, wooded area with hills in the distance, bordered by moorland. No sign of civilisation, and the silence embraced them in a strangely comforting way.

"By my estimation," Gerant began, in the measured tone of a cautious librarian, "the tunnel ran eastwards, which was a stroke of luck for us. We've moved away from Bellingham and Gribthorpe. Those lights to the south are from Inglebruk, and that wooded area to the east must be Hackthwall Forest; beyond it are the Hills of Malair Volpe. That's where we must go."

Cane didn't need to be a mind reader to see that the men weren't exactly thrilled about heading toward the cursed Hills of Malair Volpe. They shifted uneasily into a huddled murmuration. No one wanted to march straight into the land of bygone witches and unknown magic, but what choice did they have?

Captain Almfred, a man known for his candour and courage, finally voiced what everyone else was thinking: "But what of our families? We can't just leave them behind. And what of our quest to overthrow the Duke? Does that all mean nothing now?"

Their sagging morale and confusion thickened the soupy silence. Cane could sense it squeezing out what little hope remained. Though visibly weary, Gerant attempted to calm the tension.

"Our plan didn't go as well as we'd hoped," he admitted. "Foiled by the trickery of a sorceress. And now, we are what's left. We must stay together, find a place to hide and rest. They'll be coming after us; you can be sure of that."

The men grumbled, their dissatisfaction clear. Cane saw it in their eyes—the stubborn clinging to thoughts of their families, their homes, and the seeming futility of their situation.

"We're going back," Captain Almfred declared, stepping forward as the group's spokesperson. "We'll head west, split up, and return home, pretending we were scouting. If we play by their rules now, they'll leave us alone. Staying with you will only bring us more danger, because it's *her* they're after." He jerked his square chin toward Agatha, who shrank back and lowered her head, her shame palpable.

Cane's worry surfaced. He didn't blame the men for wanting to leave; it was the logical thing to do when faced with the choice of either going home or face a bewitched wilderness with no resources and a target on their backs. But logical didn't always mean right, and he had a sinking feeling that this decision was one they'd come to regret.

"As you wish," Gerant said, his tone resigned. "I am neither your keeper nor your master; you are free to choose. But I fear that once you return to Bellingham, you may never know true freedom again. We can do more for our loved ones by staying out here, uncaptured."

The men said nothing, their silence confirming their decision. They weren't ready to sacrifice everything for the cause—not yet. Without the promise of a positive outcome, without evidence that these noblemen could lead a victorious fight, their choice was easy. One by one, they turned and began to head west across the open fields.

"Do not return directly to your loved ones," Gerant called after them. "They will be tracking you. Going home will only put them in danger."

Captain Almfred nodded solemnly.

"We wish you well," Gerant added, sincerity clear in his voice.

Almfred paused for a moment, then replied, "We wish you well too." With that, they slipped into the night.

"We'd better shut this tunnel in case they follow," Bain suggested. "Sealing it might buy us a few more precious minutes."

Blake immediately perked up, already rolling his shoulders in anticipation. "I'll handle it," he said with the same bravado that had served him well moments before. The group watched as he bent down, grabbed the discarded grating, and lifted it effortlessly, holding it over his head like a champion weightlifter. With a grunt of exertion that seemed more for show than necessity, he jammed it back into place, crumpling the surrounding metal and stone like it was tin foil. Blake sealed the tunnel entrance shut and stood back, looking immensely proud of himself.

"There we go. Tight as a drum," he declared, dusting his hands off.

Felix let out a chuckle. "Well, it's certainly handy having your around these days."

"Handy?" Blake repeated, flexing his biceps. "My skills are downright dazzling."

"Not quite as dazzling as Cane's attire," Felix cast a sideways glance at Cane's purple smoking jacket, which was practically glowing in the moonlight

Cane suddenly felt increasingly—his hurried choice of attire was woefully inappropriate.

"You know, Cane," Gerant said, walking beside him, "if we wanted to signal our exact location to the enemy, we could have just lit a bonfire."

Cane sighed. "I know I'm sorry. It was the first thing I grabbed in the rush."

Before anyone else could add to the mockery, Bain stepped forward, pulling something from his pack. "Here," he said, handing over a familiar dark cloak. "I picked this up for you, back at the monastery. Thought you might want it back."

Relieved, Cane took his Imperial Guard cloak. The weight of the fabric instantly reminded him of the years of effort and sacrifice required to earn it.

Bain met his gaze with a knowing look. "I understand what it takes to get one of these. Figured it shouldn't be left behind after your, uh, striptease on the roof."

"Thank you, Bain."

"Right!" said Gerant. "Now that Cane doesn't stand out like a lighthouse, let's move on."

Felix did a quick headcount. "So, it's ten now, eh? A much better number, I feel. Sixty-six didn't quite sit right with me. Too many mouths to feed, you know."

Ten? thought Cane, *I thought we were only nine.* He glanced at the white-haired prisoner who had chosen to stick with them, despite the odds.

"Who do we have the pleasure of addressing, sir?" Cane asked, noticing the man's worldly air and the deep-set eyes that had clearly seen more suffering than any soul should.

The man's face, lined with the harshness of captivity and malnutrition, suddenly transformed with a broad, beaming smile. "Why, Cane, do you not recognise your own father?"

Cane's heart nearly stopped. For a moment, the world seemed to tilt on its axis. He blinked, his mind struggling to process the revelation. Then, with a choked cry, he lunged forward, wrapping his arms around the man he had thought was lost to him.

"Father!" he gasped, tears spilling down his cheeks as he hugged the old man. "I thought you were dead! This—this is unbelievable!"

The embrace was tight, desperate, as if Cane feared his father might vanish if he let go. Bain, with his typical bluntness, interjected, "Let the Earl breathe!"

"Sorry, Father," Cane apologised, stepping back but keeping his hands on his father's shoulders, as if needing the physical connection to convince himself this wasn't some dream. "Where is mother?"

The joy on the Earl of Cromlech's face faded as sorrow replaced it, cutting Cane to the quick. "I'm afraid your mother didn't make it. The prison conditions were abysmal. Without enough food or hope, her body finally gave in to starvation and despair. The women were treated worse than the men. They had little use for them, especially those more senior in years. The men could work, and the younger women... well, they had plans for them later." His voice cracked as he recounted the horrors he had witnessed.

Cane felt as if the ground had dropped out from under him. He had lost his mother once, and now, knowing the suffering she had endured, it felt like losing her all over again—this time, with the added weight of guilt. She had been so close, within reach, he could have saved her. His heart throbbed with pain, swelling until he thought it might burst from the sheer agony of it.

"My sweet mother." His tears fell unchecked. "She did not deserve this end."

"I know, son, I know." His father pulled him into another embrace, though this one was gentler, an attempt to comfort rather than a reunion. Cane's shoulders shook as he mourned, his mind filled with memories of his mother's kindness, her unwavering devotion to her family, her quiet strength. The thought of her dying alone, in such a cruel and unfeeling place, tore at his soul.

After a few moments, Bain's voice broke the bubble of grief. "There is no tactful way to say this, but I hate to rush you, Cane. We have to move. This head start is the only thing standing between our lives and death."

Cane nodded. He pushed the lugubrious lump of grief down into his heart to deal with later. His mother was gone, and though the pain of her loss was unbearable, he couldn't let it paralyse him. Not now. He still had his father, and that was something to hold onto—something to keep him moving forward. His father was a strong man, steadfast and reliable, and though he was weakened by his ordeal, Cane could see the life still burning in his eyes.

"I'm ready," Cane said, his voice rough but determined. He took a deep breath, squared his shoulders, and with his father by his side, rejoined the group. The others had already secured their belongings, ready to continue their journey east toward the ominous Hills of Malair Volpe.

Chapter 18

THROUGH NEVER-NEVER LAND

T REKKING THROUGH THE HEATHER and bracken, Cane, caught up in conversation with his father, had forgotten about Agatha. He jumped at the sound of her voice.

"Sorry for being ignorant of such matters, but why are we going to these hills, and why are they called the Hills of Malair Volpe?"

"Because no one dares go there," Gerant replied. "They believe it's enchanted because the Gaene Kin used to do magic there. You know, silly stories, vamped up each time they're retold, so now it's believed these wolves are ten feet high and have the fangs of a dragon."

"These hills are the only place one would find wolves in Valoria," added the Earl of Cromlech. "The Malair wolf packs are said to be the last of their kind."

"Are they dangerous?" she asked.

Percy frowned. "I'm sure they're very dangerous to anything alive and worth eating."

"Well, that counts you out, Percy," Tristan laughed. "Who'd bother gnawing on your meatless bones?"

"Speaking of food," Felix said, rubbing his growling belly. "Isn't it time we made camp, Gerant?"

"Good idea," Gerant replied. "There's a little clearing just ahead."

The woods provided a much needed change from the endless open moors they had been traipsing through, and they welcomed the prospect of a rest. Cane sat down opposite his father, his back against a sturdy oak. Soon the group settled around a warm fire burning at the centre of their makeshift camp. They washed down hard bread, cheese, and pork with light ale.

Cane watched as his father warmed his previously smooth now calloused hands in the fire; a familiar look of anticipation lit up his weathered face. He had seen that look before—a spark in his father's eyes that usually meant a tale was coming. He wasn't wrong.

Agatha turned her bright green eyes to the Earl. "Please, sir, tell us why the Malair wolves are only found there."

Cane smiled. He knew his father had been itching for an opportunity to spin this particular yarn since they entered the woods.

The Earl cleared his throat. "Gather 'round, my friends, and I'll tell you a tale older than the hills themselves."

The men visibly relaxed, their tired faces softened by the fire's glow and the anticipation of a bedtime story. Even in the dim light, Cane could see the satisfaction on his father's face as he began, his words floating out on the frosty night air.

"It is said that the Malair wolves were not ordinary animals, but guardians summoned by higher beings. Along with the bears, they were tasked with protecting a sacred building—the 'Sylphic Sanctum', constructed by the Octules, an ancient race long forgotten by most, but not by those who know the old stories."

Cane found himself drawn in despite himself. He had heard his father tell countless stories before, but there was something about the way he told them that made them feel magical every time. His words pulled them in like bees to honey. This story was all the more fascinating because they were a part of it.

Gerant, who had been carrying the key, suddenly looked up. "Do you think the Octules also carved this?" He held the key out toward Godfrey, who examined it with a discerning eye.

"Indeed, it bears their mark. The Octules were master craftsmen, engineers beyond compare. They were entrusted to build the Sanctum for that very reason, and it seems this key might be one of their creations as well. These lines resemble their workmanship."

Felix slapped Cane on the back. "So, you're not just all looks, eh, Cane! Your father's brains have rubbed off on you after all!"

Cane shifted uncomfortably, he didn't like being praised. "My father taught me well," he said, hoping to deflect the attention.

Godfrey handed the key back to Gerant, who explained how it had come into their possession. "Duke Nieman gave it to the Baroness," he gestured subtly to Agatha, "as a wedding gift. We're not sure why exactly, but it seems she needed to keep it very safe."

Cane noticed the way his father's expression softened as he smiled at Agatha, who blushed under the Earl's gaze. "Well, young lady, you've kept it safe, and now it's in even safer hands."

Agatha seemed pleased, and Cane couldn't help but admire how easily his father charmed people. He was a man who knew how to command a room—or, in this case, a campfire.

Returning to his tale, Godfrey continued. "The Octules, as I mentioned, were master craftsmen known throughout the ages. They built the Sanctum atop a conflux of the air element—a site where currents of energy converge, lending the place immense power. Mystics believe these confluxes trace along ley lines: invisible veins of energy that run beneath the earth, much like blood through our bodies. Scholars argue over their existence. Some see them as mere superstition, a convenient myth to explain why so many churches and sacred places were built on specific sites, places rumoured to hold forces beyond human sight.

"The Octules chose such a place for the Sanctum, a revered gathering site of the Gaene Kin, wise women and seers with a divine connection to the elements. But the Sanctum needed more than walls for protection. So, wolves and bears were summoned—not ordinary beasts, but legendary creatures, each bound to the essence of the air itself. They are said to hide like mist, vanishing as easily as shadows, and even slip into the minds of men, as extensions of the air."

As Cane listened, his thoughts drifted between the tale and the key Gerant held. The woods, the wolves, the Sanctum—they all blurred together in his mind.

"So," Godfrey said, "one could say these wolves, and bears, are guards to the world of air. Specifically chosen for their loyalty, fairness, and strength. The Malair wolves are our air guards."

"Air guards indeed," Felix chuckled, though he seemed a little less certain. "Sounds like a bedtime story to me."

"Guarding air? You can't even see it," Blake sneered.

Godfrey winked. "Only those with second sight can communicate with them."

"Oh, how very convenient," said Blake.

"I have never read anything about air guards," declared Rowan aloofly.

"And he's read a lot of words," added Blake. "More than he has spoken."

"These are tales passed on by word of mouth," explained Godfrey undeterred.

"Are there more places like this Sanctum?" Percy asked.

"Not that I know of," said Godfrey. "But who's to say if these confluxes in the ley lines are real? The Gaene Kin used to pilgrimage there every year to pay homage to the air spirits. I believe they are called sylphs, hence the name 'Sylphic Sanctum'."

"And why guard the air?" Tristan asked. "After all, like Blake says, it's invisible. And you can't touch it. You can't pack it up and run off with it."

"Legend has it," Godfrey said in a hushed voice for dramatic effect, "that if you control air, you can enter people's minds, manipulate thoughts, see into the future, past, and much more. The Sanctum is the gateway to this conflux of power. Many versions of the same tale float from one mouth to the next ear. One says the Gaene Kin knew the power held within the Sanctum could lead to the downfall of man if it fell into the wrong hands. That's why it's so well hidden."

The group fell silent, the crackling fire the only sound. Even Bain, who was usually all business, seemed softened by the mysteriousness of the story.

Finally, Percy couldn't help himself. "My mother used to believe in magical spirits. She told me gnomes planted the mushroom rings in our garden as meeting places. They're little folk, so the mushrooms were perfect stools for them to sit on while they held councils."

"Made-up stories," Tristan muttered. "She'd tell you that because you'd always play up at bedtime, and the only way she could get you to sleep was with tales of little gnome men."

"There's a drop of truth in every handed-down tale," Gerant said, giving Tristan a fatherly look.

"Quite so, Gerant," said Godfrey. "The Gaene Kin believed in such spirits and called on them for healing and wisdom. Another tale floating on the winds of legend whispers that the Sanctum is full of treasures. Naturally, thousands went in seek of these treasures, thinking them gold and silver. But of course, they never found it. Perhaps the real treasure is knowledge—or something less tangible, like air. Who's to say?"

"Maybe *we* will find it," Agatha said, her voice filled with a childlike hope that made Blake laugh.

"Yes, where thousands have failed, we will prevail!" Blake mocked, but Cane's stare silenced his laughter.

"Maybe with the help of someone as knowledgeable as the Earl of Cromlech," Agatha said, flashing a charming smile at Godfrey.

"Oh, well, maybe," Godfrey stammered, caught off guard by her flattery. Cane couldn't remember the last time he'd seen a woman make his father blush like a schoolboy—not even his mother.

Exhausted from the day's events and lulled by the comfort of the fire and Godfrey's tales, they drifted off to sleep. The harsh ground did little to keep them awake, and soon, their heavy breathing was the only sound in the quiet wilderness. Cane, despite his weariness, slipped into a fitful sleep, his dreams filled with images of wolves, the mysteries of the Sylphic Sanctum, and—oh no, not again—Agatha.

As dawn's light grew, it revealed the breathtaking beauty of their surroundings. Cane had seen his share of woodlands, but this forest seemed to have been designed in a fairy tale.

Moss draped the trees like fine velvet, their bark and the nearby stones covered with a mosaic of green and turquoise lichen. Dewdrops sparkled on leaves as though the trees had dressed up for their arrival. Fungi dotted the forest floor, some scaling the trunks like miniature staircases for tiny woodland creatures. Life was all around, yet everything was eerily still, as if the entire habitat and its inhabitants were watching, waiting.

After a morning of hopeful but fruitless walking, they stopped for a quick break.

"How are we supposed to find this place if nobody has ever seen it?" Tristan asked, stretching. It was the same question Cane had been asking himself. As in many fairy-tale forests, the only maps they had were old legends and a gut feeling.

"We're heading in the right direction," Gerant replied with the kind of confidence that usually preceded getting lost. "I can feel it in my bones. Plus, we're moving toward the hills, and that's something solid to trust."

"So how come no one's ever found the Sanctum?" Tristan pressed.

"Fear drove most people to turn back," said Godfrey.

"Fear of what?" Percy asked, glancing around like something might jump out of the bushes and say, "Boo!"

"The wolves and bears, dummy," said Tristan.

"And don't forget," said Godfrey, "the Octules hid it from sight. They were no fools."

As they reached the base of the green hills, Gerant speculated aloud that the Duke's men would be too afraid to follow them any further. If only that comforted Cane. It wasn't just the Duke's men that troubled him—it was the beasts from the legend that gave him cause for concern.

They started the climb, and Cane's sharp eyes spotted something—a trail, faint but unmistakable. Dropping to a crouch, he studied the prints. "Foxes, large dogs... or legendary wolves," he muttered, tracing the path with his fingers.

Godfrey peered over his shoulder. "Where'd you learn to do that, son?"

Cane shrugged, not wanting to make a big deal out of it. "Training for the Imperial Guards. We had to track each other in drills. Animals aren't much different—just a bit less predictable."

Felix squinted at the ground. "I don't know how you can see any footprints. I can't see a thing down there."

"That's because your belly's in the way," Blake teased.

"Very droll," Felix grumbled, rubbing his stomach as if offended on its behalf.

"Thank goodness we have you, Cane," Percy said. Cane couldn't tell if it was genuine praise or just Percy's way of covering his nerves.

He appreciated the vote of confidence, but it didn't quiet the nagging doubt in his mind. He had failed to protect the king, and now they were on a fool's errand through a cursed forest. Was he really the best man for this job, or would he just bring more danger?

Part of him envied the men who had turned back to Bellingham, in search of the normality of their families. For some reason though, he was more pulled by the mutual faith shared with his travel companions. If they ever needed him, he was going to do his damnedest to never fail them again.

As they neared the top of the hill, he noticed the grass on the circular plain was strangely short—not overgrown and wild like the rest of the landscape. Bushes and ivy encircled the area, framing it as if it were an arena. Drawn to its centre, he looked around, searching for the next path. The others followed.

Then he heard it—the low howling noises coming from within the darkness of the encircling trees. They stood perfectly still. It grew louder as though the conductor of mourning instruments had directed his musicians into a final crescendo of heavy, sonorous battle cries. Panic and uncertainty took hold of their thoughts. The legend of the wolves—the one they had happily dismissed in the safety of the campfire—suddenly didn't seem so far-fetched.

Chapter 19

OF WOLVES AND MEN

WOLVES EMERGED FROM THE trees—hundreds of them. They quashed all doubt of who was in charge with their unhurried advance. Their lush white fur and oversized paws gave them a mystical appearance. Within seconds, they had underscored this statement of power by exposing their impressive fangs. The breathtaking pack closed in on the trespassing party, their cold piercing stares and assured steps entrancing them. Their dominance was overpowering.

"Where did they all come from!" Percy squeaked, his knees knocking in fear.

"Now the number sixty-six is starting to sound a lot luckier to me," said Felix.

Gerant shifted uneasily. "I thought we'd get close, but not *this* close."

Cane resisted the urge to draw his sword. Perhaps if they showed no aggression, the wolves would not attack. "Fall into formation—back-to-back."

The wolves closed in, their fangs bared in a clear, wordless warning. The leader, a massive wolf with a streak of grey across his muzzle, approached with deliberate, menacing slowness. He studied them, pausing as he sniffed at Gerant, who stood frozen, sweat glistening on his high forehead. Silently, the leader moved on to Agatha. It growled loudly at her but made no attempt to attack. Agatha remained rooted to the spot, her wide eyes locked on the wolf.

Cane wasn't about to leave anything to chance. Without a second thought, he stepped between Agatha and the wolf, his hand raised. "No! You will do her no harm."

If the wolf had been a person, an onlooker would have said he took a moment to consider Cane's words. He sized him up, not in anger, but more like curiosity. Cane wished he could convey the sentiment: *We mean you no harm.*

As if understanding his thoughts, the leader let out a soft growl and stepped back, slowly retreating toward the rest of its pack before giving a commanding howl. The wolves parted, creating a path for the group to pass through unharmed. But their sharp, intelligent eyes tracked every movement, a quiet reminder that they were still very much in control.

"Thank sweet lady mercy," Felix exclaimed, looking to the skies. "What did you do, Cane? Can you speak wolf tongue?"

"Well, that was uncomfortably close," said Gerant, wiping the sweat of fear from his brow.

"The legends are true!" squealed Percy excitably.

"I bet you think little gnome men are true now too," mocked Tristan.

"Let's follow Lycus," said a starry eyed Rowan, watching the wolf leader disappear into the trees.

"Ah, our poet," Felix sighed.

They trailed behind their newly christened guide, Lycus, who led them eastward through the woods.

As the walked, the inspired Rowan shared his verse:

> "By Lycus' grace, these guardians roam,
> With fangs like spears and eyes of stone.
> Through forests deep they tread unseen,
> Fur-clad shadows, fierce and keen.
> Where Lycus leads, no man dares claim,
> A hidden path to an ancient domain.
> In silence still, their power speaks,
> His spirit free, the air he keeps."

Lycus occasionally paused to let them catch up, and Cane had to wonder if the wolf actually sighed, examined his claws, and picked at his fangs each time he waited—or if Cane was just imagining it.

The forest floor was a minefield of fallen trees and protruding moguls, strategically placed as if to trip them up. It felt like nature had a personal vendetta against travellers, turning every step into a test of agility. Cane had nearly sprained his ankle twice already, and the terrain was starting to resemble an obstacle course designed by Percy's bedtime gnomes—except of the sadistic variety.

The ground had morphed into a rich brown grid of decay, adorned with sporadic patches of moss that seemed to glow with an oddly enthusiastic brightness. Sunlight, reduced to a game of hide-and-seek, managed to sneak through the canopy, casting golden beams in playful diagonal lines. It was all quite picturesque, if you were into that sort of thing. Cane had to admit, though, that the sight was rather magical.

When they finally emerged from the gloomy embrace of the woods, an iridescent haze of gold awaited them, as if the sun itself were trying to say, "Look at me, I'm fabulous!" Once their eyes adjusted to the bright light, they were met with an unexpected sight: a meadow of cottontail grass. The scene looked like it was from another world, with white fluffy tutus on stalks swaying in a delicate dance. Cane was amused to see that the wolves had effectively blended into the meadow, as if they'd been invited to nature's own camouflage party with a 'white coat and tails' dress code. Maybe this was why people believed they turned into mist.

Wading through the sea of white, Cane noticed Lycus waiting at the edge of the field, a regal figure against the backdrop of jagged rocks and a small stream trickling down from the hilltop.

Suddenly, Felix's excited shout shattered the tranquil atmosphere. "A bear!" In his shock, he promptly tripped over an extremely well-camouflaged wolf. Under different circumstances, the scene might have been funny—but they were too scared to laugh.

Felix, stumbling back to his feet, blurted out, "Four bears! I thought they'd been wiped out!"

"Looks like these ones didn't get the extinction notice," said Bain.

"Wiped out?" whimpered Percy. "More like, will wipe the floor with us!"

Blake set down his backpack. "I can handle them. Any chance they're long-lost cousins of yours, Felix?" he laughed. "There's an uncanny resemblance to your frizzy beard and big—"

Felix wasn't about to let that pass. "I think *you're* the one that should watch out, Blake. They probably think you've stolen one of their cubs and are holding it hostage under your nose."

Godfrey turned to Cane, raising an eyebrow. "Do near-death experiences always turn your friends into comedians, or is this new?"

"Relax, lads," said Blake. "I've got this." He cracked his knuckles and rolled his shoulders like a man about to wrestle a bear—which was exactly what he was considering. "Prepare to be dazzled."

"Blake," Cane warned, "I don't think that's a good—"

But before he could finish, Blake strode forward with all the confidence of someone with super strength. "Watch and learn!" he declared, charging at the largest bear head-on.

He wrapped his arms around the bear's midsection, trying to wrestle it to the ground. For a heartbeat, Cane expected some miraculous display of strength—but nothing happened.

The bear didn't budge. In fact, it looked more confused than threatened, as if it couldn't quite figure out why this little human had decided to hug it so enthusiastically.

Blake, however, seemed to be the last to realise something was wrong. His face reddened as he strained, giving a series of increasingly desperate grunts, but the bear remained firmly in place, not shifting an inch.

Felix, watching with amusement and no concern, said, "Blake, I think your super strength has worn off."

"Wait, wait! What? Oh! Wait!"

But the bear didn't wait. With a casual nudge, it sent Blake tumbling head over heels into a nearby bush.

"Well," Godfrey said, "that could have been worse. You could easily have been its next meal."

Blake sat up, twigs sticking out of his hair and his bruised ego lost in the undergrowth. "I'm, uh, not as strong as I thought."

"Or as clever," added Gerant, shaking his head. "Why go rubbing a bear up the wrong way? They've done nothing to us. Next time, maybe let the bears decide if they want to join the wrestling match."

Felix was thoroughly enjoying Blake's embarrassment. "Looks like that magical Baron brew wore off, eh?"

Blake groaned, brushing twigs off his clothes. "Great. Now I'm back to being just *amazingly* strong and not *super* strong."

"On the bright side," Cane said, eyeing the bears, "they're not aggressive and they seem to have enjoyed the show."

The largest bear, still looking vaguely bemused, gave a great yawn and settled back on its haunches, as if to say, *Well, that was fun. What's next?*

Despite their imposing size, the bears regarded the group with a gaze more curious than threatening, like wise, oversized teddy bears sizing up an unfamiliar species. They made no move to attack, merely observing their small visitors with the air of creatures who had seen far too much to be easily impressed or scared.

Feeling oddly reassured by their silent, furry audience, the group tentatively resumed their trek, following Lycus. The bears maintained their watchful presence, an odd sort of companionship growing between the two parties. It was an unusual, mutual understanding: the adventurers respected the bears' right to look absolutely terrifying, and the bears respected their right to pass through the meadow unharmed.

Cane was beginning to think their journey was less a noble quest and more a farcical comedy in the making. "The Chronicles of Delusional Men Lost in the Woods, Who Somehow Thought Giant Bears Were Friendly."

"Let's find a cave or at least some decent shelter before the light fades," Gerant suggested, scanning the rocky terrain ahead.

In pairs, they searched for a suitable hideout. Rowan and Felix headed to the right-hand side of the stream, while Gerant and Bain scrambled up the rocks like arthritic mountain goats. Percy and Blake ventured further left along the rocky facade. Meanwhile, the Earl took a more leisurely approach, sitting on a boulder and giving Lycus a well-deserved scratch behind the ears. Agatha remained Cane's unshakable shadow, as usual.

"Hey! Who threw a rock at me?" yelped Felix, nursing a freshly acquired bump on his forehead. "And it was a big one."

Before Felix could accuse Blake, Percy, who was running to help, was knocked flat to the ground—by nothing at all. Rowan, close behind him, soon followed suit, adding his own cry of pain.

"Who's throwing rocks?" Percy demanded, rubbing his head. "Come out and face us!"

As the three men struggled to their feet, the others gathered near Cane, squinting up at the craggy hill. Bain shielded his eyes from the sun, trying to get a better view. "I don't see anything. We've been led into a trap!"

Tristan shot a glare at Lycus. "There's definitely mischief afoot—magical or not. Either those wolves are up to something, or the Gaene Kin laid traps."

"Let's not jump to conclusions," Cane said, attempting to rein in Tristan's usual rush to violence as a solution. "Look, over there!" He pointed to the summit of the crag.

A small, cat-like creature—about the size of a dog but with the refined gait of something that had clearly attended all its etiquette classes at Feline Finishing School—made its way down from the summit. Backlit by the sun, its silhouette was a dark, mysterious shape with impressively large, pointed ears.

As it approached the edge of the crag, where nothing but a sheer drop awaited, the group held their breath, fully expecting a tragic plunge. Instead, the animal sat down and began calmly licking its paws, utterly unfazed by the precarious situation. To the group, it appeared as though it was suspended mid-air.

They gasped in collective awe.

"What is it?" Percy asked, eyes wide. "Is *that* what's been chucking stuff at us?"

"Animals like that can't throw stones, you nincompoop," Tristan laughed. "It has paws."

Gathering closer in the shade, its features became clearer. Godfrey's eyes widened in utter astonishment. "It's a lynx. The rarest of animals. Also thought to be extinct."

"It's beautiful," murmured Agatha.

The lynx, indifferent to their gawking, continued its grooming, perfectly content to lounge on what appeared to be thin air. They huddled closer, perplexed by the gravity-defying feline.

Percy scratched his head, completely bewildered. "It must be some kind of magic or illusion. How can it just sit there... floating?"

"It's not Gaene Kin magic. Just a trick of the eye," Bain clarified.

"Plain talk, please," Blake grumbled.

"Oh, I see!" Tristan and Percy exclaimed in unison, their expressions brightening.

Blake, however, looked more confused than ever. "Well, I don't," he admitted.

With a grin, Bain took Blake by the arm and guided him forward, placing his hand in the air. "Feel the stone?"

Blake's face lit up as he felt the solid surface beneath his hand, though it remained invisible. The others followed suit, tentatively reaching out, each with their own mix of confusion and enlightenment.

"How did you figure it out?" Blake asked, eyeing Bain, who looked rather pleased with himself.

"The sun cast a shadow. No shadow without something solid, right? Simple."

Blake scratched his head, as if trying to dislodge a particularly stubborn idea. "Simple, yes. Of course. Simple."

"It's clever camouflage. The stone is coloured to blend with the surroundings, breaking up the building's form and confusing the eye. If you look closely by the lynx, you can just make out the surface—using it as a reference point."

With Bain's explanation, they quickly understood: the lynx's perch marked the building's height. The structure was a smooth, polished, amphitheatre-like stone blocks, partially built into the hillside, which explained the lynx's easy access to the roof. Rowan, having mysteriously reappeared after circling the hill, confirmed as much.

"So, we did find the Sylphic Sanctum after all," Agatha said, giving an almost indiscernible 'I was right, you were wrong' grin to Blake. Undiscerned by all save Cane, who thought her triumphant grin very out of character.

"Has anyone found an entrance?" Godfrey asked, running a hand over the smooth stone wall.

The wolves, uninterested in their plight, were either playing or napping in the nearby cottontail field. The bears had retreated to the woods, but Lycus stood beside Godfrey, looking on with an almost bemused expression.

They scoured the walls, moving clockwise, groping for hidden seams or doors, but found nothing. Disheartened by their fruitless search, they regrouped by the Earl on the bank of the bubbling stream.

Blake, pacing with sudden inspiration, snapped his fingers. "I've got it! The carving from the Octules! Remember, Baroness—when the Duke gave it to you, he said it could unlock doors to another world. By the gods, this place has to be that place! It has to be!"

Felix smirked, leaning lazily against the wall. "Glad you could join us, Blake. You're only about five epiphanies behind the times. Shall I go over the highlights for you, or are you good to wing it from here?"

"We know we have the key to the Sanctum, Blake," Gerant said with saintly patience. "We just haven't found the door to put it in."

"Oh, right," Blake muttered, rubbing the back of his head. "Well... just stick it in anywhere."

"As if that's going to work," Bain scoffed, taking the key from Gerant. "You really think poking it around at random like this is going to unlock anything?" He jabbed the key at the air.

Before he could add, "I don't think so", a low, grinding sound proved Blake right. The camouflaged wall slid open, revealing an entrance.

For a moment, they all froze, filled with caution and curiosity. The animals remained unfazed—clearly, they'd seen this before—but some wolves formed a protective circle around the perimeter, standing guard.

Without hesitation, Cane stepped up to the threshold, throwing a 'here goes nothing' look at the others before entering. Tristan followed closely.

A beat of silence passed.

"Well, I'll be!" Cane's voice echoed from within. "You *have* to see this!"

Chapter 20

BURNING WITH FURY

DAGMA SAT IN A plush velvet armchair, a vision of porcelain calm in contrast to the Duke's seething frustration. She idly stroked Galcion's head, a practiced gesture that soothed both her and the husky. Nieman, on the other hand, was a whirlwind of agitation, pacing furiously in front of his grand stone fireplace, spinning his ruby ring incessantly around his finger. His black hair, slicked to perfection, looked as though it might catch fire from his temper alone.

"Why do these useless scouts always come back with nothing?" His question was aimed at the inanimate, unrepentant ceiling. "Sodding hell!"

Dagma, who had the grace to look mildly concerned, remained silent behind her white mask—one of a whole collection she'd had made for different occasions, turning her unsightly misfortune into the springboard for a new line of fashion accessories. The Duke's frustration was almost endearing; she loved watching the irate peacock trying to take flight in a very cramped cage.

"Atropa is going to be pissed." His face contorted with worry, he stopped in front of the large, gilded mirror and tweaked his goatee, clearly thinking himself handsome. "Ah, that's a little better."

How vapid can this man be? Dagma wondered. *His thoughts should not be on his facial hair.* Secure in his wealth and borrowed power, he was completely blind to the fact that a handful of men had outwitted him. The trickster had become the tricked.

"Damn those rebels! They're playing me for a fool."

Not too difficult, Dagma thought, her mind wandering to how much she loathed the Duke's constant, fruitless pacing. It was like living with a large pet weasel—a very well-dressed weasel—always ferreting about. Did he ever tire of his own rants, or were they somehow energising for him?

"And this Gwaine!" the Duke fumed, trying to disentangle the pointy tip of his elaborate boot from the rug pile. "Where is his fear? Doesn't he know every man has a price? Or is his price just suffering and more suffering?"

Dagma's expression remained inscrutable, though a sneer threatened to break through. "It's not his fear you need to worry about, dear Father. It's the source of his hope. I've encountered people who can withstand anything as long as they cling to even a sliver of hope. Remove that, and they turn to putty in your hands."

The Duke grumbled something about needing a new approach. "I'll make him talk. If need be, I'll string up their families and hang them in the streets!" He knelt beside Dagma's husky, Khyro, his mood softening as he stroked its thick fur.

But then, forgetting himself, with a sudden, sinister shift, he tightened his grip around Khyro's throat.

"I'll squeeze the information out of him," he smiled cruelly. "Just as I'll squeeze the life out of their—"

The dog let out a low, warning growl, and the Duke leapt back. His eyes met Dagma's objecting stare that slithered over his skin like cold jelly.

"Don't ever touch my dogs," she growled, her voice dangerously low. "Unless you wish to *never* see another sunrise."

Regretful and rattled, the Duke made a hasty retreat toward the door. Just as he reached for the handle, one of his guards burst in, out of breath and wide-eyed.

"My lord, there's news from the watchmen!" the guard exclaimed, barely pausing for breath.

"Speak, man!" the Duke demanded, his irritation and Dagma's death promise momentarily forgotten.

"The watchmen spotted a dozen or so men entering the town from the east. Then more men, at different times, but all from the same direction. About sixty in total. Some say they're your emissaries, but we sent no ununiformed men to scout."

A slight furrow creased the Duke's small brow as he heard the word *emissaries*, but he grasped the gist of the message, his face brightened. A rakish grin expanded within the confines of his immaculate goatee. "Good, good. Let them be for now. Keep an eye on them. Make sure they're followed."

The guard, who also sported a slick goatee, saluted proudly. "Already on it, sir."

"Good," the Duke said. Just as he was about to dismiss him, Dagma spoke.

"Then drag them from their homes at first light," she said, her tone as unforgiving and deliberate as a nail driven into a coffin. "Let their families witness their execution in Traitor's Square. After a few pointless hours of mourning, bring out their families—women and children alike—to meet the same slow end. Children first. Mothers last."

Visibly shocked by her brutality, the Duke fidgeted with his ruby ring.

"That's how you make people understand who's in charge, dear Father," Dagma added with haughty satisfaction. "That's how you show traitors there is no mercy."

Despite his discomfort, Duke Nieman sanctioned Dagma's orders with a stiff nod, his gaze never leaving hers.

"Now go remove the last grain of hope from Gwaine!" she ordered.

Dagma followed Duke Nieman down into the grimy cellar, her steps silent. The stench of damp stone mixed with sweat was rife. She waited at the top of the stairs unnoticed, observing. She watched the Duke tiptoe into the dank space as though he were afraid of what might be lurking in the dark shadows. The manor's cellar had everything one might expect of a prison, complete with archetypal stone floors, blackened walls, and a wooden barrel serving as chair. He straightened his embroidered doublet, checked his reflection in a guard's empty metal luncheon plate, and put on a ridiculous air of self-importance. He relished the power he imagined he had here, but Dagma saw through his thin veneer of control.

Inside the cell, Gwaine sat as if he were in a quaint little garden rather than a foul prison cell. The man appeared to be meditating—or perhaps waiting for the right moment to pull out a violin and serenade his captor. He should have been broken by now, begging for mercy, or at the very least showing signs of wear. Yet here he was, calm and collected, as if this filthy cell were a holiday retreat.

"Your friends," Nieman began with his predictable display of superiority, "have met with defeat. They've come crawling back—like lost lambs into the laps of their shepherds." His theatrics always grated on her nerves. "By the end of the day, they'll be arrested. By tomorrow, they'll be dead. Their families will follow soon after."

Gwaine's response was as steady as it was vexing. "I will still tell you nothing. You have taken all I loved."

The Duke's face reddened, not just from anger but also from the effort of keeping his composure. "Then I'll enjoy putting down another traitor in my lands."

"They are not *your* lands, they are the *people's*. Our ruler is King Aurelius."

With a flourish, Duke Nieman drew his sword, pointing its sharp tip at Gwaine's throat through the bars. "I'll throw you to the murderous wolves you call your people. They'll stone you. They enjoy that. Your death will be far worse than if I skewered you with my sword."

Gwaine responded with the irritating calm of a philosopher-come-priest. "Such anger will cause acidity in your stomach, Duke Nieman. Before long, it will consume you to your own slow, agonising death." With a flick of his sword, Nieman cut off Gwaine's blindfold.

Dagma was impressed—not by the Duke's sword skils but by Gwaine. This simple groom had understood Nieman to be a weak aggressor. Watching Nieman squirm in his own fury was almost worth the trip down to the damp hellhole.

The Duke's frustration boiled over, visible in the tightness of his jaw and the whiteness of his knuckles. If he had the nerve, he would have gutted Gwaine on the spot—but of course, he didn't.

"I'm in charge! You're the one behind bars. I'll tell everyone you're a traitor. They enjoy a good stoning. Nothing like a good stoning to lift the people's spirits."

Dagma had heard enough. She swiftly returned to the study, already predicting the Duke's final childish exit: a contemptuous smile at Gwaine and overly grandiose march from the dismal cell.

Back upstairs, Nieman strutted into his study with two senior guards in tow. Dagma barely looked up from the map rolled out before her, her fingers tracing the forests to the east where she suspected the rebels were hiding. Flushed from his encounter with Gwaine, the Duke straightened up and tried to look composed.

"Take the prisoner to Traitor's Square," Nieman commanded, his voice ringing with false boldness. "Spread the word that Gwaine the traitor has escaped. By tomorrow, he'll wish he'd chosen our side. Together with the returning emm, emiaries, emisseries... uh, we'll have plenty of entertainment for the people of Bellingham for a whole week."

"Did you break him, Father?" Dagma asked with disinterested curiosity.

The Duke avoided her gaze. "Yes. Good and proper. With the prospect of a stoning, he's feeling miserable."

"So, in other words, you didn't. He gave you no news of their whereabouts or plans." Making Nieman flounder was a game Dagma never tired of. "Anyway, onto more pressing matters. Those fake monks and Agatha—you conveniently forgot to mention them—aren't among the ones who returned. They're still out there."

The Duke deflated, his gaze dropping to the map. "Ah."

"Yes, 'ah'," she said coldly.

"The fake monks are still out there? What hope do they possibly think they have without their troops?"

"The weaker ones may have returned, but their leaders, and my dear sister, would never give up so easily. They're on the run. Fortunately for us, a handful of men and a woman won't be hard to spot."

Nieman a forced smile, trying to regain his composure. "Of course."

Dagma continued studying the map, her huskies lounging contentedly at her feet. Nieman wasn't just outmatched by her cruelty; her strategic mind was beyond him too.

"I'll continue my location ritual. It will be easier now that I've narrowed down where they are—somewhere here in the east. But still, send out scouts. Tomorrow, we'll watch the thrashing of the returned fake *emissaries*. You'll join me," she commanded.

"Yes, of course. I planned to anyway," the Duke replied feebly.

"Nothing makes victory taste sweeter than tasting the fear of the vanquished. On a side note, I regret I won't be marrying Cane of Cromlech after all. His prolonged absence suggests he's either joined the rebels or died."

"I'll host a banquet every night until you find a worthy match. Will you manage without a lady-in-waiting? My steward says she likely got caught up in the fight at Bellingham. She hasn't returned to Malcrov Court since that night."

"Well, considering I'm little more than the charred remains of a woman, she had very little to do in terms of my toiletries or hair. I dismissed her." She laughed. "It's going to take one desperate nobleman to marry me, or I'll need a particularly strong love potion."

Dagma did not reveal the truth—that in fact she was rather pleased when her lady-in-waiting had not shown up for her duties. She did not want the Duke to feel that anyone was beyond her control. Privately, she assumed the woman had either eloped or met a violent end. Either way, she didn't care. It made her nocturnal activities in the barn easier. As for Cane, losing him as a potential husband didn't actually bother her. Her own husbandry project was underway: breeding an army. All she needed now was more space.

The incubation chambers she had crafted—unbreakable crucibles—were the hatching grounds for her drones. Unlike her mother, she couldn't breed any other kind of Calderian, only the lowly drone. They were dullards, but they followed orders. Given their formidable adult size, she would need more space. In addition to the barn, she was already eyeing a large cow shed on the outskirts of Malcrov Court.

"Yes, keep hosting those banquets," she said with a smile hidden behind her pale porcelain mask. "I'm sure there's a nobleman out there desperate enough for wealth to take on a bride as... unusual as me."

But it was not all smiles with Dagma, far from it. The very thought of her sister being alive and safe somewhere out of her reach dogged her. Her smoke-filled camphor sessions revealed nothing of Agatha's location, stoking her frustration. She needed that key before her mother returned—why had that fool of a Duke entrusted it to her? Humans were truly confounding imbeciles.

"In fact, I intend to locate them now," Dagma declared abruptly, rising from her chair with sudden purpose. Without waiting for a reply, she swept out of the study, her huskies obediently at her heels.

She left the Duke in mid-sentence, some grovelling nonsense about how they had the upper hand thanks to her.

Once inside her bedchamber, she bolted the door, moving with calm precision as she prepared for the locating ritual. Every action was deliberate, the tools laid out with practiced precision.

She set a bowl on the hearth, pouring in a dark liquid with steady hands. Muttering an incantation, she sprinkled silver dust into the water, followed by dried herbs that released a pungent, earthy scent into the air. The mixture began to bubble and froth.

Closing her eyes, Dagma focused on the image of her sister. Agatha's face, her voice, her aura. She reached out with her mind, trying to pierce the barrier that obscured her. But an impenetrable fog shrouded Agatha from her sight. Frustration surged as she pushed harder, straining to force her way through, but the more she pressed, the more elusive her sister became.

With a snarl, Dagma slammed her fist onto the hearth, sending the bowl skittering across the stone. She couldn't find them. They must have reached the Sanctum, under the protection of the veil of the air spirits' whispers, blocking even the most skilled seekers like her.

"Darkness consume them!" she shouted, ripping off her mask in a fit of anger. She glanced down, irritated to see a lock of hair stuck to the inside lining, creating yet another bald spot on her already patchy scalp. Staring at the strands, a thought sparked in her mind. She smiled wickedly. *I know exactly how to reach you, sister dearest.*

She slipped into the corridor, checking no one was there, then made a swift dash to Agatha's old room, her huskies following close behind. Everything remained untouched in her sister's quarters, as if frozen in time. The baroque furniture gleamed, undisturbed, no dust settling on the glossy black fabrics.

Dagma moved quickly to the damask headboard presiding over the large bed, brushing her hands briskly over its silky upholstery. Without any care for the mess she had made, she hurried back to her own room where she set to work.

Into a small bottle, she poured vinegar, dropped in three rusty nails, and added soil from a tin labelled 'Unnamed Grave, collected under October's waning moon'. Then came liquid from a vial marked as 'Lightning water', followed by the yolk of a black egg, and three drops each of vetiver oil and attar of roses. She shook it vigorously, watching the mixture turn a deep, blood-red hue. Finally, she added the strands of silver hair she'd plucked from Agatha's headboard, whispering words of invocation:

May the forces of pain ravage you from within, just as you have ravaged my flesh with your flames of rancour.

May the hand of malice strangle your inner soul, filling your blood with anguish, leaving nothing but heartache and dolour.

She chanted the malignant words of acrimony over and over. When she was done, Dagma placed the open bottle on her window ledge, letting it bathe in the moonlight. Under the darkness of the next new moon, she would smash it—and Agatha would feel her anger. Even though she could not find her, she could reach her. Yes, her sister would feel the pain.

Chapter 21

LIGHT THE WAY

THE DOME-SHAPED SANCTUM OPENED into a vast interior that seemed designed by the heavens themselves. Cane marvelled at how the space stretched on endlessly, like the sky.

"Wow, I can't believe we're actually inside the Sanctum," Tristan said, gazing up at the vaulted ceilings. "It's like something out of a dream. It feels like everything is floating."

One by one the others entered.

Bain ran his fingers along the walls. "These walls... they're cold, covered in alabaster." He drifted into another room. "I feel like I could just float away without even trying." He vanished from sight, leaving Gerant peering into the space he had just vacated.

"What's in there?" Gerant asked, stepping in after him.

Cane followed, entering the adjoining room to find Bain's face lit with wonder. Soft light emanating from phosphorescent plants on the walls filled the space.

"The ambiance is so relaxing," said Felix. "Makes me wish for a hammock and a little tipple."

"Everything makes you wish for a little tipple," said Bain with a grin.

"Ah, the Gaene Kin's altar room," Godfrey declared with an air of grand revelation.

Percy approached apprehensively. "Is this where they... sacrificed people?"

"Ha, no, no need to worry, young Percy," said Godfrey. "This would have been where the Gaene Kin prepared themselves before summoning the sylphs."

At the far end of the room stood an altar, carved from a pale, moonstone-like material, its surface neatly arranged with glass bottles and clay herb pots. A mirror, set within an ornate silver frame, hung on the wall behind it.

"This must have been used by the High Priestess," Godfrey said, tracing the mirror's frame. "A tool for self-reflection and introspection."

"Or just doing their hair," suggested Blake. "Women are always rearranging their hair."

Tristan spotted a wardrobe in the corner. "Ooh, I found something for you, Percy!" he exclaimed, pulling out a dark green cloak made of the lightest, almost translucent fabric. "Ceremonial robes—just your size!"

"Stop mucking about, you silly bugger," Felix scolded, though his tone lacked any real sternness.

"Yeah, show a bit of respect," Percy added, as Tristan twirled dramatically in the gown.

The room was alive with a gentle buzz—the soft whistling of wind through unseen cracks and the rhythmic cascade of water from a fountain in the corner. It was a serene soundscape, one that could have put an angry troll to sleep. Yet Cane felt anything but tranquil.

While the others basked in the room's peaceful ambiance, Cane's mind was a battleground, a whirlwind of vivid, unsettling images spinning wildly in his head. It was as if someone had cranked up the volume on his memories and mixed in a dash of trauma to the psychedelic cocktail.

He moved toward the wardrobe to trade his purple smoking coat for a large white tunic that hung loosely from its hanger. The fabric was cool against his skin as he slipped it on. When he stepped toward the mirror to check the fit, what he saw was far from reassuring.

The moment his gaze met his reflection, the visions surged with merciless clarity. Haunting images of lost souls trudging toward an endless land of darkness flooded his thoughts. At their head was a shadowy woman crowned with flames and fire leaping from her eye sockets. A sinister smile splintered across her pale face, and a shimmering, blue lizard-like tail curled beneath her flowing robes. Cane shook his head furiously, desperate to expel the ghastly images.

"Come to me," a soft voice coaxed. Cane turned, and by the fountain stood an enigmatic figure, her watery features melding with the limpid pool. She had delicate, spectral wings and a voice like an angel's sigh. "I'll show you secrets."

No, this isn't right. I must resist. Cane fought to hold onto reality, but disarray overtook his mind. Memories of his childhood—a cherished moment of joy with his mother—were plaited into something unfamiliar and unsettling. Her face, once a source of warmth, now seemed foreign and strange. His reflection in the introspection mirror was the face an older woman with grey-blue eyes. No crown of flames, yet her intricately braided hair piled atop her head like a regal headdress, and eyes that spoke of wisdom, gave her the bearing of a leader.

As he viewed the mirror more closely, his vision blurred, and the room around him dissolved into chaos. He saw a world engulfed in death, with skies darkened by flying beasts wielding terrible powers. Cities burned, fields flooded, and people perished. Devastation engulfed him. He clutched his chest, his heart pounded like a war drum.

Unable to look away, the images clung to him, chained extensions to his mind. In the next moment, he was in the midst of a joyful celebration—a wedding. Laughter filled the scene, and around him were familiar faces, friends, a radiant young woman, his daughter perhaps, smiling warmly at him. Beside her stood a tall man. But the happiness was false, thick and oppressive. He had to stop the ceremony.

A sudden sensation—fingers clasping his hand—yanked him back into the present with a jolt. He lashed out instinctively, panic blinding him. There was a cry—a woman's cry—and the visions shattered, leaving Cane gasping in the real world.

The room reassembled itself, his mind snapping back to find Agatha sprawled on the floor beside him, clutching her cheek.

"Cane!" Gerant's voice broke through, sharp with concern. "Get a hold of yourself, man!"

Cane's pulse pounded in his ears as he knelt beside Agatha, horror spreading across his face. "I... I'm sorry," he stammered, reaching out to help her up.

She recoiled, and it was Gerant who stepped forward to assist her, glaring at Cane as he did. "You hit the Baroness!"

"I didn't mean to," Cane whispered, mortified. "I—I don't know what came over me." His mood switched instantly. "If you didn't stand so close to me all the time, it wouldn't have happened."

"What in heaven's name has come over you?" Gerant demanded sternly.

His usual kind nature restored, Cane apologised again.

"It's this place," Rowan said matter-of-factly. "There's trickery here."

"Are you alright?" asked Cane.

"Yes, yes... I'm sorry. It must be this place," Agatha replied quietly, holding her burning cheek.

Cane caught his reflection in the mirror once more. Behind his own face, he saw the woman from his vision—her visage entwined with his mother's. There was something oddly... good about her, an aura of benevolence.

"Gawping at yourself in the mirror," Gerant said incredulously. "You could at least offer a proper apology to the Baroness."

But Gerant's voice was distant, a hum Cane barely registered. He couldn't tear himself away from the mirror. The woman's gaze felt... knowing. Then, deep within him, a voice—his own—rang out with sudden clarity: *You will soon see!*

"I am truly sorry," Cane said, turning to Agatha with earnest remorse. "I never meant to hurt you."

"You must forgive my son," said Godfrey. "When I told you the sylphs are known for entering the mind, I failed to mention... they aren't always a force for good."

"What do they do, then?" asked Bain.

"Well," Godfrey began, unbuttoning his top collar button. "I'm no expert, but according to my readings, sylphs are like airy personal gurus. They impart the spiritual powers and energies of air. This translates to clear thought, imagination, creativity—all the qualities leaders love to brag about and the rest of us pretend to have at social gatherings."

"Sounds handy," said Bain.

"You'd think so, wouldn't you?" Godfrey continued. "But sylphs are notoriously playful. They rarely offer a straightforward answer. Instead, they present you with a buffet of possibilities, none of which are particularly helpful when you're searching for a clear solution. Unless, of course, you're a seer."

Cane's mind wandered back to the visions that had overwhelmed him moments ago—one of fiery destruction, the other of jubilant celebration. Was he peering into the future or simply being toyed with by some bored 'playful' air spirit?

Meanwhile, Rowan had sauntered over to a shelf beneath the altar and pulled out an ancient, dust-covered book. He began muttering aloud, "Place the cauldron at the southern watchtower and repeat these words: May the guardians of—"

"Be careful!" the Earl interjected sharply. "You never know when you might accidentally cast a spell."

Rowan's face flushed with embarrassment, and he quickly slammed the book shut. "Sorry! I thought it was poetry, most of the writing rhymes."

"Yes, invocations and spells often rhyme," the Earl explained, as though discussing the merits of a fine wine. "Makes them easier to remember."

"What's this book?" Rowan asked, eyeing a larger, more ornate volume.

Godfrey took it from Rowan's hands, flipping through the pages. "It's a Book of Shadows, like a journal," he said. "A witch's diary, if you will. It records recipes, formulas, thoughts, and—" He paused, reaching the final entry. "Ah! I think you should read this, Gerant. You've got the loudest voice."

As the group settled on the fountain steps or leaned against the pillars, Gerant began to read aloud:

It is with a heavy heart and a burdened spirit that I pen this account, for the shadows of treachery loom large over our sacred Sanctum and covenant. The time has come to record the bitter truth of our conflict with the High Priestess, a truth that speaks not only of strife but of an insidious ambition that has sought to endanger all we hold dear.

The discord between us, the Gaene Kin, and the High Priestess has reached a crescendo. Our fundamental beliefs about the sylphs and their place in magic have driven a deep and unbridgeable divide between us. While we honour the sylphs as spiritual guides and sources of inspiration, our High Priestess has become fixated on harnessing their powers for her own grand designs. Her motives are driven not by reverence but by a craving for dominion and control.

In her boundless ambition, she has invoked a powerful spell to seal the Sanctum. Her aim is not merely to assert her will but to seize the key to our sacred sanctuary and banish us, the Gaene Kin, from the annals of society. Her intentions are clear: to tarnish our reputation and rewrite history, branding us as charlatans who exploit divine magic for selfish gains.

The High Priestess has wielded all four elements with formidable prowess, and her dominance over air has granted her the power to manipulate minds and traverse the realm in spirit form. It is this very power she has used to sow distrust and incite fear, positioning herself as the sole arbiter of magical authority.

We, the Gaene Kin, have no choice but to witness the undoing of our sacred bond and the triumph of a force that seeks to overshadow all we have cherished. This entry serves as a cautionary tale—a record of the High Priestess's treachery and the betrayal of our sacred trust.

"It is signed with the initials, VV," Gerant said, closing the book.

"And that marks the end of an era," said Godfrey, "and the beginning of a new chapter in the saga of magic."

"More importantly, a new chapter on power," said Bain.

"So," Tristan said, "it could be said we're up a certain creek and the High Priestess has the only paddles. She can manipulate minds, flit about like the wind, take on other people's forms, and see the future. What chance do we have?"

"Don't give up hope, young Tristan," Felix said with a smile. "At least there's only one of her."

"Yeah, but there's only ten of us, and now that Blake has peed out his Baron brew, our combined magic score is a solid zero. I don't really fancy our odds."

"Let's not lose heart," said Gerant. "We'll explore the rest of the Sanctum and see what else we can find."

"Agreed," said Bain. "We should assess the whole place before we decide to risk staying. A camouflaged Sanctum like this could make the perfect hideout. We'd be as safe as kittens."

"As safe as kittens in a knotted sack dangling over water," Rowan muttered as they moved into the next room.

Blake's eyes lit up as he spotted a wall of portraits, each depicting beautiful women in dark green robes. "I think I've died and gone to heaven. Who are these stunning ladies?"

"If only your intelligence matched your looks," Felix sighed. "They're the Gaene Kin, obviously."

The room was framed by elegant white marble pillars, leading to a central aisle of the same stone. A shimmering blue surface, like liquid silk, bordered a small platform with a statue. Percy cautiously tested the blue surface with the tip of his shoe. "You can walk on this!" he exclaimed. "It looks like water, but it's solid. Amazing!"

Blake approached the island, where the statue of a woman more beautiful than beauty itself stood in serene splendour. Her form, sculpted like a siren emerging from water, had arms stretched out between the thrones, her cape unfurling like angelic wings.

"Who... who is th- th- *that*?" Blake stammered, his gaze locked on the statue as if it were his life source.

"Stop panting like a dog on heat," Felix scolded. "Let the Earl have a look."

"The lady is the first Sovereign Adviser, Lady Seraphina," said Godfrey. "The first Sovereign Adviser to King Valerian, more precisely."

"Blake's in love," Percy said playfully. "Bit too old for you, though."

"Bit too dead," said Tristan.

"Not sure that would stop him," said Bain.

"Well, *that* was distasteful," Felix said, shaking his ginger locks.

Godfrey continued his recounting. "Her ability to foresee the future and predict adversaries' strategies was unparalleled."

"Fountain of knowledge, your father," Gerant said, impressed. "Good job we broke him out of that prison."

"I'm grateful for so many reasons that you're with us, Father," Cane added. "Come, let's move on—the light's fading." He struck the flint stones together, igniting the torches. The flames danced to life, creating a warm glow as they pressed deeper into the heart of the Sanctum.

The grand foyer opened into a sparsely furnished room, exuding an air of serene potency. The dome-shaped ceiling opened to the sky, allowing natural light to filter in. Their gaze was drawn upward by the soft scratching of claws.

"Must be the lynx trying to find a warmer spot in the setting sun," said Cane.

Most of the floor was taken up by an elaborate ritual circle, large enough to accommodate a dozen Gaene Kin. At its centre was a compass, with hands pointing to each cardinal direction. Four tall, slender pillars rose at the ends of each arrow, their surfaces carved with flowing patterns.

Gerant studied the carvings. "Each pillar represents a direction. See, the eastern one has stylised clouds and lines. But here," he pointed to the southern pillar, "we've got suns and salamanders."

"This westward one is clearly water," Bain noted. "The curves must be waves and—"

"And these are the curves of a woman," Blake interjected, tracing the outline of a figure with a long stick he'd found. His smile drooped as he spotted fins instead of legs. "On no, no thank you. Very unattractive."

"Water nymph, I'd say. You know, mermaids," Bain said.

"And what about this one?" Percy asked, pointing to the final pillar.

"Not sure, maybe trees," Gerant said, peering closer. "The woodlands—"

"Ah!" Godfrey exclaimed, as if struck by sudden inspiration. "It's a ritual circle. North represents earth, and the others—yes, you're right—fire, water, and air."

"What's it for?" Tristan asked. "Is it where the fighting took place?"

"Hardly!" said Godfrey. "The Gaene Kin would enter this circle as a safe space. When they summoned the sylphs, they used it to call upon the four elemental guardians. The pillars served as watchtowers, ensuring no one could enter or leave once the circle was activated."

"So, they were sealed inside this?" Blake asked, absentmindedly drawing a circle in the air with his stick. As if on cue, a gust of wind whipped through the room. The men instinctively stepped back from the centre—but found they couldn't move beyond the circle's bounds. Agatha, the only one outside, tried to reach in.

"What did I do?" Blake asked, staring at the end of his stick in confusion.

"What's happening?" Cane shouted over the gusts of wind.

"I think we've unknowingly triggered the summoning process," Godfrey shouted back. "Blake must have activated the circle by passing through the entry point between the East and South watchtowers—and waving that wand about. The circle is now sealed."

"Oh bugger," Blake said, regarding the smooth stick in his hand with dismay. "I thought wands were supposed to be smaller."

And so, trapped within the ritual circle, they were with faced the irony of the situation: caught in a magical trap set by the very power they sought to understand, all thanks to Blake's ill-timed wand-waving antics.

They barely had time to reprimand Blake when the atmosphere abruptly shifted.

Without warning, a beam of light shot up from the circle, stretching towards the high, domed ceiling like a heavenly spotlight. The air sizzled with electricity. Then, with a crackling sound, like a sputtering wick, a sylph began to materialise within the circle. It appeared slowly, heralded by a gentle glow and the whirr of wind that swirled around the men like a flotilla of fluttering butterflies.

"What's happening?" Percy's voice came out in a squeak, his eyes wide as saucers. "Shouldn't we try to run?"

"We can't get out!" Tristan shouted over the rising wind. "We're trapped in this bloody circle!"

Before Percy could blurt out his worried reply, the entire room erupted in a brilliant white light. Cane blinked furiously, his eyes watering as he tried to block out the intense glare. Just when he thought it couldn't get any more fantastical, a shrill, high-pitched ringing pierced the air—a noise that could only be described as the unholy offspring of a thousand crickets wailing in unison. The screeching set every nerve on edge. They instinctively cupped their ears, but it was as futile as trying to scoop a giant wave into a teacup.

The noise wasn't just loud; it seemed to be drilling into each ear drum, leaving them feeling as muddled as if they'd just downed an entire barrel of ale in one go.

Through the blinding light, Cane saw a small, luminous figure emerging, barely knee-high.

"Wow!" Percy gasped. "Gnomes *are* real!"

"Aw, is that it?" Tristan said, relieved. "It's not scary. In fact, it's quite cute."

"Just a wee tot," said Felix, his own nerves evidently calmed by the sylph's diminutive stature. With a chubby hand extended as if he were about to greet a new friend, he moved forward. "Hello, pleased to—"

His words cut off abruptly as the sylph, offended either by the notion of a handshake or being referred to as a gnome and 'wee tot', suddenly metamorphosed from an adorable light cherub into a cyclonic blur of blues and greens. The transformation was so swift, Cane barely registered it before the wind darted in and out, thin as branches and faster than any human eye could hope to follow.

Felix moved with an agility that would have impressed his friends under different circumstances, ducking under the lash of blue-green wind with just inches to spare.

"Well, by my beard!" he grumbled. "It just goes to show, not everything small and glowing is friendly!"

Chapter 22

FOR WHOM THE BELL TOLLS

T HE GUARDS UNCEREMONIOUSLY HAULED Gwaine's bedraggled body from Malcrov Court, yanking him through the grand front entrance for all to witness the fate of a traitor. His head lolled like a marionette with half its strings cut, and his swollen, bloodshot eyes struggled to stay open. Given the spectacle awaiting him, closing them might have been a mercy. The guards tasked with taking him to Traitor's Square were all too eager to do their job, rough handling adding to his bruised and battered state.

He was bound for a square that had once been a place of joy—a communal green where Bellingham's people had gathered under the benevolent rule of Aurelius. Families had picnicked on the lush grass, children laughed between market stalls, and orators spun stories from Speaker's Corner. But since Duke Nieman's arrival, that same square had become a stage for barbarity, where the 'disloyal' were stoned and flogged by the same townsfolk who had once toasted to their good health.

The guards manhandled Gwaine down the stone steps, painfully wrenching his arms, lugging him around like an unwieldy sack of potatoes. With a graceless swing, they tossed him into an open wagon, where he landed with a bone-rattling thud. The wagon itself was a gloomy relic, last seen in the days of the great plague when it had clattered through towns, collecting the dead. The disease, like Duke Nieman, had wormed its way into the everyday lives of the unwitting people of Valoria.

As the wagon creaked and groaned out of the Malcrov estate, passing rows of quaint cottages with tidy gardens, Gwaine tried not to think of the last time he'd travelled this road to Bellingham's market. Back then, his wife had been at his side, the townsfolk waving and smiling. Now, those same people were likely choosing the sharpest stones to hurl at him. He closed his eyes, hoping to retreat into some corner of his mind where the pain couldn't follow. His only comfort was the thought of joining his wife. He was still shocked they had killed her. Soon, he'd be free of this wicked world, mottled with wanton greed and gratuitous loyalties.

After just a few moments of stabbing jostling, the wagon came to an impromptu halt, and a new noise penetrated Gwaine's bleeding ears—garbled voices, like an impossibly slow flapping of wings. He forced his eyes open, but the world around him was a dizzying blur. Shapes moved too fast, then too slow; the ground seemed to tilt beneath him, and he could swear he saw stars, despite the bright midday sun.

Closing his eyes again, he strained to listen, hoping his ears might make sense of what his eyes could not.

A woman's voice rang out, clear and authoritative. "Then I suggest you take the matter up with Lady Dagma. If you have a death wish!"

"Fine, but we need the wagon for body collection," said a gruff voice.

There was a brief pause, followed by a flurry of activity. A guard lifted him out of the wagon, his arms screaming in protest. He slumped heavily against whoever had caught him—someone smaller and slighter than the brutish guards who had tossed him around. The rustle of skirts told him it was a woman, but his vision remained blurred and the hood of her cape hid her face.

"You'll have to do better than this, Gwaine," she ordered urgently but quietly. "Unless you fancy ending up in Traitor's Square."

Gwaine squinted. In the distance, the silhouette of the wagon meant to be his hearse trundled on toward the capital, its empty boards no doubt ready to be loaded with the dead.

"You need to move," the woman urged, pulling his arm tightly around her shoulder. "Before they realise we're heading the wrong way."

Summoning every scrap of strength he had, Gwaine forced himself to move, leaning heavily on his mysterious rescuer. Leaning on her for support. Leaning on her for hope. "As my saviour and rescuer," he gasped, managing a weak smile, "didn't you bring a horse?"

"You're a real comedian, Gwaine," she replied. "I cancelled the luxury horse and chariot. Thought you might enjoy the walk."

The banter, absurd as it was given their situation, brought a small measure of normality back into his fractured world. With determination, and not much else, he shuffled forward, the woman practically dragging him along.

"We've still got a way to go," she said. "But trust me, any pain you're feeling now is nothing compared to what you'd face in that square."

Gwaine knew she was right. He had endured enough pain for several lifetimes, the kind that didn't fade with time or salves, and he wasn't keen to add more. The memory of his wife's smile and touch stirred in him the need to act, to avenge her. Her savage death was his fuel for moving, his fuel for living. His physical pain was easier to compartmentalise and bear, so, he quickened his pace as best he could, knowing the aches in his limbs would help dull the ache in his heart.

After what felt like miles but was only a few furlongs, they finally reached their destination—a stone hut, nestled deep in the woods. Smoke curled lazily from the chimney, and there wasn't another soul in sight. The woman pushed open the door—just a makeshift contraption of battered planks that groaned in protest—and ushered Gwaine inside.

The moment he crossed the threshold, a wave of exhaustion claimed him. Here, at last, he allowed himself to feel safe enough to collapse on a chair by the door.

⚫

Across the cramped foyer, Holly pushed open the door to the main room, letting it creak in protest as she stepped inside. "Father, it's only me, Holly," she called out gently, though she wasn't sure if her father, half-asleep and half-deaf, would hear her anyway. The interior was as familiar and comforting as ever, despite the draft that always seemed to sneak through the gaps in the old stone walls. A fire burned in the hearth, filling the single-room dwelling with much-needed warmth.

Gwaine, barely conscious, slumped over her shoulder. For someone of her slight frame, she bore his weight with surprising ease. She watched him slump into the chair. Holly felt a pang of sympathy. He'd been on death's door when she found him, and if she was honest, he still wasn't far from it.

"Well, he's had a rough day," she muttered under her breath, dragging him to the only bed in the room—a lumpy old thing that had seen better decades, if not centuries. As she lowered him onto the mattress, his unconscious mind seemed to finally surrender, giving him the peace he desperately needed. Holly pulled a threadbare blanket from the foot of the bed, draping it over his battered body with the tenderness of someone far more accustomed to care than combat.

Her father, a frail old man with a beard that had gone from brown to grey to something resembling dusty cobwebs, barely glanced up from his perch on the tatty daybed. He grunted in recognition but seemed far more interested in his own hazy thoughts—or perhaps the fire, which crackled merrily enough to keep him entertained.

Once Gwaine was settled, Holly removed her hooded cape, revealing a plain but pleasant face framed by soft auburn curls that refused to stay neatly in place. She set to work, tending to his wounds with herbal remedies and a practiced touch that came more from experience than instinct. This wasn't her first time patching someone up, though she hoped it would be one of the last.

She hadn't always lived like this, playing nursemaid to fugitives and invalids. Not long ago, she had served as lady-in-waiting to the formidable Lady Dagma at Maicrov Court. Before that, she had enjoyed a far more stable life. She was the daughter of an esteemed scholar, a man once held in high regard for his knowledge of law and ancient history. They had lived modestly but comfortably, their small estate supported by her father's work advising local lords and teaching their children. Holly, having been raised in such an environment, had an education that few women of her standing could boast.

However, her father's outspoken nature soon became his downfall. He'd made the mistake of advising against a particularly ruthless law passed by the Duke, and in doing so, he earned the Duke's quiet enmity. First, they lost his position, then their home, as debts piled up and their patrons mysteriously vanished. It wasn't long before Holly found herself and her ailing father cast out, forced to live in a crumbling hut on the outskirts of the Malcrov estate, scraping by on what little they could grow or gather.

The shock of it all seemed to unmoor her father's mind. He began to retreat into the past, his sharp intellect dulled by confusion. Now, he spent his days muttering half-forgotten memories and muddling through the present, unable to recall where he was or why they had fallen so low.

When Lady Dagma had offered Holly a position at Malcrov Court, it had seemed like a stroke of luck—a chance to lift them both from the edge of poverty. But that life had soured quickly, and Holly was glad to be rid of it, despite the income. The final straw had been Dagma's casual poisoning of her own sister. That was when Holly realised she couldn't stay—not if she wanted to keep her conscience, and perhaps her organs, intact.

Saving Gwaine had been an easy decision. By some miracle, she'd overheard a guard bragging at the market about how Gwaine was being sent to Traitor's Square. The guard's glee at the prospect of another public stoning had infuriated Holly, and before she knew it, she was concocting a plan to rescue him.

Convincing the guards had been easier than she expected. A simple story about Lady Dagma needing Gwaine's body for one of her 'experiments', and they handed him over without a second thought. To her relief, she hadn't even needed to explain what the experiment was. The quicker they let her go, the less likely they'd have to face Dagma's wrath, and that seemed enough for them.

Over the next few days, she nursed Gwaine back to something resembling health—it was slow and arduous, more like a marathon than a sprint. Her father, who hadn't had company in ages, was positively delighted to have someone new to tell his old stories to. He spent his days watching the fire, occasionally offering advice that was equal parts wise and inapplicable. Holly was just glad he didn't object to the intrusion. The old man wasn't much use these days—he could barely feed himself without spilling half the bowl—but she still enjoyed his presence.

One afternoon, when she returned from the market, Gwaine was lucid enough to string together a coherent sentence. "You're the lady-in-waiting that disappeared, aren't you? Why did you rescue me?"

Holly didn't answer right away. She handed him a basket and gestured toward the door. "Let's pick some wild garlic and talk. Fresh air will do you good," she suggested in the same firm motherly she often used with her ailing father. No sense in coddling Gwaine—he needed to move or he'd rust like an old gate.

They wandered through the woods, the small river Ribble babbling alongside them, while Holly filled her basket with wild garlic. The scene was almost peaceful—if you ignored the tyranny taking root at Malcrov Court just across the water. The once-productive fields were now choked with rotting vegetables.

"There's a great darkness over our lands," Holly began. "The people of Bellingham are drunk on dreams of riches and idleness, blind to what the Duke is doing to our country." She pointed across the river, her face hardening. "See over there. Mountains of waste that could be traded. Food rotting in the fields while people starve. The Duke's poured his poison into our minds, and we've become blind to it. This abundance... it doesn't nourish the soul. It corrupts it."

Gwaine followed her gaze, his heart sinking at the sight of the land dying under its own false prosperity. "This isn't the result of hard work," Holly continued. "It's the result of enslavement—enslaving our minds and turning us against one another. I feel a deep shame. Not for myself, but for what Valorians have become."

"When did you start to see all this?" Gwaine asked, placing a handful of crisp leaves into his own basket.

"When the barons and earls began to disappear. When sweet Agatha was sent off to marry a man twice her age. When Dagma's heart filled with a black jealousy for her sister—black enough to poison her. Take your pick."

"Tell me everything!" Gwaine's curiosity was unmistakable, and so were the sniffing sounds coming from the woods.

"Hush," she said, grabbing his arm. "Lady Dagma's dogs. They're searching the woods." Two big huskies prowled through the underbrush, their noses low to the ground. "Hide yourself. Say nothing until they're gone. I swear those beasts report back to her."

They stood completely still, listening as the jangling of the dogs' collars like a gaoler's keys faded into the distance.

Later, over the fire, Holly prepared a simple soup from the wild garlic they had gathered, while Gwaine quizzed her as he busied himself laying the table and cutting the slightly stale bread. "And what of the rebel patriots? Any news?"

Holly stirred the soup as she spoke. "Nieman's scouts are combing the land in every direction, though they're focusing mostly to the east. Men are guarding the borders, and I think they're searching for some monks. I overheard talk of a key. Lady Dagma is especially keen on finding it."

"So, they're still out there, still fighting." Gwaine's voice grew sombre. "Maybe my wife didn't die in vain."

Holly's stirring slowed. "Oh, Gwaine, I didn't know. It was that witch Dagma, wasn't it? She redefines cruelty."

Gwaine's jaw tightened. He nodded. "Thank you. I didn't know how far her wickedness reached. Still, even if I'd told her what little I knew, I don't think it would've saved her." A pause, a quiet moment for the memory of his wife. "But those men can't hide forever." Holly saw grit in his expression. "When they return to overthrow Duke Nieman, I want to be there to help them!"

"But there are only two of us," Holly reminded him, nodding toward her father, who was slowly spooning soup into his mouth with a trembling hand. "He doesn't count."

"Well, that's one more than I thought," Gwaine said with a grin. "Besides, there's less chance of us being spotted." He paused, thinking. "We'll have to disguise ourselves. The guards likely reported back to Dagma that they handed me over to you. That's probably why she's sent her huskies—they know your scent and mine."

They spent the rest of the afternoon plotting their next move. Sitting idle was no option, not when so much was at stake. Holly scattered chopped garlic around the perimeter of the hut, hoping to throw off the dogs' noses, while Gwaine gathered winter roses from the woods. Together, they soaked their clothes in rose-scented water.

"Here we are, two unlikely insurgents holed up in a decrepit hut—well, it's mine, so I can call it that—battling a tyrant's regime with little more than herbs and hope." Holly was quietly congratulating herself for saving Gwaine.

That evening, they devised a plan to become something no one would ever suspect. For their first attempt at espionage, they chose scarecrows. The fields surrounding Malcrov Court were littered with these straw-stuffed figures, and they felt confident they could blend in. The local tradition of the Scarecrow Competition had once sparked fierce rivalry between the towns of Gribthorpe, Bellingham, and Stoketon. Farmers would spend weeks crafting their entries, hoping to win a year's supply of fodder. The results were bizarre, ranging from impressively lifelike to utterly ridiculous.

Some scarecrows sported tunics with embroidered edges, while others had painted faces that were far too jolly for their intended purpose. A few even came with families: scarecrow wives and scare-children, and, for the particularly enthusiastic, the occasional 'scaredog', usually an old boot stuffed with straw and given button eyes. The more exuberant entries featured twirling contraptions and rotating heads.

Given this eccentric tradition, they figured they'd fit right in. In fact, being too lifelike would have earned them a few extra points, if the competition were still running.

Their disguises were simple but effective: oversized, ragged clothes stuffed just enough to bulk them out, and large hats pulled low over their faces. Gwaine insisted on stuffing the straw with dried lavender, to help offset the pong of muck on the fields.

Each morning, before the first light of dawn, one of them would shuffle out to the fields, assuming the position of a particularly observant scarecrow. The other remained closer to the edge, ready to sound the alarm—or leap into action—if any suspicious activity, or any overly inquisitive animal, threatened to blow their cover.

By the end of the week, they had learned more about the comings and goings at Malcrov Court than they had ever thought possible.

The Duke was predictable to the point of tedium: a man set in his ways, who liked to survey his land at the same time each day, his hands clasped behind his back as he walked with the slow, deliberate steps of someone who believed every inch of soil belonged to him personally.

The merchants and tradesmen were equally regular in their visits, bringing goods up to the court in creaking carts weighed down with barrels and sacks. The farmers were a dull, shuffling lot, herding their sheep and cattle with the enthusiasm one might reserve for counting grains of sand. The clergyman's visits were punctual, and Holly noted with amusement how he always seemed to swagger a little more on the way out than when he'd arrived. The guards, too, were a clockwork routine—marching, training, and saluting like wind-up toys.

Duke Nieman had everyone in his pocket.

But amidst all this predictability, Lady Dagma's routine stood out like a wolf among sheep. Every night, while the rest of the court settled into their usual rhythms of snoring or scheming, she would slip out to a large barn on the estate's perimeter. The first time they mentioned it in their daily debrief, they'd brushed it off as another of Dagma's oddities. But when the visits continued, always at the same late hour, they knew they were onto something.

"Maybe she's been using her magic herb powers," Gwaine suggested one evening as they ran through their list of sightings for the day. "I've heard the cattle have become inexplicably thinner lately—sickly even. Maybe she's trying to cure them with some natural medicine."

Holly scoffed, shaking her head. "Curing cows? That doesn't sound like her at all. She's more likely the one making them sick in the first place. There's no way she's suddenly developed a soft spot for farming—or anything, for that matter."

"So, why is she making secret trips to the barn? It's full of cattle, for goodness' sake. What possible interest could she have in a barn of cows?" Gwaine frowned, rubbing his chin thoughtfully. "Maybe she's trying her hand at poisoning cows now that poisoning sisters has lost its thrill."

Holly shook her head again. "No, there's something else going on. Something worth digging into."

It was time to up their game. Watching from afar wasn't enough anymore. If they were going to uncover Lady Dagma's secrets, they needed to get closer—without ending up as unwilling participants in one of her infamous experiments.

"Tomorrow night," Holly's voice bordered on excited, though she was nervous as hell, "we're following her. And Gwaine—try to lay off the lavender this time. Anyone who didn't know better would think you're prepping for an old ladies' dance, not a rebellion."

Gwaine's eyes lit up at the word *rebellion*, like a man who'd just found his calling.

Chapter 23

SHADOW AND LIGHT

THE SYLPH'S COARSE FORM, a swirling mist of light and air, hovered just above the ground. At first, Cane thought it was a cloud trying to grow limbs. The little air spirit raised what might have been a hand—though it resembled more of a tuft of mist shaped by a breeze. It turned to Felix.

"Listen, wide one, we are not *cute*. And how dare you, narrow one, call us a gnome!! We are mighty!" it shrieked, its voice like a choir of shattered glass. The deafening sound ricocheted off the Sanctum's smooth walls.

Felix winced, muttering, "Small, but clearly not in the mood for small talk."

"We see all, we are everywhere, we *are* the air," it declared, with the kind of arrogance only an immortal being could pull off. "Why have you summoned the sylphs?"

"It was an accident." Gerant's voice, normally steady, warbled under the weight of the sylph's stare—and the absurdity of his answer. The sylph rose above them, its form billowing out like a storm cloud, all delicate menace and airy disdain.

"Then why do you come?" it demanded, sounding more annoyed by the minute. "We ask *him*." The sylph extended what resembled a finger, sharp and thin, stopping mere millimetres from Cane's chest. Energy crackled in the air around it, making his heart race in response to the invisible pull. "This one," the sylph continued, its voice like the swish of a blade being drawn, "whispers thoughts that are not his own. We hear it. We *feel* it."

Cane swallowed hard. The sylph floated closer, its form expanding, as if drawing breath—or whatever sylphs did when they were displeased. For a moment, Cane half expected it to blow him away like a stray leaf.

"We didn't mean to," Gerant explained, shooting a brief, accusatory glance at Blake, who wisely kept silent. "We seek refuge from those who wish to kill us. We believed this place might offer us safety. We have the key."

The sylph's response was swift and dismissive. "We are not a home for vagabonds and fugitives," it glowered, waving a misty hand as though brushing away an inconsequential speck. "We care not for the key. That is a human construct. *We* cannot be locked in—or out."

Cane looked at the others. Fear and confusion mirrored in their faces. They were trying to negotiate with a knee-high puff of air that clearly had the upper hand.

The sylph continued in a condescending hiss that filled all space. "We exist for life, not for you. Your kind always believes everything revolves around them. We live alongside you because we must, but do not mistake that for servitude."

A chill ran down Cane's spine. The sylph's penetrating gaze—or whatever passed for eyes—pierced right through him. Despite its diminutive size, it had an undeniable presence, one that made Cane feel like an insignificant dot on life's canvas.

"What we are not," it continued, its misty form swirling with righteous indignation, "is a homeless shelter. This site is our hub, the beating heart of Sylphic power. To have you stumble in here like a pack of buffoons is insulting."

Cane braced for more verbal lashing, but then the sylph's gaze fixed on him with an unsettling intensity. "Except you," it said, shifting from disdain to curiosity. "You're... different. A male, too. Hmm, not seen that before. Come closer."

Cane froze, his feet rooted to the spot. As the sylph drew near, he instinctively backed up, he collided with something solid—the invisible barrier at the edge of the glowing circle painted on the floor.

"Come closer!" the sylph commanded. Cane turned to his companions, but they looked as bewildered as he felt. With no real choice, he took a cautious step forward, the air around him growing more energised. He closed his eyes and stood rigid, half-hoping that, like a child pretending monsters didn't exist, the sylph would just go away. "We mean no harm. I am of no importance."

"Oh, but you are." The sylph hovered inches from his face, its cloudy form anchored to the ground by streams of light. Thin tendrils of mist extended from its fingers, curling towards his head, probing. Every instinct screamed at him to move, but the invisible wall kept him trapped.

Meanwhile, Tristan and Percy—gallantly or idiotically, the jury was out—were swinging at the sylph with wild punches. Their fists passed harmlessly through its body, causing little more than a mild ripple in its misty form.

"Get off him! Get away!" they shouted.

"What can we do?" Felix cried helplessly.

Since escaping was clearly out of the question, Cane did the only thing left to do. He drew his sword. The finely forged blade gleamed, sharp enough to cut through steel. But the sylph let out a laugh that sounded like a thousand bells rolling down a mountain. "That won't help you," it said with an airy smugness. "You cannot cut air."

In an instant, the sylph's misty tendrils invaded his senses, slipping into his ears, eyes, and nose. It was like being submerged in an ice-cold fog. Cane's face remained impassive, as though he hadn't just been turned into a vessel for a nosy cloud.

"Oh," Tristan observed, lowering his fists. "That's not what I expected."

"I think it's just having a poke around his mind," Godfrey suggested. "They are masters of thought streams, after all. They move on waves of thoughts and visions. Doesn't mean they'll do any harm by poking around in there. I hope."

"Not good," Rowan disagreed firmly, pointing at Cane. "His eyes are like the spinning wheels at the solstice firework show."

"Stop, you little idiot!" Bain bellowed, shaking his fist at the sylph as though scolding a misbehaving grandchild. "You can't just waltz in there! That's private property, you hear? Keep out!"

"What are you doing, you little upstart?" Gerant added, equally indignant. "Get out of his head!"

Just as it seemed Cane might start losing his breakfast, the sylph withdrew from his mind with a satisfied sigh, like a busybody neighbour retreating after inspecting every corner of a house. Much to everyone's relief, Cane's eyes mercifully stopped spinning. But the sylph wasn't done with him yet.

"Very interesting," it mused. "You have much to give, potential as yet untapped. The portal has been slightly opened, most likely by a shock or trauma. You begin to see and sense things, don't you?"

Cane, who was now the colour of a pale cabbage, felt as though something had pulled him inside out.

"Are you alright, Cane?" Gerant rushed over to help him. "You look like a poor sailor fresh off a stormy sea."

"A little green around the edges," said Felix.

"I feel as if all the air has been sucked right out of me." Cane struggled to catch his breath.

"There, there, easy does it," Gerant soothed, guiding him to sit, propped up against the invisible wall. "Breathe deeply and slowly." Gerant turned his anger back on the sylph. "What did you do, you little nitwit?"

"Less of the heightist insults, please. We opened his portal to unleash his full potential. No need to thank us." The sylph performed a graceful, almost mocking bow. "He will be more useful to you, and us, soon enough. We've seen things in his mindstream—he is needed. Now we understand why you are here even though you do not," it added cryptically. "Things couldn't wait for him to catch up at his usual pace. It may have taken too long."

Gerant's furious glare didn't faze the sylph in the slightest. "What have you done? Look at him! He can barely breathe!"

"You humans and your fixation on the material body," the sylph exhaled sharply in disapproval, then glided over to the others, peering into their eyes. "His body vessel will recover soon. He is a strong young man, although... he does resemble a woman in a certain light. Quite pretty features, really."

Cane impulsively touched his shoulder-length hair. He'd never let it grow this long, but he certainly hadn't been expecting to be mistaken for a woman.

"We wonder," the sylph continued, almost conversationally, "if that's why he's the first man to—" The thought was cut short as the sylph darted towards Blake with surprising speed. "Wait! Let's compare with a more masculine type—"

"Shoo!" Blake said, waving his hand as if swatting away an annoying fly. "There's nothing to see here. Move along."

"Quite right," the sylph agreed, sounding bored as it moved on to Rowan, who was doing his best to edge out of view without being noticed. "Ah, graceful qualities here as well. Let's try in—"

The sylph broke off, its attention suddenly grabbed by Agatha, who had been sitting quietly by the fountain, watching everything with an unreadable expression.

"Ah," the sylph said. "We thought we felt you. You're not supposed to be here, are you?"

With a wave of its airy hand, the sylph opened the circle. The invisible wall shimmered, dissolving into a cascade of tiny, glittering stars that fell around them like a twinkling waterfall, leaving Cane to fall flat on the floor.

The sylph glided toward Agatha, its once delicate form now bristling with jagged intensity. "There are two persons of interest in your group." Its misty tendrils twitched in agitation darting back and forth. "But you—*you* should not be here at all!" Its voice rose to a shrill pitch that set Cane's teeth on edge.

Agatha looked stricken, her hands clutching her ears as if she could block out the sylph's invasive presence. Her head bowed, tears welling in her eyes. "No! Please, no! Go away!" she cried, her voice breaking.

Cane tried to stand, but his legs felt like lead. He barely managed to lift his head before Gerant's voice stopped him cold. "Stay there, boy," Gerant ordered, leaving no room for argument. Flanked by Tristan and Blake, he advanced on the sylph with a determination that would've been admirable if it wasn't so utterly futile. "Get away from her!" he shouted, brandishing his small sword as if it might actually make a difference.

The sylph paid no heed. Instead, a multitude of smaller sylphs appeared, each no larger than a teacup, whirling around Agatha in a curious frenzy—a concerto of rings and swirls.

"You are a hybrid child!" thundered the larger sylph. It swelled into a stormy thundercloud, absorbing the mini-sylphs into its mass until it nearly brushed the domed ceiling. "You should not *be!*" The booming voice shook the very stones of the Sanctum, and for a moment, Cane was certain the entire structure would collapse under the sheer force of it.

The men exchanged panicked glances, clearly out of their depth. "What does it want?" Percy asked, hiding behind Tristan.

"Maybe if we give it an offering, we can appease it," said Godfrey.

"I'm too young to be a sacrifice," Percy whimpered, clutching at Tristan's arm. "I don't want to die!"

Tristan put an arm around Percy in a weak attempt at comfort. "Nobody's being sacrificed, brother... I hope."

"What did the Gaene Kin give as an offering?" Bain asked, turning to Godfrey.

"I—I can't remember exactly," Godfrey stammered, looking as though he'd aged ten years in the last ten minutes.

"Think, man, think!" Bain's politeness gone as he eyed the growing storm above crackling with energy. "The giant sylph storm is ready to explode!"

Godfrey's eyes darted around the room, searching in vain for inspiration. But the barren stone walls offered nothing—no answers, no solutions.

It was then that Cane heard a calm voice rise through the mounting tension, soothing as a cool breeze on a sweltering day. It was his voice. "I know," he said, surprising himself as much as the others. He pushed himself to his feet, smoothing back his windswept chestnut hair. "I don't know *how* I know, but I know."

Everyone turned to him. Even the sylph seemed momentarily intrigued, its stormy form shrinking slightly.

"We honour you, your sylph mightiness," Cane began, fumbling for the right words to address a fluffy godlike spirit. "Master guardian of the air. We honour all that you know and do. We are humbly grateful and indebted for your services to our human kingdom." He bowed his head but never broke eye contact with the sylph, which slowly returned to its smaller, pint-sized form. As he spoke, Cane felt lighter, as though the air around him had bolstered his strength. His mind was clear, yet brimming with a knowledge he couldn't explain.

"I know what the Gaene Kin offered in return for your powerful services," he continued, the words coming to him as naturally as breathing. "We are not prepared. We tell no lies. We cannot offer you the wind chimes to help carry your messages, nor the incense to clear and purify the air. Not yet. But we can bring you music, to show our reverence and help you focus and synchronise."

"We can?" Felix asked, looking as baffled as the rest of them.

"Yes," Cane replied with a certainty that left no room for doubt. He turned to Agatha, still trembling. "Baroness, please find the strength to sing."

"Ah, yes," Felix said, his face lighting up in relief. "Yes, Baroness, please sing. If nothing else, it'll calm *my* nerves."

Agatha twisted her hands together, her fear evident in every line of her grimace. "I—I'm not sure I can," she stammered. "I'm scared."

"If you do not sing," the sylph interjected coldly, "we will suck one of your minds as payment."

Blake's eyes bulged like a toad's. "What? No, that's cruel!"

"Don't worry," the sylph said with a dismissive wave. "It won't be yours. We enjoy fuller minds, and we're also partial to young minds." Its gaze slid pointedly towards Percy and Tristan, who both paled to match the whites of their gaping eyes.

"Oh dear, well... in that case," Agatha said, forcing courage into her trembling voice. "I'll do my best."

An expectant silence fell, all eyes on Agatha. Even before she began, there was something spellbinding about her, as if the air held its breath in anticipation.

Her voice was an instrument in its own right, weaving through the room like a ribbon of sound. Each note carried a delicate sweetness, wrapping everyone in a rocking embrace of calm. The sound flittered through the air, casting a spell of peace and tranquility over the group. Unbidden smiles spread across their faces as their worries momentarily dissolved.

None of them understood the words she sang, but that hardly mattered. The meaning was irrelevant; it was the beauty of her voice that worked its magic. It filled everyone with a tangible sense of peace. Everyone, that is, except the sylph.

Its reaction was unexpectedly dramatic. "No!" it shrieked, its voice tearing through the room like a tempest. "Not like that! That's boring! We want lively! The Gaene Kin always come here cooing us with sleepy melodies, like we're children at bedtime!" If the sylph had feet, it would've stomped like a wild child in the throes of a tantrum. "Impress us! You call us by accident, use us as a guesthouse and you think this will do? We demand *exceptional*!"

Agatha, a picture of worry, glanced at the men, who were just coming out of the spell of her voice. "Um, oh dear, I don't think I know any, um, lively songs," she stammered.

"I do," Felix said, shuffling confidently to the front. "Feel free to join in. You'll know this one." He winked at Tristan and Percy, who looked unsure but nodded, nonetheless. "It's a modern one." Felix cleared his throat, tapping his foot with exaggerated flair. "One, two, three, four!"

He launched into a jaunty tune, his strong voice bright, full of timbre but slightly off-key:

"Hey, you with wings on your feet,

dancing around, never missing a beat.

Life's a breeze when you're floating on air.

A little bit of magic everywhere!

If you've got a special beer,

sip it down, feel the cheer.

So bright and clear, a rainbow in your eyes. Everywhere you look, it's a sunny surprise!"

The men looked at each other bemused, unsure whether to cringe or applaud. Felix, however, was undeterred, grinning from ear to ear as he belted out the tune. To their astonishment, the sylph was no longer scowling. Instead, it was tapping its cloud-like foot to the beat, an expression of unmistakable glee on its misty face.

Tristan and Percy, emboldened by the sylph's reaction, jumped in enthusiastically with the chorus:

"If you've got a special beer,

sip it down, feel the cheer.

So bright and clear, a rainbow in your eyes.

Everywhere you look, it's a sunny surprise!"

By the time they reached the final crescendo, the whole group was swept up in the moment, delivering a spirited—if not entirely polished—rendition:

"So let's toast to the magic, raise our glasses high,

with wings on our feet, we'll reach for the sky!

Rainbows in our eyes, smiles on our faces.

Life is a journey to beautiful places!

If you've got a special beer,

sip it down, feel the cheer!

So bright and clear, a rainbow in your eyes.

Everywhere you look, it's a sunny surprise!"

The sylph clapped its fluffy hands with unrestrained joy. "Yes, yes, yes! Finally, something uplifting! Thank you, thank you! You know, we had no intention of harming the young lady. We can't. We're not allowed to intervene directly. And as for sucking your minds? Pfft! What a foul idea! We leave that to lesser deities. But," it added with a mischievous glint, "we are a sylph of our word. So, in exchange for the wide one's excellent song, we'll divulge one thing you wish to know."

What a twisted sense of logic, thought Cane.

"Just one question?" Bain grumbled, folding his arms across his broad chest. "Surely that performance earned at least two."

"Do not push your luck, big man," the sylph replied with a pointed glare. "One question."

Chapter 24

THE FORGOTTEN TALE

Blake seized on this opportunity to ask one question to satisfy his personal curiosity. "Could you tell us what happened to the last beautiful High Priestess and, uh, where she is now?"

Gerant rolled his eyes so hard Cane was surprised they didn't pop out the back of his head. "Always thinking with your John Thomas and not your brain," Gerant muttered under his breath.

The sylph, however, seemed entirely unperturbed by his question. "That's two, we'll answer the first only. Atropa held the title of the last High Priestess. She was responsible for—"

"Wait!" Gerant interrupted. "That is *not* our question!"

But the sylph was as compassionate as a judge handing down a sentence on a guilty man. "The question was asked, and so must be answered."

"We have more important and pressing matters to clear up. Let us confer!" Gerant insisted.

"No! You sing, we offer, you ask, we answer. That is the law."

"What if I sing you another song?" Felix cleared his throat ready to launch into another operatic performance. "Do we get another question?"

"One question per solstice cycle."

"What's a solstice cycle?" Tristan asked, looking as if he wished he had paid more attention during whatever lesson covered this.

"The longest day in the summer and the shortest day in the winter," said Rowan. "You know, the firework shows."

"Bugger, that's at least half a year away," Tristan groaned.

Ten pairs of eyes immediately turned to Blake, who was suddenly fixatedly interested in his own shoes.

"It's not such a bad question," Cane said. "Gwaine spoke of Atropa returning to claim Valoria. If we know more about Atropa, we might find out more about what she plans to do. Maybe even when she is coming. It could shed some light on the Duke's immediate plans as well, since he is obviously working with her." He glanced at Agatha, who was still sitting meekly by the pool. "And maybe something about how Agatha fits into all this."

The sylph, no doubt on a busy schedule, did not wait for them to confer. Its misty body dispersed into millions of droplets, creating in a visual projection of women in dark green capes roaming through the countryside, gathering herbs.

"We begin."

Suspended droplets refracting light into a prism of colours brought the room alive with hues that slowly shaped into graceful figures dressed in flowing robes and floral headpieces. The Gaene Kin walked in a solemn column.

Gradually, the woodland tones in the droplets darkened, turning into ominous purples and blacks. A figure shrouded in darkness formed in the mist. Around her, the land withered and died, the once-lush fields turning to ash and dust. A chill swept through the group, their breath visible in the now-cold air, as the tale descended into darkness.

"We present to you the tale of Atropa, High Priestess of the Gaene Kin, adviser to Sovereign Valkarse, great-granddaughter of Lady Seraphina, and instigator of the Sorrel Schism," the sylph announced, pausing dramatically. The men lapped up every word like parched nomads savouring the first drops of water from a mirage oasis—except for Blake, who looked confused.

The sylph's voice softened. "Long ago, before your memories began, the Gaene Kin ruled not as kings or emperors, but as watchers—stewards of the ancient balance. They could speak to the elements, commune with the winds, and summon the power to heal. Their strength was drawn from the earth itself, and in return, they nurtured it, ensuring that life flourished in harmony. They were more than mere humans; they were listeners, attuned to the whispers of the world around them. They would visit the Sanctum to seek our wisdom, for we know all," it added with a self-satisfied puff. "We flow through every crevice of the world, privy to all its secrets."

"Ew, that doesn't sound right," Percy squirmed.

"Bit full of itself, isn't it?" Tristan whispered back.

"Silence!" The sylph, irritated by the interruption, continued. "But as with all things, there were those who coveted such power. Within the hierarchy of the Gaene Kin, there was always a High Priestess—not necessarily their leader, but the one most attuned to the Earth's hums and the whispers of the wind."

As the sylph narrated the ancient lineage of the High Priestesses, the coloured droplets painted a procession of women through the ages, serious and mystical. "The

High Priestesses held a special role, gifted with foresight and the ability to channel the elements. But this power," the sylph intoned darkly, "was a double-edged sword. Atropa's great-grandmother, the first High Priestess, used her powers for the good of mankind, advising Sovereign Valerian to maintain peace and prosperity. But Atropa..." the sylph's voice dropped to a dramatic whisper, "...was another story entirely. Atropa became the spark that ignited the Sorrel Schism."

"What does that mean, exactly?" Blake asked, still confused.

"Silence!" the sylph snarled, making Blake jump. "We tell. You listen. No questions. Understand what you can and figure out the rest later."

Satisfied it had reestablished control, the sylph resumed. "High Priestess Atropa saw herself as superior, her lineage and knowledge of magic granting her a status above the Gaene Kin. She believed she was a sacred vessel of divine energy, her powers directly linked to the Earth's essence. But this," the sylph's tone hardened, "was not the way of the Gaene Kin. This is not the way of nature. She was born a conduit, not a manipulator. If people could claim ownership or shape the Earth's energy to their will, it would unbalance the natural stasis."

"Like giving a toddler a dagger to play with," Felix whispered to Blake to help him grasp the situation. "Bound to end badly."

"Blinded by ambition and arrogance, Atropa did not see the danger. She abused her position, dismissing the Gaene Kin and their practices as beneath her. Exerting her influence, the Gaene Kin were declared outcasts, shunned by society. And *that* is the Sorrel Schism." The sylph turned to Blake, as if daring him to ask another question.

"Atropa seized our knowledge, learned to harness the intrinsic power of nature and all its elements. She believed herself invincible. In some ways, she was. We did not see this in the future threads. So miniscule was its likelihood, we paid it little heed. We were unprepared for what came next. She did the unthinkable."

"What did she do?" asked Tristan, barely able to contain his curiosity.

"To better understand, we will *show* you the turning point."

The sylph's misty droplets rearranged themselves into a new scene. Cane watched as King Valkarse, a man who looked like he never passed up a chance to strike a heroic pose, sat on his throne, addressing his court with heavy-handed solemnity. The grand hall of the Palace of Bellingham was packed with glittering courtiers.

"This is King Valkarse making his grand proclamation to the Octule ambassadors, in an effort to appease them."

"Take my High Priestess as a token of my good faith," King Valkarse declared.

The sylph's form presented a new scene, its mood now sombre. "That proclamation sealed Valoria's fate and marked the beginning of Atropa's descent into black sorcery."

The droplets showed Atropa before her departure from Valoria with the Octules. She was whispering insidious words into the ear of King Aldric, sovereign leader of North Valoria. "She used her position as the adviser to manipulate King Aldric, planting seeds of distrust against King Valkarse. She portrayed him as a treacherous power-hungry monarch. King Aldric, ignorant of Atropa's true intentions, was swayed by her deception. He prepared for battle, setting the stage for a clash of powers. In her first step toward revenge, she pitted North against South."

The droplets spun together, filling the air with colour to create a vibrant jungle landscape teeming with life. Giant trees stretched skyward with emerald leaves, and exotic creatures darted through the dense undergrowth.

At the heart of this verdant world stood the towering figures of the Octules. Despite their imposing size, they moved with a fluid grace. Their world was one of harmony and boundless energy, a place where nature and the mystical were inextricably linked.

"Atropa's time in Octavia with the Octules was a happy one. We saw her gain many things from them. Yes, they gave her a great gift. She had a—"

"So why didn't she stay there?" Tristan asked, completely caught up in the tale.

"Because, her heart, twisted by revenge, compelled her to return to Valoria. Hatred triumphed over happiness. She gathered her faithful, the Army of the Bleak—Valorians disillusioned by the rule of self-proclaimed kings—and took her seat in Illminster in the north."

The sylph's form shattered into black droplets, depicting the bleak, marching army. Before them a gruesome battle came to life, so visceral that even Bain recoiled. Above the carnage, Atropa stood on the gothic castle ramparts, looking down with cold satisfaction.

"In the final battle between King Aldric and King Valkarse, when both leaders stood at the precipice of their reigns, locked in fierce combat, neither realised their battle was nothing more than a smokescreen for Atropa's true plan. She appeared before them the moment Aldric drove his sword through Valkarse's golden armour. Her cruel smile told them everything—they had been mere puppets. But it was too late. Not only had they destroyed each other without her lifting a finger, their senseless warring had weakened Valoria. At that moment, Atropa descended with her Army of the Bleak, leaving a trail of scorched earth in their wake. Valoria was hers for the taking."

"How come she isn't still here then?" Percy asked, daring to break the sylph's narrative flow.

The sylph's tone softened. "The Gaene Kin, though they owed mankind nothing after being cast out, could not stand by and watch Valoria destroyed. In secret, they reinforced the Valorians' efforts, calling upon the elements of air and earth to push Atropa back."

Cane watched as the sylph's droplets painted a vivid picture of the Gaene Kin in action, their magic all around them like a protective barrier. "They summoned the animal kingdom and crafted potent potions. Though they could not kill Atropa, they forced her from Valoria and drove her to Caldera, an archipelago of volcanic fury."

The imagery was so lifelike, Cane could almost feel the intense heat of Caldera, its rocky formation shaped like a giant brooding dragon tempered by the ocean's waves crashing against its scissor-sharp shores.

"Atropa's once grand image was now marred with defeat. Her forlorn followers retreated with her, their spirits as bleak as the blackened land they now called home. With nothing left to lose, her Army of the Bleak gave up their lives and souls in the name of revenge. Atropa, obsessed with her vengeance, experimented on them, using black sorcery to create the unthinkable. She forged an abomination, a species that was not meant to be. An unthinkable fusion of man, wasp, and roach. These spawn serve her alone, driven by a hive mind that cares nothing for individual lives. They are the greatest threat to our natural balance." The sylph raised a cautionary, wispy finger. "We were shortsighted, unable to foresee such cruelty. Atropa too was blind. Her new army are carnivores, feeding on flesh. When they deplete all food sources, as they inevitably will, only one will remain—themselves. Self-extinction. But not before they wreak devastation on the world first."

"O-kay," Blake said, clearly overwhelmed. "This is kind of out there. You know, really over my head. Is anyone else having trouble getting to grips with what Mr. Fluffy is—"

"We are not fluffy!" the sylph looked daggers at Blake.

Cane quickly stepped in. "We believe she is to return to Valoria very soon. Is she? How can we defeat her?"

"No more questions! We cannot intervene. We have already overdelivered and answered both questions."

Cane understood the sylph was duty-bound to stay out of human affairs. Sharing this story was most likely overstepping its remit as guardian. Trying to get more from it was pointless. But he had to try, surely this was an exception.

"Wait!" Cane pleaded. "This affects you too. And if we all die, if there is mass extinction, you'll have failed as guardians."

The sylph hesitated, clearly wrestling with the truth of Cane's words but reluctant to concede. "To maintain natural stasis, we cannot directly interfere. Every living thing has a role to play. If we start taking on roles that are not ours, instead of fulfilling the one accorded to us, boundaries become blurred, confusion takes over. We must abide by the laws of nature placed on us. Find out what must be done, Cane, for the battle is inevitable.

It's coming, whether you want it or not. Whether you're ready or not. Best make sure you *are* ready."

It paused briefly. "It won't be long now." And with that, the sylph dissolved into the air calling out, "Bring us our chimes and incense. You owe us these offerings."

"Blimey!" Felix exclaimed. "This Atropa is the boil on Beelzebub's backside. What possesses someone to do such hideous things?"

"So, those pasty predators at the monastery," Blake said, "they were like... her Bleaker soldiers?"

"Maybe something like them," said Cane.

"Atropa and her lot don't sound so sexy now, do they, Blake?" said Bain.

"No." Blake shuddered. "And according to that little white thing, she's coming back with more."

"How are we supposed to fight them?" Tristan asked, worried. "We barely kept them away by playing the organ."

"Oh no!" Blake exclaimed, slapping his hand against his forehead. "How are we going to carry the organ into battle?"

Bain sighed. "Are we sure the human race is worth saving?"

Chapter 25

MISTRESS OF PUPPETS

THE DUKE STARED MOTIONLESS at the impressive collection of swords on his study walls. Hung like the sharp and gleaming trophies of a warlord, these were symbols of violence and authority. Yet in his hands, they were about as useful as a quill to a pig. Dagma knew exactly what his staring meant: he was thinking. And when the Duke thought, everything else stopped. His limbs went limp, his mouth muttered nonsense, and the tiny blob in his skull, which might have passed for a misplaced slug in an autopsy, strained to produce a single coherent idea.

Leaning back, Dagma waited. She could almost hear the rusted gears in his head creaking as they tried to grind out a plan—something, anything, to prove he wasn't just a puppet on her string. The poor fool didn't seem to realise that without her family's backing, he'd still be a nobody, scrounging for scraps in the streets. Yet, here he was, with the King of South Valoria locked up in his dungeons, completely oblivious to the fact that she had handed him that feast on a silver platter.

His eyes, still blank and unfocused, drifted over to the glass chessboard where he'd been pretending to play against himself. It was painfully obvious he had no idea how the game worked. He moved a bishop forward, then shoved a pawn three squares diagonally, and then... stopped. The movement had apparently scrambled his brain, forcing him to freeze again as he tried to shift gears.

"Yes! Yes, that's it!" he suddenly shouted.

Dagma prepared herself for whatever half-baked scheme was about to spill out of his mouth. The Duke's plans were always as dull as ditchwater and just as useful. Maybe this time he'd surprise her—even a blind squirrel finds a nut once in a while.

"I'll order puppet shows!" he declared with pride. "With the king as the main puppet! We'll poke fun at him for being greedy, his fancy ways, the bad stuff he's done to the people. The shows will—"

"Ridicule and demean him," Dagma supplied, not even bothering to look up from her nails.

"Yes, yes!" he continued, as if he'd thought of it himself. "We'll turn the sovereign name into a symbol of... of..." His eyes darted around the room, searching the room as though the right words might be hiding behind the drapes.

"Treachery and deceit," Dagma offered.

"Yes, yes! Treachery and deceit!" he repeated his enthusiasm. "We'll drag him before the drunks in the taverns, let them laugh at him... and things."

Dagma took a slow, steadying breath, watching the Duke as if he were a child determined to eat soup with a fork. She'd explained their plan to him a dozen times by now, yet here he was, pacing his study with a gleeful grin, conjuring ideas for puppet shows in which he would dangle the king like his own personal plaything on a string.

"Look," she interrupted, fixing him with a stare, "as fun as it might sound to turn the king into your personal sock puppet, remember the goal here is to keep him intact—a ruler, not a ridicule."

The Duke squinted at her, fingers pausing mid-air as if pondering this new revelation. "Right, right... keep him as the king. But what if we did just one show—a short one, just to let the people have a laugh? A little puppet king wouldn't hurt."

Dagma pinched the bridge of her nose. "For the last time, we already have a stand-in on the throne—a double, remember? The whole idea is to keep up the illusion, so no one suspects anything."

His face lit up as though hearing this for the first time. "Ah! Yes, yes, the stand-in! So, we don't need to use the real king for the show... we could use a different puppet!"

Dagma sighed, a long, slow exhale. "The *point* is no puppet show at all," she said, each word measured. "Just the quiet ruse of a stand-in, ruling peacefully. No theatrics, no shows, just... quiet."

The Duke blinked, clearly struggling to compute a world without his puppet show. After a long pause, he gave her a thumbs-up. "Got it. No shows with the *real* king. The dummy will do nicely for that!"

Dagma simply closed her eyes and shook her head. "No shows, full stop. Now, go and bring me Aurelius."

She watched him go. "I guess that squirrel doesn't have any nuts," she crooned lovingly to her huskies, "or brains."

In the quiet of Malcrov Court, the guards tied Aurelius to the same chair where Gwaine had once resisted her probing methods—how long would the king last? Dagma circled him like a predator savouring the thrill of the hunt. To her, Aurelius was more than just a deposed king; he was a treasure trove of knowledge that she intended to plunder.

"You have nothing to fear, sweetie," she drooled, waving a hand delicately in front of her mask. "Behind this, I'm all smiles and puppy dog tails." Her huskies watched, loyal as ever, their eyes never leaving Aurelius.

She leaned in close, her breath warm against his face, though her voice was anything but kind. "My first question, you sap, concerns the Gaene Kin. Tell me all you know."

Dagma believed the Gaene Kin to be the one group that had slipped through the cracks of her mother's otherwise meticulous planning. Atropa had been vague—deliberately so, as usual—ranting about how she'd been wronged, convicted without trial, and chased from Valoria like a common dog. But Dagma wasn't about to charge in blindly. If she was to be a key player in this grand scheme of revenge, she needed to know every detail, every threat. And right now, the Gaene Kin were the only wild card left on the table.

Knowledge was power, and Dagma was about to arm herself with a weapon far deadlier than any sword in the Duke's showy collection.

A small flame danced on her fingertip, hovering just beneath Aurelius's ear. His cry ripped through the silence—a sound so raw and wretched it might have softened even the hardest of hearts. But not Dagma's. She was busy enjoying the power play; each anguished scream was like music to her ears. The flame traced a path from one earlobe to the other, eliciting a continuous chorus of desperate cries. Even her fearless huskies skittered back, their sensitive ears bombarded by the screams.

"I know silence is your main line of defence, you spineless sap," Dagma hissed, circling him like a vulture with a vendetta. "I know the real you—leader in title, but never in action. Always dodging decisions, sitting on the fence. Look at you—your high brow, that ridiculous mane of tarnished gold hair. You've got all the shine of a leader, but none of the balls."

Her hand shot downward, her grip closing around his testicles like a vice. "Shall I set these alight?" she asked with a sadistic smile. "You've clearly never used them—not even to make an heir. What use are they to you now?" Her fingers tightened. "I've always preferred to go straight for the pain points. Consider yourself lucky I'm not after the balls in your head. But these two," she gave another vicious squeeze, "will do nicely. I'll pickle them as a memento."

Aurelius's face contorted in agony, tears spilling down his cheeks, yet still he refused to speak. The flames on Dagma's fingertips flared brighter, throwing a menacing glow over his suffering. Despite the torment, his lips remained sealed.

Frustration rose in Dagma's eyes, but then gave way to cold calculation. She stepped back, extinguishing the flames with a sharp snap of her fingers. "Fine," she spat, her tone resolute. "If physical pain won't make you talk, let's see how you handle the death of innocents. I'll kill a child every hour until you spill what I need to know about the Gaene

Kin. Tell me what's in that stubborn old head of yours, or I'll crack it open like a walnut if I must—feed what's left of you to my huskies."

Aurelius finally broke in horror at her threat. "The Gaene Kin were a society of women," he began, his voice shaky.

"Ah, there we go," Dagma said, lounging into a plush chair as if settling in for a nice story. "Finally he speaks!" Her bony fingers drummed lazily against the chair's armrests, her eyes alight with triumph.

Aurelius fought to steady his voice. "They were skilled in harnessing nature's power. Healers. Their knowledge passed from mother to daughter, generation after generation. They understood the natural world, how it was tied to the well-being of the people. They made medicines, salves, and healed the sick. And in each generation, one among them served as adviser to Valoria's sovereign leader."

Behind her mask, Dagma licked her thin lips, like a snake flicking its tongue, collecting each morsel of information.

"They were called the High Priestesses of the Gaene Kin. The last of them, an adviser to King Valkarse, banished the entire order, casting them out of society. That's all I know."

"Liar!" Dagma shot up out of her chair, her fiery figure towering over him. "You're lying! Tell me more!"

"A royal decree in my father's time forbade everyone from speaking of them," Aurelius stammered. "They were dubbed witches to be feared. That is why no one of this generation remembers them." His head slumped, as if weighed down by guilt or exhaustion.

Furious, Dagma struck him hard across the face, her hand leaving an angry red welt. "Wake up, you spineless worm! Who banished them? Why? Where did they go?"

"I—I..." Aurelius hesitated.

The predator sized her prey. "Shall I fetch the first child to be slaughtered because you're too cowardly to speak the truth?" She paused, her expression shifting from rage to a sly realisation. "You're protecting someone, aren't you? That's why you're holding back. Who are you protecting? I demand to know!"

She stomped her foot, and sparks shot up her leg in a display of light that sent her huskies scampering into the corner, tails tucked between their legs. They knew their mistress's hot temper all too well.

"No! No! I will tell you," Aurelius gasped, desperately. "Please, don't harm anyone."

"That's better," the predator knew her prey had finally succumbed.

Aurelius was a pitiful sight. Her mother would have loved it. His waxy face was slick with sweat, each drop reflecting twofold in the fire's flames like a melting candle. Poetic in a way. But Dagma wasn't here for poetry—she was here for information.

"The last High Priestess saw herself as superior. She claimed dominion over the meeting place... where the coven gathered." Aurelius finally croaked out, each word sounding like it was being pulled from him with hot, iron tongs. "No one knows where it is, and she alone has the key."

Dagma's mind worked through the implications. *So, the Sylphic Sanctum is where the Gaene Kin gathered. Why did you not mention that, Mother?* she mused. Conveniently, Atropa had left out these crucial details, claiming only that the Sanctum was to serve as the watchtower in the east. It seemed integrity was not a strong suit in her family.

"After the High Priestess turned on her sisters and branded them as witches, their sacred places—once revered and respected—were abandoned. The knowledge they held was lost."

She had to be sure this was her mother. "Give me the High Priestess' name!"

"Atropa," Aurelius responded instantly, like a schoolboy reciting a well-rehearsed lesson. "The last adviser to the southern sovereign, King Valkarse. My father."

Oh, the irony. On one side, her mother—self-proclaimed ruler of Creation—had turned against her own kind, banishing them instead of using them. She'd feared their power and ousted them. On the other, this pitiful king had reduced the banishment of an entire section of society to a mere footnote, more concerned with the loss of their knowledge than their existence. Like a scholar mourning a burned library. Pathetic.

So, Mother dear, you thought them beneath you? Not worthy to mention? Turned against your own kind, did you? No wonder you skipped this little chapter in your story. A classic sign of megalomania—hoarding all the power for yourself.

But Dagma wasn't done. She had only just begun to wring Aurelius dry.

Chapter 26

No One Else Mattered

D AGMA LET THE QUIET stretch, watching Aurelius, waiting for the signs of discomfort that always surfaced when people did not know what was going to happen, but sensed it would hurt.

Predictably, he began to squirm.

Satisfied, she finally asked, "Did you ever meet any of the Gaene Kin?" Her tone was deceptively casual, as though asking what he'd had for lunch.

"As far as I know, they are dead," Aurelius muttered, clearly hoping to close the subject.

"That was not my question, you useless sap," she snapped, irritation flaring. "I need to know more. Salves. Healing. Banishment. Honestly, you *are* just a puppet—all show and no substance. You never really cared about your people, did you? Did you ever lift a finger to help them? You live off the reputation of your golden King Valerian, the first true sovereign. Now *he* was impressive! But you? What have you done? Nothing original, nothing of worth. All for show. Nieman was right to parade you like his little puppet on a string. That's all you are. Aesthetic. A beautiful palace. Beautiful clothes. But no beautiful wife or—"

Dagma stopped mid-rant, her sharp eyes catching a telltale twitch in Aurelius's expression. His pupils had undeniably dilated at the mention of a wife.

Oh, this is interesting.

"Well, well, what have we here?" she asked with a hungry lion's growl. "I do so love the human body. You men have certain signs you just can't hide when... *aroused*." Her gaze briefly dropped to his groin—not that there was anything to see—but the dilation of his pupils told her she'd struck a nerve. "You've known love, haven't you? Still do, by the looks of it."

Aurelius wriggled in his chair. He pulled his saggy, old arms futilely against the ropes binding him.

"It's no use, my regal friend," Dagma laughed, thoroughly enjoying herself. "You're not going anywhere. Now, tell me about this love of yours."

"Never!" Aurelius cried.

Dagma's non-existent eyebrows arched behind her mask. "Interesting how you react so passionately when I ask about your *lady* friend. Matters of the heart, it seems, mean more to you than your kingdom and your people. Now, I *definitely* want to know more."

"There's nothing to tell. Certainly nothing to tell you," Aurelius lashed out with uncharacteristic defiance.

Dagma, more amused than offended, cocked her head. "Oh, don't get your hackles in a twist, my regal sweetie. You seem to have forgotten who's in charge." She was inwardly thrilled to have hit such a sensitive spot. She hadn't expected this kind of reaction from the usually docile king. "Remember those little tots? Pop, pop, pop!" She sang it like a twisted nursery rhyme "Off with a head every hour, because Lady Dagma has the power!" But Aurelius's face only hardened.

"You wouldn't dare," he sneered. "Committing such an act of cruelty would turn the people against you. That would be counterintuitive to all you've done thus far. You've wanted the people on board. You wouldn't dare."

His smugness was as short-lived as it was ill-founded.

"As you should know by now, appearances can be deceiving," Dagma's tone was syrupy and sinister. "I don't give one iota what the people think. My plan—*our* plan—has always been to take over leadership of Valoria. And we've been successful there." She brought her fiery fingers under his chin, the heat making sweat pour down his face like a doll left too close to a fire. "Now, where were we? Ah yes, you were about to tell me about this lady love of yours."

Aurelius, now visibly shaking, clenched his jaw. But Dagma could see the cracks forming. He was oh-so-deliciously close to breaking.

Then, irritatingly, his demeanour shifted. The panic drained away, replaced by an unexpected calm. He was staring off into the distance. His eyes fixed on some invisible point in the corner of the room. It was as if he were no longer there, no longer bound by ropes of fear, but somewhere far from her reach, in a world of happier memories. It was revolting, really—how people could retreat into their own minds like that.

"It's not such a great secret, I suppose. Servants do gossip," Aurelius began, his voice softened by nostalgia. Dagma groaned involuntarily. *Of course,* she thought, *he's going to launch into some weepy tale of lost love instead of getting straight to the good stuff. Why did everyone insist on turning everything into a melodrama?*

"She was not only the most beautiful woman I had ever seen," Aurelius continued, now speaking as though narrating a love story to a room full of lovestruck romantics, rather than a fiery sorceress quickly losing her patience, "she was also the most talented. I hadn't meant to fall in love. I was set to marry another for duty, as tradition dictated. I accepted that. But she came to the palace one day with other healers. I had sprained my ankle while learning the dance for my wedding. My overprotective mother insisted it be healed immediately, so she brought them in to tend to me."

He paused, his eyes glazing further, as though he could see that long-ago day playing out before him. "I was no more than a boy really, on the verge of twenty. I had no control over my heart, and when I saw her, it was hers from that moment on. Since that day, nothing else has mattered—only her."

Dagma could practically feel the sentimental love seeping from his words. Her fingers twitched with the urge to slap him. But instead, she patiently folded her hands in her lap and verbally sliced through his fairytale cake with a heartless cynic's knife. "And then what? Come on, sweetie, spill the beans. Get to the good part. You lost your heart, your head, and clearly your virginity—then what?" Still, his gaze remained distant. "What happened?!"

Aurelius broke from his daydream with a jolt as Dagma gave him a sharp thump on the thigh. He let out a yelp, more from surprise than pain. "Goodness, woman, do you know no decorum?"

"Decorum?" Dagma laughed, the sound sharp and metallic. "I've no need for decorum. I'm a powerful sorceress, not some debutante at a coming-out party. Now, get on with it—and her name. I want the name." She snapped her fingers, each click sending small bursts of sparks into the air.

Aurelius sighed, the weight of the situation pressing down on his shoulders. Reluctantly, he continued, his nostalgia tainted with a bitterness that hadn't been there before. "Her name was Edina." Dagma couldn't believe how easily the name rolled off his disloyal tongue. "My mother instantly saw the connection between us when Edina came with the other healers. She told me it was a forbidden love—Edina was beneath my station."

"Excellent!" Dagma clapped her hands, creating sizzling, little flames. "Wait! You said she came with other healers. That means—oh, this is rich—that means there were *more* Gaene Kin!" She practically bounced in her seat, barely containing her malicious glee. "I love it, I love it, I love it! I could not have designed this better myself. My mother despises the Gaene Kin, and she hates *your* kind. Your lineage, your ancestors, and—" Dagma paused as a thought struck her. "Is there anyone my mother doesn't hate?"

With a dismissive wave, she continued. "Anyway! A descendant of the regal bastards she despises falls for a descendant of the witchy lowlifes she loathes. Oh, this is too delicious." Aurelius looked as though he wished the floor would open up and swallow him, but there was no escape. Dagma, practically vibrating with delight, hovered like a spider poised over a fly wriggling helplessly in its web.

"Tell me more," she insisted with foul, mock sweetness. "Don't leave out a single detail."

She paced back and forth, her thoughts spinning. Unlike the Duke, who could barely manage a coherent thought while on the move, Dagma thrived in motion. Walking fuelled her brain, each step generating new ideas and possibilities.

"Those healer witches must've had children. Which means they're still around. Still alive. Still a potential threat." She hadn't necessarily meant for her musings to be heard by Aurelius, whose shoulders somehow drooped even further.

"I think you'll find that highly unlikely, if the tales are true," Aurelius corrected her, his voice hollow. "After they were banished, they remained isolated on an island, separate from society. Being all women, their line will end."

"Hmm, possibly." Dagma considered that he might just be trying to throw her off the scent. Switching tactics, she asked, "How were they allowed into the palace, then? How did your mother even find them if they were hiding on some secluded island?"

"You're right to ask," Aurelius sighed, utterly defeated. His whole being seemed to sag, from his muscle-less shoulders to the folds of despair hanging under his eyes. "The Gaene Kin went into hiding. Only women knew of their whereabouts. Men weren't part of their circle. As for my mother, she was obsessed with appearances. She couldn't stand the idea of me limping at the wedding. Of course, our chief physician had no instant cure. You see, she didn't want to wait for my ankle to heal naturally, so she sought them out, the Gaene Kin, to relieve the swelling instantly."

"Where are they now? Where is your love now?" Dagma demanded, her face now inches from his, her black eyes boring into his soul through the slits of her porcelain mask. "You must know, for she's your life, your love, your *everything*."

"I don't know," Aurelius replied sadly.

Dagma shrieked with incredulity, "How can you not know? What kind of idiot are you? Is Valoria full of idiots? You love this woman, you don't marry her because of some tradition nonsense, and then you just lose her?"

Aurelius hung his head in shame. "Yes, I lost her. But not through any lack of effort on my part. Edina had feelings for me too, but she didn't want me to suffer. She hid herself away."

"How do you know this? You couldn't have seen her more than a handful of times."

"We met in secret," Aurelius admitted, the confession a bitter pill. "I promised her I'd be with her, give up the crown, everything. I even called off the wedding."

"Ooh, big promises from a big king," Dagma jeered. "I'd never have guessed that of you. Clearly, this woman motivated you to take action more than the entire population of Valoria."

Aurelius flinched but pressed on. "When she visited me last, she told me that life on the run with a hunted witch wasn't what she wanted for me. I haven't seen her since." His voice broke, and tears welled up in his eyes, his long-buried sorrow finally spilling over.

Dagma fell silent—not out of compassion, but because she knew, without a doubt, that Aurelius was telling the truth. There was no need for further threats, no reason to make him drink the elixir of truth she had prepared just in case. This oaf, this empty vessel of a man, had given her everything he knew. In his bumbling way, he had unwittingly given her even more.

She considered the situation. No young girl in the throes of first love would have given up so easily. A life on the run would have seemed like an adventure, not a burden—unless something weighed more heavily on her. Something like the demands of motherhood.

"Where is the child now?" Dagma's question struck like an arrow to the heart, hitting Aurelius with unexpected, callous clarity.

His body stiffened against the chair's restraints, as if he could somehow back away. Eyes wide and dry, he stared at Dagma as though she had spoken an impossible horror. "What?"

"Oh, you really are a moron," Dagma cackled. "You didn't know, did you? You didn't know Edina was with child!" She laughed long and hard. "Mother will love this story."

She moved to leave. Her hand hovered on the door handle, but she paused, as a wicked afterthought crossed her mind. "Oh dear, I almost forgot to say goodbye, didn't I, regal sweetie?"

With a sudden, savage motion, Dagma lifted her arm and struck Aurelius hard across the face. The blow was so fierce that Aurelius slumped in his chair, knocked unconscious by the force of it. Dagma stared down at the crumpled, useless heap with a satisfied grin.

"Well, I have no more need for him, do I?" She coaxed her huskies out from the corner where they'd cowered during her interrogation. "Come here, babies. He was a moron, wasn't he? But now we know. There *are* Gaene Kin out there. And this Edina—well, she's probably changed her identity by now. Though, if she fell for this bonehead, maybe she's not as bright as we thought."

She pushed her porcelain mask up to the top of her head, sighing in relief. "Bloody hot under there," she muttered. Her face, a charred landscape of scorched skin, was a piece of deviant macabre art.

"Guards!" she barked. Two men rushed in, their expressions barely concealed horror—whether at the sight of her face or their once-golden leader, she couldn't care less. "Lock the prisoner in the cellar. I'm done with him!"

The guards hesitated, their faces paling as they untied Aurelius, his regal form now a broken, sweaty wreck. One of them made a strangled noise and looked away.

Dagma rolled her eyes, thoroughly unimpressed. "Oh, come on, he's not that bad. Think of him as the loser in one of your tavern brawls." She waved them off with a flick of her wrist. "Same thing. Just another lowlife in the gutter."

As the guards dragged Aurelius from the room, limp and unconscious, Dagma laughed softly to herself. *Decorum?* she thought with a sneer. *I've no need for it. Or a face, for that matter. I'm a sorceress—with an army.*

Her huskies circled at her feet, sensing the triumphant energy radiating from their mistress.

Dagma fussed over them with affection. "Yes, my darlings, we've learned a lot today, haven't we? And this... this is only the beginning. Our baby drones are finally coming along nicely."

With her dark robes swirling around her like billows of smoke, she strode out, heading to her growing army of drones.

Chapter 27

MOTH TO A FLAME

S MELLING FAINTLY OF PINE from the resin and bark they had gathered, Cane and Gerant entered the Sanctum.

"The world drums to a different beat at dawn," Cane remarked to Gerant, glancing around. As a boy hunting in the woods of Cromlech, he'd always felt this quiet industriousness that filled the natural world as the day began to stir. It was the hour when everything felt most alive, as if every leaf, every insect, knew it had work to do before the sun rose and the day began proper.

The Sanctum itself was a hive of activity, each man engrossed in his task like busy bees. Bain's strong hands carved the oak, while Felix deftly hollowed out the wood with the same finesse he'd use to scoop a potato from its jacket. Rowan stood nearby, his arms full of hemp, which Tristan and Percy were splitting into fine, fibrous strings.

Here, in the same room where the Gaene Kin had once prepared their secret brews, they were crafting something new. Knife cuts and stains from crushed herbs still marked the surface of the large, well-worn table that dominated the room. Shelves filled with old jars and containers filled with forgotten ingredients of roots, dried leaves, and powders lined the walls.

Decades of fire had blackened the stone arch of the deep-set hearth that took up most of one wall. Now, a cheerful fire blazed within. The smell of burning wood mingled with the faint scents of the past—ghost traces of dried rosemary, sage, potions.

Settling near the flames, Lycus and the lynx basked in the warmth, their eyes half-closed in contentment. Cane wondered at the surreal sense of domesticity—a group of fugitives and legendary creatures finding shared peace in a sacred space. It was as if they'd become a family of sorts—a bizarre, mismatched family in an equally bizarre home setting.

A whining Percy, however, wasn't quite sharing in the warm feelings. "I can still hear its voice ringing in my ears," he groaned, pressing his hands to his temples as if that might somehow silence the noise.

"Careful, you'll flatten your curls," Tristan teased. "How will you claim to be the heir of the legendary Perceval if you end up with straight hair!"

Percy scowled. "It's not funny. Doesn't anyone else hear it? This unbearable ringing, like the cries of a thousand birds trapped inside my head."

"I do, brother. It's bloody maddening. But what can you do. I'm sure it'll fade. Plus, if the oldies aren't complaining—"

"I think it's precisely because we are older that we can't hear it," Felix chuckled. "Ah, the joys of being young. For me, it's more like a dull buzzing at the back of my head. Reminds me of my wife, until I lost her—God rest her soul."

That shut everyone up. Felix had been married?

"Well, I didn't *lose* her," Felix corrected. "I couldn't have lost her even if I tried. She was colossal. I looked like a juicy little berry next to a giant Samhain jack-o'-lantern at our wedding. All for the good of our families of course—you know, uniting lands and tithes and all that."

"So, what happened?" Tristan asked. "Where is she now?"

"Though I didn't have the good fortune to lose her, one could say she was taken off my hands. I was lucky enough to have her run off with our head cook. He was probably after her for her money. She told me it was because he made her feel beautiful, and I didn't. When I failed to react in disappointment at being jilted, she tactlessly detailed their numerous amorous and heated encounters in the pig shed."

The room collectively cringed.

"Now that nasty image is painted indelibly in my mind," Felix continued. "Poor pigs, how they must have suffered with all that grunting and squealing—"

"Yes, I think we get the picture, thank you, Felix," Gerant interjected, saving them all from further details.

Cane silently thanked Gerant for stepping in. The mental image was beginning to bend his mind more than the sylph had.

Felix shrugged. "Anyway, that's why I got into cooking. So, even my large, unfaithful wife story has a silver lining."

"Well, Felix, I think I speak for all of us when I say we're eternally grateful your marital misfortune turned you into such a culinary wizard. Your stews are the only thing keeping our spirits up some days."

The others nodded in agreement, relieved by the change in topic.

"Honestly," said Gerant, "if it weren't for you, we'd probably be roasting our boots by now or scavenging poisonous roots. So, here's to you, Felix—the man who turned marital misfortune into mouthwatering meals."

Smiling, they resumed their crafting in silence until Percy asked, "Do you think the sylph will help us once we've given these offerings? The ten of us can't go up against a whole army."

"I don't think they're here to help," Bain said bluntly. "They're here to tell it like it is. They've probably had it up to here with watching the same screw-ups over and over."

"Then why don't they just tell us what to do so we don't keep messing up?" Percy asked.

"It's not that simple," Godfrey said. "They don't see things as right or wrong—just different outcomes. In nature, things sometimes have to fall apart for change to happen. Their job isn't to make everything perfect; it's to keep the energy moving, to make sure life keeps communicating."

"Well, they're a bit full of themselves, aren't they?" Tristan grumbled. "There are other essential things in life after all. What makes them think they're the best?"

"Probably because without air, everything else would die," Bain pointed out.

"Oh," Tristan said. "I didn't know that."

"Because you never paid attention to our tutors," Percy tattled.

"Without air, fire wouldn't burn," Godfrey added. "It's in the water, too. It makes sure the earth breathes. Without it, plants wouldn't grow. So, I'd say the sylphs have a good reason to feel superior."

His eyes glazing over, Cane couldn't help but feel he had a more pressing mission in mind: to find Agatha. Rising to his feet, barely aware of the growing restlessness tugging at him, he walked out of the room as though some unseen force guided him.

A pang of concern crept in with each moment he couldn't find her, growing into an unexplained urgency. Had she been taken by the Duke? Or worse, was she off doing something reckless? With thoughts bouncing between mild panic and paranoid suspicion, Cane knocked on the door of the small room she was supposed to be using. No answer. Fantastic. The teeter-totter of anxiety in his mind swung wildly as he rushed from chamber to chamber—still no Agatha.

Only one place left to check: the ritual room. He entered, half-expecting to find a note saying, *Gone to kill my sister, back later!* But no, it was just an empty room with an electric hum in the air. He caught sight of the silver-framed mirror and moved as far away from it as possible, keeping his gaze down.

His ears pricked at the sound of splashing, drawing him to the fountain. The surface lay undisturbed, smooth as glass. Just as he began to doubt his senses, Agatha rose from its shallow depths, her presence both sudden and surreal.

Cane nearly jumped out of his skin. "What are you *doing* in there?"

"Oh, you startled me!" she said guiltily, as though she'd been caught trespassing.

"Why are you in the water?"

"At first, I just wanted to bathe. I'm not used to going for days without washing." She smiled sheepishly. "Then, I had the strangest notion that I needed complete silence," she explained, her excitement growing. "Everywhere I go, I hear things; even at night, the trees rustle, the owls hoot. I hear the others turning in their beds. I hear the fountain. But under water, the world turns silent. When the water stops flowing, there is complete silence down there. I only hear the beating of my heart and my thoughts. And finally, there, in the solitude and cradle of the water, I found my memory."

Cane offered his hand to help her out of the pool, doing his best to ignore the fact that she was only in her undergarments. *Bold*, he thought quickly averting his eyes. Not seeing her clothes anywhere, he handed her his cloak, all while wondering if she'd walked through the Sanctum like that.

They headed over to the benches by the wardrobe that held the Gaene Kin's robes. As they sat down, Cane couldn't help but admire how beautiful she looked, her wet hair swept back with a few undone plaits framing her face.

"What did you remember about your past?" he asked quietly, trying to focus on the conversation instead of her beauty.

Agatha turned away, fiddling with a brass ring on her finger. Cane couldn't tell if she was being shy, thoughtful, or just trying to figure out how to drop some earth-shattering news on him. She started talking about a necklace that used to match her brass ring. Something about not exactly having time to pack when they left the castle in such a hurry. She laughed nervously.

"I can't really turn that day you found me into anything funny, can I?" she said coquettishly.

Cane was trying to keep up with her words now, his brain was starting to feel like it was wrapped in a thick blanket. *What's happening? Why is she talking about jewellery?* Was he losing his grip on reality, or had the sylph rewired his mind? Agatha slipped her small hand into his, and suddenly, a wave of warmth shot through him, followed by a surge of... *something*. Something hot. Something awkwardly passionate.

Mortified by the direction his thoughts—and certain other *things*—were heading, Cane shot up from the bench and began pacing like a man who just realised he had sat on a nail.

Agatha's expression turned to one of hurt and confusion, her big eyes glistening with tears waiting to fall. "Oh. I'm sorry," she said. "That was tactless of me."

"No, no, don't be. I er, I er—" Cane had no idea how to politely explain why he had turned his back to her. *God, if only I hadn't given her my cloak—at least then I could hide it!* Panicking, he made straight for the wardrobe and yanked out a long black robe with silver-embroidered birds on its cuffs. "Which one do you think the High Priestess wore?" he asked, trying to sound casual but probably looking insane as he held the robe up to his body.

Agatha blinked in bewilderment, watching him dive into the wardrobe like a child playing dress-up. "I'm not sure," she replied, clearly puzzled by his sudden fixation on fashion. She watched as he pulled out another robe, this time a deep purple number that would have made any gothic underlord proud. "Must have been this one, wouldn't you say?"

"Are you feeling alright?"

"Yes, yes, quite alright. Very alright, too alright," Cane blurted out, grinning like an idiot. His composure long gone, leaving him stranded in a sea of awkwardness.

"Or maybe this one?" he said, his hands now moving at top speed as he flung robes in and out of the wardrobe. Why wouldn't this problem just go away? He couldn't very well sprint out of the room and leave her there, could he?

"Maybe the sylph did something to your mind," Agatha, suggested with genuine concern. "You're not acting quite yourself."

"Oh, well maybe, yes. I am feeling... oh god, yes, I am feeling," he said, words tumbling out faster than he could catch them. "I am feeling very much, err, yes. Feeling very much."

Before he could spiral any further into his word salad, Agatha approached him, calm and collected. She gently took the robe from him and placed it back in the wardrobe, while Cane tried to keep his composure from unravelling like a knitted jumper. He realised with some relief that she was behind him now—out of sight, out of problem.

But then she tried to guide him back to the bench to help him recompose, and Cane found himself doing some bizarre side-step dance to keep his back to her. By the fifth round of this ludicrous waltz, Agatha finally gave up and placed her fingers on his temples. Cane's heart nearly exploded out of his chest. *Please don't let me be drooling.*

"It must be something that spirit did to you. Here, let me help you relax," she said soothingly, her fingers moving in slow, deliberate circles. Cane felt his tension—well, *some* of it—start to melt away. She gently nudged him to sit down, and, like a crab scuttling sideways, he manoeuvred himself back onto the bench, careful to keep his back to her.

Agatha continued massaging his temples, and Cane was quickly turning into a blur of bliss and forgetfulness. Every touch sent shivers through his body, each one more inebriating than the last.

"There, that's better," she said, her voice as sweet as honey.

Cane's mind was doing somersaults. His thoughts seemed to have taken on a life of their own, blending together into one big, confusing hodgepodge.

"Are you from Caldera as well, then?" Why had he asked that? His mouth was working independently of his brain, like a ship's rudder detached from its wheel. "Why don't you answ—, ans-swear?" he stammered, his words as slurred as his thoughts. Was he drunk on love, or was it Agatha's touch? Not that it mattered—he was swimming in bliss and had no intention of throwing himself a lifeline. "No, seriously. I'm sincerely interested in your past, Agatha. What did you remember in the fountain pool?"

He heard his voice, but it still seemed to be operating on its own accord, and not a particularly competent one at that.

"You'll most certainly forget my words. You won't remember that I am indeed a daughter of Caldera. That I came to Valoria with my sister Dagma. We had a mission."

"How exciting for you." Cane's eyelids drooped as if weighted down by invisible anchors.

"You see, I knew you wouldn't be interested," Agatha said, disappointed.

"No, no, please go on." Cane tried fight off a yawn that could have been measured in leagues.

"I remembered my home is called Caldera. The land of fire." Agatha's voice guided him over to the large stone table, and he followed her like a happy puppy. She opened a massive leather-bound tome of land maps and constellations, turning to a specific page without even seeming to touch it. "You see, on this page, the map plotted by the Octules, that is where Caldera lies."

Her words tripped over each other in his brain. Jostling this way and that like loose coins. Cane squinted at the map, trying to make sense of the details. His mind felt like it was wading through treacle. "But how did they travel between these lands?" he asked.

"Most likely by sea and air. The Octules come from Octavia, a hidden tropical land." Agatha pointed to a distant marker on the map. "That's Octavia."

Cane blinked, trying to stay focused on her words. "I always thought the Octules were... well, that they never really existed. My father talks about them like they were lur-gends," he slurred, his tongue seemingly deciding to fold in two and take a nap.

"They had to have existed; otherwise, this Sanctum wouldn't be here, and we—"

"—and we would be outside!" Cane chuckled at his own joke. "Oh, sorry for interrupting. What were you saying?"

"It is I who should apologise. I am boring you, aren't I?"

"No, no, noooo. Not at all. What else do you remember. Did you love that old Baron?"

Cane was barely holding onto the thread of the conversation—or maybe he wasn't holding onto anything at all. Somewhere in that haze, he realised he'd asked a rather idiotic question about the Baron. Why did he even care? But Agatha's tears pulled him back to reality—or whatever version of reality he was currently experiencing.

As she wept softly, he awkwardly wrapped an arm around her, and she rested her head on his shoulder. He could feel the fog in his head thickening, as if someone had stuffed his skull with cotton. His eyelids drooped, but he fought to stay alert, even as Agatha decided it was time to call it a night. "Yes!" Cane jolted upright, suddenly wide awake and disoriented, like a startled cat. Had she answered his question? "I'll walk you back home. You never know who's out on the streets at this time of night." He zigzagged with Agatha to her room, managing to avoid walking into walls by sheer luck.

"You need to get into some dry clothes. Sleep well," he said, trying to sound composed, though his mind was still spinning like a top. Oh god, he wanted to kiss her, but instead, he stared at her emerald eyes, sparkling like jewels, and the way she absentmindedly twirled her silver hair on her finger. When she handed back his cloak with a grateful smile, he nearly melted into a puddle right there in the hallway.

As she turned in for the night, Cane stood there, cloak in hand, pondering like a man who'd misplaced his wits. Should he go back in? He shouldn't go in. But hadn't he already been in? The sequence was fuzzy, but the scent of her now lingering on his cloak was not. He took a deep whiff, grinning like a lovesick fool.

Dazed, Cane wandered back to the others by the fire, sliding down the smooth alabaster wall, staring dreamily into the flames. Agatha had mentioned something about a land of fire, but that thought drifted away as sleep claimed him.

Watching him stupefied, his friends weren't exactly thrilled. "Hey! Are you going to help or what?" Blake's voice rang out, but Cane was far too deep in his stupor to respond.

Blake approached, hand raised.

"What do you think you're doing?" Bain quickly grabbed Blake's hand before it could make contact.

"I was just going to give him a little tap on his handsome face to wake him up," Blake said earnestly. "Without my super strength, it wouldn't have hurt. Promise."

"I have a better idea," Bain said, his tone suggesting he'd just had a stroke of genius. He spooned some resin they had collected for the sylph, put it in a cup, and hung it over the fire. Within seconds, the room filled with sweet-smelling smoke.

"Bloody hell," Percy muttered, waving his hands futilely as the smoke swallowed him whole. "I can't see a bloody thing."

"What did you do that for?" Gerant asked, eyes watering.

"When Cane spoke to the sylph, he said the resins cleared the mind and purified the air," Bain said. "*I* was listening."

"There was nothing wrong with the air before," Percy grumbled, still flapping his hands around.

"No, but there was something wrong with Cane's mind, so I thought I'd clear it."

"Excellent idea, old chap!" Gerant said, impressed. "If nothing else, we won't smell as bad after so many days without washing."

"Ah! What a heavenly aroma," Rowan sighed, inhaling deeply like a man who'd just discovered the meaning of life. "Intoxicating. It fills my senses."

"Nectar of the gods," Felix added in agreement.

"It actually is," said Godfrey. "Food for the gods, I mean. The queen of such resins is copal, used by the Tunderians to summon the gods and placed in the mouths of the departed to nourish them in the afterlife. Some use it to communicate with the dead."

"It's enough to raise the dead," Percy coughed, clearly unimpressed by Godfrey's trivia.

"Goodness, Father, is there anything you don't know? You're like a walking encyclopaedia of esoteric trivia."

"Never mind that. What have you been doing?" Godfrey asked.

"I have no idea," came the sleepy reply.

Chapter 28

EDGES OF MADNESS

"F INALLY!" BAIN SAID, USING a stick to remove the cup from the fire. "Cane has returned to the land of the living."

"Someone open the Sanctum door," Felix groaned, squinting through the smoke. "All this clarity of thought is unbearable. I'm not used to it." He tipped back his flask of port. "This'll help dull it."

Cane, still feeling as though his brain had turned to honeycomb, was startled by the sound of his father's voice. "What happened to you, son?"

"I'm not sure what you mean," Cane replied, though truthfully, he wasn't sure what *he* meant either.

"You were gone for hours, then you came back and fell into a dead sleep."

"Oh, really? I just went to make sure the Baroness was alright and—"

"No need to explain," Blake interrupted with an exaggerated wink that looked more like he had something stuck in his eye. "I'd have done the same." The insinuation flew right over Cane's head.

"Yes, well, she *was* alright—"

"I bet she was," Blake snickered, clearly relishing Cane's confusion.

"—so I escorted her to one of the rooms, and she's resting now," Cane finished, still oblivious to Blake's innuendo. "Seems like I missed out on all the action here."

"Oh, I don't think you missed out on *any* action!" Blake grinned like the cat that got the cream, his eyebrows bouncing up and down.

"Have you got something in your eye, Blake?" Cane asked in all seriousness.

"Alright, Blake," Gerant cut in. "Enough teasing the poor lad. We have more important things to do. We need to make plans."

"And bigger chimes," Tristan added, fiddling with his small creations. "These ones wouldn't even get a bat's attention."

"I suggest we all get some proper sleep," Gerant said.

They bedded down around the fire in the resin-scented room, and Cane, still in a fog, soon drifted off. His dreams were vivid, so much so that he half-wondered if the sylph had put something into his mind while he was probing around, opening portals. Sylphs mess with thought and time—

It felt like only seconds later when, before he could even finish that thought, when everyone woke up.

Awake, the group was abuzz with energy. Gerant was beaming like the sun. "I've got a corker of a plan. It came to me as if hand-delivered by the god of cunning. I know how to get the people back on our side."

"I know how to make bigger chimes!" Tristan whooped, practically dragging Percy outside before his brother had time to protest.

"Me too!" Percy echoed, though it was hard to tell if he was genuinely excited or just caught up in Tristan's rush of enthusiasm.

"I've come up with the best menu you could ever dream of," Felix announced, rubbing his hands together. "Rowan, will you help me gather supplies?"

"No," Rowan replied politely. "I have some of my finest poetry I must commit to paper. I fear it will take me at least a week."

"I'll help," came Agatha's voice. Cane's heart flip-flopped.

"Oh! Where did you come from?" Felix asked, startled. "I mean, thank you, Baroness."

"Any flashes of inspiration on your end, Bain?" Gerant asked, keeping the momentum going.

"Actually, yes," Bain replied, though with less enthusiasm than the others. "I've thought of a better way to collect, store, and burn the resin more efficiently." He turned to the Earl. "All good with you, sir?"

Godfrey, smiling serenely, nodded. "Yes, thank you. I spent a lovely evening with my wife; it felt so real." He glanced over at Cane. "And you, son? Did the resin smoke affect your sleep?"

Cane rubbed his forehead, feeling as though a tiny but persistent hammer was tapping away at his skull. "I can't seem to think straight. My thoughts are all jumbled. That sylph did something when it was in my head."

"It said it unlocked the portal." Godfrey's reply didn't bring Cane much comfort. His brain felt like it had been not only opened but turned inside out and given a vigorous shake for good measure.

"Come, son, let's go for a walk and talk. That helps to ease my thoughts sometimes."

A walk sounded like just the thing he needed to try and make sense of the pandemonium that had set up camp in his mind—and perhaps clear some of the fog.

"Good idea, I'll meet you shortly." Cane went to gather his hunting gear.

As he stepped into the crisp winter morning, the bite of cold air lifted his mood instantly. He blinked away the watery tears, taking in the scene before him—Percy and Tristan tumbling through the field with the wolves, who seemed to have forgotten they were supposed to be fearsome beasts and not oversized playmates.

Beneath a large oak, Gerant was casually taking notes while a bear cub snuggled in his lap. If anyone could make a bear cub look like a lapdog, it was Gerant. Nearby, Bain emerged from the Sanctum carrying pouches and tools, his expression set in quiet determination.

"Take your time," Blake said, clapping a reassuring hand on Cane's shoulder with enough force to make him stagger. "Things will get clearer."

Unconvinced, Cane nodded more out of politeness than conviction.

"Things never stay the same!" Felix said cheerfully. He was with Agatha, both of them carrying baskets. "Good job those Gaene Kin left all these behind—perfect for scrumping and harvesting!"

Agatha held up the tiniest, most impractical basket shaped like a mushroom. "Even a little one for mushrooms." It would struggle to hold a single sprig of thyme, let alone a mushroom.

Though he felt like a shirt buttoned up all wrong, Cane managed a smile. "Did you.... sleep well?"

"Yes, very well, thank you," Agatha replied sweetly.

"Come along, Baroness! No time for dawdling!" Felix called, already marching ahead. "We've got hungry mouths to feed—and then Tristan and Percy, the bottomless pits!"

With a hasty lift of her skirts, Agatha hurried after Felix, her tiny basket swinging uselessly at her side.

Felix turned back, raising his voice for Cane to hear. "And while you're out walking, Cane, shoot us some grouse—or maybe a deer!"

Grateful for the excuse to focus on something practical, Cane secured his quiver and hooked on his bow. Shooting arrows was second nature to him. Far easier than undoing the knot in his chest and head.

Just as he was about to set off, his father called to him. "What happened to our walk and talk?"

A pang of guilt stirred in him. "Father, I... I think I need to take this walk alone. I'm sorry."

"No need for apologies, son. I fully understand. I was a young man once too, remember."

Cane's throat tightened as his father embraced him. It was the kind of hug that used to make everything better. Yet, when he stepped back, he felt like something had slipped away, something he couldn't grasp or put back. He resisted the urge to hold onto his father. This was *his* burden to bear, *his* muddled mind to sort out.

His thoughts spiralled into a double helix of grief and confusion. He wanted to cry out, to tell his father everything—about how his grip on life was crumbling, how the world he once knew had vanished, how he missed his mother, so deeply it hurt to breathe. But the words wouldn't come.

Instead, he simply nodded. Without another word, he walked into the forest, the weight of the new world pressing on him.

The trees' cool embrace, at least, offered a quiet refuge, where he could wrestle with his thoughts in peace, away from the watchful eyes of those who might expect answers he could not give. Tall and ancient, they shielded him from the events that had recently upended his life. Here, beneath nature's canopy, time slowed, and for just a moment, he could pretend that everything outside these woods did not exist.

He knew, of course, that he could not avoid his tangled thoughts forever. They lurked just beyond the edges of his mind, waiting to ambush him the moment he let his guard down. But for now, the simple act of walking was helping. The repetitive rhythm of his steps opened up space in his head—space where the fog began to lift.

Just as he was starting to appreciate the clarity, a movement caught his eye. A deer—a beautiful beast, all grace and innocence, completely unaware of the world's troubles. Cane stilled, taking aim. The focus required to line up the shot silenced the noise, pushed away unwelcome thoughts. For a brief, blissful moment, his mind was clear.

But as soon as he noticed the silence, the floodgates opened. In an instant, his mind was awash with a torrent of thoughts: *How can I kill such a majestic creature? What happened with the Baroness last night? Who is Atropa? Why do the shadows whisper her name? Why do I sense things before they happen? And what's with those dreams about volcanoes and bubbling heat? Are the plants talking? Why do I know what this herb does?* He glanced down at the plant by his feet, recognising its properties without ever studying it. *Why do I know and hear these things? Did my father teach me this as a boy?*

The onslaught of thoughts rose to a deafening crescendo, a cacophony that drove Cane to his knees. Hands clamped over his ears, as if trying to drown out the din inside his own skull. Eyes squeezed shut, he released a strangled scream of anguish. It tore from his soul, clawing skyward like a desperate plea for mercy.

Startled by his sudden collapse, the deer fled into the forest, grateful not to be the one in pain.

Cane's stifled cry raged on, a tortuous mass of grief, anger, and loss that coiled tightly in his chest, constricting his throat until he thought he might choke on it. His eyes stung with tears that refused to fall, and he couldn't tell where the pain began or if it would ever end. He was powerless, a man coming apart at the seams.

Then suddenly, he was running. He didn't remember getting to his feet, his body had taken over, demanding air to fuel his desperate flight. He sprinted through the forest, his long legs carrying him faster than he knew they could. The roots and underbrush that should have tripped him seemed to part in his wake, as if the forest itself were clearing a path for him.

As he ran, the knot of anguish in his chest began to loosen, slowly unwinding. He could almost see it now, this dark, coiled mass of pain, leaving his body and dissipating into the air around him. Just like that, it was gone. Vanished. Though his chest heaved and his legs felt numb, his mind was his own again. For the first time in what felt like a lifetime, Cane smiled. A real, genuine smile.

Relief flooded him. He was fine—no, he was more than fine. He was free. He felt weightless, running through the woods like a man reborn. Laughter bubbled up from his chest, the wild, euphoric cry of someone who had discovered the alchemists' secret formula.

He slowed, eventually stopping to catch his breath. Everything around him seemed impossibly beautiful. The world wasn't wicked; it was magnificent, pulsing with life. And Cane wanted to be part of it. He *would* be part of it. He *would* help his new friends, fight for them, and do whatever it took to protect this world.

But then, a thought struck him like an icy splash of water. *Wait—where am I?* Glancing around, he realised he had no idea where his impromptu run had taken him.

"Well, being a crazy person might have its upsides, but getting lost definitely isn't one of them," he chuckled to himself.

Despite the disorientation, a warm feeling filled him. His father, his friends—his new family—were waiting for him. They needed him. His father especially, after all he had endured. A surge of purpose swelled within him, a deep-seated need to protect and help those he cared about. His mind felt clearer than it had in days.

He knew exactly where he was headed. Well, except in the immediate sense. Somehow, in the rush of it all, he had lost his way in the woods—a rare occurrence for someone nicknamed the walking compass by his school peers, but even the best lose their bearings sometimes. Now, which direction?

Voices reached his ears—men's voices. Cane froze, as still as the deer he'd seen earlier. In a fluid movement, he crouched down and hastily covered himself with soggy leaves and snow, blending into the forest floor as best he could. The snapping of frozen twigs under boots grew louder. Through his cover, he glimpsed the glint of metal—a sword, a helmet—catching in the sunlight. He held his breath, every muscle tensed, hoping the dead leaves would be enough to hide him.

"Search over there!" a gruff voice yelled.

"I 'ave! There's nothin' 'ere!" came a grumbling reply, thick with a local Bellingham accent.

"Do it again! The lady's growin' anxious. We've gotta find somefin'," the first voice insisted.

Cane pressed himself deeper into the earth, almost willing the ground to swallow him. His mind sifted through his options: *Don't move, don't breathe, don't even think too loudly.* If they found him, he would be placing his friends in danger. Footsteps crunched just inches away, close enough that he could see mud-caked boots, guards' boots. Nieman's guards, bearing that ridiculous dragonfly crest. His heart pounded so loudly in his chest, he was sure they could hear it. A cough tickled the back of his dry throat. Desperately, he clamped a hand over his mouth, barely smothering it in time.

"What woz that?" the gruff voice demanded.

"Ah, noffin'. Just a rat ferretin' about… or maybe the wind. You take this job too serious, like. Long as we're out 'ere long enough, you'll get paid. Now come on, I'm starvin'," the other guard muttered, more interested in his next meal than the search.

"Me too. 'Ungry and firsty," the first guard grouched with a rough laugh. "Let's hit the Pinky Tavern in Milsop, get trollied for a few days, then go back and tell the missus we ain't found nothin'."

"Yer, sounds good, let's do that."

Cane dared to let out an exhale slowly, praying they would soon be gone. But then one of the guards spoke up again.

"Wait, 'old on—wot's that?"

"Wot?"

"Ooh, check out this bit of tomfoolery."

"It don't sparkle. It ain't worth nothin'. Leave it."

"You daft?"

The question seemed to stump the second guard for a moment.

"Uh, no. Don't fink so."

"We'll take it to the lady. Shows we've been searchin', don't it? She'll re-compense us."

"I've never been compensed in me life. Me parents weren't even religious."

"Nah, block 'ead. She'll reward us."

"Oh, yeah, that. Can we still get trollied?"

"A celebratory drink, is in order. She might make us sergeant."

Their laughter faded as they moved away. Cane didn't dare move. He stayed perfectly still, every muscle locked in place, even as his mind threatened to betray him. The thoughts, those cursed thoughts, rushed back in. Images, words, sensations—none of them his—swirled in his head, pushing him to the brink of madness. He closed his eyes, fighting to keep a scream from escaping his throat, knowing that any sound could give hi m away.

Was it Agatha's jewellery they found? Flashes of her ring, something about a matching necklace scorched through his thoughts. Had she dropped it on purpose?

Time lost all meaning as Cane lay there, his earlier breakthrough now muddied with doubts about Agatha. Were the guards still nearby, or had they gone? *How long should I wait?*

Then, he saw it—a familiar tail brushing above the delicate cottontail blossoms. Lycus. The sight of the wolf's tail was like a beacon in the storm of his thoughts. Lycus nudged him gently, the wolf's calm presence a godsend, his guiding angel on four paws.

Cane slowly pushed himself up, his limbs stiff from lying still for so long. He followed Lycus back toward the Sanctum, the wolf leading him through the thickening forest. Along the way, they paused to hunt grouse. Focusing on the hunt—on the arrow, the target, the silent synchronisation between man and wolf—calmed the remnants of his mental maelstrom.

As they walked on, Cane let the quiet sounds of the forest wash over him: the soft swish of trees, Lycus's gentle pitter-patter on the ground. It was a welcome reprieve. Yet, beneath this outward serenity, an inner conflict denied him true peace. Suspicion simmered. His instincts screamed: *She dropped it on purpose.*

Chapter 29

A Thorn Within

K NEELING IN THE FROSTY grass, Agatha dutifully foraged for anything remotely edible. So far, she had only managed to scrape up a few scraggly fennel plants. Hardly enough to impress anyone, especially Bain, who seemed to hold a particular grudge against her. *It's that fire incident at the monastery*, she thought with a sigh. *And, of course, it was all Dagma's fault.* Her sister's insufferable competitiveness had always left Agatha picking up the pieces.

She shook off the thought, trying to focus on her task. If she could just find something more substantial, they might start to like her. At the very least, they wouldn't see her as a burden, or worse, as if she might sprout fangs at any moment.

Lost in her thoughts, she jumped when a hand suddenly touched her shoulder.

"Oh, Earl of Cromlech!" She spun around to see the elderly nobleman smiling down at her. "You startled me."

"Apologies, Baroness," Godfrey said with an apologetic grin. "I've been waving for a while, but you were miles away. I was wondering if you'd help me collect some watercress by the stream. The stones are a bit slippery. At my age, well, I'm not as spry as I used to be."

Relief warmed Agatha. *At least someone here doesn't think I'm entirely useless.* "Of course. I'd be glad to help." She glanced over at the stream, where a thick patch of watercress flourished. *This could be my chance to win them over.*

"Thank you." Godfrey handed her his basket. "I'll take over the fennel hunt, then." He glanced at the pitifully tiny basket. "Maybe I'll fetch another one."

"Oh, no, we can share." As they walked to the water's edge, Agatha allowed herself a small smile. She could contribute, she could be useful. Maybe, with time, even *likeable*.

She was just about to gather the watercress when she spotted Cane emerging from the woods. His clothes were torn, twigs stuck in his hair, yet somehow, his disarray only enhanced his appeal.

Oh, for heaven's sake, she scolded herself, her pulse quickening. *How is it possible for anyone to look that good?* From her spot by the stream, she had the perfect vantage to observe him—and observe she did. His strong arms, broad chest, and complete obliviousness to his own beauty. *It's almost unfair. No one person should have all that beauty to themselves.*

She admired his modesty, too. Cane was a man bound by duty, a man with morals—oh, hadn't she learned *that* the hard way! The memory of their night by the fountain made her blush. Most men would've taken advantage, but not him. *He's not boring*, she reassured herself, though she couldn't help but compare him to the others—Gerant with his commanding presence, Blake with his boldness, Rowan with his poetry, and the charismatic Felix, always so uplifting. Cane didn't have their outward flair, but maybe that was why she found him so intriguing. He didn't flaunt his qualities.

Her thoughts wandered as she watched him, noticing how his torn shirt revealed his muscular arms and torso. Her heart knocked in her chest like a giant on a door, demanding entrance. *Get a grip, Agatha,* she mentally slapped herself, but her body was not cooperating. Heat flushed through her, as though she might combust on the spot.

The only solution was to cool down before she did something embarrassing. Stepping into the stream, she splashed herself with icy water, steam hissed from her skin. *Much better*, she thought, her pulse returning to a somewhat reasonable pace.

Yes, Cane is attractive, she admitted, *but I can't go around acting like some doe-eyed schoolgirl.* She tried to distract herself by thinking of something less appealing—Blake's bushy moustache popped into her head. She shuddered in revulsion. *How do women find that attractive?* It was no surprise her tastes weren't the same as most in Valoria. She'd never imagined herself being so drawn to a man, especially not one like Cane. That Baron had been a beast by comparison. *Well, he's with his love like he wanted*, she thought with a giggle.

Felix's voice interrupted her thoughts. "You've been gone for an age, Cane. What happened to you?" He was already busy plucking the grouse Cane had brought back. "You look like you've been dragged through a hedge backwards."

"They're still searching for us," Cane said.

Agatha, now fully recomposed, returned with Godfrey to join them, listening intently to Cane's news.

"It was the Duke's men. They're searching for us under Dagma's orders. They mentioned a 'lady', I'm sure it's her; though they didn't seem very thorough. They found a necklace. I couldn't see it. Then they went off to Milsop where they'll get drunk and hide out long enough to convince Dagma that they've done a proper job before heading back."

"We have to move faster," Gerant said. "We have but a few days at most. And no more venturing beyond the cottontail field. What kind of necklace did they—"

But Agatha didn't hear the rest. One moment, she was gawping at Cane, admiring the firmness of his torso and hoping she was not slabbering; the next, the world flipped upside down. Literally. The sky vanished, replaced by darkness. *What in the blazes is happening?* Her head throbbed, and she realised with a start that she'd been hit. *Dagma.* The name careered through her mind. *This has her written all over it. "Slight your sister's eyes", or "Darken your sibling's sight"—some stupid spell with an equally stupid title. I wish I'd been an only child.*

She could hear voices around her, but she couldn't see a thing. *Great. Just great. Now I'm blind and possibly concussed.*

"Oh dear, oh dear!" Godfrey's voice sounded panicked.

"What is it?" Bain's rational tone cut in. "What was that crashing sound?"

"Oh dear, it's the Baroness. I think she's fainted."

Fainted? Agatha fumed inwardly. *That's a safe assumption, unless I'm taking a nap in the mud!*

"Help me get her up!" *Cane. Finally!*

Agatha felt hands fumbling to untangle her dress and hair from the thorny bushes. *Who on earth is handling me like a trussed-up pheasant?* Then came a more pressing concern—*whose hands are on my thighs? Please don't let it be Blake,* she prayed silently.

Blake had been giving her that smarmy 'I'm available' look since the day they met. How any woman found that ridiculous broom of a moustache of his attractive—*Focus, Agatha!*

But before she could drop into another mental rabbit hole, the hands on her thighs lifted her up, only to drop her like a scorching coal.

"Oh my god, she's boiling hot!" Bain's voice. *Well, thank the stars, it wasn't Blake after all. Small mercies.* "She's burning up!"

Next thing she knew, she was being bundled into what felt like every cloak the Gaene Kin owned and carted off to the Sanctum. *Lovely. Now I'm wrapped up like a roast dinner.* Gerant took charge, as usual. *Of course he did. One day Cane will realise Gerant has limits, but today is not that day.*

"She has an extremely high fever," Gerant said. "Cane, fetch cold water and cloths. Felix, Godfrey, bring garlic, feverfew and yarrow." He rattled off a list of more herbs for them to gather, clearly thinking a handful of plants could cool her down.

"How can we help?" came Percy's scrawny but earnest voice.

"What can we do?" Tristan asked.

Bless them both, Agatha thought fondly. *Hopefully one of them will think of something other than seasoning me like a Valorian hotpot.*

"Check the Gaene Kin books," Gerant ordered. "Find a salve, ritual, *anything* that can break a fever."

Oh, brilliant. The boys are off on a magical mystery tour hunting for witch's potions while I'm bubbling like farts in Satan's bath water.

Agatha could hear the genuine panic and concern in the men's voices, and, despite the circumstances, she was touched. *They actually care.* It was a novel feeling for her, one she might have enjoyed—if she weren't a human bonfire.

Something was very wrong. She had never felt this hot before, not even when her thoughts wandered to Cane's... finer attributes. *Why hasn't this idiot Gerant figured out that I need a freezing cold stream, not a ridiculous herbal tea?* she fumed silently. *This poxy little cloth on my forehead is about as useful as a snowflake in a furnace! I need to cool down before I burst into flames!*

"Gerant." Cane's voice, so soothing through the sweltering heat. *Oh, thank heavens, his voice.* It was like a balm to her fevered mind. *He'll know what to do.* "I don't have any experience in such matters, but this doesn't seem to be working."

Thank you! Finally, someone with sense. She could have wept with relief if she hadn't been trying to avoid choking on the foul yarrow-garlic concoction Gerant was determined to pour into her barely responsive mouth. *STREAM! I NEED A COLD STREAM, YOU FOOLS!* Her inner rant was starting to sound suspiciously like her sister's, which stoked her frustration.

Then, as if by divine intervention, Cane spoke again, and his words were like a chorus of angels to her ears.

"Why don't we lower her body temperature by putting her in the stream?"

Yes! YES! At last, someone using their brain. Cane, you brilliant, beautiful man!

Hands lifted her again, and she could only hope the ones around her waist belonged to Cane. Moments later, the icy water of the stream welcomed her like an old friend, instantly quenching the fiery heat that had been consuming her. *Sweet relief,* she thought, as the cold water worked its magic.

"It's working!" Cane's voice, full of relief. "She's smiling, she's coming back around. Let's get her inside."

Of course I'm smiling, Agatha thought, feeling a faint flicker of hope. *This is heavenly.*

But the sensation was short-lived. Her relief was quickly overshadowed by a new, unsettling feeling deep within her. *Uh-oh.* The hope ebbed away as she realised her torment was about to get even worse.

"We've tried every homeopathic way we know." Gerant's weary voice. *Ah, finally admitting your limits, Gerant? Took you long enough.*

"She's pregnant," Godfrey's voice. *Good god Godfrey, I thought you were the clever one.*

"Oh!" Blake's idiotic voice piped up. "So she and the Baron must have got it on after all."

"She just needs rest," Godfrey again, the voice of reason.

Yes, rest. Rest sounds good.

————◆○◆————

Agatha's consciousness wavered in and out like a candle in a drafty room. Somewhere in the dark, she felt the sharp sting of a needle plunging into her belly. Panic flared. *What in the nine circles of hell are they doing?* The freezing stream had cooled her and broken her fever. She wanted to scream at them to stop, but the darkness surrounded her like a spider's shroud.

The needle pierced deeper, and a realisation, more horrifying than any fever dream, dawned on her. The pain was erupting *inside* her.

This is it, she thought. *This is how I go—skewered from the inside out by some idiot's attempt at pointless midwifery.* But no one was touching her. What was it?

Searing pain ripped through her, spreading outward like wildfire. Every nerve in her body ignited in agony, and she could feel her muscles contracting violently, as though her bones were being bent and wrenched apart. *What fresh hell is this?* Her heart pounded so erratically she expected it to burst out of her chest like a jack-in-the-box. *Oh, lovely. Dying from an exploding heart is just the icing on top of this infernal cake.*

The pain was all-consuming, each breath felt like inhaling shards of glass. Her skin burned with fever, yet she shivered uncontrollably, her body caught between the fiery heat and ice-cold tremors.

A primal scream clawed its way up her throat, but she couldn't muster the strength to release it. *How poetic*, she mused darkly. *I'm dying and I can't even scream about it. Typical.*

Her limbs grew heavier. Every movement required superhuman effort, like wading through quicksand while the world shrank around her, leaving her alone in a battlefield of pain. Something inside her was waging war, and she was the unfortunate collateral damage. *Dagma*, she thought bitterly. *This has to be Dagma. Only she could concoct such a miserable way to die.* Agatha held onto this thought like a lifeline. If a hex from her sister was tearing her apart from the inside, then this was a battle of wills—she'd be damned if she'd let Dagma win.

I'll strangle her. No, I'll gut her first, then strangle her. Damn you, Dagma. I won't let you have the satisfaction.

Darkness swallowed her again. When she next became aware, voices hovered at the borders of her consciousness, distant, as though spoken through water.

Snippets of conversation floated around in her mental pool of swirling eddies. "Here are some more de-hexing rituals from the Gaene Kin's Book of Shadows," someone said—Rowan? Percy? She couldn't tell. *Oh, great. More nonsense rituals. I'm pregnant, not cursed, you dolts.*

Wait. The realisation slammed into her like a lightning bolt. *I'm pregnant. I'm actually pregnant! That was a lot quicker than I expected!* A giddy joy welled up in her. *Take that, Dagma! Mother will be over the moon. You may have hexed me, but I'm the one who's pregnant. Ha!*

"I still think that magic stuff won't work if we do it." *Pragmatic and down-to-earth as ever, Bain. But kudos for trying.*

"Get Cane to say it, at least, since the sylph seemed to think he has some—" Bain continued, but Agatha was slipping away again, the darkness closing in. Next time she came to, she heard Cane's soft voice shining through the darkness like a light.

"Spirits of the wind, ancestors of the past, we call on you to help this soul. Break the chains of poison, cleanse this body. Release the poison from its flesh fabric. Protect, infuse with light. Banish the poison to the darkness."

In Agatha's fevered mind, Cane's soothing words began to blend with the sharp, venomous tones of her sister, Dagma:

<May the forces of pain ravage you from within, as you have ravaged my flesh with your flames of rancour.>

What the hell, sister? Agatha's thoughts screamed, though her body remained limp, like a rag doll at the mercy of an evil toddler. *You infernal witch!* She could almost see Dagma's cruel smile, her sister's words like serpentine vines, wrapping around her every muscle and blood cell, constricting her in a vice of pure malice.

But Cane's words—those soft, earnest words—were like beams of light cutting through the vines of Dagma's curse. It felt like two opposing sides fighting inside her, Cane's incantation trying to pry loose Dagma's malevolent grip:

"Restore peace, we honour you and respect you."
< May the hand of malice strangle your inner soul.>
"May the light of these candles guide you to us."
< filling your blood with anguish.>

Agatha could feel the two forces clash within her, Cane's words illuminating the darkness that Dagma had so gleefully unleashed. *I swear, Dagma, if I survive this, I'm going to find you and*—but the thought was lost in the next duel of pain and light:

"We offer our love as a shield."
< leaving nothing but heartache and dolour.>
"We ask for the renewal of her energies, rebirth."

With that, Dagma's curse cracked, the fiery chains loosening their grip. Agatha felt it deep in her core—Dagma's hex was breaking. Hope lit up in her as Cane's voice fully exorcised Dagma's evil:

We offer our love as a shield.

Each word from Cane peeled away a layer of darkness, banishing the hex. Agatha felt life returning as Dagma's venom was finally purged.

"Oh, my unfaithful wife, strike me dead if that isn't Beelzebub himself!" *Always the charmer, Felix, but your oddball humour is not appropriate now.*

"Bloody hell!" Tristan exclaimed in shock. "What is that?"

"Bugger me!" Percy blurted out. Agatha wondered for the hundredth time if he was hoping someone would take him up on that or if it was just his go-to expletive.

"What in the devil's name is *that*?" Bain's voice joined the chorus of confusion and horror.

Okay, now I'm worried. What the hell are they looking at? Agatha braced herself for whatever horror her sister had concocted this time.

"Keep going, Cane!" Gerant urged. "I think it's working."

"Yes," Rowan added in his soft, serious tone. "And after all the black has gone, we'll need to seal her in one of those ritual circles for protection."

"I've never seen so much blackness." Felix sounded impressed. "Not even a burnt pig on a spit creates such bellows of black."

I'm being compared to a smoking pig carcass! Damn your soul, Dagma, Agatha thought, half in disbelief, half in grudging admiration. *What kind of hellish hex did you put on me?*

Chapter 30

KEEPERS OF POWER

A GATHA FELT COOL NOW, as though the infernal heat that had been roasting her alive had finally been doused. Cane's voice sailed over her like a serenade for the newly undead:

> "Guardian of Earth's ancient wisdom,
> Sculptor of stone and wellspring of creation,
> We summon you to watch over the Northern tower.
> Mistress of the Waters,
> Mother of oceans, rivers, and springs,
> We call upon you to protect the Western tower.
> Lord of Flames,
> Bearer of lightning, wrath, and renewal,
> We beckon you to guard the Southern tower.
> Spirit of the Winds,
> Seer of secrets and messenger of destiny,
> We invoke you to safeguard the Eastern tower.
> The Four Keepers of Power, we summon you
> to seal this spirit, safeguarding her from harm."

Someone anointed her forehead with a cool liquid. *Ah, finally, it's over.* She felt... well, not quite herself, but certainly better. Still, she couldn't move. She was trapped in darkness. How long have I been here? And who was holding her hand? Wait, no, they weren't holding her hand—they were checking for a pulse. *Do I not have a pulse? But Dagma's hex was lifted!*

"They just suddenly appeared!" That was definitely Felix's voice. "Her eyes filled with blood, and then her body went limp and then—"

Wait, my body is limp? Am I... dead? But she was moving. She could feel herself moving. *Yes! And now I can see again.*

She blinked, and there he was—Felix, his two chins wobbling over her. Agatha had never thought she'd be so relieved to see his pudgy face. He was mopping her brow. *How kind of him... Wait, something's not right.*

She wasn't looking *up* at the wobbly chins.

She glanced down and immediately wished she hadn't. There she was—or more precisely, half of her was—lying in bed. The other half? Well, let's just say that part of her had sloped away on its own... quite literally. Blood covered everything. Black blood. Whatever battle had ruptured inside had materialised all over the marble floor. Only the top half of her torso remained on the bed, her eyes mercifully closed, as though she were peacefully napping.

At least I am pretty when I'm dead, she thought, just as Cane rushed in. *Be still my beating heart—oh wait, no, it already is.* Her real lips would have been smiling because Cane's face was a picture of genuine concern.

"What are they?" His voice, usually so dreamy, now held a note of surprise and—what was that? A hint of repulsion? *Cane, how could you? It's not my fault my lower body decided to implode from the inside. That sister of mine will pay dearly for this. If I had any hands, I'd strangle her myself. But what are you staring at?*

Cane's eyes were glued to two small oval objects on the floor by the bed. They were no bigger than hen's eggs, one with a bluish-black exterior, and the other a shiny gold. Both were made of tightly woven layers of fine silk. The blackberry-coloured egg had been torn open, and from it emerged a small, sinewy blue limb, glistening with a viscous, iridescent fluid. The tiny tentacle-like appendage probed the air, searching for its target. It was covered in fine, needle-like barbs, each one pulsating with venomous intent.

With lightning speed, the tiny tentacle lashed out.

"Stand back!" Cane shoved Felix out of its trajectory. *Ah, Cane, the selfless hero. And you,* she glared at the tentacle, which hungrily sought its next victim, *you were the bastard thing that did this to me.*

"Something or someone is coming!" Percy shrieked.

Chaos ensued. Cracks of light tore through the air, and out of them, figures began to emerge. It was mind-blowing, jaw-dropping, leaving the men struggling in the speech department.

"I think it's the g-g-guardian k-k-ke-keeper things!" Tristan cried out, keeping well back from the small tentacle egg, his trembling hand inadvertently ringing the chimes.

"Oh... I didn't actually expect them to appear," Rowan said, clutching the Book of Shadows as if it were a shield. "I thought it was all symbolic or... through intention, not—"

The Keepers of Power were coming.

Well, thought Agatha, floating above what was left of her body, *this just got interesting.*

The sylph appeared first in its heavenly light. For once, it did not seem angry. It took its place to the right of the bed, radiating an air of superior knowledge, as if it had been expecting this all along.

Next, a stunning nymph-like undine revealed on the opposite side. *Well, well, well,* Agatha mused, *aren't we the glamorous one!* The air rippled around her as she took her place, her fluid beauty captivating everyone in the room. The men were practically salivating unchecked, their eyes glued to her ever-shifting form.

The undine was not just beautiful—she was hypnotic, a living work of art living up to tales of the legendary allure of her kind. Tales of how men could lose themselves just by looking at one. And it was true—the undine's beauty was not static or conventional. Her torso, formed from the clearest water, sparkled like moonlight on a calm sea, while her aquatic lower half undulated with the grace of ocean waves. Her hair flowed like an effervescent waterfall, and her eyes—two deep pools of wisdom, compassion, and just a hint of mischief—drew everyone into her enchanting orbit.

While the men were busy gawking at the undine, Agatha noticed the third guardian slithering in—decidedly less appealing, but no less impressive. Heat radiated from his long, blue-scaled body, so intense that Agatha felt grateful for her current non-corporeal state. He moved with a sinuous, unnerving grace, his limbs slender but strong, pushing his slick body along with an asynchronous rhythm. There was something unsettling about his movements that made even the other two guardians avert their gaze. His thin, purple tongue flicked in and out.

"We appeared because we sensed a disruption in the natural order," the sylph said in its all-knowing, slightly shrill voice.

"You're always so perceptive, so wise," the undine's words flowed forth like seafoam, full of benevolent charm. But the sylph did not have long to bask in the compliment.

"You're too late," growled the Fire Keeper in a voice of raw and ruthless power. His presence seemed to shrink the room, displacing its air and sending shivers down everybody's spine—well, everyone with a spine still attached to their body. "Your perceptions should have been acted on the moment that idiot Valkarse handed Atropa over like a trophy to be bartered. *That* was when the balance of the world as we know it was lost forever."

The Fire Keeper turned his blazing eyes to Cane. "Even you, pretty boy, are too late. Things are already in motion. The Army of the Bleak will bring darkness and flame upon these lands."

His gaze shifted to Tristan, who was trembling so violently that his foot-long chimes were still jangling uncontrollably.

"You!" the Fire Keeper hissed. "Stop that infernal ringing already!"

"Oh!" Tristan dropped the chimes as if they had suddenly turned into hot coals. "Yes, sir. I mean, no, sir—"

Thankfully, the salamander-like creature's attention was drawn back to the other Keepers. "Speaking of late, where is my friend of soil and stone? Not like him to—"

Just then, the floor beside the eggs split open, and a stout, bearded figure clambered out. He brushed off his short body, chuntering to himself.

"Sorry we're late," the newcomer rumbled amicably like distant thunder. "We were having a nice chat with the notoriously verbose earthworm chieftain, Ver, on our annual underground spa day when we heard the summons. Then we got lost in a fungus forest and got our foot stuck in a knot of roots. Funny, really, as I was just telling Ver, that he needs to have a word with those moles. They're wreaking havoc down there—"

"Enough chitter and chatter, Master Pygmy," the sylph interrupted, raising a bossy fluffy hand. "We must decide what is to be done."

"*That* tiny man is guardian of the earth and—" Tristan's mouth snapped shut when the Earth Keeper's gemstone eyes locked onto him.

The pygmy spat on his calloused hands—first left, then right—rubbing them together with a rough, gritty sound. He flexed his fingers and then eyed the silky eggs.

"Right, which one are we snatching?" the pygmy sneered, his voice as gravelly as the ground it came from.

Still floating above the scene, Agatha was both amused and annoyed. *Of course,* she thought, eyeing the pygmy puffing out his chest as if he'd just won first prize for best garden at a village fair. *They came for my eggs. And here I was, hoping they'd at least try to put me back together.*

"You turned up just to take the eggs?" Bain asked. "That's unbelievable!"

"Why, of course," the pygmy replied, as if it were the most obvious thing in the world. "Think yourselves lucky. Normally, we don't turn up at all. We get summoned all the time by amateur witches or people begging for some petty nonsense like more wealth, more power, a new wife, a new horse, better looks, better cards..." He shook his head. "Mortals, honestly. We only ever show up for the Gaene Kin. *Now,* there was a lot that knew how to be respectful to their superiors!" He smiled, a hint of nostalgia twinkling in his sparkling eyes. "And even then, we'd only send ambassadors, sub-versions of us. Naturally, we've got more important matters to attend to."

"Like spa days," the undine said.

"Well, that was an exception," the pygmy coughed.

"Why did you come today?" Cane asked.

"Because, as we said," the sylph replied, "nature's balance has been disturbed. Someone of your kind has been mixing and messing with things that shouldn't be mixed and messed with. That sets off a chain of cataclysmic events, and we need to get ahead of it. So, we're taking these eggs before they become what no one can name and unleash deeds no one can imagine."

With a speed that belied his stout form and stubby legs, the pygmy darted toward the golden egg, grabbing it and hugging it close, like a child clutching a prized toy. "Beat you!" he declared triumphantly, smiling smugly at the undine.

"Or you think you have," the sylph replied condescendingly. "Nothing is swifter than air." And just like that, the sylph produced the golden egg, cradling it in its transparent hands as if it had been there all along.

They're all just a bunch of show-offs, Agatha thought, watching their theatrics.

The pygmy looked down, huffing in frustration. He had grabbed Agatha's shoe.

"Where's the other egg?" Cane asked, scanning the room.

While everyone had been distracted, the Fire Keeper had quietly picked up the torn egg in his mouth. His fiery eyes stared at them, daring anyone to intervene. His thick, muscular limbs moved with deliberate menace; the scrape of his claws against the floor making every one of Agatha's dead hairs stand on end.

"So much for divine intervention," said Rowan. "Cane read out the protection summoning spell to help the Baroness, and yet here you all are, bickering like children trying to outdo one another. I sincerely hope there's a higher echelon governing you four."

With a final, defiant glance, the salamander-like Keeper slipped back into the shadows, leaving worry and fear in his wake.

"Stop! Where are you going? Why did you take that? Come back here!" Tristan shouted in panic. "You can't just let him take it!" He turned to the sylph, imploringly.

"Oh yes, we can," the pygmy chuckled. Without another word, he turned, and sank back into the floor. The ground closed up behind him as if he had never been there at all.

"We, the Keepers of Power, restore and maintain natural balance. We do not pander to the whims of mortals." The undine spoke as if she were explaining a simple truth to a child. "We are too late to help the mother. One egg has been claimed by our darker kin, and the other must now remain in the rightful guardianship of the light."

Tristan's frustration boiled over, his face turning crimson. "You can't just take them!"

"We have no intention of taking it," the sylph replied, its words light and effortless. With a nonchalant flick of its wrist, it tossed the golden egg straight toward Cane. He caught it with surprising ease.

"You're supposed to help us!" Rowan's shout trailed after the fading form of the sylph, but his plea was met with nothing but the whisper of the wind as it dissolved from sight.

⸻ ◆ ⸻

It wasn't every day that nine grown men found themselves paralysed with fear over something no bigger than their hand. But today wasn't exactly like most other days. Agatha knew each one was silently waiting for a terror to crawl out of the egg. They awaited a cannibalistic crawler. Or something even worse—a fusion of man and squid like the Baron and Arabella.

And what about me? Agatha was trapped in her own invisible box. Whatever unseen barrier separated her from the living muffled her cries. Desperation scrambled her thoughts. *I'll go mad in here. All alone. Someone, anyone—help me!* She screamed to an audience of none—or so she thought. Someone was watching her.

She turned to meet the undine's eyes, those impossibly deep pools of wisdom fixed on her. *You can see me?* Agatha's ranking on the hope-ometre soared. *You can hear me? Help me!*

But the undine had no intention of helping. With a gentle but firm wag of her watery finger, she tutted at Agatha, then pressed that same finger to her lips. "Shh," was all she said before turning her attention to the men, leaving Agatha stunned and utterly deflated. *Great. Just great. Silenced by a glorified, sexy fish.*

Meanwhile, the undine addressed the men. "The egg is now yours to watch over. You are its guardians."

"But what do we do with it?" Blake asked, looking more stir-crazy by the minute. "I'm too young to be a father! There's so much I haven't done yet—and so many women I haven't—"

"If it were my egg, I would put it in water," the undine suggested serenely.

Felix latched onto the idea and rushed forward. "Right. Water! The fountain!"

"If it were the Fire Keeper's egg," the undine continued, "it would be nestled in smouldering coals."

Felix froze mid-step. The image of cooking the egg clearly brought him up short.

"And the Earth Keeper would surely bury it deep within the ground," the undine added, as placidly as a still pond.

Felix, usually so jovial, was vexed. "Now you're just messing with us. How are we supposed to do anything when you tangle us up in your riddles?"

The undine responded with a cryptic, knowing smile—serene, enigmatic, and maddeningly composed—that silenced any possible retort.

Cane, however, remained unfazed. "And what would the Air Keeper do with it?"

"Ah, the Air Keeper," the undine sighed with a touch of affection. "A pleasurable mystery. We combine so well together and yet are so different. Air, too, is life-giving yet capricious. It is the breath of life, but also breathes life into fire. That egg should be with the sylphs. But they are unpredictable by nature—sometimes benevolent, sometimes mischievous, a gentle breeze on a warm day so welcome, or a howling blizzard that clears forests to wastelands. Duality, like humans: both an inspiration and a scourge." A dark undercurrent seeped into her words. "Perhaps they would kill it. And perhaps they should. A spawn of deviant lineage—something that should not be. But we Keepers, we cannot want or act on such inclinations. If we did, we'd be no different from mortals like you."

Her voice swelled, a rising tide of fury. "If we wanted all descendants to be wiped out, we'd eliminate all that fuelled this miscreation." But as quickly as the tidal wave had come, it shrank to gentle ripples. "If the sylphs were to care for this egg, they might sing to it, share words of assurance and wisdom."

"Riddles!" Gerant exploded, his frustration matching Felix's. "These are all riddles. They are of no use to us."

"Riddles. Resolutions. Reasons." The undine's sing-song voice calmed them. "How to see the single solution. Which is right, which is wrong? Even to refrain has repercussions. How to read the riddles in the rivers of your reality." Her words rocked them gently like a boat on a calm sea. "Any more questions?" she asked, but her form was already dissolving.

There were, of course, plenty of questions, but none of them managed to form before the undine vanished, leaving the men in mesmerised silence.

One question did cross Agatha's mind, though: *Where did that oversized lizard take my egg?*

Chapter 31

A MEMORY REMAINS

CANE'S AND SIXTEEN OTHER eyes fixed on the small, glistening egg.

"Let's smash it and be done with it," Tristan suggested, punctuating his point by punching his right fist into his left palm.

Tristan's default solution to anything he couldn't open was always to bash it in. Applicable and effective in some contexts, say a locked treasure chest, but probably not the nuanced approach they needed here.

"Tristan's propensity for wanton violence might be a good idea," said Bain. "You heard what the Water Keeper said—wipe out all descendants of this deviant species."

Rowan interjected with the voice of reason—or perhaps naivety. "But it might be harmless."

"You're such a softie," Tristan scoffed, punching his palm again like that was going to settle the matter. "Smash it before it smashes us."

"Or I could make an interesting omelette, if we follow the Fire Keeper's way." Cane couldn't tell if Felix was joking or seriously contemplating the culinary potential of the golden egg. Either way, not the helpful suggestion they needed either right now.

The egg drew everyone's eyes to it like a magnet, as if sheer concentration could prevent it from doing whatever wicked thing it was destined to do. Perhaps they feared that the moment they stopped staring, the egg would hatch into something unspeakable and gnash their faces off.

"This is ridiculous," Gerant said finally. "It's just an egg. We'll monitor it. Then, if anything remotely evil-looking crawls out, we'll kill it. How hard can it be, it'll only be the size of—"

"Blake's brain?" said Tristan, laughing.

"Hey," Blake was affronted. "At least *my* biceps are bigger than an egg."

Cane was not sure about Gerant's plan. None of them had any experience in raising non-person persons, potentially malevolent ducklings or whatever was to hatch out of it. And that made it hard to formulate his argument for putting it in the fountain water.

"Or we could study it," said Godfrey, with a note of excitement that Cane found slightly disturbing.

"Yes," agreed Gerant. "There is always *that* option."

"It is a new species. We could learn from it, and it could learn from us. We could teach it our ways—the path to kindness and compassion."

Whatever his father had been smoking, Cane feared Gerant was now packing the same fanciful blend in his pipe.

Gerant lit the tobacco and puffed decisively. "Right. For now, we need to put it somewhere safe while we decide what to do with it."

"Percy, how about you put it in that green pouch of yours you're always carrying around?" Felix suggested. "It's the perfect size, and I don't think I've ever seen you without it."

"Uh, um, er," Percy stuttered in embarrassment. "Well, that's actually occupied at the moment."

"What do you mean, 'occupied'?" Felix asked, his ginger eyebrows creeping up his forehead like caterpillars making a break for it.

"Well, I was given the great honour of guarding my legendary great-great-uncle Perceval."

"Oh, it was you they chose for that, was it?" said Tristan. "I'd wondered where old Perceval had gotten to."

Felix's caterpillars raced up for cover under his hairline. "D'you mean to say that you're carrying a *dead man* around with you?"

The tension that had gripped the room since Agatha's death ruptured like a dam giving way. Laughter erupted, shoulders relaxed, and the atmosphere lightened for the first time in what felt like days. Cane found himself chuckling along with the rest. Percy's earnestness made the whole situation even funnier.

"You have been lugging around your dead uncle!" Blake wheezed, clutching his sides. "When Gerant said to only pack the essentials, you brought a corpse." His cheeks flushed from the effort of laughing so hard. "Percy, you're too much. One of a kind!"

Percy, red-faced but determined, defended himself. "I don't see what's so funny about that. None of you would want others to abandon you just because your body stopped working!"

"Alright, alright, enough," Gerant intervened, still wiping tears of laughter from his eyes. "We all know how much the legendary Perceval means to young Percy. I'll put the egg in my tobacco pouch for now."

Cane watched as Gerant carefully picked up the egg, his fingers trembling slightly. "This is disturbing," Gerant muttered, as he nestled the egg among the soft tobacco leaves. His gaze shifted uneasily to Agatha's chewed-up body on the bed—a morbid reminder of what had transpired. Her legs lay somewhere near and under the bed, but no one wanted to look. Cane had to admit, it was a sight that could turn the strongest of stomachs—including the one behind Blake's chiselled abs.

Gerant cleared his throat, trying to bring back some semblance of order. "Let's deal with practical matters and clear up this mess." He pointed his pipe to the carnage on the bed.

"Which of us is man enough to, uh, help me take care of the Baroness?" Bain asked, rolling up his sleeves.

"It's more like which of us is strong and unfeeling enough," said Felix.

"Well, that rules Rowan out," said Bain. "You, young man, have far too many feelings racing through you. But Blake," he clapped Blake on the shoulder. "I'd say you're the most manly of all of us."

Normally, Blake would have revelled in the rays of such a compliment, but even he couldn't pretend to have what it took for this job.

"Ah, yes, well, cleaning is more of a woman's job, isn't it?" Blake mumbled, scraping the bottom of the excuse barrel.

"Well, since the only woman among us is dead," Gerant replied, "why don't we *all* get on with it?"

Cane knew that no matter how Gerant divvied up the tasks, the situation was far from under control or normal. They had an egg to babysit, a bloody mess to clean, and no real idea of what to do next.

⸺⬥⸺

He knelt beside what remained of Agatha, now a bundled mass under the blanket. He did his best to wrap her up neatly, but there was only so much you could do when you had to criss-cross legs over a torso to make everything fit. The process felt more like packing away a banquet's leftovers than giving someone a proper burial. It wasn't like when normal people passed, where the grief was clean and sharp, a clear loss. No, this felt messier—like the end of a long day at the butcher's shop.

As he considered Agatha's form, now just a bi-limb lump under the blanket, Cane realised he wasn't sure how to feel. She wasn't Agatha anymore—not the graceful woman he remembered, who once cradled a baby and plucked the harp with such delicate fingers. This wasn't Agatha. This was something else. Something that had once been a person but was now just a task to finish. Parts of a body to bury and effluence to mop.

Bundled up now, out of sight, he could think about her more clearly. It was odd, but he felt more at ease now that she was hidden from view. Maybe it was because his feelings for her had always been contradictory: drawn to her, enchanted by her beauty, but also frightened—not because of anything she did—because of how she made him feel. Unbalanced. Confused. People always said love did that, messed with your mind, made you act foolish. But with Agatha, it was something more, something that had shaken the foundations of his world the day they met. She had been the catalyst for everything that followed—the new friends, the reunion with his father. Her impact on his life was immense, but whether it had been good or bad was still up for debate.

"Cane," Bain's voice pulled him from his thoughts. "Let's finish this. We've dug the grave. You can bring her out."

With a grimace, Cane got to his feet. Blake helped him lift the blanket, which was bulging and dripping—far from a dignified end. Felix followed behind with a mop, while Percy carried a bucket, looking for all the world like they were cleaning up after a particularly messy and brutal boxing match. Any remaining traces of Agatha's life were being wiped off the once spotless alabaster floor.

Not thinking properly, Bain and Gerant had hastily dug a standard-shape grave, not accounting for Agatha's newly reassembled limbs. Fitting her in was a like shoving a grand piano through a hobbit's front door—parts needing to be repositioned.

Meanwhile, Godfrey and Rowan took on the more ceremonial task, sprinkling hops on and around the grave.

"To purify the soil and her soul," Rowan explained, as if quoting scripture. "I read it in the Gaene Kin's 'Book of Shadows'. Since the Sanctum is such a spiritual place, I think we should honour their traditions."

Cane wasn't sure how much spiritual purity a handful of hops would provide after what had just happened. Nonetheless, a prayer and a blessing seemed like the right thing to do. Agatha had not exactly met an end anyone would wish upon their worst enemy—*except maybe Dagma*, thought Cane. *She had been Agatha's worst enemy*. Not knowing how to develop this thought further, he filed it away for later under: Vindictive Sibling Hatred.

The odd-looking group congregated around Agatha's grave. Even the bears, wolves and lynx came to join them, sitting respectfully just a few metres away. Lycus stood by

Cane's side, his presence grounding him. None of them were particularly religious, so they improvised the eulogy. The men's sonorous voices filled the cold afternoon air as they delivered their makeshift prayer and blessing to ease the parting of Agatha's soul:

Withering maiden at peace be
Withering maiden be set free
Countless dark nights
Countless bad sights
With this song we banish
With these petals they vanish.
Feel the sun of tomorrow
Feel no more deep sorrow
Withering maiden be set free
Withering maiden at peace be.

"Poor girl," Felix sighed. "She was only a slip of a thing. Not wanted by her mother, mistreated by her father, ridiculed and abandoned at the castle, poisoned by her sister. The world has only shown her its cruel side, and yet in return, she gave music and light. She was a beautiful sight, and what a voice."

"That's all well and good, Felix," Bain said, as blunt as the edge of a worn axe, "but your summation is a little misguided. I suspected something was not right about her from the start. You missed out a major point: that thing in the grave is not like us. It may not even qualify as human. No woman I've ever known has laid an egg."

"Me neither," said Blake, as though he were a self-appointed authority on women's reproductive systems.

"She was still a part of our group," said Gerant. No one could argue with that.

They bowed their heads for a few moments, giving Agatha the kind of silent respect that only comes when no one knows what to say next. Awkwardness permeated their mood.

Percy finally broke the tension. "Well, since we're here, why don't we bury the egg like the watery woman said the Earth Keeper would do?"

"No!" said Cane. "It can't stay in the ground. It needs to go in the water."

"What?" Gerant looked at him as if he'd just suggested swallowing the egg whole. "Why would you say that?"

Cane hesitated. How could he explain something he barely understood himself? "I suppose because Agatha was always happy in water," he said, knowing full well how ridiculous that sounded.

"Well, there's only one way to find out," Felix said with a shrug. "Let's put it in the water."

With a mix of excitement and nerves, they went back inside the Sanctum and carefully placed the egg into the fountain. They all gathered around, eyes wide, breaths held, expecting... something. A magical light show, an explosion of tentacles, maybe even a celestial choir. Instead, nothing happened.

"Bathos," Rowan muttered.

"Is that some fancy poetic word for bathing?" Blake asked. "Why can't you just say 'bath'?"

"It has nothing to do with washing," Rowan replied. "Bathos means a massive anticlimax."

"Another gem from our literary prince Rowan," said Felix, just before his stomach growled loudly, breaking the tension in a primordial way. "And that, gentlemen, is the onomatopoeic term for 'it's time to eat'."

As Gerant carefully dried and put the egg back in his tobacco pouch, it suddenly hit Cane that they hadn't eaten in over a day. As usual, Felix took charge, rallying his 'sous-chefs', Percy and Tristan, to help him prepare the long-overdue meal of roast grouse, fennel and watercress.

Before long, the enticing aromas of their dinner filled the Sanctum. They gathered around the stone table and long benches in a room that had likely seen many serious discussions among the Gaene Kin, now repurposed for a far more basic need.

Chapter 32

REBELS WITH A CAUSE

"WELL, GENTLEMEN, ANOTHER FINE feast," Gerant said, lifting his cup in a toast to Felix. "A toast to the chef! And his helpers, of course!" He nodded to Tristan and Percy. The brothers were very chipper—more thanks to the wine than the praise.

"We found the wine under the altar," Tristan said proudly, holding up a half-empty bottle as if it were treasure. "Those Gaene Kin ladies must have had a few knees up in here, I bet."

Cane felt they'd had more wine than was wise—but then, after a day dealing with apparitions from a different realm and a woman who could lay eggs, what was a little indulgence? The wine provided a much-needed escape, a nurse tending to their sorrow, softening the sharp edges of their fear.

He leaned back on the rough wooden bench, his stomach pleasantly full, and his head fuzzy from the wine. It had been an enjoyable meal, considering the circumstances. The others seemed in good spirits—or at least, sufficiently tipsy to forget, for a moment, the dilemmas they faced.

"I believe," Gerant began, his tone sinking the jubilant mood like a heavy stone on a lily pad, "there is one area where we cannot congratulate ourselves. We are no closer to a solution. No closer to saving the good people of Valoria."

"Botheration, Gerant!" Bain interrupted, filled with irritation—and wine. "We've been a tad preoccupied with sylphs, keepers, and Agatha's whole egg-death debacle! Give us a break. Besides, how are we supposed to save Valorians who don't even want saving? We're landowners, not magicians."

Tristan, far deeper into the elderflower wine than anyone else, lifted his cup swaying slightly. "Our world is under the rule of a tyrannical usurper," he slurred. "And we shall all become… fodder for pasty hellspawn… who wear no clothes!" He paused for a hiccup.

"I say... enjoy the now." He raised his cup higher, nearly toppling over in the process. "Tomorrow izzz another day."

"Thank you, Bain and Tristan for your useful contributions," said Gerant. "Now, if I may finish."

He scanned the table, daring anyone to interrupt. The group fell silent, recognising the serious air about him.

"We are all guardians now. Guardians of—"

"I wanna be the Fire Lord!" Tristan blurted, full of drunken enthusiasm. "Did you see how cool he was? The way his big muscly legs moved, and he just took that egg and left like he didn't give a f—"

"Thank you, Tristan, again," Gerant said, his patience wearing thin.

"No, no, no," Percy slurred, pointing at his brother. "You can't be the evil, fiery one. You're the gnomey... pygmy one. You're short and—"

"Noooo!" Tristan's hazelnut eyes crossed as he tried to focus on Percy. "You're shorter." He pointed a wobbly finger at his brother. "And Gerant can be the bossy siff. 'Ooh, I can't tell you what you need to know because I'm *so* mysterious and know *so* much.' Squeak, squeak, squeak!" He jumped to his feet and began whooshing around the room, dramatically imitating the sylph. "'I'm sooo powerful and all-knowing that I can't do anything useful!' If I were a siff, I would—"

"A sylph," Percy corrected, standing precariously on a small stool.

"That's what I said," Tristan insisted. "If I were a siff, I would tell us everything, we're a nice bunch. Help us out, you know." With that, he collapsed face down on the floor, snoring almost instantly.

"Good," said Gerant. "Maybe now I can tell you my plan. It came to me in a flash when we burned that resin earlier. Brilliant it is. Three-pronged of course! I feel we should cut to the chaste."

Blake opened his mouth, but Gerant beat him to it. "It's a figure of speech, Blake." Blake closed his mouth. "What are the facts? We're guardians of an egg. We don't know where the other egg is, so no point dwelling on it just now. We're also guardians of an important key. So, we must keep that safe too.

"We can save the people of Valoria and we can oust that tyrannical usurper!" Gerant's rallying speech had their attention. "First, we warn the people—let them know something's off, that the Duke is deceiving them."

Percy looked perplexed. "How? We can't just knock on doors and say: 'Hello, I'm a nice person, you can trust me! Follow my advice and your soul won't burn in hell forever for siding with the dippy Duke and being a weak little tw—'"

Gerant raised a hand to stop him. "We use the printed word. Posters, pamphlets—dozens of them—questioning who this Duke really is. Where did he come from? Why are we fighting our own people when, under Aurelius's rule, there were no wars?"

He paused. "Second, after we've sown the seeds of doubt, we'll swing them back to reason. Now, can anyone guess how? What do the people of Valoria look to as a symbol of mystery and mastery?"

Percy scratched his head, rocking unsteadily on his stool.

"The perfect wife?" Blake suggested, his own faculties fogged by the wine.

"For the love of the gods, Felix," Bain groaned, "did you slip something into this wine? It's numbing our brains faster than valerian root."

Felix, half dozing, replied, "Who me? Nooo. Just a few dried mushrooms and such in the sauce."

"I think these young men have had too much sauce," sighed Bain.

"Ooh! Ooh!" Percy suddenly exclaimed, bouncing in his seat like an excited child. "I know! Ask me, pleeeease!"

"Alright, Percy, before you explode," Gerant sighed.

"The Devil's Needle!" Percy shrieked, beaming as if he'd just invented the wheel. "A massive monolith! A symbol of heresy and heraldry with the power to fascinate, frighten, delight, distress, enchant, enthral—"

"Alright, Professor Percy," Bain cut in, sparing them from Percy's descent into a drunken monologue. "We get the picture. End of sermon. Take a breath."

"Yes, Percy," Gerant said. "The Devil's Needle."

"Great," Blake said sarcastically. "A giant rock. What are we going to do—throw it at them?"

"Nooo," Tristan slurred, rising from his drunken stupor like a ghost from the grave, making everyone jump. "We use what it *symbolissses*." He slung an arm around Gerant's shoulders, grinning like a fool. "Right, Gerant, m'lord."

"Exactly what I had in mind. What it *symbolises*." Gerant gently peeled Tristan's arm off his shoulder.

"Is someone going to explain this, or am I supposed to piece together the breadcrumbs like always?" Blake grumbled.

"Well, today's full of surprises—a self-deprecating metaphor, from Blake," Rowan clapped his hands, delighted. "Looks like Blake's swashbuckling machismo is shrinking."

"Yup," Tristan agreed, wobbling as he struggled to stay upright. "You could even slip it into the pouch with old Perceval, it's so small now." He tapped Percy's green pouch.

Godfrey, also a little worse for wear thanks to the sauce, stepped in. "The Devil's Needle is an immense stone in Mort Valley, a deep gorge between Bellingham and Ironholme—known locally as the Devil's Apron. The stone itself stands five metres high, tapering toward the sky amidst a collection of enormous rock formations. One story would have us believe it is a Gaene Kin petrified by the Devil. Another legend claims that the markings on the stone were left by the talons of an ancient, angry deity. The monolith has stood over the Rudston moors for as long as anyone can remember. So potent was its presence that the Cretyne monks built their monastery as close as possible, hoping to align themselves with its power. Folklore says the smaller rocks clustered in circles were once gods themselves, whispering to one another. The Gaene Kin, too, used the site to hear these whispers—"

"Somebody stop him please," said Blake. "My mind is going to explode with too much information. And I still don't see how we can use it."

"If there's one that gets thing people going, it's fear," said Gerant, "especially if laced with the divine. And if we play our cards right, the Devil's Needle might just be the symbol we need to stir imaginations and ignite fear to galvanise the Valorians into action."

"If the Gaene Kin visited there," Cane mused aloud, "could that not be an earth or stone conflux, like the Sanctum is for air?"

"Possibly," said Gerant, though he was keen to move on. "Put a pin in that thought, Cane. Let's focus on now."

Focus—something Cane found increasingly elusive these days. While Gerant launched into the details of his plan, Cane's thoughts meandered back to the idea of elemental confluxes. The Sanctum for air, the Devil's Apron for stone; surely, sites for fire and water existed too. Were the Gaene Kin interested only in foresight, hence their connection to air? Air, after all, was the dominant element; without it, none of the others could—

"Are you daydreaming, Cane?" Gerant asked.

"Perhaps," Cane admitted.

Determined to share his *brilliant* idea, Gerant moved on to what he clearly considered the highlight of his plan. "So, my plan is to set the Devil's Needle on fire."

It was not met with the approval Gerant was expecting. Cane wondered if he had misheard. He was not the only one. Bain looked at Gerant as if he had gone mad. "Have you quite lost your senses?"

"We can't set stone on fire!" Blake pointed out the obvious.

"Not the stone itself," Gerant clarified, his eyes gleaming with manic enthusiasm. "We set fire around the stone to make it look like it's burning. If they see it in flames, they'll think something extraordinary is happening. No one dares go near the Needle, but it's visible from Malcrov Court, where they are most likely holding our sovereign leader captive. That brings me to the third prong of my plan: we save the king."

"Don't you think the dippy Duke will have taken over his palace? That power-hungry twit loves all things that symbolise power to pump up his manhood," Felix said, gesturing in a way that left little to the imagination. "What better way to pump himself up than by sitting in the king's seat? You know what they say—the flashier the man, the smaller his—"

"Yes, we get the picture, Felix," Gerant cut in before Felix could finish, but not before Percy and Tristan dissolved into fits of giggles.

Gerant, growing more serious, pressed on. "I doubt he would push his luck with the people that far. The palace symbolises the sovereign lineage; the Duke is establishing a new power base. I think he'll be at Malcrov Court. The dummy king will stay at the palace. It's only a few miles from the Devil's Apron—a short ride by horse."

"What if something happens to us for messing with the Devil's Needle?" Percy asked, sobering at the thought. "What if the Gaene Kin punish us? What if we're cursed, like the ancient gods—turned to stone for meddling with sacred stuff?"

Tristan was also unnerved now. "Or worse, we could break a spell—like Blake did in the ritual circle, or Cane when he summoned those Keepers. We might end up releasing the Devil himself, opening the gates of hell."

"Keep it real, Tristan," said Gerant. "Punishment is coming if we don't act. We'll just rot here if we do nothing or they'll find us eventually, whether it's the Duke's soldiers, Dagma's sorcery, or those wretched crawlers. We need to set things in motion. We've risked our lives—and the lives of the Bellingham soldiers—for nothing if we fold now. It is not us who will bend to an old wives' tale." He looked at Bain. "We *are* magicians now. Using trickery to make our audience believe. By dripping tar down the side of the Devil's Needle and setting it alight, we can make it look like the stone is on fire."

Cane had to admit the plan was feasible with just a handful of men—that was all they had now. They were the small rod that could lever the immense boulder of public opinion. Felix seemed to realise this too, his ginger whiskers twitching with excitement. "I see your intention, Gerant. We'll set it ablaze to make the people think the gods are angry—that something's wrong."

"But then what?" asked Bain. "How do we win them back from the Duke's grip? Once we've got their attention with the fire, how do we lead them back to reason?"

Gerant was one step ahead. "We'll seal the deal with a speech at Speaker's Corner. I'll handle that."

"There's merit to your plan, Gerant," Cane said. "But what about Atropa's return—the warning Gwaine gave us? And the Army of the Bleak the Fire Keeper said she'd have at her side. How can we prepare for that?"

"That would require a fourth prong," Gerant smiled. "And my fork only has three. Let's focus on what we *can* do, Cane."

"It had better have a fourth," said Bain. "Someone's got to stay behind and look after that egg. We can't just take it with us. What if it hatches and we put people in danger?"

"I had intended for Cane and Godfrey to remain here to guard the key," Gerant explained. "It may seem like the easiest job, but the key is high on Dagma's list." Gerant looked around the table. "Any objections or suggestions?"

"You've not failed us yet, *Your Great Gerantness*," Tristan slurred, swooping into a low curtsy. "We've dodged being imprisoned by the Duke, survived mutant cannibals, fought in a real battle to save our king—and don't get me started on Dagma! Honestly, what could possibly surprise us now?"

Chapter 33

IF DARKNESS HAD A DAUGHTER

A T NIGHT, WHEN MALCROV Court was draped in the stillness of slumber, Dagma would slip silently from her chambers, moving like a wraith down the grand staircase. Her steps were deliberate, careful to avoid the creaky spots that might betray her secret nocturnal activities. Such was her scariness, the imposing portraits that lined the walls seemed to hold their breath when she passed, as if too afraid to draw her gaze.

Her destination was always the same: the barn, to check her drones were progressing to plan. After ensuring everything was on schedule, it was time for some self-care. No pomade or cream could erase her scars. Her charred, broken body craved the restoration only fire could bring. Although the flames had taken parts of her, they could also give something back. For Dagma, physical perfection was a fleeting vanity; power, true power, was what mattered. She needed the fire though, to heal.

Barefoot, with her a ghostly veil night robe flowing behind her, she entered the empty ballroom. The vast room felt cavernous in the dark, the only light the faint glimmer from the chandeliers, their crystals catching the small beam from the waxing moon.

With a snap of her bony fingers, black nails clicking sharply, she summoned the fire. The enormous central fireplace roared to life, its flames greedily lapping up the oxygen. At her side, Galcion and Khyro knew this routine well. They sat patiently, then slumped to the floor, curling up, waiting for the end.

The ballroom doors clicked shut behind her. Now, it was just Dagma and the fire.

From the pocket of her robe, she pulled a smooth quartz crystal and a small vial of oil flecked with pyrite pieces, nails, and sprinkles of gold. Her white robe fell to the floor, pooling at her feet like milk, exposing the charred and scarred flesh beneath. Firelight danced across her body as she poured the oil over herself, the liquid catching the light and making her skin glisten like molten metal. With slow, deliberate movements, she pressed the smooth quartz pebble to her skin, tracing the spirals of bulging veins and the taut muscles of her arms and legs. It moved upward, gliding over her inner thighs, across her abdomen, her breasts, and finally to her forehead, where it lingered, drawing in the fire's power.

She stepped into the flames, calling on the spirits bound to her long ago.

"Come to me, spirits of fire. Fill me, spirits of fire. Come to me, flames of life. Fill me with healing and power."

The fire rose in response, wrapping around her like a lover's embrace. Dagma caroused in it, feeling the energy coursing through her, the flames licking at her skin with a heat that would have incinerated a lesser being. She spread her arms wide, her voice rising in a crescendo as she repeated the invocation, her body moving in a hypnotic dance, swaying and gyrating as the fire filled her with its potent energy.

"I am a Daughter of Caldera. I am a portent of power. Marvel at me!"

Her body, usually a vessel of strength and control, jolted and thrashed, caught in the tantric throes of a fiery ecstasy. But tonight, something was wrong. Her movements became erratic, a sharp, stabbing pain cutting through her euphoria, searing through her belly like a hot knife. Panic flooded her mind as she realised something was wrong. Terribly wrong. The trance shattered. She leaped from the flames, landing on the cold marble floor in painful shock. Her grip faltered, and the quartz pebble fell to the floor with a lifeless clink. It was no longer warm and vibrant, but cold, slimy, and devoid of the power it once h eld.

Emptiness engulfed her, seeping deep into her bones. She staggered, her vision blurring as Galcion and Khyro rushed to her side, their large, worried eyes reflecting her distress. Like a soldier being dragged from the battlefield, she clutched their fur as they shoved her robe back on and pulled her to her room.

She collapsed onto the bed, shivering uncontrollably. What had happened? Had she angered the Fire Keeper? She had always been his faithful servant. And now—nothing. Only terrifying silence. No comforting presence. No fiery warmth. Just a cold vacuum.

Her eyes darted around the room, landing on the vial she had prepared for her sister's hexing. The sight of it brought a bitter taste to her mouth. The glass was cracked. The angelica root inside had swollen and burst the bottle before she could smashed it on the night of the new moon. Now, the dragon's blood resin she had injected into the hex vial was oozing out, staining the glass with its thick, dark essence that may as well have inked out: 'Return to Sender'.

Dagma's mind raced. It had worked—of that she was certain. Agatha had suffered; the pain had been real. But why, then, did she feel so miserable? The realisation struck her sharp and sudden, like a dagger to the chest. Agatha was dead. The hex had gone too far.

For a fleeting moment, guilt twisted in her gut, a foreign and unwelcome feeling. She had caused her sister's death. But the guilt passed quickly, replaced by an uncaring, more satisfying thrill of conquest. With Agatha gone, nothing stood in her way. Valoria would be hers.

She would show her mother how it was done, prove that she was the one destined to rule.

Damnation, why can't I be rid of this guilt? It nagged at her, a persistent itch she couldn't scratch. "Well, it's your fault, Agatha," she muttered bitterly. "If you'd done it my way, you wouldn't have had to suffer. But no, you thought you knew better. Off you went with those monk men and Cane."

Pain throbbed through her body—the same pain she had inflicted. "Oh, hell! This is what she felt!" She curled inwards. "Make it stop."

The pain didn't stop. It stretched on for hours, a relentless, torturous ordeal that left Dagma sprawling on her bed like a sacrificial offering. Sweat soaked the sheets as she lay spread-eagle, her chest heaving. Finally, the agony began to fade. The hex she'd cast had released its grip, leaving her exhausted but oddly satisfied. *There's always a price to pay with a hex*, she thought. *Worth it, though*. But next time, she'd remember to invoke a protective shield. Even the most seasoned practitioner could have a lapse in judgment—something she wouldn't let happen again.

Galcion whined beside her. She turned her head, still half-delirious, reaching out to stroke the loyal dog. "And you," she uttered, giving an absentminded pat to Khyro as well, "thank you for saving me. Both of you. Such good protectors."

Her hand froze mid-pat. *What now?*

A soft singing interrupted the quiet. It seemed there was truly no rest for the wicked. She rose slowly, the haunting melody drawing her from her bed, pulled her like a magnet down the spiral staircase, her feet moving of their own accord, the blood and sweat from her ordeal leaving dark stains behind her.

Had anyone else in the household seen her, they would have been numbed with fright—a phantom figure, drenched in blood and sweat, floating through the darkened halls, she was a ghastly vision. Fortunately for them, and for Dagma, no one was around.

Where is that noise coming from? Damn this infernal merry-go-round! The song like a siren's call luring sailors to their doom, drew her into the hidden inner courtyard.

The pool glistened, catching faint beams of light from the overhead windows. Like a sleepwalker, Dagma stepped into the calm and inviting water until it reached her chin. Its coolness was a stark contrast to the fire that had consumed her earlier. She floated there, until a sudden thought struck her. *What am I doing here? Agatha loved this pool, not me.*

Before she could react, something yanked her ankles hard, dragging her under. Panicking, she thrashed, trying to break free, but the hands gripping her ankles were impossibly strong, dragging her deeper. She managed only a few desperate gasps of air before her vision blurred, and she caught a glimpse of the figure holding her down.

It had to be her. The undine. The queen of all oceans and waters, keeper of the Earth's tears. Why was she here now?

Why are you doing this? Dagma's thoughts screamed as she struggled to free herself. *What do you want from me?*

The Water Keeper was merciless. "You must die. All descendants of the abomination must die."

"I'm sorry!" Dagma's plea was frantic. "I'm sorry I killed my sister! I'll make it up to you!"

But the Water Keeper was unmoved. Her grip tightened, and Dagma felt her lungs burning, the need for air becoming unbearable. The huskies leaned over the edge of the pool, their eyes wide with helplessness as they watched. *Yes*, Dagma thought, *they'll jump in and save me!*

Salvation didn't come from her canine friends. Instead, a raging inferno spread across the water's surface like a wildfire. The Water Keeper shrieked, her hold weakening as the fire scorched the pool. Boiling water seared Dagma's skin as the undine dissolved into nothingness.

The water evaporated in an instant. Dagma stood in the middle of an empty pool, her blood-streaked robe now dry and stiff against her raw skin. She span around frantically. *Where are my huskies?*

The scent of burnt fur reached her. She dared not move at first, fearing another unseen force would strike. Her eyes checked left, then right. Nothing. The courtyard was unnervingly quiet, as if the murderous moments before had never happened. Tentatively, she took a step forward, then another, until she reached the side of the pool. *All safe? Maybe. Maybe not.*

She walked past the burnt remains of Galcion and Khyro, their smouldering fur and bones brought tears to her eyes. *I'll clean them up later,* she thought, trying to ignore the pang of sorrow. She needed to get out of there, to escape this cursed night alive.

Then, she heard it. Drums. A deep, rhythmic pounding that echoed through the halls. Battle drums. The thumping growing louder, dragging her back to the ballroom. "Curse it all," she thought out loud, "what next? I haven't got time for this."

She reached the ballroom doors, her patience worn thin. Then, as if in answer, the massive doors flung open. A fiery face infused with thunderous ascendency, bellowed at her from within the central fireplace.

"Get in here, you power-hungry underling!"

Okay, maybe talking my thoughts out loud wasn't such a good idea. Dagma scurried in like a frightened mouse. Inside, the central fire roaring with life once more. From behind the immense column, a blue-scaled salamander-like creature slithered into view. Its body so long that its tail remained hidden in the shadows even as its head loomed inches from her.

"Hello, Dagma," he hissed. "So nice to finally meet you. Your nightly rituals, your chants—oh, we hear them. Although, we do feel you get more pleasure out of them than we do."

His amphibious, yellow eyes blinked upwards and downwards in a disconcerting motion to places she most certainly did not want them looking.

Her hands flew instinctively to cover herself, her bony fingers hovering over her womanly triangle. She gulped. *What a mess, tonight is one nightmare after the other.*

The Fire Keeper's laugh was a low rumble. "Oh, Dagma, you have no idea what you've gotten yourself into, do you?"

Tiny flames glinted in his yellow eyes as he circled Dagma, his tail coiling around her like a noose. "Nothing to say? You're usually so talkative. So needy," he hissed, his tail tip brushing against her scorched face. The skin there had once been smooth, beautiful even, but now it was a crusty reminder of the price she had paid for jealousy.

"Poor thing," the salamander continued with mock sympathy, "always in your sister's shadow."

Her teeth clenched, Dagma resisted the urge to slap the overgrown lizard's smug face. He was right, of course. She had spent a lifetime being eclipsed by her sister. Always second to Agatha. Always the backup plan. But she was not about to let this flaming lizard patronise her. Keeper or not.

Dagma's words rolled off her tongue before she could stop them. "You can take your observations and shove them—"

The Fire Keeper's slitted eyes gleamed. "Ah, there's that fire I've heard so much about. Shame it's so... small. Well, well, let's not dwell, we have more important things to discuss.

"My Keeper companions don't want your kind to live, but we do. We are curious to see what will happen. Evolution, perhaps? Or at the very least, some entertainment." His forked tongue snaked in and out. "Unfortunately, as the laws of nature would have it, we cannot intervene directly in your realm. Though our sister of the tides violated those doctrines tonight trying to drown you, we play by the book. We have a gift for you."

His tail uncoiled, flicking toward the fire. The flames leapt up, growing as though they had been summoned.

Dagma, relieved to be released from his grip, edged cautiously closer to the fire. *A gift? How exciting. New powers? More power? Finally, some recognition.* But as she squinted into the flames, her anticipation plummeted. Nestled in the fire was a small, bluish-black egg.

"I don't do breakfast." She was not impressed. "What am I supposed to do with an egg?"

"Well, that's up to you. We cannot intervene. But we assure you, it's not for eating. We thought it fitting that this egg, hatching prematurely because of your hex on your own sister, should now be your responsibility."

Marvellous. Bloody marvellous, Dagma thought. *A bloody egg without instructions.* Tentatively, she reached into the fire to retrieve it.

"No! Not yet! She is not ready," the Fire Keeper roared.

Dagma jumped back. The flames rose. From the fire, they emerged—the fire spirits she had only heard of, never seen, no matter how fervently she had chanted.

Though no bigger than her hand, the small fire spirits were a fearsome sight. Each one had its own unique mask and costume. One wore a mask of fiery scarlet and black with bat-like wings; another was clad in brown leather and fur; others had ram's horns, or feathered masks that only revealed glowing red eyes.

Together, they chanted in unison, lifting the egg high into the flames:

"Behold, the flame maiden of Caldera,
Behold, she is born into the fire,
Behold, an angel of purity and new beginnings,
Wielder of flame and stone, mistress of the Earth's core,
A messenger of the Fire Keeper."

The chanting rose to a fevered pitch. Then, as suddenly as they had appeared, the fire spirits melted back into the flames, their forms flickering out like dying embers.

The egg, now glowing with an intense inner light, began to grow.

Dagma spotted the Fire Keeper's reptilian smile just before he slithered back into the darkness. Loud crackling sounds made her swing back to the fire. The egg was splitting. Were those small hands?

Tiny blue fingers gripped the edge of the cracked shell, followed by a scrawny, blue-skinned body pulling itself free. Dagma's breath caught in her throat.

"From salamander of fire to maiden of fire," came the Fire Keeper's voice from the shadows.

Before her eyes, the blue figure transformed. The scrawny body shifted, limbs elongated, skin smoothed. In a blink, the salamander became a girl—a girl with jet-black hair down to her ankles, and hauntingly familiar azure eyes. Agatha's eyes.

Dagma's heart skipped a beat. "Are you—?"

"Thank you for giving me life," the girl said, her voice sizzling like the fire that birthed her. "I am a child of the fire. Daughter of Caldera. Harbinger of darkness."

"Okay." This wasn't the gift she had been expecting. She hated children. Two replacement huskies would have been more her choice. But after nearly being drowned by that bitch of a water nymph, this was... better. She could not deny, the girl was magnificent.

"You're magnificent," she gasped, almost involuntarily.

"I am a child of the fire. Daughter of Caldera. Harbinger of darkness," the girl repeated, her tone mechanical, like she was reciting some memorised recital.

"Alright, got that the first time." *This might be more challenging than at first glance.* "Come, let's get you down from there." She held out her hand. It was a bony charred hand and she was dressed in blood-stained night robe. Not the best first impression.

Dagma beheld the girl standing on the edge of the fireplace. Her delicate skin unmarred by the fire's cruelties, yet her eyes already darkened with bitterness. The black hair spilling down her back sparked with the flames behind her, a sight that would have left most mortals quaking in their boots. But Dagma knew better. This child was not afraid of the fire—she was *of* the fire.

Well, at least she's got that going for her, Dagma thought, as the girl regarded her with an emotionless gaze. There was a coldness in those azure eyes that even Dagma found unsettling. The girl placed her small hand on Dagma's head.

For a split second, Dagma felt like her scalp, or what was left of it, was being sucked into that tiny palm. A blinding light flooded the room. She braced herself for the worst.

Other than a bright blinding light, nothing seemed to happen.

Then the girl removed her hand and said in a flat tone, "Thank you for the human words."

Oh great, Dagma thought, *she can talk now. Who knows what else she just plucked out of my mind?* She was not accustomed to being used—the thought of it made her uneasy. This had to be fixed, and fast. After all, this girl was *her* asset, a gift from the Fire Keeper.

"Come," Dagma said, forcing a note of kindness into her voice. "Come, and I will look after you. Um, did the Keeper give you a name?"

"He is the *Fire Keeper* to all who serve him," the girl corrected her angrily.

Dagma bit back a retort. *Cheeky little madam, isn't she?* But there was no denying the power radiating off the girl, and Dagma couldn't help but admire her audacity. "I meant no disrespect," she said smoothly. "Did the *Fire Keeper* give you a name?"

"No need for names," the girl replied, her tone as flat as before. "Only here, where everything has to have a word. I choose Queen. Since I will be the next queen of the hive."

Well, there's no stopping this rolling boulder of self-confidence. "How about something more unique. We already have lots of queens in our annals of history. Maybe something still royal, but more extravagant. Regina? Reina? Or—."

"Yes. Reonia," the girl said decisively. "I am Reonia."

"Okay, bit of a tongue twister. Not sure that's a name, or even if I can say it," Dagma muttered under her breath. "But if you want it, it's yours." *Difficult name for a difficult girl. Perfect.* Dagma straightened, adopting a more authoritative tone. "We have much to discuss, Reon... Ree-on-ya—"

"Reonia," the girl corrected

"That's what I said!" Dagma snapped, though she knew full well it wasn't. "Anyway, you can trust me. I'm your aunt, after all."

"I know, I killed your sister. Just like you wanted."

Dagma felt something heavy fall inside her—like a lead anchor sinking to the pit of her stomach—as her eyes met Reonia's unblinking gaze. *This girl is outdoing me on all levels of evil,* she thought with trepidation. "Oh, um, thank you," she said awkwardly. "So, she is, er, quite dead?"

"No, not quite dead."

Dagma was surprised to feel relieved—until Reonia added, "Completely dead. There is only one kind of dead." Her voice was utterly devoid of emotion. "I pierced my egg early with my tentacle and filled her belly with fire. She is *completely* dead."

"Ah, yes," Dagma forced a smile. "Just as I requested—ravaged from within. But I don't recall asking for her to *die*. Heartache and pain, yes, but not—"

"Not my fault." Reonia shrugged, utterly indifferent. "These things happen."

Dagma swallowed hard. It dawned on her that this girl was more than just evil—she was unstable. Unhinged. Reonia's premature hatching had likely caused some issues. The girl might look physically perfect, even strong, but mentally? Well, that was a different story. To say Reonia was a little deranged would be the understatement of the century.

As if to prove Dagma's hypothesis right, Reonia asked, "When do we start killing humans?" looking around with disinterest, as though slaughter was just another mundane task on her to-do list.

Did the Fire Keeper bring me a gift or a potential liability? She couldn't afford to let this girl—this tinderbox—loose without a plan. "Patience," she said. "First, we need to locate the Sanctum and get the key. We can't just start a slaughter without a strategy."

Reonia stared blankly. *Of course, she doesn't care about strategy.*

"Thankfully some of the idiot Duke's men found Agatha's necklace by Hackthwall Forest. You know who the Duke is, don't you?"

"Yes, I mind-sucked you. I know all," came the unemotional reply.

"Good, right, yes. I've been mind-sucked. Anyway, where was I? Ah, yes. So, it's likely she and the key will be near there. Mother said the Sanctum was by some woods."

"Then let the slaughter begin there."

"No!" Dagma was on the verge of losing her temper. "Locate the Sanctum. Then get the key. *Then* we can discuss other activities."

Reonia nodded perfunctorily. Dagma exhaled slowly. *Had she understood?* This wasn't going to be easy, but she would find a way to control this portent of power she'd been given.

For now, she had to keep Reonia on a short leash—and keep her pointed at her enemies to make sure she didn't become the next target of the girl's terrifyingly casual bloodlust.

The Rite of Balance

As it is above, so it is below; the celestial order mirrors the terrestrial. We are called to impart that which is eternal, to mend that which is fractured. By decree of the ancient order, the sacred law of nature, we bestow upon you, the elemental forces of wind, flame, water, and stone. The Covenant of the Keepers rebirths you as the sacred equilibrium. So it is willed, so it shall be done.

We impart the wisdom of the winds, the sighs of time, and the fidelity of thought. Let your mind be as boundless as the sky, carrying the echoes of the ages and the whispers of unfolding destiny.

We infuse you with the purging fire, the relentless force that drives anger and hatred. Your spirit, born in the flaming crucible of adversity, will sear away weakness, and forge within you the unyielding strength to endure.

We temper the fire with the cooling waters of clarity. Healing powers flow within you, bringing compassion for sorrow, and deep, abiding equanimity. A calm as deep as the ocean's depths runs within you to navigate the warring tides with grace.

We restore balance. You stand firm, grounded in the bedrock of existence, unwavering amidst the chaos. Your deep connection to the natural world imbues you with the ability to draw upon the deep, nurturing strength of the land.

As steady as stone, as fluid as water, as fierce as flame, and as free as the winds that guide you.

Chapter 34

FADE TO GOLD

S HE FLOATED IN A warm, comforting darkness, cocooned in the water's buoyancy. The voices outside had been there for as long as she could remember, their mutterings soothed her as she drifted in and out of sleep. She didn't know what she was, not yet, but she felt safe—safer now that the other presence, the one brimming with anger and venom, was gone. It had left an ache in her; she pushed those thoughts away. She needed to sleep.

But the voices outside wouldn't let her.

"Shush, stop your moaning, I said," an older voice grumbled, breaking through her drowsiness.

"Can anybody else hear that?" another man asked.

"Yes," a whisper responded. "It's like crunching twigs under boots."

"Uh oh, they found us!" a young one yelped.

"No, no, listen," the second man cut in. "It's not getting louder. It should get louder if they're approaching. It's coming from in there." A pause. "It's stopped."

"There it is again," said another, more frantic voice. "It's like crackling. Oh!"

"Oh, bugger me!"

"It's the bloody egg. What's it doing in the fountain?! Get your sword out, Blake!"

"I took it off to get changed," came the reply, more annoyed than alarmed.

"Well, a dagger or something."

"They're all over there on the table. I'm not going past the fountain to get them."

"Then get Thunder and Lightning out!"

"Let's stay calm," the older voice intervened again.

She stirred. *They're coming closer.* She wasn't sure how she knew, but she felt them moving toward her. Their voices grew louder, their tones more frantic.

"Look, the water is bubbling!" one of the voices squealed.

"And the egg, it's the size of a football now!"

"It's probably putting it in the water that triggered it to hatch!"

"We don't know that," the older man insisted.

"Well, whatever it is, it's started now. Whatever it is," a younger man said.

I have to get out, she realised. *They need help—and I can help them.* She didn't know how she knew they were good people, but she felt it, deep inside. Her mother had known it too, she was sure of that. And if they were good, then she had to help them, protect them, fight for them—whatever that meant. There was no time to lose, even though a part of her longed to stay in this warm, safe space, free from that evil presence that had haunted her.

Her compulsion to wake up, to break free, was too strong to ignore. She banged against the inside of the egg, the walls that had protected her now feeling too tight, too confining.

"Stand back, it's coming out."

"Get your swords ready."

"Why? Are we into killing babies now?" a voice asked sarcastically, followed by a calmer one suggesting: "Maybe we should get a spell ready instead?"

"What do we know of spells? Remember the last time we did one. No, thank you."

"It doesn't really matter because we have a whole library of spells here." She heard the sound of flipping through pages—not that she knew what books were, let alone pages. "Look what I found. A failsafe plan—a 'Protection Spell', to keep those spirits and fairies away."

"What on earth are fairies?"

"They're trickier and nastier, and smaller versions of our sylph."

"Is that even possible? Our sylph chum is a pretty tricky little character."

"Well, maybe it's too risky, and maybe we should not meddle with stuff we don't know about."

"Oh, but it's okay to set the Devil's Needle on fire even though that might invoke the reincarnation of Beelzebub himself!?"

"Rowan has a point there," someone conceded. "Anyway, we have more important matters at hand right here."

She listened to their back-and-forth with a mixture of amusement and frustration. *They're overthinking it. I'm coming out whether they're ready or not.* She was growing too big for this tiny space, her body pushing against the walls of the egg. The water around her bubbled and swirled, a sign that something was happening—something important.

"Did you already cast a spell? I mean, why did the water suddenly start bubbling? Did you put something in it?"

"No, of course not. I wouldn't do anything behind your backs."

"But you pickpocketed me and put it in the fountain, didn't you?"

"Sorry, I felt it was right; it was all that wine and mushroom sauce."

"So, it was in the fountain all night, unattended. Anything could have happened."

"What could have happened? There's nobody else here."

"Apart from the Four Keepers of Powers that can come and go as they please."

But something had happened, she thought, though she couldn't fully grasp it yet. *It must have been the Four Keepers of Power—who else could it be? They had come. They spoke those confusing words.* Their influence had seeped into her egg, changing her in ways she couldn't yet comprehend.

The tingling had started when a whispery wind suffused her. The sounds had trickled like a breeze through her thoughts. Then the searing heat had pulsed through her, only to be quenched by cooling waters, its lulling leaving her a little seasick. Finally, the four voices had quieted, leaving her with that solid weight pressing into her awareness.

Whatever the Four had done, it was done. And now, she was ready to come out.

—◆◇◆—

A crack, then another. The egg splintered. The voices outside stilled mid-argument. There was light.

Without knowing why, she felt an impulse to stretch, to reach toward that light. Pushing at the confines of her once-safe, now suffocating shell, she pushed through the remaining shell. She braced herself. *Now,* she thought. Oh, that was much better. It had been getting awfully tight in there.

Her tiny mind buzzed with the burst of new sensations, sights and smells. Out here everything was sharper, louder, brighter.

She elongated her 'self'—the part with the legs and arms. The top of her 'self'—which held thoughts and images—could now see 'things'.

Her 'seeing-things' took in the world beyond the darkness of the shell. So many *things,* so many *talking things.*

"She's just like the nymph," said one of the talking things—the one called Percy.

Her gaze swept across the group of talking things. The one called Rowan was staring at her like she was a rare gem, his eyes wide and unblinking. He seemed especially fascinated by her hair.

"Ah, her hair. It flows like liquid gold. Her eyes, they gleam like golden orbs. She's beautiful." She noticed there was water in his eyes. Was he part nymph too? She felt a sudden urge to connect with this being that made water from his eyes. Share her water. He was leaking—surely he needed more?

Summoning the water around her, she made it bubble with a frenzied energy. It was exhilarating, feeling the water respond to her call, moving with her thoughts. She was alive, free, and full of power. Oh, how she liked this feeling.

But then, the Rowan thing backed away in fright, his words bursting her bubble of joy. "She's dangerous! We need to perform a ritual to protect us from her evil. Nymphs are related to sirens and undines, all temptresses that seduce men."

She tilted her head, confused. *Seduce?* What did that mean? It didn't sound very friendly. Or fun.

"I'm ready to be seduced," piped up the one they called Blake. He made her want to giggle and cringe at the same time. The black bushy line on his face twitched as he spoke. "Besides, she's so small. How could she possibly harm us?"

The one called Tristan stepped back from the fountain, his eyes wide with fear and curiosity. "What's she doing?"

What *was* she doing? She wasn't sure, but it felt exhilarating.

"I don't know," said the one called Gerant, scratching his hairy chin in what she later recognised as a thinking pose.

The Bain thing—oh, he was *stern*—frowned deeper, his thin lips drawing into a tight line. He didn't look like someone who enjoyed surprises.

"It can think. It is looking at us."

Her mouth pouted at that. She was more than just some 'it', thank you very much. *I'll show them.*

"Should we catch it?"

Before anyone could answer the Percy thing, the fountain exploded in a sparkling show of liquid fireworks, the water shot upwards in a dazzling display of light and colour.

Gasps and shouts filled the room, but she barely noticed. Inside her watery tower, she felt the change.

Growing. Transforming. Her limbs began to reshape themselves—scales giving way to soft skin, webbed fingers becoming delicate digits. She ran her new fingers through her hair.

"She is a waterfall of gold," the Rowan thing pined.

The Cane thing finally spoke. "No. She's just a girl."

She turned to him, drawn by his simple truth. There was something different about him—something solid, steady, like the stone beneath her feet. Where the others reacted with awe or fear, Cane saw the girl.

Meanwhile, the 'Bain thing', tall and stern, studied her closely. His eyes bored into her as if trying to look inside her.

"Definitely not the Baron's," he said, staring into her golden eyes and then turned to Cane. "An uncanny family resemblance."

"How can that be?" asked the bushy thing—no, it was Blake, the one *behind* the 'bushy thing'. She was starting to get the hang of this whole name malarkey.

"Ha! So, no longer the expert on women's reproductive systems," chuckled Felix, rounder than the others and sporting a surprising amount of ginger hair around his speaking hole.

"But he met the Baroness less than nine months ago," Blake said, his voice higher and defensive. The furry bits above his eyes shot up, which she found out later meant surprise. This was all very fascinating.

Just as confused as Blake, she was lost in what all this talk meant. If anyone had answers, surely it was Cane. Mother had trusted him most.

Before he could move, she placed her hand on his head. A blinding light filled the room, and Cane's loud noise—*scream*, yes, that's what it was—rang in her newly understood 'hearing things'. *Ears.* Humans screamed when scared, even without pain. That was odd.

Ooh, I've got lots of new words now, she thought.

She moved on to the next one—the bushy-faced Gerant. His authority was evident from the way the others deferred to him. *He'll know some useful things.* She reached out to place her hand on his head, but for some reason, he ran away.

Why were they always running from her?

When she caught up with Gerant, he screamed too. It was the same: blinding light, loud noise, no pain, just fear of the unknown. She sighed inwardly. *Humans are so weird. Why scream like they're being stabbed when it's just fear?* Oh well, at least after mind-sucking all of them, she'd learned that none of them knew what she was either. How disappointing.

Even though, after all the screaming and running, she still had no idea who or what she was, she had picked up some useful titbits: words, a plan to overthrow a *dippy Duke* (that sounded like something she could help with), and Blake's imprescriptible belief he was God's gift to women!

Maybe if they knew she wanted to help, they would stop all this pointless screaming and flailing.

She decided to speak. But when she opened her mouth, a high-pitch screech ripped out. Oh dear, that didn't sound good. She hadn't done this before—used human words. Everyone's eyes bulged, showing mainly white, and they clutched their ears in pain from her banshee-like scream. Where was the right channel?

The second time, she accidentally shot out flames accompanied by a foreboding tone of doom. *Whoops*, that wasn't it either. She half-singed Blake's beloved 'bushy thing'.

Moustache, she remembered smiling proudly. Blake was *not* smiling. He looked furious, his face a shade of red she identified as *high-level human anger*.

This was not going well. *Okay, third time's the charm.* That was one of Tristan's sayings.

"Hello," she tried again, this time managing a soft tone. Much better. The men seemed calmer now, no longer on the verge of bolting or grabbing the nearest object to hurl at her.

"Thank you for giving me life," she said, her voice soft and musical, like the tinkling of a thousand bells. The men stared at her, entranced by her voice. "I am a child of the water. Daughter of Caldera. Harbinger of light."

The spell she had unknowingly cast over the room broke when Cane coughed awkwardly.

"Ah... she's... not wearing anything." He coughed again, louder.

Rowan mumbled something about modesty and rituals, as he hastily looked away. Percy and Tristan, their faces cycling through every shade of crimson, tried very hard not to stare.

Oblivious to their embarrassment, she smiled. These men were odd, but she liked them.

She shivered. The chill of the air prickled her newly formed, smooth skin. Cane approached her cautiously. Unfastening his cloak, he held it out like an offering.

She blinked at the cloak, puzzled. Was it a gift? Did it have powers?

He gently draped the cloak over her bare shoulders. The fabric was warm and comforting. Well, this was certainly better than being cold.

"Hello. I can help. I *want* to help."

Not convinced, Felix, held out a wooden spoon. "Stay back, don't come any closer!" he jabbed the spoon at her, his hands trembling.

She blinked. Was this a ritual? She glanced around and spotted a similar object with a handle—Blake's dagger on the table. Mimicking Felix, she grabbed it and jabbed back, her expression intensely focused. *Is this how humans communicate? Do we just poke each other with things?*

Felix's eyes nearly popped out of his head. "Arghh!!" he screeched, backing away.

She lowered the knife, realising this might *not* be the best way to make friends.

"Arghh!!" Felix continued screaming, as he ran from the room.

Surprised, she dropped the knife and, for some reason, found herself running after him. "Arghh!" she copied him, figuring it was just what humans did. Her bare feet pitter-pattering against the cold stone floor as they raced into a large hall, the others trailing behind. *What strange creatures,* she thought, giggling at the sight of Felix's tummy bouncing up and down as he ran.

"She is evil! She doesn't want to help us at all!" Felix was still screaming.

That didn't sound promising. Quickly, she scanned her newly acquired knowledge for anything useful. A memory popped up, one of Tristan's from when he was a boy: "You must not laugh at your brother, Tristan, just because he's smaller and has curly hair. It's not kind. You must help other people."

"How do you know that?" Tristan asked, stunned.

The men warily gathered around her in a circle. She said, "I want to help you."

Cane's cloak, now heavy and hot from all the running, felt oppressive. She shrugged it off.

"No, no, no, put it back on!" Cane quickly wrapped the cloak over her shoulders. "Thankfully, your hair covers you," he muttered under his breath.

"Too hot," she protested, tugging at the cloak.

He gently guided her to a bench at the side. Meanwhile, the others continued to stare, making her feel even hotter. All she could think about was water—cool, refreshing water. She felt *so* hot. Like Mother. Would she die too? But she'd only just got here.

"How about this!" Percy reappeared, holding up a small gown, clearly meant for someone small, like her. This made her smile—I'm not going to die!

"Thank you," she said, taking the dress from Percy. "I am very hot." But just as she took the dress, she noticed something new happening—steam was rising from her arms. Wait, no, not steam, smoke. She was on fire.

"She's on fire!" Tristan yelled in full panic mode. "Bloody hell, she's on fire and blinking and that's not normal."

"Oh, I am not normal." She looked at them for help, suddenly sensing the full extent of her predicament and her helplessness. She had to get back to the fountain, quickly.

Cane scooped her up and sprinted for the fountain room, the others close behind. Why did they always follow? He plunged her into the cool water, her fiery skin hissing as it met the water. *Relief.*

The men watched hesitantly at the edge.

Exhausted, she closed her eyes. She didn't know how long she'd slept, but when she opened her eyes again, the men were no longer staring. Instead, they were huddled together, whispering loudly with their backs to her.

"We cannot trust her," Bain was saying, his voice harsh and suspicious. "Given her lineage, she—"

"Yes, I am part of that lineage," Cane cut in. "Somehow. So, she can't be *all* bad."

"We can't destroy something living just because we don't understand it," said Gerant.

"Fine, we'll give her a chance," Bain conceded grudgingly. "But remember, the sylph said we need to eliminate all descendants to vanquish the miscreants. There's *something* evil in her. Nobody normal burns like a furnace and survives. Well, apart from Lady Dagma, and there's nothing normal or nice about that nefarious necromancer."

She didn't like the sound of that. Being lumped in with evil was *not* what she wanted. The spawn in her mother had been pure evil, and she was determined not to be anything like it.

Resolute in proving them wrong, she raised her hand, conjuring a tiny spark of light. She blew on it, sending it floating toward them. It grew into a warm, glowing ball that divided into dozens of smaller lights, filling the hall with a festive, comforting glow.

The men quieted, their harsh whispers fading into silent awe.

"See," said Cane. "She means well."

"Or she's a trickster," Bain said looking at her with distrust.

She sighed. *These men are so hard to please. But at least they're not running and screaming anymore. Progress!*

Chapter 35

DAUGHTER OF LIGHT

AYS HAD PASSED, AND she was in a perpetual state of confusion—hot, cold, and, like any normal teenager, mostly just tired. On top of it all, the men were a riddle she couldn't crack. One minute they trusted her, the next, they looked at her as if she had just sprouted wings. She spent her time either soaking in the fountain pool or huddled by the fire in the room where they ate. It wasn't a kitchen; she'd gathered that much from Godfrey's mind-suck. His thoughts were neatly arranged like a librarian's filing cabinet. A kitchen, it seemed, was a different kind of place entirely, just like this marble building was part of a much wider world.

Godfrey knew a lot. Cane knew even more, though his knowledge was the kind you couldn't pin down with words—more shapes, sensing, and just knowing.

They still didn't trust her enough to see this wider world, but for now, the Sanctum was enough. Baby steps. Or, more accurately, *hatchling* steps.

What am I doing wrong? she wondered. *This is my... my what? My family? Yes, that sounds right. I have to fit in here. Because if I don't fit in here, where will I fit in?* That thought made her pause. Cane wasn't with his family but he seemed blissfully unaware. Bain didn't even *like* his family, yet he was perfectly content. So, why was she so desperate to be accepted?

Probably because she felt isolated. Probably because she didn't know *what* she was.

She'd seen her reflection. She was different—shorter, skinnier, a wild mane of golden hair and big golden eyes. Her brow and face resembled Cane's, but her hands were much smaller, delicate even, and she lacked the roughness, the face fuzz, the deep voice. Her own voice was squeaky. None of the men ever caught fire or conjured glowing lights, and they all slept in beds, not pools of water.

Oh dear, the list of differences is endless, she sighed, resigning herself to being an anomaly until one commonality came to mind: *We all eat!*

An idea took root. *I'll surprise them with a meal! That'll show them I can fit in.*

The next morning, she got to work.

She rummaged through their supplies, poking curiously at raw ingredients like a mad scientist assembling a potion. Bread? Check. Meat? Well, meat-like. Something red and squishy. She grabbed a few jars of honey, balancing them precariously in her hands, and found a bowl of salt—that must go with everything, right? She dumped it in for good measure.

Frowning at the fire pit, she had no idea how to get it lit—so she decided to use her own tiny finger flame. A burst of fire shot out from her palm, igniting the logs in an instant but also setting the corner of the tablecloth aflame. Panicked, she doused it with a nearby jug of water. That should've solved the problem, but now the table was wet, and everything on it looked like it had gone for a swim.

Undeterred, she dumped all the ingredients—meat, bread, eggs, honey—into the cauldron. She stirred vigorously, glancing over her shoulder as footsteps approached. *Oh! They'll be here any moment,* she thought excitedly.

When a bleary-eyed Felix stumbled into the room, she beamed with pride.

"What have you done?" His shriek was so loud that Tristan and Percy came rushing in, daggers drawn.

"I made breakfast!" she said, practically glowing with delight. "Just like you. For you."

Felix stared at the table, horrified. The cauldron bubbled frantically beside her, an unidentifiable mass of goo swirling within.

"Ah, well, thank you, dear, but normally we, um, cook the meat and toast the bread over the fire. We don't boil *everything* in the cauldron. That's, er, just for soup, you see."

Her smile slid off her face. "Is it not right?" she asked in a small voice, her excitement deflating. She had to admit, the soggy food spread across the table didn't look like what Felix usually prepared.

Tristan tried to make her feel better. "Well, at least the logs are burning nicely now."

"I'm sure the boiled rabbit will be edible," Percy said, sitting down and chewing with a valiant effort on a stringy piece of meat.

One by one, the other men drifted in, tactfully navigating around her unique breakfast spread. Bain asked her to sit with them, and her heart fluttered with hope, as if, just maybe, she was finally being accepted.

Bain settled himself in front of some grey gloop. "Right, young lady. You made breakfast, and I promised to give you a chance, so let's start, shall we?"

Filled with hope, she passed him some burnt bread, her small hand brushing his. He quickly pulled his hand away. The sting of rejection hit her hard. *Not again,* she thought, as tears blurred her vision. She'd grown tired of this—of always feeling on the outside, always missing that happiness she'd glimpsed in their minds.

Bain cleared his throat, his voice quieter now. "I'm sorry," he muttered, his large hand hovering awkwardly before resting over hers. It felt warm, rough—like a shield.

The tears kept flowing, but this time they felt different, lighter, almost like they were lifting something heavy off her chest. And then, suddenly, she felt it—a warmth spreading inside her, a fluttering sensation in her belly. Was this happiness? It felt like magic, filling her up from the inside out; she felt like she could float.

Around her, the smiles grew, and something warm blossomed in her chest, spreading out to her fingertips. *Is this happiness? Does it just keep growing?* She felt like her body might burst with it. Her cheeks hurt from smiling so much. And then, something even more wondrous happened—her body started shaking. Her tummy tightened, and a funny sound burst out of her mouth. *Oh my, is this laughter? It's even better than the happiness! Is there another level? This is... this is... heavenly!*

But just as quickly as it had come, it began to fade. The smiles around the table were smaller. Her body stilled, the laughter fading, but she still felt good. Very, very good.

So, this is what happiness feels like, she thought, still luxuriating in the glow of it. *Maybe I'm not so different after all.*

"You know what, little thing," Bain said, catching her attention, "we don't even know your name."

"Neither do I," she replied, po-faced. That statement, for some reason, sent the men into fits of laughter. She blinked at them, perplexed. "I don't even know *what* I am." Their laughter doubled.

She crossed her arms, frowning deeply. "I hardly see what's funny about that. How would you like it if you didn't know you were a man?"

The switch from laughter to awkward silence was instant. Feeling a twinge of guilt for killing the mood, she tried to placate them. "I feel lost, like I don't belong. I know I'm female—a girl—but not a human girl. What am I?"

"We don't know," Cane admitted. "But somehow, you're partly, well, partly me. Somehow."

"Why are you not sure?" she asked full of innocent curiosity.

"Well, it's not easy to say," Cane replied, rubbing the back of his neck awkwardly. "I have no clear memory, just hazy flashbacks and—"

Gerant came to Cane's rescue. "I think such conversations are best saved for when you're older," he said with a wink. "You shouldn't feel alone. You have us. For now, let's focus on getting you familiar with the basics, like reading, writing—"

"Cooking!" said Felix.

"Yes, cooking, sword fighting and horse riding. Then we can go kill the dippy Duke!" she cheered.

The men erupted into laughter again. *What is wrong with these people?* she wondered. *Is my ferocious tone in this girl voice not getting through to them?* Maybe she'd stuttered. Deciding to give it another go, she pulled her shoulders back and summoned her deepest, most menacing voice.

"We will kill the dippy Duke," she declared making the men jump back in their seats.

Oops, she thought, realising too late that she'd accidentally scorched the table.

Felix chuckled, putting out the small fire with a damp cloth. "Good thing it's a stone table!"

"Alright," Gerant said, easing back into his seat, warily keeping one eye her, "let's give our little fire-breathing dragon a name."

Suggestions flew around the table like sparks from a fire.

"Firefly," Percy suggested, and she wrinkled her nose.

Rowan threw in his poetic two pennies worth. "Drakona!" She shook her head.

Then came more like 'Wyverna' and 'Sirena'—and Blake's 'Dora' was met with a flat stare all round.

"How about Luciana, since she is the harbinger of light?" Cane suggested.

Felix was clearly enamoured with his suggestion. "Oh yes, I like that."

The men nodded in agreement, and she found herself liking the sound of it too. "Luciana," she repeated, testing the name on her tongue. *I like that.* "I have a name."

The days that followed were more perfect than Luciana could have dreamed of. Freed from the confines of the marble walls, she walked with the men, finally exploring the world beyond her sheltered existence. She helped where she could—lighting fires with just a touch, reviving frozen plants, and even healing small wounds they incurred during training.

One night, Luciana lay floating above her bed—yes, a bed, since she'd mastered her water powers, and yes, floating, because her air powers still weren't fully under control—when she felt a strong presence sweep through the Sanctum. It was like a cool breeze, with a hint of mischief. The shrill voice of the sylph floated into her mind. *That's the voice that gave me the wisdom of the winds and the sight of time,* she thought, perking up. *What's it doing here again?*

Her curiosity got the better of her, and she tiptoed to the ritual room. Peering inside, she saw the men gathered, looking tense and alert, their eyes fixed on the little sylph.

"Why have you come?" asked Gerant. "We did not summon you."

"We have come of our own free will," the sylph trilled. "We cannot intervene directly in human affairs or the way of the world. We ride on the whispers—"

"Yes, yes, very poetic," Bain interrupted, sounding as if he'd heard this kind of speech a thousand times. "What do you want, riddle master?"

"We only wish to say thank you for the offerings. We hear the chimes daily and have enjoyed the clarity of your resins and—" It played coyly with one of its wispy tendrils.

"And what?" asked Bain angrily.

"And that if, hypothetically, you were planning a three-pronged attack, now would be the best time. The lines of the future are favourable."

"Oh, I see," said Bain. "That was unexpectedly helpful. Thank you."

"Do I need to sing again?" Felix asked, ready to burst into song.

"No need, wide one." The sylph sounded amiably amused. "But should you wish to hum a tune once we are gone, we would take great pleasure in your tenorous songs."

Tenorous? She didn't know what that meant, but maybe sylphs were allowed to make up words.

"Why the sudden generosity?" Tristan asked suspiciously. "Very fishy if you ask me."

"We do not dabble with fish," the sylph was in a huff. "That is the Water Keeper's job. We are messengers of the timelines. We come to those in need."

"When it suits you," Tristan shot back.

"We are not used to such insubordination and disrespect," the sylph huffed. "We came to help and, well, now we are leaving."

Luciana watched the Keeper swish upward and vanish, leaving a trail of sparkling mist.

Tristan wasn't done. "We don't know where the other egg was taken. Would it be too much to ask for a clue?"

"Yes," came the bodiless reply from somewhere far above.

"Blast," Tristan grumbled. "He does that just to annoy us, I'm sure. Little bugger."

"We can still hear you," the sylph's voice called back.

Luciana burst into the room with the enthusiasm of a child about to blow out the candles on her birthday cake. Excitement sparkled in her golden lion eyes. "So, are we going?"

Gerant, like a gentle giant, placed his large, hairy hand on her small shoulder. "*We* are," he said kindly, "but you, little one, will stay here with your... um, Cane and Godfrey."

The sparkle in Luciana's eyes dimmed. "Oh." She looked like someone had not just stolen her birthday cake but made off with the presents. "But I can help! I'm very useful. You know, with my dragon breath? I've been practicing!"

She took a deep breath, puffing out her cheeks dramatically as if ready to blow fire across the room.

"No, that won't be necessary," Gerant was quick to stop her. She'd already burnt several chairs and useful blankets during her 'practice'.

"And I can use the wind to move!" she added. With a sudden whoosh, she vanished from one side of the ritual chamber and reappeared on the other in the blink of an eye. "See? Super fast!"

The men glanced at each other, half impressed, half alarmed.

"And I can call on water!" she continued, flipping her little hand with a flourish. A playful, star-shaped stream of water flowed out of the fountain, darting around the room. She grinned, proud of her aquatic acrobatics.

Gerant's eyes widened as he saw where her hand was pointed next. "Luciana, wait!" He grabbed her outstretched hand just before she could direct her magic toward a load-bearing stone column. "Let's... let's not move the stone, alright? I'm sure you have mastered that just fine, too."

Luciana pouted but didn't resist. She wanted to be helpful, but apparently hers wasn't the kind of help they needed.

They busied themselves with simpler tasks. Luciana watched as they collected sap from the trees to brew into ink, gathered nettles for paper, and plucked feathers to fashion into writing quills. It all seemed terribly boring to her, but they insisted it was necessary.

"We're making posters," Gerant explained patiently. "Just as we planned. We'll plant seeds of doubt in the people's minds. Let them ask questions: 'Where did Duke Nieman come from? What has Duke Nieman done for our peaceful community? Choose Nieman. Choose war!'"

Luciana scrunched her nose. "Why don't we just zap him with fire and tell them the truth?"

"If only it were that simple," said Gerant.

"Why posters?"

"The posters and pamphlets are the rousing whispers before we set the Devil's Needle on fire," Gerant said, with a look that suggested this was very important grown-up talk. "They'll get people thinking about their lives before the Duke. A time without fighting, without fear. Once they start remembering, they'll see how much blood has been spilled since his arrival. And since the posters are delivered anonymously, they are neutral messengers."

"But can't the Duke's men just take them down?" asked Blake.

"Yes, they can," said Gerant, "but not before people have read them. Not fast enough."

Gerant went over his three-pronged plan again.

"Some of us must stay behind to guard the key and keep the sylphs' gateway safe. That'll be you, Cane, along with your father and Luciana." He looked at Luciana, who was busy trying to spin a star-shaped puddle to hide the fact she was sulking. "I doubt they'll attack; they don't know we're here."

Gerant turned to Percy, Tristan, and Blake with a serious expression. "To pull this plan off, I have a big ask of you. I hope you're ready for it."

"We're ready for action," the brothers said in unison.

"Especially you, Percy," Gerant added with a knowing smile. "Rowan, their disguises, please."

Rowan brought out the gowns of the Gaene Kin.

"I thought I was staying here," said Luciana.

"These are not for you," replied Gerant looking at Percy.

"You've got to be joking," Percy groaned. "I'm not dressing up as a woman. It was bad enough as a monk—so breezy around the legs."

"No way!" objected Blake.

"You just don't want to shave off your lip rug!" said Rowan .

Blake stroked his large black whiskers with a pained expression.

"You don't have to shave off that hairy mouser living under your nose," Felix said, laughing. "Some of the women in Bellingham could give you a run for your money in that department!"

"Percy might make a fine young lady, but not me," Blake continued to complain. "And I'm not getting rid of Roderic."

"You named your moustache?" Percy burst out, unable to contain his laughter.

"It's a part of me," Blake said defensively.

"And of all the names, you called it *Roderic*?" said Tristan. "I mean, Lotharion the Lady Charmer would have been better. But *Roderic*?"

"Or Leo the Lusty Lip Serpent!" Percy said, doubling over with laughter. "Roderic! Do your special lady friends get to call it *Eric* or *Roddie*?" The others burst into fits of laughter.

"Don't worry, Blake," Gerant said, trying to keep a straight face, "you are going as Rowan's husband."

Blake stood as big and wide as he could. "That doesn't sound much better. Skinny and pale, he's not my type at all. Think of my reputation with the ladies. I have standards to uphold."

He shrank under Gerant's serious gaze. "Oh alright, to save mankind, I can do it just this once. Better than parting with *Roderic*."

"We thought Percy would prefer to go as a foot masseur." Felix winked, taking a bite out of an apple.

"And you, Percy," Gerant continued, "being the, um, not so tall one, are going as your brother's wife."

"Ready to help," Percy said, slipping into his gown with as much dignity as he could. "And being a lady is miles better than a foot masseur, so no complaints here. Plus, at least I don't have to be married to bushy Blake with his pet *Roderic*. But I must say, I was hoping for something more action related."

"Oh, there'll be plenty of action Percy," Gerant reassured him. "You and Tristan will be one couple; Blake and Rowan the other. Distribute the posters but try not to be seen."

The wives-to-be tried on their gowns. The were the plainest in the wardrobe.

"Oh! This dress lets in all the cold air," Percy grumbled as Tristan tied a cord sash around his waist.

"I think you should keep our trousers on underneath," said Rowan from beneath his hooded gown, not entirely thrilled with his new role either.

Luciana had a flash of inspiration. "Percy and Rowan need wigs to complete their look." Without waiting for a reply, she cut off all her golden hair and with nimble fingers moving at the speed of light wove the strands together. "Had far too much of it anyway," she said, beaming as the men admired her handiwork.

With every smile, every word of thanks, her own silly grin grew and grew until there was no more room for it on her face.

"Thank you, Luciana," said Gerant. "That really adds a convincing touch. It doesn't change things though, we need you to stay here and guard the Sanctum."

"You're welcome. But there's no need to keep on lying, Mr. Gerant. Even if it's just a white lie. I know I'm not *guarding* the Sanctum. You're leaving me here because I'm volatile, unpredictable and potentially a target. Papa Cane and Godfrey are the real guards here, along with the wolves and bears, of course. Don't look so surprised—I'm onto all your plans."

Gerant did look surprised. "Ah, yes. I forgot you can enter our thoughts."

Luciana grinned cheekily. "That's true, but I'm also very good at eavesdropping."

Chapter 36

THINGS THAT SHOULD NOT BE

Night had fallen. Gwaine and Holly huddled in their less-than-ideal hiding spot, deep in the cover of darkness. Their noses wrinkled against the stench of manure, but at least it masked their scent from any hunting dog, or worse, Dagma. They had a simple plan: figure out what the witchy woman was up to and then get the hell out. Unfortunately, this meant staking out the smelliest corner of a cow shed. Gwaine couldn't decide what was worse: the cold numbing his limbs or the anticipation of what they were about to see. After all, Dagma wasn't exactly known for quiet nights of cocoa and bedtime reading.

But it wasn't just Dagma's delightfully crispy face that greeted them this time. She had a young black-haired girl with her, bright-eyed and bouncing with excitement, like she was about to step into a candy shop.

"I want to show you what I've been preparing for great Atropa's arrival," Dagma said.

"The *great* Atropa!" the girl squealed, clapping her hands.

"Yes, yes, but hush now. Follow me."

"Yuck, to the dirty cow sheds?"

"Exactly. The Duke thinks I'm better suited to curing cows than taking over Valoria. Let him think that. It's the perfect cover."

As Dagma creaked open the barn doors, Gwaine and Holly seized the opportunity to move closer. They scooted to the other side of the barn, footsteps muffled by the groaning doors. Peering through the loose wooden slats, they were about to see enough to populate their worst nightmares for the rest of their lives.

Inside, Dagma shoved aside a few pitiful-looking cows, who moaned in protest but were too weak to resist. She led the girl up to a rickety mezzanine with nothing but a shabby workbench, a few dusty sacks, and a rusty shovel that looked like it hadn't seen a day of honest work in years. With a flourish, Dagma pulled a small bottle from her gown, uncorked it, and poured its contents into a tray filled with something thick and opaque.

Gwaine wasn't a betting man, but he'd wager that gloop wasn't the overcooked custard it resembled.

"What is that yucky stuff?" asked the girl.

"These," Dagma replied, as if discussing a baking recipe, "are my eggs. I take a small amount of male human blood, usually while they sleep. That triggers my eggs to develop. Now, if I had my good looks or could enter minds, I'd seduce a man to fertilise them and make queens. But I don't."

"No, you're really ugly."

Gwaine couldn't help but smile at the girl's brutal candour.

Dagma, ignoring the insult, continued. "I mean I don't *want* to make queens. I want to make drones. All males. Once these little beauties are ready, I inject them up the cow's arse. Here."

The girl scrunched up her face. "Arse? Do you mean the anus? That's where stuff comes *out*. Why do you put it *in*?"

Gwaine's stomach flipped. As far as barbarism went, this was a new level of depravity.

"It's just easier," Dagma explained, as if still guiding the girl through a recipe. "The larvae travel up the digestive tract into the cow's belly, where they feed."

"Yuck, they eat that rotten grass in the cow's belly?"

"No, no. They eat the cow's soft tissue. And when they're ready, they burrow their way out."

The depravity level had just sunk to a new low. *Oh, it just keeps getting better. Flesh-eating larvae.* He looked at Holly. Her dark brown eyes were silently screaming in revulsion. Gwaine wished he could unhear this entire conversation, but the sordid details kept rolling in, like a horror story that didn't know when to end.

"Doesn't the cow make a lot of noise? Won't people notice?" the girl asked.

"Our clever little larvae release a poison first that paralyses the cow. Then they chew their way out with their sharp mandibles. It will soon be time for them to birth."

Dagma sounded so upbeat, Gwaine expected her to do a little jig. He found himself wishing for the simple life—a cottage with a garden, maybe some hens, no murderous larvae—the girl's monotone voice brought him back to the gruesome present.

"But then there will be lots of dead cows lying around."

"No, my dear Ree-on-yee-ha—"

"Reonia," the girl corrected.

"That what I said. Anyway, that's the wonderful part. Once the poison wears off, the cow revives. It even cares for the newly born larvae, thinking they're its young. Happens with the bulls, too."

"Oh, how sweet."

Gwaine nearly choked on his own disgust. *Sweet?* More like the kindling of insanity's fire. How could anyone see this as anything but repugnant? There was more to come. Dagma pulled out a mysterious bag.

"And now for these little treasures," Dagma said with Christmas-morning excitement as if she were handing Reonia her stocking.

Gwaine gritted his teeth. *How on earth did I end up here? Hiding in a filthy barn, spying on a witch with a penchant for cow-anus shenanigans?*

Meanwhile, Dagma was rubbing her hands together, creating a dry rasping sound. Beside her, Reonia mimicked the motion like a mini apprentice of evil. Gwaine and Holly were doing their best impressions of statues, though the rancid air was practically chewable.

Curiosity got the better of them, and they leaned forward for a better view. Immediately, they regretted it.

Whatever was in that sack... *oh no. No. No.* It looked like it had crawled out of someone's sick imagination and then gone back in for more.

"This is the second batch," Dagma announced with a hint of disappointment, as if her cake hadn't risen properly. "Something went wrong. I think the man I used was subpar. These turned out mutant."

Reonia pointed to a nearby barrel painted with a sloppy '1'. "And the first batch?"

"Oh, that lot?" Dagma sighed theatrically. "They went wrong too. I used mother's foolproof formula. Even made crucibles for spawning pools. But I've never been great with water magic. Or maybe it's because I didn't feed them meat. I enchanted the water with nutrients, but it just bubbled and cooked them to death."

"So, what will you do with them?" Reonia sounded as if she was asking about leftovers.

Dagma replied dismissively, "Fodder for the next batch, of course."

Gwaine, who was still reeling from the idea of bubbling larvae soup, had to admit he was wrong—he had thought things couldn't get any more disgusting.

"That's very efficient. So, they eat themselves?"

"They eat anything. Flesh is their preferred dish. Like sheep eating grass, but more carnivorous."

"Why make them if all they do is eat?"

"They'll follow my commands. They're our army."

Reonia's eyes widened. "An army of flesh-eaters? Do they grow as fast as me?"

"Faster. They will be full-sized in just a few weeks after coming out of the host animal, and already with the strength of ten oxen. When they're born, I'll bind them to me."

"How will you do that?"

"I use a fragment of my fire power, infuse it in them. This binds them to me through sound—so I can command them with my voice."

"Why aren't you making any queens?"

"We don't need any more queens. We have *you*," Dagma replied, her voice softening unnervingly. She reached out, her charred hand caressing the girl's porcelain-like face. For a fleeting second, Gwaine could almost convince himself that Dagma's eyes softened with something like tenderness. Though he'd have to squint really hard to believe it.

"And my sister," Reonia added, her tone as casual as if she were talking about a pet hamster.

Dagma nearly dropped the sack of dead larvae she'd been holding. "What? Your sister? There's another?"

"Yes. Only one other. And she was weak. I could feel her. Stupid golden egg—she just wanted to sleep all the time. Hide and sleep. I got out. She's stupid."

"Another potential queen." Dagma's voice quivered with unease, a rare crack in her usually confident facade. "Where is she?"

"With the stupid men at the marble place," Reonia said offhandedly.

Gwaine's stomach plummeted. *Two of these miscreants.* And if one of them was with Gerant and the others. His dread deepened. They might not even realise what they were dealing with.

"The marble place?" Dagma asked. "You mean the Sanctum?"

"I don't know if it's the sank-sancta-sancto, whatever—how should I know? The Fire Keeper came to get me and brought me to you because I'm special and shouldn't stay with stupid people in boring white marble places."

"Yes, the Sanctum," Dagma muttered more to herself than to the girl, her mind probably already plotting ten steps ahead. "Well, we'll deal with that soon enough. We should have sufficient drones to handle her and all those silly—"

"When I mind-sucked you, I saw Atropa," Reonia interrupted. "Ah, mighty Atropa. She is magnificent. I am magnificent."

Dagma stiffened. *Was that a tiny twinge of jealousy she felt?* Gwaine looked at Holly, who must have sensed it too as she returned his look with a silent nod and a smirk.

"And your point is?" Dagma asked, trying to keep her tone neutral, but Gwaine could hear the irritation in her tone.

"She told you her plan was to capture the old man Aurelius and his family so they could watch her return and take over this place. She wants you and that Duke man to infillate—"

"Infiltrate," Dagma corrected, her voice a bit sharper now.

"Whatever," Reonia shrugged. "Not build an army. That wasn't in her plan. Capturing, brainwashing and making human-type babies to infillitate and take over power and all that. Not fight with drone armies. What are you doing, Auntie D? Is Auntie D a bad auntie? Why isn't Auntie D making babies? Stupid Mother did. Atropa will be happy with Mother and angry with Auntie D."

If Dagma had any nostrils, they would have flared like trumpets. "Agatha is dead. Atropa will be happy with *me*." Then, catching herself, she added, "No, well, what I mean is, that's all wrong."

"Explain," Reonia demanded, clearly not ready to drop the subject.

"Auntie D is a *clever* auntie," Dagma began, using the same condescending tone one might use to explain that water is wet. "Auntie D is helping Atropa—in case her plan that moves at the speed of a glacier doesn't work. Your stupid mother, Agatha, ran off with the stupid men. And Auntie D has no intention of sharing anything with human men, let alone having things grow in her tummy. Auntie D is smarter than that." She stopped, probably tiring of referring to herself in the third person. "I don't even touch the human men. I apply my special pheromones, target a suitable one, extract what is required, and induce a state of forgetfulness and delirium with a lovely blend of poppies, passionflower, dogwood, and valerian slipped into their drink or food. Easy as that!"

She stopped, possibly wondering if she'd given too many details for a girl born just a few days ago. "Having an army of drones will make sure the humans do what *we*, I mean, Atropa demands when she arrives."

Reonia was hanging on her every word, eyes wide with admiration. Dagma seized the moment to cement her influence over the girl. "Come, Reonia. You will be a part of this. You can bind a unit of drones to your command." Now there was an auntie who knew the way to her niece's heart.

"Yay, my own drone army!"

Up in the rafters, Gwaine felt hope slipping away. That was it—the girl was putty in Dagma's hands now. Holly's expression mirrored his dismay as they watched the two head to the back of the barn. They crept silently along the beams for a better view, dodging creaking wood and holes.

"It is important we're not discovered, so everything is kept out of sight. Do you want to see some that are already eating their way out?" Dagma asked, with the same casual tone one might use when offering a tour around a well-kept garden.

Reonia nodded eagerly, the grin plastered on her face since Dagma had dangled the prospect of commanding flesh-eating drones. As Dagma moved to the opposite side of the barn, Gwaine's eyes darted back and forth through the slats, taking in the scene below.

What he saw was far worse than Dagma's scorched face up close.

Eight—or was it ten?—tiny, vaguely human-shaped aberrations were wriggling out of the leathery hide of a cow. Their amber-coloured bodies, slick with whatever vile substances had been brewing inside the poor beast, glistened as they chomped their way to freedom. Their hair-thin limbs twitching distortedly as they squirmed out.

Gwaine fought a wave of nausea. *Stay quiet, stay hidden.* Beside him, Holly's face had drained of all colour.

He couldn't look away, though. Neither of them could. Because what they were witnessing wasn't just revolting, it was a sign that the situation had gone from bad to apocalyptic. They needed to know all.

Down below, Dagma looked on with motherly pride. "Ahh, they are adorable," she cooed, and Reonia nodded enthusiastically. Gwaine could only think that 'adorable' was about the last word he would ever use to describe the writhing, insect-like abominations. But Dagma was in her element—a paradise of the macabre.

Against his better judgement, Gwaine forced himself to keep watching. The foetuses floated in a creamy, translucent liquid that glistened unnervingly in the dim barn light. Their amber skin was so thin it was nearly transparent, revealing unexpected internal structures: skeletal ridges along their spines that looked like they could sprout wings at any moment, bulbous, oversized nodules on their heads that might one day become antennae, or worse, horns.

Gwaine wasn't exactly an expert on creepy-crawlies, but he knew enough to see this was some sickening hybrid of human and insect.

"Auntie D, you *are* clever. Atropa will definitely be pleased with you—better than my stupid mother who fell in with humans and tried to save those ingrates."

"Reonia, you say the sweetest things." Dagma's grin was disturbingly wide. Thanks to the lack of skin and her exposed teeth, she had a permanent skeletal grin. She had that whole *cliché villain* vibe, complete with the burnt-in-hell look.

"Ready to perform your first ritual, Reonia, with our—no, *your* army?" Dagma was laying it on thick. Not a bad idea to get the evil child on her side, then she wouldn't have to sleep with one eye open for the rest of her life.

"Listen and learn," said Dagma. She began reciting a dark incantation.

"By the ancient flame that burns within, I, Dagma, Daughter of Caldera, Mistress of the Darkened Fire, summon you" Her voice swelled, filled with dark wizardry, invoking sparks, flames, and wind.

"We have to see," Gwaine whispered urgently to Holly, his voice barely audible over the growing hum of magic.

He spotted a somewhat crumbling section of wall that might serve as a makeshift ladder. Silently cursing his now gaunt physique—thank you, captivity diet—he scrambled up, finding tenuous holds on the protruding crossbeams. Reaching the roof, he peered through the shabby rafters. Below, Dagma and Reonia were doing their best to make his darkest fantasies come true.

Reonia's small form stood confidently in a circle of cows who were unknowingly giving birth to an army of flesh-eating horrors for her to command.

"Protectress of the flame, harbinger of darkness, bringer of pain, I, Reonia, Daughter of Caldera, Commander of Drones, order you to come forth and be claimed," Reonia chanted like a natural-born overlord. Gwaine grimaced. *Great, just what the world needs, a mini-megalomaniac with a natural flair for the demonic.*

Dagma sprayed something from tiny bottles, the contents of which glowed blue and sparkled like fairy dust—an evil fairy dust with a vendetta against all things good and kind. The blue mixture landed on Reonia's hand, and she cast it over her newly claimed army with all the skill of a deranged sorceress.

The transformation was instant and horrifying. Each tiny body absorbed a grain of the blue sand, and before Gwaine's disbelieving eyes, the minuscule figures began to change. Their translucent amber skin grew dark and hard. Folded wings hummed to life, their forms solidified into obsidian black shells, and they grew—oh, how they grew. Spiked bristles sprouted from their strong limbs, and large heads with bulging eyes stared at Reonia, awaiting her command.

Then more emerged. And more and more, all munching their way out of the cows. Gwaine's heart stopped as hundreds of drones, now standing a terrifying seven feet high, pounded their spine-covered arms against their chests. The rhythmic thuds reverberated through the barn like the march of hell's army.

Heaven help us! he thought. *This is it. This is how the world ends.*

Gwaine tried to grasp the full horror of what he was seeing. It wasn't just the sight of Dagma's horrific brood that terrified him, it was the fact that these monstrous hordes were under the control of a power-crazed little girl. If Dagma was the wicked witch, Reonia was a demon in pigtails.

He glanced at Holly, who was pale but resolute. The unspoken understanding between them was clear: things had gone from terrible to 'I want to curl up and cry' in the blink of an eye. But both knew they couldn't afford to fall apart now.

God willing, we'll live long enough to warn the others, Gwaine thought. *Not that it'll matter. All we have is a scraggly army of men and women at best, maybe a few pitchforks, to take on an army of giant, man-eating insects. Piece of cake.*

"Your first proper meal. Eat up!" Reonia tipped over the barrel filled with failed foetuses that resembled skeletal eels. "Ooh, they've gobbled them all up so quick!"

The cannibalistic frenzy below was the final straw. Gwaine could feel the bile rising, but he fought it down. *Don't retch, don't retch,* he chanted silently to himself. But it was no use. His body rebelled. He dry heaved—the first time.

Gwaine's stomach lurched. Scrambling to get away from the edge, his foot slipped on the rotten wood. Before he knew it, he was slipping down the barn wall. He landed with a silent thud, the impact shooting pain up his leg. He swallowed a cry of pain.

Holly was beside him in an instant, pulling him out of sight into a pile of manure. Gwaine had never been so grateful to be buried in shit in his entire life. As he lay there, the stench burning his nose and his leg throbbing, he knew the muck was the only thing between them and a very grisly end.

Gwaine held his breath as he listened to Dagma and Reonia move down the staircase.

Minutes dragged by, each one filled with the gross sounds of drones feeding on cows. Gwaine caught Holly's eye, and with a grim smile, he palmed some of the muck onto her, trying to ease the tension. "Very funny," she mouthed. Her eyes watered, though whether from the smell or relief, he couldn't tell. He'd ask her later—if they survived this.

Gwaine's blood ran cold. It was only a matter of time before those drones would finish eating and potentially start hunting them, as ordained by an evil child with a god complex. They had to move. Fast.

He motioned for Holly to help him up. Every step sent jolts of pain through his sprained leg, but he gritted his teeth and pushed on. He wasn't about to become a snack for insectoid monsters.

They crept out of the barn as quietly as possible, the sickening buzz of the drones' feeding frenzy still ringing in their ears.

Relieved to see the open sky, they couldn't afford to stop for even a second to sigh in relief. They had to get as far away as possible, find help, and pray to whatever gods might be listening that they weren't too late.

"Come on," he whispered to Holly, limping along as fast as he could manage. "We've got to warn the others."

When they were clear of the estate, they turned to see the impossibly large humanoid figures 'buzzing' around the barnyard.

"If I were a cat, I'd have seven lives left," said Gwaine.

"But you're an unemployed groom, so really you have minus two."

Gwaine chuckled at Holly's bleak observation. "At least I don't smell like lavender anymore."

Holly laughed. "God, I wish you did!"

Chapter 37

SETTING THE STAGE

"Mr. Fluffy let something slip." Bain's characteristic seriousness clashed with his choice of words.

Gerant nodded, stroking his beard thoughtfully. "Yes. Without intervening directly, it helped. It's clear now," he said, as if the sylph's cryptic message had transformed into an enlightening revelation instead of a riddle wrapped in a mystery inside an enigma.

Blake, still tangled in that enigma, looked confused. "What is clear? How did it help? Because it told us to go now before the spring rains come?"

Bain chuckled, shaking his head. "I don't think the sylph sees itself as a weather forecaster."

"More like a future forecaster," said Gerant. "The sylph wouldn't have appeared without reason. Telling us to act now means they need us. It also means there's a future thread where we beat Dagma, Nieman, and maybe whatever mess this Atropa has brewing."

"There will also be future threads containing our defeat," Rowan said gloomily, as though it were in his genes to be the wet blanket if the mood was getting too positive.

"Ah, Rowan, chin up," Gerant said, clapping him on the shoulder with enough gusto to almost knock the pessimism out of his slight frame. "Remember, wherever your thoughts flow, your actions follow. Let's stay on the path where we don't die, shall we?"

Rowan grumbled something under his breath, about how being positive was overrated, but he did not push his point.

"Fortunately, we're ready," Gerant announced, squaring his broad shoulders like a heavyweight about to get in the ring. "Get your disguises and supplies."

"Yes! Let's get that dirty Duke," Luciana squealed, her enthusiasm nearly as explosive as her actual firepower. Gerant gave Cane a knowing glance, who gently took Luciana's hand.

"Listen, firecracker," Cane said, kneeling down to her level. "I know you want to help, but you're staying here with me and Godfrey. That's been the plan from the start."

Luciana pouted, her golden eyes watery. "That was when I was a little and you didn't know what I'd be. I'm grown up now. Don't you trust me?" She looked less like the Bringer of Light and more like a sulky street urchin with all her golden hair chopped off.

"It was just last week!" Softening his tone, Gerant tried to placate her. "It's not about trust. Just because you're getting stronger doesn't mean it's safe. We don't want you hurt."

Luciana nodded reluctantly, though it was clear she wasn't happy about being left behind.

"It's fine. We'll probably have our hands full with the forces of evil here anyway," she said, attempting to sound hopeful.

While the men transformed themselves into the most mismatched group of recruits imaginable, Cane took Luciana outside.

After much tying and patience, Gerant emerged looking every bit the part of an old beggar. "We're ready." Behind him trailed his peculiar platoon: two odd-looking couples, Bain pretending to be a cripple, and Felix, a bent old man.

Godfrey, who had seen many things in his time, couldn't help but remark, "Not exactly the conventional cast of heroes destined to save a nation."

"Ah, but that's the beauty of it, Godfrey," Gerant said with a grin. "Trouble always comes from where you least expect it. That's why it works—no one would ever believe this lot could be a threat."

Godfrey nodded. "You're right there. Godspeed, and may fortune favour you."

"I look forward to seeing your real faces again soon," Cane added, watching as Luciana gave each man a tender hug before they left to cross over the hilltops of Malair Volpe. Even the wolves watched them go with a sort of sad, knowing look.

Riding over the hilltop route, Gerant and his crew were blissfully unaware that Reonia, leading a five-hundred-strong unit of spiky humanoid figures, was already circling the base of the hills, dragging some large spherical object on wheels. Luciana had unwittingly been right: Cane and Godfrey, along with the wolves and bears, were going to have their hands full. But for now, Gerant's group was ignorant of this looming threat, and ignorance, as they say, is bliss—at least while it lasts.

Once clear of the forest, the group split into pairs to avoid drawing attention.

After a few days of uneventful travel, Percy and Tristan were the first to enter the perimeters of Bellingham.

"You make a fine wife!" Tristan teased, eyeing Percy's awkwardly masculine gait beneath the frock. Percy, red-faced beneath his bonnet, muttered something unintelligible, but there was no denying his youthful features lent him a plausible touch of femininity.

They worked quickly, surreptitiously sticking posters to the municipal hall's pillars, slipping pamphlets into unsuspecting bags, and sliding them under doors on the town's south side. A breeze caught the edge of one poster as it fluttered, drawing a passerby's curious gaze. They stopped to read it.

It had begun.

Across town, where the streets were busier, Blake and Rowan, an even stranger-looking pair, were doing their best to blend in.

Blake adjusted his cloak, ensuring it hid his considerable bulk as they discreetly dropped pamphlets near the White Stork Tavern. Each time he glanced over his shoulder, a sense of urgency drove him—a need to get this done before anyone caught on.

To keep their charade real, the mismatched couple, wandered toward a roasting chestnut stall.

"Two bags of roasted chestnuts, please," Blake ordered shiftily.

The elderly vendor smiled warmly as she handed over the bags, her eyes twinkling with mischief. She winked at Rowan. "Ah, young love," she said, nodding approvingly. "Got yourself a right keeper there, haven't ya, love?"

Rowan, fully committing to his role as the bashful wife, fluttered his long eyelashes and gave Blake's arm an exaggerated squeeze. "Oh yes, he's just the best," he squeaked, voice pitched high enough to make Blake wince.

With a theatrical huff, Blake pulled Rowan into a bear-tight embrace. "And you're just the sweetest, my petal." Rowan wheezed and shot Blake a sideways look of panic, struggling to adjust his precarious wig with one hand while clutching the chestnuts with the other. "Careful, darling. Remember your strength."

The stall lady laughed, oblivious to the farce. "True love, bless your hearts. Enjoy your nuts!"

As they moved away, Rowan sighed dramatically. "You *are* nuts. Hug me like that again, and I may never breathe again."

"Sorry, sweetheart," Blake chuckled. Rowan couldn't help but laugh. Both enjoyed a moment of respite in their panicked state.

Back on the north side of town, Gerant, along with Felix and Bain, were playing their parts as enfeebled old men. Felix, with a patch over one eye and hunched over a cane, and Bain, who had tied up the bottom part of his leg to look like a one-legged cripple, made for the most pitiful—and least threatening—duo Bellingham had ever seen. As they stuck up posters, Gerant noticed a shift in the town's usual rhythm: hushed grumblings from small clusters of townsfolk, promenades interrupted by nervous huddles, a general sense of unease creeping in. The plan was working. The people would soon know.

"This is doing nothing for my posture," Felix complained, rubbing his aching, crooked back.

"And you think having your leg bent double is any more pleasant or comfortable?" Bain winced in mutual agony as he shifted his weight. The scouts are looking for able-bodied men, and the pain was worth enduring if it meant avoiding a long-stay booking in Gribthorpe's dungeons.

While Gerant moved deeper into the city, trusting his companions to handle their end, Bain and Felix mounted horses they had previously 'borrowed' from a pair of drunken men at the White Stork Tavern and rode out into the dark moors.

As the unlikely agents disappeared into the night, Gerant smiled to himself. *Not the most glamorous of plans,* he thought, *but then again, heroes come in all shapes, sizes, and dresses.*

He had volunteered for the riskiest role, moving through the town of Bellingham with the calm of a man who had seen a thing or two—or three—before breakfast. Wrapped in a shabby grey cloak, he hobbled along the cobblestone streets, blending in like a well-worn part of the town's scenery. But beneath that calm exterior, his mind was sharp—eyes scanning every corner, every face, and every hint of movement.

Out on the dark moors, Bain and Felix rode their horses with the kind of caution lesser man reserved for sneaking away from a tavern without settling the tab. The uneven ground was treacherous, thick bracken threatening to trip up the horses at every step. Despite visibility reduced to little more than a few feet in the murk, Bain had the uneasy feeling that someone, or something, was following them.

"We must be quick," Bain whispered, his voice barely carrying over the dull stomp of the horses' hooves. "If the Duke's men catch us, the whole plan's foiled."

Felix nodded, his usually cheerful smile replaced by a tight thin line. As they pressed on, the landscape began to change. Low-standing rocks appeared, gradually giving way to larger formations, jagged and sharp, with the ominous spire of the Devil's Needle looming in the distance.

The narrow path wound between towering stacks of boulders, forcing them to dismount. Bain kept a firm grip on the horses' reins—both animals were twitchy, their unease contagious. Maybe the emptiness of the moors or the strange rustling that seemed to shadow them, had spooked them. Bain wasn't about to let them bolt—on foot, he and Felix would be sitting ducks.

Felix worked quickly, pouring the tar around the base of the towering megalith like a thief on borrowed time. The strong smell of the tar failed to mask something far more pungent that wafted under Bain's large nostrils.

"Hurry up, Felix," Bain urged. "There's something evil at work here."

"Yes, I'm pretty sure it's me," Felix muttered as he struck the flint, sparking the tar. "May the old gods, if there are any, forgive my sacrilegious act."

As the tar caught, flames licked up the ancient stone, casting an unholy light over the scene. Both men stepped back, half expecting the ground to open up and devour them whole. But the foreign presence was not in the earth—it lurked in the shadows beyond the firelight.

Two silhouettes advanced slowly. Their forms growing bigger and bigger.

"Bloody hell! Where did they come from?" Felix jumped behind Bain.

"Who cares where they came from? What do we do now?" There was no doubt they were the figures' target. Bain drew his sword, the steel glinting in the firelight, but in that moment, all Cane's training evaporated, replaced by fear.

Then, in a twist so bizarre that Bain wondered if they'd inhaled some hallucinogenic fumes, Felix's expression transformed from fear to sheer joy.

"It can't be!"

"It can't be what?" Bain growled, not understanding why Felix looked like a starving man who'd just spotted a tasty pie.

"It's our friend, Gwaine!" Felix's was practically singing with glee.

Bain squinted as the figures drew closer. One limped, supported by the other—a woman, it seemed, both in rags. Though shivering, the woman clutched the man.

"Gwaine?" Bain asked, lowering his sword slightly. "What in the name of—"

As they neared, Bain's relief was quickly tempered by the overwhelming stench that accompanied them.

"My word, man, what is that awful smell?" Felix covered his nose, recoiling as the full force of the manure hit him.

"All in the line of duty, Felix," Gwaine replied. "We've not had the luxury of making contact with soap these past days, on account of the fear being hunted by flesh-eating monsters. Cow muck makes for excellent camouflage."

"It's good to see you alive," Felix said in earnest, though he hesitated to embrace his friend. "What's this about monsters?"

"We," Gwaine gestured to the woman beside him. "Sorry, this is Holly, former lady-in-waiting to Lady Dagma. We took it upon ourselves to spy on Nieman and almost ended up being a side dish for some cannibalistic beasts."

Remembering Tristan's confessional report, Bain gave a curt bow to the brave woman with the auburn curls. "Tell us more as we go," he urged, motioning toward the horses. "Gerant's speech should be underway by now. We've got a lot to catch up on."

Bain helped Holly and Gwaine onto one of the horses. As they set off, they recounted their harrowing tale of espionage and the chilling news of the army Dagma was amassing—an army of unnatural brutes, led by the deranged Reonia.

"I'm afraid," Gwaine admitted, "after having to lay low out of sight of these deviants of nature, we haven't had the opportunity to bathe. We've been branded as traitors, but we had to come find you."

Bain began to piece things together. This was the fourth prong of Gerant's fork they had not prepared for. At least, the other three prongs were progressing. By now, Gerant's speech would have begun, igniting the townsfolk. His thoughts turned to Bellingham. He knew they had to get back to the city to warn them—and quickly.

Chapter 38

UNLIKELY HEROES

A S NIGHT'S BLACK CANOPY settled fully over Bellingham, the aroma of roasted chestnuts and strong coulain filled the air, mingling with the sound of hushed conversations and the clinking of mugs filled with warm, sweet ale. Perfect conditions for the townsfolk to notice the posters and pamphlets scattered throughout the streets. Gerant could see a few clutching the leaflets, brows furrowed in thought as they read the incendiary messages.

This was the moment Gerant had been waiting for. His destination: one of the Speaker's Squares, formerly green patches of land where people could sit and listen to the speaker of the day. The tradition of speaking one's mind in public had been a proud one in Bellingham—until the Duke got his grubby hands on the city's spirit, bending it to his own ends.

Gerant arrived at a square that had seen better days. The sign, once proudly declaring it 'Speaker's Square' had been defaced. The word 'Speaker' was crudely scratched out. Now it read: 'Traytor's Square', a reminder of how far the city had burrowed into the Duke's grip.

Gerant shuffled unnoticed into the square, his bent posture adding to the illusion of frailty. To anyone passing by, he was just another old beggar, down on his luck and looking for a place to rest his weary bones. He had chosen this square deliberately. Despite the city's altered spirit, it still attracted people—though these days, they came for stoning and heckling more than for sharing stories or listening to legends.

A group of about twenty men loitered near the square's edge, their eyes darting nervously as two lifeless bodies were dragged away by guards. Gerant recognised the unfortunate souls—Almfred and Ralding, brave men who had turned back too soon after their escape through the tunnels. They had not been granted the soldier's death they deserved, dying instead as nameless traitors. Their unheroic deaths saddened Gerant.

Couples idled on the steps in front of a nearby church, the softly lit market stalls illuminated the white stone and the square in front. A large fire burned in a metal barrel at the centre, where passers-by gathered to warm their hands. The setting lay quiet, almost serene—perfect for the storm he was about to whip up.

Now or never, he thought. *Bain and Felix should have finished.*

He tottered over to a low wall, leaning heavily on his cane, and waited. He knew that timing was everything to catch the crowd when they were at their most restless and ready to listen. And listen they would—whether they wanted to or not.

More people drifted into the square, drawn to the warmth of the communal fire, their faces lit by the flames. The promise of company and distraction pulling them in. *Moths to a flame,* Gerant thought. *Let's light it.*

He cleared his throat and slowly straightened up, letting his cloak fall back just enough to reveal the strength in his shoulders, the sincerity in his eyes.

"It's funny, isn't it?" he began, his voice carrying just enough authority to make heads turn. "How a square once meant for the voices of the people now bears the mark of tyranny."

A few people stopped and looked at him, curious. Gerant saw it—felt the shift in energy. His voice grew louder and stronger, each unexpected word breaking through the hum of conversation.

"Traitor's Square, they call it now. But tell me, who are the real traitors here? Those who dare speak the truth, or those who fear it?"

The square quieted. Eyes began to turn toward him. He was no longer just an old beggar. He was someone to be heard.

With a swift motion, Gerant threw off the shabby cloak, revealing himself fully to the crowd. The transformation was complete. He stepped up onto the box that had served countless speakers before him, filling his lungs and bellowing, "Let me be heard, o' people of Bellingham!"

Worried chatter spread like wildfire: "Who is that?" "What's going on?" "Is he allowed to do that?"

Drawn by curiosity and the irresistible allure of something forbidden, the moths flew in closer. Mothers nudged their children forwards, eager for them to hear the tale this mysterious old man was about to spin. The spark had been lit, they couldn't resist the light.

Gerant stood tall on the box, his voice rich and commanding, drawing them in as easily as a fisherman reels in his catch.

"I say, let me be heard, o' people of Bellingham. I've a story to tell—a grand one! It's sure to delight and thrill. The tale of a great empire, ruled by a great man. His benevolence and powers were legendary. His will alone made birds sing and crops flourish."

The crowd edged in closer, anticipation buzzing through them. Children sat cross-legged, their faces glowing in the firelight, utterly entranced by the tale of a mighty emperor brought low by a fearsome dragon. Gerant painted scenes the of destruction that followed—the emperor's palace laid to waste, the rich landowners' homes crumbling, and the people turning on one another in a desperate struggle for survival.

Just as the crowd was hanging on his every word, a panicked shout exploded through the rapt audience.

"The Devil's Needle is on fire! The Devil's Needle is on fire!"

From a narrow alley, three men burst into the square, their faces pale with fear. The crowd swelled into a sea of swivelling heads and anxious whispers, searching for answers in its confusion.

Gerant smiled inwardly. The plan was unfolding perfectly. Tonight, the people of Bellingham would remember what it meant to have a voice—and the Duke would learn just how dangerous that voice could be.

"What do you mean it's on fire?" one man asked, his voice sharp with fear.

"It's burning!" panted one of the three men, still gasping for breath. "It's alight—somehow!"

"But stone doesn't burn," protested another onlooker.

"Well, this one does!" the man replied, shaking his head in bewilderment. "I saw it with my own eyes as I was coming through the main gates. It's not a stone like others. It's made from the Devil's own flesh!"

"Look! You can see the flames from here!" a woman shouted from one of the upper terraces of the White Stork Tavern. She clutched her shawl tightly around her, as if it might ward off the terror taking hold.

"It's a sign!" someone shouted.

"It's a sign," came the collective cry.

"The ancient gods are angered!"

"What have we done?"

Panic spread through the square, just as Gerant had predicted. Their fear, their confusion, it all funnelled back to him. Elevated on the platform, a lone figure in a sea of uncertainty, he was suddenly the authority they sought, their instinctive leader in this moment of chaos.

"What do we do?" a man called out desperately.

"What should we do? They'll soon be after us in our homes!" cried another.

"What have we done to anger the ancient gods?" a woman screeched, her eyes wide with panic.

The tension was thickening, a rising tide of fear that threatened to spiral out of control. Gerant knew he had only seconds to steer the crowd away from hysteria and toward the direction they needed to go. The success of their mission—and possibly the fate of all Valoria—depended on it.

"Calm yourselves. Calm yourselves," he called out with just the right level of authority. "If the ancient gods had wanted to unleash their wrath upon you, they surely would have done so by now." Gerant guided the crowd before him into the smooth and reassuring harbour of his deep voice. "Instead, they have given you a sign." He gestured dramatically to the horizon where the Devil's Needle burned. "The flames are not a sign of doom, but of redemption! The ancient gods are not angered—they're watching, waiting to see who among us will rise! What you see is a sign, yes, but not of wrath. It is a sign of *change*!"

Mumbles rippled through the crowd as Gerant watched the sense of hope start to weave its way back in. He had them where he wanted them.

"They have been lenient with us, but we must not waste this opportunity," he urged. "The fire is not our punishment; it's our call to action!"

His friends, all still in disguise and strategically scattered, began stirring the pot. Percy, affecting his best woman's voice, wailed dramatically, "Oh, what have we done? What have we done? Oh my children, oh my husband!" He attached himself to Tristan like a barnacle.

Tristan, in the role of long-suffering husband, made a show of trying to peel Percy off. "Oh, my darling wife, calm yourself," he said with exaggerated patience. "We can always ask for forgiveness for our sins."

"But it must be the worst of sins!" Percy shrieked, clinging to Tristan with renewed vigour. "What could we have done to anger the ancient ones like this?"

Through gritted teeth, Tristan hissed, "Very nice, but a little too convincing. You've missed your calling as a whining wife. Now let go of me."

Percy's theatrics were drowned out by Blake's booming, wooden voice. "We've done some really bad stuff. Really bad."

Though his delivery left much to be desired, Blake's voice carried impressively over the crowd.

"Yes, husband of mine, terrible things," Rowan, beside him, agreed in a womanly voice, hands fluttering dramatically. "For here we stand in Traitor's Square, once Speaker's Square, where we used to bring our children. Do you remember, darling? Such happy days, and now—" Rowan turned to Blake with an expression of exaggerated sorrow.

Blake gave a small, awkward smile, trying to appear loving and caring toward his decidedly unattractive wife. "We have brought dark times to Bellingham," he shouted loud enough to crack the cement in the city walls. People shook angry fists—not sure who they were angry at yet. They needed a name.

Just then, Bain's voice rang out from the back. The captured crowd turned as one, like an ebbing wave, to face him. He shook his walking cane furiously, adding to the drama. "It's the Duke! It's that blasted Duke! Mark my words. Ever since he's been here—"

His words were swallowed by the furious roar of the crowd, who were more than eager to assign blame for their misfortunes. They had a name. Now the crowd was ready, ripe for the next phase of the plan.

"Should we bring back Aurelius?" came a quavering voice—Felix, cleverly positioned on the opposite side of the crowd. His innocent question rippled through the masses, planting the seeds of hope and regret in the collective mind. It took root faster than Gerant had anticipated.

"Yes! He would know how to restore order, fairness, and peace!" someone shouted.

"But hasn't the Duke kidnapped him?" Tristan exclaimed, playing his part to perfection.

"No! How terrible!" gasped the crowd, their fear transforming into righteous anger.

"What a wicked thing to do," one woman wailed.

"He's a good man," another added.

"A great leader," came the chorus. "Our leader!"

Gerant could scarcely believe how smoothly it was all going. The mob's thoughts were now echoing their own scripted lines, and Gerant knew the time was right to nudge them into action.

Standing tall on the box, he projected his voice over the din, assuming the mantle of leadership the crowd so desperately wanted. "Like a rotten apple that spoils the harvest, we will pluck him from his estate and hold him prisoner in the municipal hall to stand trial. We will save Aurelius! We must act now, or risk further angering the ancient gods! If we do nothing, they will see us as indolent and worthy of chastisement!"

The mob roared in agreement, though not entirely sure what 'indolent' or 'chastisement' meant, they didn't want to risk the ancient gods' wrath. Horses were grabbed, carts commandeered, and the people of Bellingham surged toward Malcrov Court, their numbers growing. The clamour of their fury rang through the night like a flock of angry geese, all honking for justice and retribution.

At the head of the gaggle, Gerant led the charge.

Chapter 39

THE ART OF IMPROVISATION

GALLOPING TOWARD THE IMPENDING battle, Tristan struggled to keep a straight face, though the situation was far from funny. They were characters in a warped tale, off to topple the fool who wore the crown—except maybe *they* were the fools, with no experience, and no real idea of what to expect. They found safety in their numbers. An angry gaggle of geese thundering over the moors, equipped with gardening tools and kitchen paraphernalia, made for a pretty scary army.

Percy clung to him for dear life, his long hair whipping at Tristan's face, making everything even more farcical. To top off this circus, a maddening jangling racket came from Tristan's saddle pouch—his chimes.

"What in the gods' names did you bring your chimes for?" Percy griped, trying to keep his skirts from billowing up as they rode. "It's a battle, not a concert!"

Tristan laughed. "I could well ask why you brought our dead great-great-uncle along for the ride. At least *I* might be able to summon a sylph. Not sure old Perceval's ashes are much use in combat."

"Fat load of good those sylphs are, fickle as the wind they guard."

"We agree on that. Capricious little buggers. Not like we're professional fighters anyway. And you're charging in wearing a *skirt*!"

"Lots of warriors wore skirts," Percy shouted over the ruckus of hooves and war chants. "Goodness knows how they kept 'em from flying up on horseback though!"

"Ha! As Father used to say, nothing easy was ever worth doing."

"Yeah, but I don't think he meant charging into battle with no clue what we're doing. Probably more about conjugating verbs in the old tongue so we could read the scriptures."

"I don't know about you, but I'd rather be out here making a difference than have my head stuck in a book."

Tristan was proud of his brother. Percy had always struggled to measure up physically, and that was probably why he lugged around old Perceval's remains. Maybe he hoped some of the old hero's courage would rub off on him. Despite his quirks, Percy was the perfect counterbalance to Tristan's impetuous nature. Where Tristan was headstrong, Percy's caution served as a vital anchor, keeping him from leaping headfirst into disaster. And headstrong heroes didn't tend to live long—their great-great-uncle a prime example.

"Hopefully, we'll just be hanging around the edges, not diving into the thick of it," Tristan said, trying to comfort his brother's obvious nerves.

Truth be told, he didn't mind the idea of battle. They had a mob on their side, after all, and that evil sorceress Dagma was in for a surprise.

As Tristan glanced around, he spotted Blake and Rowan approaching on horseback. Rowan seemed to be fighting with his bonnet, but a second look revealed he was waving them over, not battling with the wind. Steering his horse around a cart, Tristan joined his friends, noting the alarm on their faces.

"What's the matter?" he asked.

"The groom, Gwaine—" Rowan began, but the hooves Tristan's blasted chimes drowned him out.

"It's going to rain?" Tristan yelled back confused.

"No. I said: the groom Gwaine and—" Rowan's words were lost again to the loud jangling. "For pity's sake, put those bloody things in your bag!" It was the first time Tristan—or anyone, for that matter—had ever seen Rowan anything other than calm. "Blake, you tell him! You're louder than me."

Blake didn't need asking twice. "Gwaine," he bellowed, "that groom fella from before. He's found out some important stuff with a lady who waits—one of Dagma's lot—and it's really important."

"Can't we stop to talk?" Tristan shouted.

"No time!" Blake replied, spurring his horse forward. "We're telling Gerant next!"

"Telling him what?"

"That there's an army of Dagma's *babies*!"

"An army of *babies*?" Tristan repeated incredulously.

"Yes! We have to be careful!" Blake sped off toward the front of the group to deliver his message.

"What in the bugger is he on about? Percy, did you catch that?"

"An army of babies," Percy repeated, looking just as confused.

"Oh, wait, look, Gerant's motioning to us. He's splitting the mob. But we're already at Malcrov Court. Why does he want us in that field?"

"And everyone else is heading for the manor," Percy observed. "Gerant will have his reasons."

They caught up with Gerant and the others, who had ditched their restrictive disguises. As Percy and Rowan hastily shed their bonnets and gowns, Tristan—ever impatient—demanded answers. "What's going on? What's this about Dagma's babies? Why are we in an empty field?"

He shut up once he saw the serious expression on Gerant's face. This was bad news.

"Gwaine and Holly are leading the people to find King Aurelius," Gerant explained in an urgent voice. "We have a stranger task on our hands, thanks to the information they gathered at great risk. It's worse than we thought."

"Dagma's *babies*?" Tristan asked again.

"We have to get them *before* they grow," said Gerant.

"Why? What makes them so dangerous?"

"Because they're as hard as nails, tall as oaks, and lethal as weapons. These creatures are anything but human. Dagma gestated them—in cows. Now, they're under her control."

Tristan's laughter split the air, unable to help himself. "That's a joke, right? That's impossible."

"Tristan!" Felix cut in, unusually sombre. "Does this seem like the right time for jokes?"

Tristan's laughter stalled in his throat.

"The Keepers warned us of Atropa returning with her miscreant army, but it seems they forgot to tell us her daughter is already here with one of her own. And here they come."

They crouched in the shadows of the trees, eyes wide as they took in the surreal sight before them.

"Stay out of sight," Bain whispered, his voice as steady as ever. "For now, we need to just see what we're up against."

"Oh, my giddy aunt!" Tristan's hushed exclamation barely contained his shock. His eyes, unable to register what they saw, struggled to process the unfolding nightmare.

In the farmyard, a dark army of towering figures stood in formation. At first glance, they looked like massive upright roaches or wasps, but no, these were men—or something resembling men—encased in glossy black armour bristling with spikes. Tristan heard Percy gulp beside him, a nervous sound that matched his own rising panic. There were hundreds of them.

These were definitely not the babies he had imagined.

He silently prayed they were fully grown because if they got any bigger, he doubted he would manage to fit them into his field of vision—or keep his trousers clean.

In a synchronised motion, the entire horde knelt on backward-bending knees, forming a shiny black sea at the feet of the red-cloaked sorceress, Dagma. There she was, without mask, on the barn's roof, the beating heart of this battalion of killing machines. Tristan and the others held their breath, every instinct screaming at them not to make a sound that might draw her gaze.

Ah, the pre-battle pep talk, Tristan thought, *she was about to deliver a rousing speech to send these monsters off to massacre the Valorians. Not that they needed rousing; they looked like they were built for one purpose only, and it wasn't diplomacy.*

"Ooh, ah, eeh, eeh ah!" screeched Dagma.

Tristan did a double take. The donkey-talk was *not* what he expected. The sound that came from her mouth was a strange, melodic string of syllables, reminiscent of the vocal scales his old music teacher used to make him practice. But this was much louder and, disturbingly, far more compelling.

With a long, drawn-out 'eeh', she made the soldiers rise. A sequence of 'ahs' brought them to heel, and a sharp string of 'oohs' had them falling into a terrifying V-formation beneath her, like some grisly choir of doom. The rhythmic thud of armoured fists slamming against chests added to the hellish symphonic battle cry.

The mother and leader of these savage warriors continued her haunting drill, her voice travelling up and down octaves like an instrument of war.

But then she paused, something off in the distance catching her eye. Tristan followed her gaze—Malcrov Court. A blazing fire had flared up there. The mob had set the manor alight.

Tristan watched in horror as Dagma's black horde turned its attention to the burning manor. A rapid string of sounds from Dagma—something Tristan could only translate as 'Charge!'—sent the black swarm sweeping across the field like a thundercloud, ready to rain down on the unsuspecting Valorians busy destroying Nieman's estate.

"What have I done?" Gerant murmured. "I've sent these people to their death."

"The odds are heavily stacked against us," Felix mumbled, devoid of his usual optimism.

"We still have the element of surprise," said Bain. "Cane taught us the success of this strategy in countless battles."

"How will that help us?" Gerant asked, looking more lost than Tristan had ever seen him. "There are so many of them."

"Well, actually, there is only one," Percy said quietly, more to himself than anyone else.

"What do you mean, lad?" Felix asked. "Are you blind? Can your young eyes not see the hundredfold spiked warriors beasts out there?"

"Oh, you're a genius, brother!" Tristan's face lit up as he caught on to his brother's point. "It's not *them* we need to worry about, it's just the red witch. She's the one controlling the spiky nasties."

"Yes," Gerant said, hope returning to his voice. "Gwaine said she bound them to her with a ritual. A young girl did the same with another legion, but I haven't seen her. Anyone else?" They shook their heads. "Then let's focus on Dagma."

"So, how do we break this ritual?" Tristan asked, turning to Gerant, who, rather alarmingly, looked expectantly at Percy. *This is a new one for the books,* he thought. *Who flipped the hierarchy here?*

"I don't have the answers," Percy admitted, retreating slightly, clearly uncomfortable under the pressure. "I just thought if we take her down, they'll all go with her."

"Well, we'd better figure it out fast," Bain said, as the distant, dying cries of the Valorians reached their ears.

"I can," Rowan suddenly spoke up. "Well, I have some ideas."

"Spit 'em out, lad," urged Bain.

"The 'Book of Shadows' has formulas for war water bottles," Rowan explained hurriedly. "They used them to stop demons in dreams, protect against enemies at the Sanctum, things like—"

"Okay, we get it. How do we make them? We don't have any bottles," Bain interrupted.

"I thought the Gaene Kin didn't harm or kill," Percy pointed out.

"It doesn't kill," Rowan clarified. "It can paralyse. Stop the enemy in their tracks."

"Good enough," said Felix. "If we can paralyse that witch, then her oversized insect army is as good as an oversized *dead* army."

"Gwaine said Dagma poured the larvae from vials." Gerant stepped into his leadership role again. "Let's see if she left any in the barn. Come with me. What are the ingredients, Rowan?"

As they hurried toward the barn, Rowan rattled off the list: "Rainwater."

Scanning the farmyard, Tristan noted lots of rain-filled barrels and troughs. "Easily done, there's plenty."

"Rusty nails," Rowan continued down his list of ingredients.

"Plenty of those around here, too," Felix said, already picking some off the ground.

"And the ashes of a dead person or soil from a grave."

They froze in their tracks. All eyes slid to Percy, who immediately clutched the green pouch at his belt. "No, you're not having him," Percy protested, his voice pleading.

"We have to, Percy," Tristan urged. "He'd *want* us to. He'd get to be a legend again in death—a hero, alive and dead. What could be better? I think he'd rather help stop this swarm of insectoid beasts than hang around your groin for the rest of his afterlife."

Tristan knew he had made a convincing argument. Even if it pained his brother to part with their great-great-uncle's ashes, the chance for their ancestor to go out as a hero in the ultimate battle from beyond the grave was a legacy that even a mythical afterlife couldn't top.

With a reluctant sigh, Percy loosened the cord around the pouch.

"Once we've made the bottles, we must use the element of surprise to attack Dagma," said Bain. "We'll come from outside the court, behind her. She won't expect that. She thinks everyone is already inside. But we need eyes on the rear in case that second legion—the one under the other girl—comes at us. We must act quickly, without hesitation. Cane says even a second's delay can cost a life. Once we've distracted her, the rest of you throw the war water bottles to paralyse her. We haven't a moment to lose."

Chapter 40

SAY YOUR PRAYERS

TRISTAN NOTED HOW QUICKLY everyone had all fallen into their new roles—a whole lifetime away from their easy charade as monks in the monastery. Gerant, his thick, forest beard flecked with straw, came out of the barn holding handfuls of small bottles. Big Bain followed, carrying even more. Percy, with a steady hand, was already filling them by the troughs.

Tristan smiled to see his brother so calm. "Perceval the Bold!" he proclaimed. "Don't waste a drop of our great-great uncle's magic heroism powder."

"I like the sound of that," Percy smiled.

Even Felix, usually more at home in front of an oven, now holding a fistful of rusty nails, had become an invaluable part of this makeshift militia. And Rowan, the bookworm, was needed more than ever as he recited the protection paralysation chant as though he had practised it all his life.

Tristan couldn't help feeling a little left out. Everyone seemed to have their role, except him. Then, in a flash of inspiration, he knew. Of course, he was the trickster, the distraction. He'd be the one to pull off the impossible.

"Blake," Tristan called out. "You're the fittest of us all." He watched Blake's face light up with the unexpected compliment. "You'll help me create the diversion," he added.

"I will?" Blake's initial enthusiasm wavered.

"Yes, come. It's time to get out the Legbreaker and Endmaker to distract her."

Blake's moustache curled up as a churlish grin spread across his face. "Yes!"

"Great idea, Tristan," said Gerant.

"Sounds like a suicide mission," said Felix. "We're outmanned, out-spiked, out-spooked and out of our depth."

"Then we're all set," said Gerant. "Tristan, you and Blake handle the diversion. Bain and Felix, you've got the arms for throwing—get those bottles at Dagma. Rowan, Percy, and I will carry the bottles and keep a lookout for the second army."

"How will we know when you're ready for us to throw the bottles?" Percy asked as they ran toward the flaming manor, where the battle was already in full swing.

"Oh you'll know, brother," Tristan flashed a confident smile, the kind that always managed to reassure Percy, even when Tristan himself wasn't entirely sure.

How could he be sure, he had never done this before. That was a lie, he had done this many times in his childhood as a harmless prank. He and Percy would perch high on the old stone lychgate at the entrance of the churchyard. From there, they could see the villagers heading toward the church, all dressed up for Sunday service. Their own trousers were typically covered in dirt, pockets bulging with shiny conkers they had collected from the woods.

Smack, smack, smack. With perfect aim, Tristan would knock off the clergyman's hat or make the haughty Mayor's daughter turn around in fright clutching her backside. "Naughty churchyard spirits," the villagers would mutter, unaware of the real culprits. That was until the day their father caught them. The berating they received from their father was legendary—he'd be proud of him now.

"Fill your pockets and pouches with stones," he ordered Blake. "No, not those big ones. Think crab apples."

Blake set to work gathering the right-sized stones, while Tristan felt the familiar surge of adrenaline—just like the good old churchyard pranks. Only this time, the stakes weren't about knocking hats off clergy but saving everyone he cared about.

With catapults at the ready, Tristan and Blake sprinted ahead, weaving through the trees to take their position. From their hidden perch, Tristan couldn't help but recall those innocent days of raining conkers on unsuspecting villagers. But now, the view below was anything but playful.

The courtyard had turned into a bloodbath, a scene of savagery that would be seared into Tristan's mind forever.

People tried to flee the court, but the predators—those perverse abominations of man and insect—were faster. Their spiky limbs would hook into the spines of fleeing victims, yanking them back like a spider hauling in its prey: half-alive and destined to be devoured. The beasts' human-like mouths opened wide to reveal rows of mandibles, scissoring away like a gardener on a manic pruning spree.

Bodies hung from windows, the desperate occupants preferring to fall to their deaths rather than face the jaws of the ravenous monsters. No mercy. Just an unstoppable hunger for flesh.

Blake turned away, retching into the underbrush. Tristan was thankful no one else was around to hear it. Not that he could blame him—Tristan himself would've joined in, but there was nothing left in his stomach to lose. It was time to put an end to this unrestrained orgy of gorging.

"Where's that flame-haired witch?" he muttered scanning for the conductor orchestrating the massacre. Blake nudged him, pointing toward a turret on the far side of the courtyard. There she was, looking down on her ruinous army with a wicked smile, conducting her demonic beasts to a cannibalistic score.

People screamed, "The Devil's Arrow! The Devil has returned! We are all doomed!" They let their weapons clatter to the ground, resigning themselves to their fate, their cries for forgiveness rising to the skies. "We are sinners! Forgive us!" Some still tried to fight, but their strength was fading fast. What little courage they had left was drained by the sight of a maskless Dagma, the devil incarnate.

"Formidable, isn't she?" Tristan muttered. "Don't get caught in the detail, Cane says," Tristan reminded himself, shaking off his own paralysis of horror. "Focus on your task. Let's go!"

With pockets bulging, they loaded their catapults and took aim. Together, they fired. Two large stones hurtled towards Dagma, smacking into her ankles. She glanced down, momentarily confused, but continued conducting her demonic orchestra, seemingly unfazed.

"Third time's the charm," Tristan grinned. He could see the others moving into position, ready to strike. Smack, smack—two more stones hit, this time bullseyes to her forehead.

Her chant faltered. For a heartbeat, the battlefield stilled. Dagma's army paused, their jaws still dripping with blood, as they looked around, confused. Half-chewed bodies dropped from their mandibles, and then the beasts began lumbering back toward Dagma.

"So, that's what happens," said Tristan.

"Is that what we *wanted* to happen?" Blake stammered, pointing a trembling finger at Dagma. She had located the source of her assault and was now glaring at them with a stare that could freeze fire.

"Um, yes and no. Not exactly," Tristan yelped, realising they were in deep trouble. They kept firing, desperate to keep her distracted. Below, Bain and Felix were finally in position, their 'loaders' ready to throw. "Oh God, hurry up!" he shouted, feeling the panic rise.

Dagma stormed toward their tree, her eyes locked on them with murderous intent. *Smash, smash*—two small bottles launched, hit her squarely on the back. *Smash, smash*—another pair followed. Her steps grew sluggish, each movement a struggle against invisible chains.

"What in Caldera's name is going on?!" she screamed in rage. "Why can't I move? You vermin, I will get you!" She glared at Tristan and Blake with a promise of slow, creative deaths.

"Not if we get you first," Tristan said under his breath, though he wasn't entirely sure who he was trying to convince—her or himself. "Yes! She's stuck! We did it!" Tristan exclaimed, sticking his tongue out at the paralysed Dagma. "It worked. Take that witch bitch."

Blake, less jubilant, pointed out, "She can still *groan*. She can still command them to *impale* us."

His simple yet crucial observation took a while to hit home. A high-pitched 'hee-haw' from Dagma's lipless mouth signalled a fresh command. The shiny spiky drones were turning their attention toward the tree. "That obviously means 'Go shred those two idiots in the tree'."

"What do we do?" Blake asked, his face as pale as milk, his moustache floating in contrast like a dead branch against the moon.

"It's time for the Mercy Shooter. Let's see if we can knock the witch out cold," Tristan said, rummaging in his pouch for more stones. "Blast these chimes." He pulled out one, and it jangled loudly. "Here, hold these!" *Why isn't Blake taking the chimes so I can get the stones out?*

He stopped to look at Blake. There was something at play behind his glazed eyes. It was either the prelude to a deeply embarrassing accident in the disposal of personal effluence or, the kindling of a rare, brilliant thought.

"Keep jingling those chimes," Blake said slowly, his eyes fixed on the black mass below. "I think it's blocking her signal."

"Oh my god, Blake," Tristan said dumbfounded. "I never thought I'd say this, but you're a genius."

As long as Tristan kept the chimes ringing, the bestial soldiers stumbled, looking around in confusion, their bloodthirsty rampage grinding to a halt. Dagma, now livid, was powerless.

"What do we do now?" Blake asked, still dazed as if he had just witnessed a miracle.

"Gerant will take charge. He always does," Tristan said confidently.

Sure enough, Gerant's commanding voice rang out, rallying the survivors to fight the stupefied drones. "Kill the demons! They are the servants of the ancient gods. We must destroy them to be truly free!" Many who had fled, now returned, drawn by the sight of Gerant and others attacking the beasts without being torn to shreds.

Axes, pitchforks and spades retrieved from the ground clashed against the beasts' armoured skin. People struck at the beasts with boundless vengeance. It was barbaric and messy, but Tristan could see it was working.

"Strike at their joints," Bain shouted, hacking at one of the monstrosities. "That's where they're weak."

Fuelled by rage and the loss of their loved ones, they attacked their enemy with a ferocity equal to the suffering they had endured moments before. By the time they finished, piles of dead, shiny black bodies littered the ground.

When the sun rose, it threw a stark light on the bloody aftermath. The red blood of Valorians mingled with the black blood of their enemy.

"You bastards, I will get you for this!" the Dagma statue shouted. No one paid her any attention.

Tristan and Blake climbed down from the tree. "Everyone okay?" Tristan called out, looking around.

"Anyone seen Gwaine and Holly?" Bain asked.

Dagma, though now paralysed, was still screaming furiously. "YOU THERE! Don't ignore me! I'm STILL HERE!"

"No, I haven't seen them recently," Tristan replied to Bain. "Last I saw, they were climbing over a pile of dead bodies over there, but I can't be sure."

"Since we don't know how long the paralysis will last," said Gerant, "I suggest we deal with the sorceress now."

"Yes, I *am* a powerful sorceress! I will get you!" Though Dagma screamed loudly, the fear invoked by her was severely diminished—to zero.

"There's also that girl to find," Gerant added. "And her army."

"Agreed," said Felix. "But at least now we know how to defeat them."

"I demand to be heard! Annoying people of Valoria," Dagma inhaled deeply, as if preparing for some final dark spell. "I will be done with you in an—"

There came a loud clang. Dagma's plaintive cry was silenced. Behind her stood Gwaine, kettle in hand, looking rather pleased with himself. "That shut her up," he grinned.

Holly followed up with a solid wallop to Dagma's head using her spade.

"One more for good measure," she said, looking like she wanted to do it again—and again.

Gwaine, still out of breath, wiped his mucky brow. "I really need to get fit if being a spy and man of action is to be my new vocation in life."

"You're doing just fine," said Holly warmly. She then shouted over to Gerant, "We'll check the manor. Duke Nieman and King Aurelius might be in there."

"Good idea," Gerant called back. "We need to secure the king."

"We'll come too!" Tristan yelled, "And secure some ale while we're at it!"

"Port!" Felix panted, finally catching up.

"Sausages!" shouted Percy.

Inside the fire-ravaged halls of Malcrov Court, once immaculate and now in ruins, they found no one—except a few opportunists stuffing jewels and gems into their pockets and socks.

"The Duke is not here," said Gwaine exiting at last.

"We found the king," Rowan shouted from the cellars. Blake followed him, carrying a frail and withered version of their king.

"Quick, get a cart!" Gerant ordered. Within moments, they settled the king in the back of the same cart used to wheel Gwaine off to his supposed death. Gerant commissioned a band of strong Valorians to escort Aurelius safely back to the Palace of Bellingham. They looked proud to serve, while another hundred or so battle-hardened men and women gathered, ready to follow their king to whatever fight awaited.

"Right," Gerant said, mounting a horse, "let's get back and see how Cane has fared in preventing Luciana from burning down the Sanctum."

They mounted whatever horses they could find. While Percy was reeling off his celebration menu favourites to Felix, Rowan trotted up alongside Gerant.

"Don't you think that's where the second army would go?" he asked.

"Yes, the Sanctum is most likely their target," said Gerant. "But don't worry, it is well camouflaged." Rowan still looked worried. "Plus, Cane and Godfrey have the fire-breathing dragon on their side."

"Yes, but she's the kindest fire breathing dragon ever known," said Tristan. "Not likely to harm a fly, let alone an army of man-sized insects."

"Well, not deliberately anyway," Felix laughed.

As they rode away, the sound of their horses' hooves muffled Dagma's bitter muttering from atop her fallen black army. "Fools," she spat. "I'm but a breeze compared to the storm Ree-on-yee-ha will rage on you."

Chapter 41

DAUGHTERS OF CALDERA

CANE HAD INSTRUCTED HIS father and Luciana to stay inside the Sanctum. It was the safest place, not only for its perfect camouflage but because he was confident their enemies would not want it destroyed.

Everything fell silent. Outside, he surveyed the land around the site. Maybe his mind was playing tricks on him, but he thought he heard the forest whisper to him through the quivering branches. The birds had fallen silent, and the wind carried a sense of foreboding. He could feel the anxiety in the animals—the nervous scurrying of mice retreating underground and the faint tremor in the earth beneath his feet, a warning from nature itself. Danger was approaching.

Then he saw it.

An army appeared on the horizon like a moving forest. At its head rode a girl wearing an obsidian bodice, a blood-red cloak trailing behind her like a war banner. She also wore a look of conceitedness. The soldiers following her were unlike any men Cane had ever seen—towering, monstrous figures with metal-reinforced joints, horned helms, and spikes jutting from their throats. Their eyes, black as death, promised only destruction. They were the impossibly terrifying made real.

The girl's laughter rang through the air, loud and deranged, echoing off the ravine walls. Even her Lieutenant, ten times her size, looked momentarily unnerved. "What are you looking at, you lump? Face front, ugly!" said the girl; then, she whistled sharply. Her Lieutenant obeyed, eyes forward.

Cane could see her intention to destroy and conquer was absolute. She circumnavigated trees and rocks with precision, guiding her army with ruthless efficiency. The treacherous ravine proved no obstacle for her. Those in her troop who fell were left unaided. *Merciless*, thought Cane. *If they spot us, there's no chance of negotiating a truce—nor of defeating them alone.*

At the border of the cottontail meadow, now a sea of yellow buttercups, the girl paused to study the land. The low spring sun partially blinded her, but she shielded her eyes with a gloved hand.

Snarling wolves growled from the cliffs. The girl squinted in their direction. Her Lieutenant let out a cautious grunt. Without even looking at him, she slammed her fist into his side. "Get with it, you clumsy oaf!" she snapped, whistling him back into line.

Her sneer deepened as she saw the wolves forming ranks. Two lines of them had encircled an area by the rock cliffs, their eyes glinting with wary intelligence.

The girl snapped her fingers and whistled sharply. "Prepare the contraption. Now." Her hulking soldiers obeyed, heaving a massive wooden siege device into position. The wolves crouched, ready to pounce, their eyes tracking every movement. Calmly, the girl pulled two pieces of flint from her bodice, striking them together to light the fuse on a spherical object.

"Fire!" she commanded with a cold, cutting whistle.

Soldiers severed the ropes holding the catapult's payload and the sphere soared high, arcing through the sky. The wolves scattered, most of them converging towards the advancing aggressors. When the explosion hit the ground, a shower of grass, rocks, and debris erupted. Chaos and mayhem ensued as the wolves, now caught in the crossfire, were thrown into disarray.

The girl's demented laughter returned electrified with the thrill of imminent victory. "Look at them scatter! Die! Die! Die!"

Her gaze turned to the Sanctum. Cane's heart quickened. *She knows where it is.* He had to move quickly. His father and Luciana needed to get out before she turned her focus on them. Nothing would stop her—not even the brave wolves she intended to crush underfoot.

Another sharp whistle sent her soldiers charging forward with savage zeal. The clash was immediate and brutal: the fierce mechanical beasts smashed into the wolves with all the force of a sledgehammer to a porcelain vase. The wolves, in turn, fell upon them with equal ferocity, their teeth and claws ripping into the hardened casings like they were made of putty.

From her elevated position, she fired volley after volley, her expression cold and crazed.

Cane led his father and Luciana to a concealed nook near the cliffs. "Stay here," he urged quietly, glancing over his shoulder. "The wolves seem to be holding their own, but she knows where the Sanctum is. She'll be coming for us or the key."

On the battlefield, Lycus, the silver-streaked alpha, led his pack. They lunged valiantly at the intruders. Four wolves per insectoid soldier. Each one clasped tenaciously to a limb, rendering them almost immobile. Some swung their horns wildly, attempting to fend off their attackers, but it was a losing battle. Their howls mingled with the screeches of the enemy as they tore into them. Reinforcements poured in from the forest—snarling, red-gummed wolves, their ranks moving in coordinated lines, ten deep, as they defended the Sanctum.

The girl's shrill whistle pierced through the battlefield. "Get them airborne! Now!" she commanded her Lieutenant, who ran lumberingly to the soldiers at the edge of the meadow, those not yet engaged in combat.

A deep mechanical whirring rose as the insectoid soldiers extended their arms. With a sickening crack, translucent wings unfurled from their backs. The wolves, stunned, could only watch as the soldiers took to the sky.

"By the gods!" Godfrey gasped, drawing his sword. Cane held him back.

The attackers swooped down with deadly precision, spikes extended, stabbing the wolves below. The wolves, blurs of white, darted at lightning speed to avoid the aerial assault, but their numbers were thinning fast as the drones shredded them without mercy.

"This is your end!" the girl cried triumphantly.

At the edge of the ravine, her dark red robes whipped around her like flaming tongues, she watched the carnage unfold with too much pleasure. The howls, the yelps, the blood—they were mere background noise. Victory was within her grasp, and she exulted in the power she wielded.

"This is what it means to be powerful," she growled, her eyes drinking in the destruction as if it were a testament to her might—and every death, every broken body, a personal trophy.

The battlefield was strewn with the fallen wolves. Deep sorrow pinched Cane's heart. They needed help. Something bigger and stronger.

As if summoned by his thoughts, a thunderous roar came from the forest. The giant bears charged from the trees, their bulky forms crashing through the underbrush with earth-shaking force. Rising on their hind legs, they swatted the aerial aggressors with their colossal paws, batting them from the sky. Wings were torn clean off, sending them plummeting to the ground in crumpled heaps.

The girl's grin mutated into a scowl. "Bastards!" she spat, her frustration flaring as the bears turned the battle. "They're ruining everything." She whistled even more of her winged soldiers into battle.

Cane couldn't stand by any longer. Seeing the animals sacrificing themselves stirred something in him. Sprinting into the fray, he was a lone figure dwarfed by the towering, black soldiers. His sword barely made a dent against their metallic exteriors, knocking a few off balance but doing little damage. *Soldiers of tungsten malice,* he thought. *They're impenetrable!*

Then, as if directed by the deeper recesses of his mind, he noticed their joints—exposed, vulnerable flesh beneath the armour flaps. *There.* Without thinking, he lunged, thrusting his sword into the gaps. The keen blade sliced through their flesh like butter. They began to fall.

He was making a difference. As if learning from him, the wolves adopted his tactic, abandoning their earlier tactics of recklessly tearing at the flanks. They began targeting the joints, inflicting precise, lethal wounds with fangs and claws.

Are they following my lead? The question flitted through his mind, but there wasn't time to dwell on it. The wolves worked in perfect harmony with him, as if they were an extension of his own will.

Seeing his progress, the girl rubbed her hands over the lit fuse of her catapult, fire sparking between her palms. Her voice carried across the battlefield, singsong and mocking. "Hello, Daddy. It's me. Pop, pop, pop. One, two, three—try and dodge these. You can't beat me."

Daddy? That wicked girl was in the other egg?

No time for thoughts of parental responsibility, he had to dodge the three massive fireballs heading toward him. Cane moved instinctively, each fiery orb missing him by a hair's breadth. His movements were swifter than ever before. *Are the sylphs helping me?*

Once clear, he pulled an arrow from his quiver, nocked it quickly, and loosed it toward her. The arrow found its mark—not in her, but in the eye of her unfortunate Lieutenant she'd hidden behind. The beast crumpled with a pitiful groan, dead before he hit the ground. The girl barely spared him a glance.

"Aim for their eyes!" Cane shouted.

"Where *is* that insufferable man?" The girl snapped in frustration. Arrows whizzed past, striking her soldiers' eyes with deadly precision. One by one, they fell from the sky like oversized, mechanised flies.

"Haven't lost your touch, son!" Cane, though elated to hear his father's voice, hoped he was well hidden.

The girl raised her hands, fire swirling around her. "Do you think you can stop me?" she roared. "I command the powers of Fire! I am the Mighty Reonia. Daughter of Caldera. Flame Maiden. Harbinger of death!"

Cane watched her prepare to move to a new position for another fiery assault when something flashed—a fluid streak of gold, darting from the trees toward the catapult.

What was that? Cane's heart raced, then understanding clicked into place. *I know that light.* Reonia's listing of self-proclaimed accolades had given Luciana time to move into place.

Reonia saw the flash of gold too. Her distraction lasted but a moment, but it was enough. Cane sprinted to the catapult, his steps silent and swift. He reached it unseen, tearing out the fuse just as Reonia raised her hands for another wave of destruction.

"Who put out my fire?" she snarled. "It couldn't possibly be that weakling sister of mine, could it?"

The earth beneath Reonia's horse trembled violently, as if the ground was rebelling against her presence, trying to eject her. Roots burst forth from the soil like writhing coils, winding around the legs of her horse and nearby soldiers. The once-unstoppable killing machines were dragged into the earth, as if they were nothing more than toy figures.

Reonia's horse reared in terror, throwing her off balance. She tumbled to the ground, her fury igniting. "Sister!" Her voice a scimitar, its target, Luciana.

Cane's heart leaped as Reonia scrambled to her feet, her eyes blazing with rage. She scanned the battlefield, her gaze locking on Luciana in an instant. A deadly stare-off.

Luciana! Cane ran, but he wouldn't reach them in time.

What could the genteel Luciana do in the face of this merciless antagonist? Kindness and softness were no match for Reonia's ruthlessness.

Reonia's words slithered between her pointed teeth. "How delightful. The day just keeps getting better and better."

Luciana stepped forward, her soft features a stark contrast to the chilling evil before her. Cane's worry grew—he feared Reonia's ferocity would overwhelm her.

"Oh, look at you," Reonia sneered. "The face of an angel, the spine of a jellyfish, and such a bad hairdo! I will erase you from existence, you bitch."

"Where did you learn such foul language so quickly, dear sister?" Luciana cut in, her voice calm and steady. "I've clearly kept better company than you."

Reonia's face warped into a smile that could curdle milk. "I learned it from Auntie D, darling. Far better company than your prissy lot. Don't worry, sweet sister, I'll give you a crash course in foulness and darkness—right now. One neat, brutal lesson. Your first and last."

Her black hair whipping about her like a storm gone rogue, Reonia advanced, eyes burning with a fierce blue light. "You were never meant to be here. I am the rightful heir to Caldera! You're just a mistake, like Mother. You should have died."

Luciana took a small step back, her hands raised as if to ward off Reonia's fury.

"Ha! Yes! Cower before me!" Reonia swelled with vanity. "I will incinerate you!"

With a vicious strike, Reonia knocked Luciana to the ground, sending her tumbling like a wilted flower. She towered over her, a dark monolith of doom.

"It is preordained, sweet sister," Reonia crowed with arrogance. "I am Atropa's successor. You are nothing, a weak, pathetic thing. She will choose me."

Her blue nails traced slowly across Luciana's cheek, savouring the terror in her sister's eyes. "But I can give you a small consolation before I extinguish your pitiful life. I'll take great pleasure in slaughtering Father next. And the wolves. And—"

Luciana's face contorted—but not with fear. What Cane saw now was raw, fierce, and primal. Rage. Where he had expected to see resignation, he saw an inferno of hatred.

Luciana's gaze was wild and dangerous. Reonia paused, her confidence wavering.

"You dare speak of *my* family?" Luciana growled, her voice a low, trembling storm of defiance. "Your foul mouth is unworthy to even utter their names, you feckless fiend!"

Luciana let out a primordial scream loud enough to split the heavens. The sound crashed like a wave, deafening, as though the Mother of oceans herself had roared through her.

Reonia staggered back, hands clapped over her bleeding ears. "You... you have the siren's call! But how?" Reonia, the spoilt brat at the power party, was shaken by the unexpected show of magic. "It's not fair. How many powers did you get?" Evidently unaccustomed to feeling vulnerable, she tried to reassert her dominance. "No matter. I've got fire *and* earth."

Her attempt to sound triumphant rang hollow. With no flame at hand and no time to start another with her flint, Reonia scrabbled to source the earth's power. Evidently it wasn't her natural-go-to source. It seemed to Cane she was late to the draw.

Her eyes widened in shock as Luciana began to rise from the ground, lifted by an invisible force, her arms spreading wide like wings.

"What... what are you?" Reonia gasped, stumbling backward. She stood frozen with her mouth aghast, empty of malicious words and all previous verbal incarcerations for her sister. She could do nothing but wait to see what Luciana was capable of. Even her army, without her whistling commands, had stopped. They watched spellbound as though petrified by some unseen hand of restraint.

That was Cane's moment. He led the wolves and bears into the paralysed soldiers, cutting them down like stalks of corn beneath a farmer's scythe.

Luciana's stony eyes turned away from Reonia to the towering cliffs behind them. Her body trembled with pure energy, too much for flesh to contain. With a single, swift motion, she released her energy onto the cliff face. The rock shuddered and cracked, the sound of grinding stone enough to force Reonia to her knees. A section broke free forming a colossal replica of Luciana in stone.

Their enemy slaughtered, Cane and the wolves ran for shelter at the base of the cliff on the far side of the Sanctum. Luciana's physical body hung lifeless in the air now, her strength fully transferred to the huge stone visage. Lycus moved to stand guard over her limp body.

"Impossible!" Reonia whispered, her breath catching in her throat as she watched the colossal stone version of her sister take shape. Luciana's face, massive and godlike, materialised over her.

Then, with a deafening roar, Luciana's stony face opened its mouth, and any hope Reonia had left was obliterated. The gale that followed was cataclysmic. Trees ripped from the earth, soldiers flung skyward like leaves in a storm. Reonia hugged a boulder, her fingers digging desperately into the stone as the ground itself was torn apart around her.

Luciana's stony lips cracked into a smile, rocks cascading from her cheeks, flattening rows of soldiers like they were nothing. Her lips pursed as if to blow the sails of a giant's ship.

Her intake of air must have left all the residents of South Valoria gasping for breath. As Luciana exhaled, the force was nothing short of biblical. Soldiers, trees, grass spiralled into the tornado of breath.

The detritus of Reonia's dead army was hurled away, vanishing into the sky like unwanted debris.

As the violent gust subsided, Luciana's cold, unfeeling eyes fixed on Reonia, who cowered behind a boulder near the stream. Gasping for breath, trembling, Reonia clambered to her feet. The battlefield was covered with the mangled remains of her soldiers. She was no match for Luciana.

With a panicked glance at her sister, Reonia threw herself down the ravine. Cane sprinted to the edge, watching as she tumbled painfully to the bottom. Unfortunately, she survived—he saw her struggle to her feet, slipping on the corpses of her soldiers, and dodging those still raining down from the sky with the buttercups.

He was relieved to see her retreating figure, and even more relieved that Luciana was unhurt. What she had just done blew him away—though not literally thankfully. What was she?

Whatever the answer was, he was glad the Fire Keeper had not taken the golden egg. In that moment, he felt what could only have been described as his first 'fatherly' feelings for her. He wanted to protect and care for this girl.

Cane dashed toward Luciana's prone form, her previously towering presence now diminished and fragile. He caught her just as the last of her radiant features faded into the rocky wall. Cradling her in his arms, the sight of Agatha cradling a baby all those months ago flashed in his mind. If anyone was 'the one', it was this girl in his arms. And yet, how small she looked, how light she felt—despite the weight of the world she had just carried.

"Luciana! Are you alright?" His voice wavered between hope and dread, the words barely escaping his throat. She stirred, her eyes fluttering open.

She managed a quiet 'yes' through dry lips. "Is it over?" She tried to sit up, wincing. "Where is she?" Panic set in her voice as she looked for her sister.

"Gone. She knew she couldn't defeat you." Cane shook his head, struggling to reconcile the enormity of her actions. "What you did was, well, it was nothing short of miraculous. Not one of them left standing."

Relief was short-lived. A knot of dread turned like a screw in his stomach. *Where's Father?*

Luciana sat up. "What is it?"

"My father," Cane said, panic rising. "I left him in the nook." He bolted back to their hiding spot, only to find it empty. His heart sank, heavy as an anchor in a cruel, unpitying sea.

Peering over the ravine, he scanned the scattered, mangled bodies below. Each broken carcass seemed to mock his hope. Then, the sound of soft sobbing pulled him from his search. Turning, he saw Luciana kneeling beside a motionless figure, sword in hand.

His father.

No! No!

Cane's entire body went numb. His legs could no longer hold him. The sight of his father's broken body crushed him. He had only just found his father, to lose him twice was a sick joke. The thought of mourning his parents *again* hit him like a wave, leaving him marooned in solitude.

Luciana's gaze met Cane's, her eyes filled with sorrow. She moved aside to give him space.

Godfrey's breath was shallow, his lips pale, the shadows of death gathering around him. His voice strained with effort. "I know what you're thinking, son," he rasped. "Dying twice on you... a real family tradition. Now you've got to mourn me all over again."

"No, Father, don't—"

"Listen," Godfrey interrupted, his voice breaking, blood trickling from his lips. "You're not alone, Cane. You've got friends... family. And I'll be joining your mother soon, my love, my beautiful wife—" His voice trailed off into a soft cough. His hand, though weak, clung to Cane's. "You are not alone."

"Father, we need you," Cane said, his words choked with grief. These were the last words Godfrey heard before he drew his final breath.

Cane sat in silence. The world around him seemed to stop, every sound muffled by the cloak of grief enveloping him. His chest ached, an open, unrelenting pain.

Luciana watched him from a few steps away, her face streaked with quiet tears. He glanced back at his father's lifeless body, the reality of the loss sinking in. Despite the deep ache in him, he acknowledged what his father had said: this time was different. He wasn't alone. People needed him now, depended on him.

With a heavy heart, he released his father's limp hand and took Luciana's small one. The tears streaming from her golden eyes spoke volumes. Though an adolescent in body, she had the life experience of a babe. He had to look after her.

The unspoken grief was yet to be felt in full. Not just his grief. There was grief all around him. Wolves and bears were tending to their wounded. After the fighting came the mourning.

Chapter 42

WHERE EVIL LIES

S EVERAL DAYS LATER, CANE was digging yet another grave for the wolves when he saw Gerant leading the returning party across the field. The horses moved slowly, picking their way through the newly made carpet of corpses.

"Hail brave warriors!" Gerant called out cheerfully. "I see you've been unequivocally successful in your battle."

His broad smile sagged when he saw the rows of graves.

"Not entirely," Cane said, gesturing to the wolves and bears nearby solemnly nursing their wounds. "And my father."

"No," said Gerant sadly.

"But we're out of danger. For now."

"What a waste of good lives," Gerant murmured. "Your father was an exceptional man. I'm sorry, Cane." He paused as the others bowed their heads in respectful silence. "There's a morsel of comfort I can offer in knowing they fought for something worth fighting for. The people of Bellingham have found reason again. Our king, and the life we've fought for, are nursing themselves back to health."

The returning group dismounted and Luciana came running out with a pail of water and a ladle for the thirsty travellers. She hugged each of them in turn—even Gwaine and Holly. This small act made the mood lighter.

The group dedicated their time to helping Cane bury the dead. Each grave an act of remembrance.

As they dug, Gerant moved beside Cane.

"So, what happened?" he asked.

Cane's eyes darkened. "Luciana's evil twin paid us a visit—along with a few hundred of her giant, battle-frenzied insectoid friends."

Gerant raised a bushy eyebrow. "A lovely family reunion, I'm sure. We had a similar run-in ourselves. How'd you manage to send them packing?"

"I didn't," Cane said, casting a glance at Luciana. "The animal guardians fought bravely, and Luciana, well..." He shook his head in admiration. "She was beyond incredible."

Gerant's eyes widened with a grin. "Our little firecracker got her moment to shine, eh? Let me guess, you finally nailed that fire-breathing dragon trick?"

Luciana paused mid-gulp, the ladle she'd been drinking from dripping water down her front. Her cheeks were flushed from the praise. With a smirk, she wiped her mouth with the back of her hand. "Actually," she said with a glint in her eyes, "I picked up a few new tricks along the way."

Cane chuckled. "You'd have been proud of her. She isn't just a fire-breathing little dragon, she can turn into a golem the size of a mountain."

Those who had not witnessed Luciana's transformation exchanged uneasy glances, unsure whether to laugh or believe what they had just heard. A few managed awkward smiles.

"And your mission?" Cane asked.

Tristan stepped forward, his face lighting up with a cheeky grin. "Oh, ours was a little more understated. No giant golems, just two catapults, ten small bottles and one crazy, *dead* sorceress."

The men burst into laughter, breaking the sadness that had come over them since seeing Godfrey and the dead guardians.

"Understated but effective," Felix added, clapping Tristan and Percy on the back. "It was a great plan lads."

"Aurelius is being escorted back to Palace of Bellingham," said Gerant. "Once he's recovered from this ordeal, he'll resume his duties as our king. It will take time to restore both his health and the palace. We've agreed to visit him when he's back on his feet. As for the Duke—nowhere to be found. And Dagma—dead on a mountain of enemy corpses."

Cane was disappointed the Duke had slithered away but given what they had overcome and just been through, he was last on his list of concerns.

Gerant continued, "The people of Bellingham are busy finding survivors and building pyres for those black *things*."

"Sounds very thorough," Cane congratulated them.

"And the key?" asked Gerant.

Without hesitation, Cane reached under his tunic and pulled out the large key. "Safe and sound."

Bain frowned, scratching his beard. "But why do they want it so badly? That Atropa could come and go as she pleases."

"Ah, but with the key," Cane said, "so can we. Atropa locked the Gaene Kin out. She doesn't want anyone here, not us, not them. There's something she's hiding. Something she's afraid we might uncover. Perhaps there's something the sylphs foresee that she doesn't want us to know."

"What do you think that might be?" Gerant asked.

Cane shrugged. "Could be anything. A secret only the key can unlock or something she's desperate to keep hidden."

He moved toward Gwaine and Holly, hand extended.

"Pardon my manners. I see we've gained a couple of new faces," he remarked.

"I'm Holly," she introduced herself, "and Gwaine, well, you already know."

"Pleased to meet you," he replied, bowing his head slightly. "Gwaine, I'm very pleased to finally put a face to your valorous name. I thoroughly enjoyed your labyrinth for the Unity Trials."

"Ah, pleased to hear it," said Gwaine with two red circles of modest pride colouring his cheeks. "Those were the days."

Bain stepped toward Holly, offering a gallant smile. "May I escort you to our makeshift bathing area?"

A blush spread beneath the muck on Holly's face. "That would be most kind," she said, giving Gwaine a 'me first' look and beaming as they followed Bain.

<hr />

For the rest of the day, everyone focused on cleansing—physically and emotionally. They prepared the fallen guardians for their honourable burial, while the living worked to cleanse their sorrow. As dusk handed over to night, the Sanctum's grounds grew quiet, holding a sacred stillness during the burial rites.

Once the rituals were complete, minor wounds tended and manure cleaned, they gathered around the stone table, too exhausted to make the journey back to Bellingham—a semblance of normalcy restored. Apart from the abundance of sausages, cheese and beer—those were a definite new addition.

"While searching for the Duke," Gwaine explained, nodding to the laden table, "Felix took off with Tristan and Percy to fulfil their priority of raiding the Duke's pantry. We brought back more weapons, and they brought back sausages and rum. But no Duke."

"Somehow," said Gerant chuckling, "between all of us, we always seem to cover all bases."

Cane got a sudden feeling of déjà vu. It was just like when he was at the monastery for the first breakfast: he felt among friends but a niggling worry floated just beneath the happy surface.

He should have been happy there surrounded by laughing friends. The sconces on the walls created a warm glow over their tired faces. Gerant puffed contentedly on his pipe, a look of satisfaction under his beard.

"There was a time," Gerant began, "when I feared this burden might be too great for us. But with the help of such... unlikely heroes, we've accomplished the seemingly impossible. Tonight, we toast not only to our victory—however brief—but also to the fallen."

Tankards were raised, and the group drank deeply. When Cane spoke, the lump in his throat kept his speech short.

"To my father," he said, lifting his drink higher. "Without his wisdom and courage, we wouldn't have made it this far. He fought with honour until the end. I couldn't have asked for a better father."

"To the Earl of Cromlech!" Gerant echoed. Then, with a smile, he added, "And a toast to Gwaine and Holly. Your bravery and quick thinking spared us from Dagma's army. Thanks to you, we didn't walk into her trap."

"And now we are better equipped for the potential armies of Caldera," added Rowan, dampening the mood as usual. "You know, with Atropa."

"Oh," Gerant groaned, dragging a hand down his face. "I'd quite happily forgotten about that."

They all wanted to forget about that. For this moment, they chose to raise their tankards again, saluting the future with forced optimism.

"With Dagma gone and King Aurelius restored to his rightful place, I believe we can look forward to a brighter future," Gerant declared.

"Hear, hear!" came the chorus and clinking. "Cheers!"

Cane cleared his throat, bringing a hush to the room. "Before we move on, I'd like to say a few words for Agatha." He looked to Luciana.

He paused, gathering his thoughts. "Agatha, whose life was cut short too soon. We owe her a debt we can never fully repay." The group nodded in solemn agreement, their faces reflecting the gravity of their shared loss. "And we thank her, for giving us the gift of Luciana. Without her, we'd have lost today. We would have lost everything."

The biggest cheer of the evening went to the red-faced Luciana, whose smile was so big it hooked over her ears. Cane leaned in and gave her a proud father hug, which made her redden even more. Her happiness eased the loss of his father.

"To Luciana!" they all toasted.

As the evening wore on, the memory of their fallen comrades remained a steady toast—that was the only thing that remained steady. Eventually, those who could still use their legs crawled into their makeshift beds, others just slumped in their seats, with a sense of contentment and peace of mind that had been seriously lacking in recent months.

Everyone but Cane.

He could not sleep; his thoughts were dogged with loss. The knowledge that Aurelius had been restored to his throne offered some comfort, but it was a costly victory. The void left by his father's death was a stark tear in his personal story, which was far from neatly resolved.

Any happiness he felt for his friends and new-found daughter was marred by the fact that his own father's life had not been spared. Fate had been as merciless as Reonia. After all the suffering he had been through and after only being reunited for such a brief time. All he loved and had fought for seemed tainted by the brush of unfairness. Agatha, though only part of his life for a short time, also pervaded his thoughts.

Not wanting to listen to his confuddled contemplations on repeat, he rose from his bed, pulling his cloak from the back of a small wooden chair. Running a hand through his tangled hair, he tried to shake the surrealness of it all—the fearsome Army of the Bleak, the epic quest as just a few men to save the destiny of Valoria from an ill fate, and last but not least, his daughters. It was all so far from his simple life as an Imperial Guard.

Slipping out of the Sanctum, he moved quietly, careful not to disturb the others and wake them from their well-deserved rest. The frigid air smacked him like an icy slap, waking him fully. Its chill sank into his bones instilling not a state of cold, but a state of clarity. A new feeling Cane liked very much.

The sky, previously a reassuring canopy of stars, was now an ominous canvas of brooding clouds. He felt a malevolence hidden in the dark. Perhaps it was the growing rumble of a far-off storm reminding him of the black clouds over Castle Gradunce and stirring these vivid sensations in him.

A storm was coming, that was all, and Cane wasn't about to let it stop him from saying his final goodbyes. He pulled his cape to keep out the bitter wind that now whistled around him in mournful lamentations—just as it had done around that lifeless carcass of a castle. Was the moody weather testing his resolve? He had endured more than a rainstorm could throw at him.

A short walk to the edge of the woods took him to the resting places of his father and Agatha. His heart was filled with unspoken words, the kind that could never truly be put to rest. After who knows how many minutes of silence, he turned to head back inside, but something caught his eye—a faint light moving in the distance.

Narrowing his gaze, he made out a small, cylindrical glow approaching through the trees. Instinctively, his hand went to where his sword should have been—only to remember he had left it inside before going to bed. Cursing under his breath, he held out his burning torch, brandishing it like a weapon, and stood his ground.

Now two lights, side by side. Whoever, or whatever, was approaching had their sights set on him.

The darkened surroundings afforded him no light to make out his prospective opponent. The shadows obscured everything but those twin points of light. Although by his judgement, the opponent seemed short—very short. Could it be the pygmy?

Cane's apprehension eased when he saw that the two brilliant discs were none other than the eyes of the lynx. He laughed out loud in relief at his own foolish fear. His tension now eased; he bent down to stroke the lynx pressing against his leg.

"You startled me, friend," he said, his voice low as he knelt to caress the animal's fur.

"What are you doing out on a night like tonight?" he asked the silent form that looked deep into his eyes as though it were trying to communicate back. Cane was rather startled to note that its eyes were of a perfect emerald green. Hadn't they been amber?

Perhaps the darkness made them seem different. He was keen to dismiss anything incongruous. He never used to put much stock in omens, but he took the lynx's presence to be a sign from Agatha since she had so admired it.

Heavy raindrops began to fall, the cold splashes landing on his hands.

"Go now and find some shelter," Cane bade the lynx goodnight, feeling more unsettled than he had before he came out. Pulling his collar up, he made his way back to the Sanctum, his heart troubled and his thoughts muddled.

The lynx watched Cane retreat into the Sanctum, following him with her gaze until the stone door slid shut behind him. As the first drops of rain pelted her fur, she blinked slowly, indifferent to the storm that now lashed the earth. The howling wind tugged at the trees, making their branches creak in protest, but none of it stirred her. There was only one worry that stirred within the lynx: how to face her sister, Dagma.

How were they to start afresh after so much time had elapsed, after so much had happened, after such an embarrassing defeat? If it had not been for their sibling rivalry, all would have gone to plan.

Agatha had chosen the lynx's body—sleek and deadly—because of its prowess and predatory skills. It suited her very well. Ever since those wretched eggs had unceremoniously hatched from her body, she had walked with the dead. Seeing that insufferable Gerant and his band of fools return victorious had spurred her into action, forcing her to seize a new body and claim vengeance. How could they have been defeated by such unworthy adversaries?

She knew Dagma still lived; she could feel her, the bond between them a thread that even death couldn't sever. If not for Dagma's insatiable greed—poisoning her babies with the Baron to claim the glory of propagating for Atropa—none of this would have happened. And Agatha, in turn, would not have been so wickedly spiteful and tried to burn her alive. She knew her unfortunate 'physical' death had been the work of one of Dagma's vindictive hexes.

The lynx padded silently over the sodden ground, the undergrowth slick with rain, her paws finding their way through the bodies of fallen drones in the ravine. She rehearsed what she might say to Dagma. There could be no mention of vengeance, no hint of anger or any potentially inciteful accusations. If only the Duke's idiotic scouts would have found her necklace sooner, she had left it in plain sight, Dagma would have known her desire for a truce.

That was all in the past. From now on, they would work together. They had to get that key.

In truth, she was rather looking forward to their scheming again. It would be such a relief from the cumbersomely slow plodding minds of men. Cane, though—Cane she would miss. She had grown to like him. He had proven to be the perfect mate. She allowed herself a self-congratulatory smile at how perfectly she had played the role of the helpless victim, despite that blasted Baron's dying last words: 'Beware the woman'. Bain had practically delivered her to them on a platter. How had they been so blind! Especially when she had launched the torch at Dagma. Flammable cloak indeed. Her devastating fire powers were sure to have vexed her sister. At least Dagma still had a body—no sympathy there. Or when Cane had found her in the fountain pool. Her skin had been in severe need of rehydration; but her mind bending had worked perfectly. Through her powers of persuasion, she had taken what she needed from him to procreate, without him even noticing or remembering. Most satisfying.

As she exited Hackthwall Forest, the storm grew more violent, a fitting backdrop for their new chapter. For this end was merely a beginning in disguise. Tomorrow, she would find her sister and finally meet her bitch of a daughter.

EPILOGUE

A New Era

I T WOULD HAVE BEEN a foolish hope to aspire to life in Bellingham ever resuming its natural course, that of peace and tranquillity under Aurelius's previously unperturbed reign. Once you have stabbed your neighbour in the back and betrayed the sons of your friends, there are no more sanctimonious hiding places to where you can flee.

The people of Bellingham did in some ways resume their everyday lives. The market trade and evening strolls went on much like before. No one spoke of the Duke. His former spies and entourage slipped back into their previous lives as though nothing had happened. The impressive grounds of Malcrov Court were transformed. The building was converted into a hospital, the cottages used for the infirm or outpatients. Because it was hidden away, this healing of the war's wounds could go on unseen. Nonetheless, stark reminders of what had happened surrounded people's lives every day. The haunting darkened thoughts of past treacherous deeds did not grow back to full health like the grass on Speaker's Corner or the grass over the graves of their loved-ones. And although they could share a cup of hot coulain with their fellow man, the people of Bellingham could never fully look each other in the eye again for fear of slipping into the infamy of their past misdeeds.

They looked to the Imperial Palace, which still shone in its resplendent exotic glory as a reminder and symbol to them. But even after being restored, the marks left by the hungry flames that had ravaged its balustrades showed through the smooth limestone surface; the cracks in the facade were getting bigger and the leaves of the palms trees aligning the front avenue all wilted under the scorching blaze of the summer sun. The hallmarks of a long and fruitful era that was surely coming to an end were fading with every day that passed.

On his approach to the once grand entrance on horseback, Cane was of a grave disposition. He had a message to impart to his dear ruler that weighed heavy on his heart and he wondered if the king's frail state would be able to bear the news. After having always been a faithful and loyal servant to Aurelius, he did not want him to feel let down by the news of his imminent departure.

Cane had decided to leave Valoria with Luciana in search of Octavia. Everything he had read in his father's library pointed to the Octules holding the answers. Travelling to an unchartered land seemed an impossibility, but when coupled with the fact Cane had neither a ship nor sailing experience, it bordered on ludicrous.

None of this deterred him. He would find a way. What troubled him was the prospect of returning to ask the king for help. As a naive Imperial Guard, he had revered Aurelius; now, as a recently promoted Captain of the Guard, he regarded him through a more pragmatic lens. Would the king be willing to invest substantial resources in a quest deemed ludicrous?

Cane believed that the threat of an invasion from the Army of the Bleak would clinch his argument.

DEAR VALIANT / VILLAINOUS Reader,

I hope you've enjoyed the story and been inspired to leave a positive review!!

As a freelance author, I rely on my readers to support me in creating more books. I do all the work myself from the idea to the editing, cover design, formatting and marketing. I thoroughly enjoy it and would like to do more.

HOW YOU CAN HELP: You already helped by choosing this book. Could I also ask that you leave a kind review to help guide others to these amazing stories and characters?

Thank you very much. Every good review and recommendation is a step closer to another magical adventure being created.

Now that you've made my day, go forth and conquer yours with magic in your heart.

For more stories in the Ascendance trilogy where you can continue to live in the magical world of Valoria visit:

www.fmhepton.com

Magical wishes,

Francesca Hepton

Also by F. M. Hepton

ASCENDANCE SERIES

The Dark Side of Reverence – Book I
Shadows over Valoria – Book II **(COMING JUNE 2025)**
Dominion – Book III **(COMING NOVEMBER 2025)**

WWW.FMHEPTON.COM

VISIT www.fmhepton.com to
GRAB YOUR FREE COPY OF CANE'S BACKSTORY

ABOUT THE AUTHOR

Born on the volcanic island of Oahu but rooted in the cold wilds of North Yorkshire, Francesca has spent a lifetime travelling the world and exploring the depths of the human experience. With a passion for languages, she speaks four fluently, allowing her to connect with diverse cultures and stories. She studied at the University of St. Andrews (MA Honours, Modern Languages) and the Université de Toulouse, and created the well-loved children's book series Kiki and Friends.

She is a devoted mother to two sons, who have kept the flame of fantasy alive, fueling her desire to write stories that dive into the unexpected and twisted facets of life. Their years of walking together through Britain's landscape, with its mysterious moorlands, ancient stone circles, dark forests and imposing gorges, serve as a constant source of inspiration.

Through her writing, Francesca invites readers to explore the unconventional, challenging perceptions of what is good and bad, and discovering the magic that often lies in the shadows.

NOW YOU'VE MET THE UNLIKELY HEROES
AND LOVEABLE VILLAINS, AREN'T YOU
CURIOUS TO FIND OUT WHAT CATASTROPHE
AWAITS THEM BY ATROPA'S EVIL HAND?
GET YOUR COPY OF BOOK TWO IN THE
ASCENDANCE TRILOGY

SHADOWS OVER VALORIA
BOOK II, by F.M. Hepton

www.fmhepton.com

Made in the USA
Columbia, SC
22 February 2025

964f8671-7c50-4ae2-aa41-40dbf16fef63R01